A KILLING RAIN

P.J. PARRISH

D0187857

P

PINNACLE BOOKS
Kensington Publishing Corp.
http://www.kensingtonbooks.com

PINNACLE BOOKS are published by

Kensington Publishing Corp.
850 Third Avenue
New York, NY 10022

All Kensington Titles, Imprints, and Distributed Lines are available at special quantity discounts for bulk purchases for sales promotions, premiums, fund-raising, and educational or institutional use. Special book excerpts or customized printings can also be created to fit specific needs. For details, write or phone the office of the Kensington special sales manager: Kensington Publishing Corp., 850 Third Avenue, New York, NY 10022, attn: Special Sales Department, Phone: 1-800-221-2647.

Pinnacle and the P logo Reg. U.S. Pat. & TM Off.

First Pinnacle Books Printing: February 2005

10 9 8 7 6 5 4 3 2 1

Printed in the United States of America

Praise for P.J. Parrish and ISLAND OF BONES

"The newest addition to Parrish's Louis Kincaid series lures readers in from the outset. World-weary, contemplative Landeta is the perfect foil for Kincaid, a true man of action. Their camaraderie and unspoken understanding, combined with Parrish's crisp dialogue and skill at stringing out the suspense, are what make this carefully constructed mystery so absorbing."

Publishers Weekly (Starred Review)

"A suspenseful read with some unusual twists and turns that mystery lovers will appreciate."

The Pilot (Southern Pines, South Carolina)

"The sins of generations past haunt Louis Kincaid and the case he takes on in P.J. Parrish's beautifully evoked, darkly moral tale *Island of Bones*, set in that coastal territory where even the elemental distinction between land and sea can be as blurred as that between good and evil."

S.J. Rozan, Edgar-winning author of *Winter and Night*

"I'm hooked on P.J. Parrish. Nobody else creates such a compelling mix of real characters, genuine emotion, and fast-paced suspense. *Island of Bones* is her best yet!"

Barbara Parker, *New York Times* bestselling author of *Suspicion of Madness*

"Island of Bones opens like a hurricane and blows you away through the final page. It's a major league thriller that's hard to stop reading."

Robert B. Parker, *New York Times* bestselling author

Praise for P.J. Parrish and THICKER THAN WATER

"Crisp prose and evocative descriptions of southern Florida set the tone for this grim mystery, but it's the story's sympathetic characters and sudden twists that will leave readers hungering for more."

Publishers Weekly

"*Thicker Than Water* is that kind of book that grabs you and won't let go. I absolutely loved it. You're going to be hearing a lot more about P.J. Parrish."

Steve Hamilton, Edgar and Shamus-award winning author of *Ice Run*

"If you want to discover the hot new mystery writers, try the very best: P.J. Parrish."

City Paper (Nashville, Tennessee)

*To my son Robert
and my Little Brother Johnnie.
Two good boys who became fine men.*

CHAPTER 1

Sunday, January 10, 1988

The road in front of him was empty. Just as it had been behind him for so long now. Straight and flat, it cut a cruel slash across the gut of the Florida Everglades. No curves, no hills, nothing to relieve the tedium of the journey.

He had never minded driving Alligator Alley during the day. Then, the harsh sun bleached out the swaying saw grass and the sky was huge and white-blue. During the day, it was easy for him to imagine he was somewhere else, maybe traveling across some Western prairie, like Shane riding in to save someone who needed saving.

But at night, like now . . .

Alligator Alley was empty and black with only the thin beams of his own headlights to show him where he was going.

He reached down and turned up the volume on the tape. Marty Robbins had been keeping him company for the last hour, ever since he had passed the toll booth back near Naples.

Ride, cowboy, ride. Don't go too slow.
Ride, cowboy, ride. You've a long way to go.

He knew all the words by heart, but he wasn't singing along with them now. He was concentrating, watching the odometer, calculating how many more miles he had to go.

The instructions had been simple. Drive exactly forty-two miles east of the toll booth. Pull off into the boat ramp parking area, turn out your lights, and wait.

He picked up his orange soda and took a drink, feeling a nub of excitement in his belly. He had waited a long time for this, a long time to feel part of something important like this. It was a simple job. All he had to do was to deliver a FedEx box and pick up another package in return.

Two grand for his trouble. Simple. Easy.

He glanced down at the big FedEx box on the seat. He knew what was in it. He had pulled over as soon as he was into the dark cover of Alligator Alley and carefully pried opened the box's flap. The box was stuffed with stacks of money, held by rubber bands. The stacks were all hundred-dollar bills. He counted twenty stacks. One hundred thousand dollars, he guessed. His hands were sweating so much he could barely push the stacks back in the FedEx box.

For a second—just one—he had thought about turning the Cadillac around and disappearing with that FedEx box. But he knew that wasn't right. He would stick to the plan. Go to the boat ramp pull-off, put the box on the trash can, and pick up the package. It was probably drugs, but hell, what did he care?

Marty started in on "A Half-Way Chance with You." He didn't like the love songs but this one wasn't too bad. He kept time to it, tapping his fingers on the steering wheel.

The headlights picked up a green road sign, the turn-off for the boat ramp. He checked the odometer. This had to be it.

He slowed, easing into the parking lot. He pulled the Cadillac to a stop but kept the motor running. He rolled down the window and scanned the empty lot. No lights, no moon tonight, just his headlights piercing the endless black expanse of the Glades beyond the low wood barrier surrounding the lot. The dashboard clock read just after four, so he knew he was only a couple of minutes late. Unless the damn clock was wrong. He felt a nervous tug in his stomach.

Then, he picked up a small glow over on the far side of the lot. He squinted and made out something parked over against the brush, some kind of fancy black truck, maybe a Blazer. The motor was off and he couldn't see anyone inside through the tinted windows. The glow grew brighter. Probably a cigarette.

This had to be the guy. No one else would be out here this time of night, sitting alone on the side of the road.

He pulled the Cadillac forward, stopping about twenty yards away. He killed the headlights and turned the tape down to a whisper. Marty Robbins was still singing his love song, harmonizing with the frogs and crickets.

The window of the truck came down and the glowing butt was flicked out. He caught a glimpse of a face shadowed by the brim of a hat. The guy was waiting for him to make the first move.

He picked up the FedEx box and opened the door. The second he was out of the Cadillac, the Blazer's lights came on. He blinked in the glare and averted his eyes, spotting the now fully illuminated trash can over by the boat ramp. He went to it and carefully set the box on the rim of the can. He backed away, edging toward the Cadillac, shielding his eyes with his hand to look back at the Blazer.

The guy sitting behind the wheel still hadn't moved.

He waited. A minute, then another. No movement from the Blazer. He heard a door open.

A shadow of a figure emerged from the backseat. He couldn't see him in the glare but then the figure moved toward the front of the Blazer.

Small with long dark hair.

Wait . . . was it a woman?

The figure moved into the beam of the headlights and he could see clearly now that it was a woman. Her long black hair was pulled back in a ponytail. Then, suddenly, there were two more with her.

Women . . . three women. He could tell now for sure that they were women from the way they stood there, huddled and scared like kittens, their long black hair swirling around their faces.

"Go. Go on now."

It was the guy behind the wheel who had spoken. He was waving a hand out his window, waving toward the Cadillac, and the three women were looking back at him, like they didn't understand what he was saying.

"Over there! Go on . . . over to that car. That's your ride. Go on now."

The women looked at each other, then slowly, moving as if they were one, they started toward the Cadillac.

He stared at them. What was this? What was going on? Was this the *package* he was supposed to pick up? Women?

A slight grin came to his face. Okay, he could deal with this. He would make the delivery and not ask any questions. Just like he had been told to do.

The woman who had come out first was barely a shadow against the trees but he saw something in the movement of her body, a small jerk of her head, that told him she was going to run. And she did, bolting into the darkness.

Shit!

He ran after her, feeling the ground shift from asphalt to grass. He was quicker and stronger and he caught her easily ten or fifteen feet from the Blazer.

He wrapped an arm tight around her neck and started to drag her back. She was light and he could almost carry her, but she was fighting, her screams screeching in his ears.

"Shut up!" he yelled.

Her nails tore into his forearm. She started kicking, her legs flailing in the air. The screams grew louder. And louder until it was all he could hear. He tried to put a hand over her mouth, but she bit him, her teeth sinking into the black leather of his glove.

When he jerked his hand away from her mouth, the screaming started up again. He almost had her back to the pavement when her foot smashed into his crotch. He doubled in pain, letting out a groan, trying to hold onto her with one hand. Her screams were piercing now.

Shut up! Jesus, shut up!

He yanked her back, throwing her against the hood of the Blazer. His eyes flicked to the other two women huddled by the side of the truck and then up to the windshield to the faceless man in the hat behind the wheel.

The Blazer's engine's revved and he felt it vibrating against his body. He knew the guy was going to pull away and that the whole thing would be messed up.

And the woman pinned beneath his body was still screaming.

Shut up! Oh God, just shut up and keep still!

But she wouldn't.

He threw his body over her, his right hand groping behind, around to his belt, around to the knife.

Shut up! Stop it! Stop that screaming!

He cut her throat.

Her body went limp. It was quiet now.

He looked into the Blazer through the blood-splattered windshield. He could see only the wide eyes of the driver.

The Blazer jerked into reverse with a roar, tossing him and the woman's body to the asphalt. It lurched forward, swerving around him and the woman, and almost hitting the Cadillac. The other two women jumped aside, and the Blazer raced out onto Alligator Alley.

He looked at the knife in his hand and at the woman lying on the ground.

Oh no . . .

The two women were standing there staring at him in horror.

Oh God, he was in trouble now.

He stuck the knife back in its sheath, his hands trembling. His eyes darted back to the Cadillac. For a second, he thought of jumping in and heading east, not stopping until he got to Miami. But he couldn't do that, couldn't just leave.

He looked down at the body. He had to hide her. But where? The parking lot had no cover and he would get cut to pieces by the razorlike blades of the saw grass if he tried to drag her out there. The canal? He could throw her in the water and maybe a gator would find her and pull her under. But she'd probably just float and he knew the fishermen would be out soon. They always got out here by dawn.

Think, think . . .

He grabbed her under the arms and dragged her over to the grass near the boat ramp. A boat . . . someone had abandoned a boat. It was old, beat up, but made out of aluminum, so maybe it would still float. That's where he would put her.

He dropped her into the boat. She lay wedged against the seat, her head at a weird angle. He hesitated, then grabbed her blouse, ripping it open. He jerked her slacks down around the thighs, paused, then gently spread her legs. A rape gone wrong . . .

The boat was sitting in some weeds and he had to push hard to get it to slide down into the black water of the canal. Once in the water, it moved easily, and he gave it a hard shove. He let out a breath of relief as it began to glide away.

He looked back toward the trash can where he had left the FedEx box, thinking at least he could return the money since he had lost one of the packages. But it was gone. Somehow the man must have taken it while he was struggling with the woman.

The other two women were huddled by the Cadillac, holding each other. He went to them. They started backing away from him, their eyes wide with terror.

"No, don't," he said, holding up his hands. "I won't hurt you. Don't run."

He opened the back door of the Cadillac. "Get in," he said.

The women didn't move.

"Get in, please," he said. He tried to make his voice sound gentle. He couldn't afford to lose another one.

The women got in the backseat. He closed the door, locked it, and slid in the driver's side, closing his eyes for a moment. Marty Robbins was whispering in his ear.

> *They say that just before the dawn*
> *That night is as black as can be-e-e*

One of the women was weeping. A wind was coming up from the north, rippling the black water of the canal and swaying the saw grass, making the tall blades sound like knives scraping on stone.

He pulled out of the lot. At the edge of Alligator Alley, he stopped. He looked right, across the flat grass to where the first thin edge of gray was shading in from the east.

He turned the Cadillac west and headed back into the darkness.

CHAPTER 2

Tuesday, January 12

His hands were sweating. And his heart was beating too fast, making his chest tight. What the hell was wrong with him? He had faced this before and survived. He knew what to expect, knew that it was only painful for the first couple of minutes and then you just went numb until it was over.

So why was he afraid this time?

Louis Kincaid got out of the Mustang and took a few seconds to just stand there, staring at the house. He glanced up at the night sky. No moon, no stars. Just a cool breeze blowing in from the gulf, whispering rain.

The porch light was on and a pale green luna moth was chasing a smaller moth, throwing itself against the glowing globe. Louis rang the bell. No answer. He pushed it again and as he waited, he watched the green moth. Now it was gripping the edge of the glass, exhausted, its wings tattered from its mating ritual. The other moth had disappeared.

He ran his wet palms down his thighs, catching sight of his black slacks. He was covered in cat hair.

Shit . . . damn it to hell.

The door jerked open.

Benjamin looked up at him through the screen.

"She isn't ready yet," he said.

Louis glanced at his watch. The dinner reservation was for eight-thirty. They weren't going to make it.

"You better come in 'cause it might be a while," Benjamin said, holding the screen open.

"Good idea," Louis said.

He followed the boy into the living room. There were some school books and a looseleaf binder scattered on the floor in front of the television. *Beauty and the Beast* was on, the sound turned down. Benjamin sat down cross-legged on the floor, his skinny brown legs protruding from baggy red shorts, his sticklike arms covered to the elbows by a too big Michael Jordan T-shirt.

Louis perched on the edge of the sofa, glancing around.

"Ben, is April coming over?" he asked.

Benjamin made a face as he busied himself with a toy car. "I don't need April anymore."

"You're too young to stay alone," Louis said.

"My friend Joshua stays alone."

"Well, maybe next year when you're twelve."

Louis glanced at his watch again, seeing his reservation for the waterfront table and the whole evening going up in smoke.

"Ben, do me a favor," he said. "Go see what's taking your mom so long."

Benjamin didn't look up. "She's doing her hair again. I heard her swearing at it in the bathroom."

Louis stifled a sigh and brushed at the cat hairs on his cuffs.

"So how come it took you so long to ask my mom for a date?" Benjamin asked.

Louis pursed his lips, trying to think of an answer. He had been thinking about asking Susan Outlaw for a date almost from the day he met her more than a year ago. But she was a public defender and he had been a private investigator working for her. An awkward situation to begin with—with no room for romance. When the case ended, though, he had asked Susan out. She had refused, saying she didn't want to get involved with anyone. It stayed that way for over a year.

One night his friend, Mel Landeta, offered some advice.

"Well, Rocky, you need to either get off your island or let her on it with you," Mel said.

"What do you mean?"

"Women like to get inside you. You got to let her in."

So he had tried. Tried the small talk, tried to be less cautious, tried even to make an effort with her son Benjamin. Benjamin warmed up to him first. Then Susan came around.

And now, here he was, sitting on Susan's sofa like some pimply prom date, complete with sweaty palms, racing pulse, and cat-hair pants.

He glanced toward Susan's closed bedroom door. It took him a moment to realize Benjamin was staring at him.

"Your pants are hairy," Benjamin said.

Louis smiled. "Yeah, I know. My whole house is hairy."

"Ma's got a lint brush. You wanna borrow it?"

"Nah, that's okay."

Benjamin shrugged and went back to playing with his toy. Louis's smile lingered. He liked the kid . . . no doubt about it. He liked the kid's mother. He liked the fact there might be a place for him in their world.

"You didn't answer my question," Benjamin said.

"What question?"

"Why it took you so long to ask Ma out?"

"Fear."

"Are you afraid of her?"

Louis didn't—couldn't—answer that one.

"Yeah, she can be mean sometimes," Benjamin said. "But it's for our own good."

Louis smiled. Benjamin was twisting the toy.

"What is that?" Louis asked.

"Optimus Prime."

"It looks like a car to me," Louis said, his eyes wandering back to Susan's bedroom door.

"Watch." Benjamin pulled and twisted on the toy and then held it out proudly. Now it looked like a robot. "It's a Transformer," he said.

Louis caught a whiff of something sweet and looked up. Susan was standing under the archway of the hall, hand on her hip.

"Makes you feel old, huh?" she said.

One glance was all he needed to take her in. Some kind of black blouse that draped nicely across her breasts, offering a peek of brown skin in the deep vee of the neckline. A spark of light at her ears that he finally saw was just earrings catching the light of the dining room chandelier.

Louis found his voice. "I'm twenty-eight but when it comes to kids, I feel fifty."

She frowned. "Twenty-eight?"

Louis realized she was looking at him like he was a bug on the wall. "How old did you think I was?"

She threw up her hands, but they just hung in the air, the fingers wiggling nervously. "I don't know. I guess it doesn't matter. I just thought . . ."

"Thought what?"

She dropped her arms. "Never mind."

Benjamin was watching them. "Ma's thirty-two," he said.

"Ben!"

Susan turned and went into the kitchen. Benjamin looked at Louis and shrugged.

She was embarrassed? But why? Not at being thirty-two, he guessed, but more so at being the "older woman." Man, he needed to fix this if the evening was going to go anywhere. He followed her into the kitchen. She was pulling steaks from the refrigerator.

The words came out before he could stop them. "I thought we were going out."

She faced him, the package of T-bones sagging in her hand. "Going out? I thought you meant . . ."

It was then he noticed she was wearing jeans. "You said you wanted a steak. You didn't say—"

She dropped the meat on the counter. "Well, shoot," she muttered. She looked around the kitchen, at the loaf of French bread on the counter, the potatoes, the colorful salad all ready in its teak bowl. Louis realized she had put real effort into this, but so had he in trying to get that special table at La Veranda, including twenty bucks in advance to the maître 'd.

Susan gave a small shrug. "I guess if you want to go out, we can go out. I can call April and we can—"

Louis held up both hands. "Relax. It's fine."

"No, it isn't. Look, you're already ticked off because you had some high hopes of—"

He touched her shoulder. She didn't move away.

"I'm not ticked off. I can do the family thing. I don't mind."

She turned and leaned against the counter, brushing a stray hair back off her face. Then she crossed her arms.

"Look, I don't know exactly what I did," Louis said. "But I'm sorry."

"It's me," she said quietly. "I might have misled you, you know, about dinner. It's just, well, I didn't think you'd come if I told you I wanted to have it at home."

"It's fine."

"It's just that it's been so long," she whispered, staring at the floor.

"So long since what, Ma?" said the small voice behind him.

They both looked down at Benjamin standing in the doorway. Susan moved away from Louis quickly and began ripping open the steaks.

"So long since what?" Benjamin asked again.

She glanced at him, then her eyes flicked up to Louis. "Since I've had a good piece of meat," she said.

Louis turned away, smiling. Benjamin slid into a chair, his car sprouting arms again. "We having steaks?" he asked. "We never eat steaks."

"Yes, we're having steaks," Susan answered.

"Is that what people eat on dates?"

Susan looked at him but didn't reply. Louis sat down at the yellow Formica dining set. He broke the awkward silence by clearing his throat. "Do you have anything to drink?"

Before Susan could answer, Benjamin jumped to the fridge, yanking open the door. He plopped a can down in front of Louis.

"Ma got you Dr Pepper. She says you like it."

Louis looked from Benjamin up to Susan. He could see a tint of red color her skin. "I have wine if you'd rather have that," she said, holding up a bottle.

"This is good," Louis said, popping the tab. He could feel Benjamin's eyes on him as he drank.

Susan brought the wine to the table with a corkscrew. "Well, I could use a drink. You mind doing the honors?"

As Louis opened the bottle, Benjamin continued to twist his car back into the robot.

"What is the purpose of that?" Louis asked.

"Transformation," Benjamin said. "You know, changing into something else."

"That could be handy," Louis said.

"Yeah, like if you're being chased or something, you could change into something else."

"Cops could be superheroes," Louis said. "Like the Six Million Dollar Man."

Benjamin made a face. "Kinda."

Louis looked back at Susan. She was watching them, and she had a strange look on her face—almost like pleasure. It took him a moment to realize that her look wasn't just at him being here on a date. It was him being here with Benjamin.

"If you could transform, what would you turn into?" Benjamin asked.

Louis looked back at him. Benjamin was peering at him with large brown eyes behind black-rimmed glasses.

"I don't know. Maybe I'd transform into head of detectives for Fort Myers Police."

Benjamin cocked his head. "But you're a P.I. That's more cool."

Louis glanced back at Susan. She was busy getting the steaks ready for the oven, but he knew she was listening to every word.

"What about you?" Louis asked Benjamin. "What would you be?"

"A bird, so I could fly."

Louis turned in his chair. "And you?" he asked Susan.

She was slicing the French bread with a huge knife and when she faced him, she held the knife up in her hand.

"I like being me," she said. "I like being a mother and I like what I do. I have no desire to be something else."

Benjamin slipped from the chair again and disappeared into the living room. Susan dumped the potatoes in a pan and put it on the stove.

She grabbed two tumblers from the cabinet and came to the table to sit down. Louis looked at the glasses, the wine bottle in his hand.

"Ben's using my only two wineglasses for a school project," she said. "They're supposed to be underwater space stations or something. They're covered with algae by now, I'm sure."

"I understand," Louis said, pouring the wine into the tumblers.

She gave him a wry smile. "I doubt it."

"I was a kid once, you know."

She took a drink of wine, her eyes never leaving his across the rim of her cup. "I'm sorry," she said finally. "It's just . . . well, you need to know what you're getting into here, Louis. Living with a child is different. There are things you have to do . . . different."

She was trying to put him off again, trying to warn him of the "dangers" and responsibilities of taking care of a child. He knew it was also her way of making sure that he understood she came with baggage that was four feet tall with glasses.

He looked at her. "Susan, I don't care about the wineglasses."

She looked away. "It's not the wineglasses. It's him. We've been by ourselves so much, and I have never brought anyone—any man—into his life for fear he would get attached when there was no chance . . ."

She rose suddenly and went to check the steaks. It was quiet for a moment.

"Susan, I promise I won't hurt him."

She didn't turn.

He let out a breath and took a drink of the wine.

"His father hurt him," she said, facing Louis. "Ben used to say his prayers every night and always ask God to bring his daddy home. He stopped asking last year, and stopped saying his prayers altogether a few months ago."

Louis looked down at his wine. For a moment, just a moment, he was back in a cold room in Mississippi kneeling on a hard linoleum floor.

If I should die before I wake, I pray the Lord my soul to take. Amen. And God, please bring my daddy back so momma will stop drinking.

Louis sat back in the chair, his fingers wrapped around the tumbler.

Tell her. If you want this to go anywhere, talk to her.

"Susan, I was . . ." The words caught in his throat and he swallowed hard. "I was a foster kid. I used to lay awake at night, too, hoping to be rescued by a man who never came. I know what's it's like."

She stared at him. He could see so many things in her face, like suddenly a mask had slipped, a crack had opened, and all her emotions were there, raw and hovering on the surface. A year to wear her down, and now here she was, wanting so hard to trust him. He could see it there on her face.

"I promise," he said. "I promise that no matter what happens between you and me, I won't ever walk out on him."

Susan looked at him for a moment, then wiped the corner of her eye with the back of her hand. "Jesus, it's warm in here."

She turned to busy herself with cooking. Louis stood up and wandered into the living room.

He took a deep breath. All right . . . that was it. He had let her onto his island, even if it was just one small step. And it didn't feel so bad. Strange, maybe, being able to share something like that with someone so suddenly. But not bad at all.

He was staring at the television when he heard the doorbell. Susan poked her head into the living room.

"Louis, can you get that please?"

Louis rose and went to the door, looking through the small diamond-shaped window.

The man on the porch was holding the screen open with his shoulder, and was straining to peer into the window. He had smooth brown skin, and was wearing a suede trench coat the color of butterscotch, a black scarf, and a black fedora. Louis opened the door and the man's brown eyes snapped back to him. For an instant, the man seemed confused, but he covered it quickly with a smile.

"Hello," he said. He craned his neck, trying to look beyond Louis into the living room.

"Can I help you with something?" Louis asked.

The man looked back at Louis. The smile was still there, but it looked forced. And the man's eyes, now focused on Louis, narrowed ever so slightly.

"Yeah, I'm Austin Outlaw."

The smile remained.

"Is my wife here?"

CHAPTER 3

Louis stepped back from the door and Austin Outlaw came inside, taking off his hat. Susan came in from the kitchen and when she saw Austin, her body went rigid. She just stood there, holding a dish towel, eyes fixed on Austin, lips parted. The air in the room was suddenly thick with a million memories and emotions.

Footsteps from the hall and all heads turned toward Benjamin. Louis watched the boy's face. It first registered shock, then recognition, then grew bright with joy as the boy rushed to his father.

"Daddy!"

Austin bent and picked Benjamin up, bringing him high into the air then pulling him against his chest. Benjamin was talking excitedly, his brown twig arms wrapped tight around his father's neck.

Louis turned to look at Susan. Her eyes were glassy with tears, and when she saw Louis looking at her, she wiped them quickly away with the back of her hand and stepped forward. She forced a tight smile.

"Austin."

Austin lowered Benjamin and moved to Susan. He took

her by the shoulders and pulled her close to plant a kiss on her cheek.

"Baby, it's good to see you."

Susan pulled away, throwing Louis a pained look, the towel wrung around her fingers.

"Daddy," Benjamin said, pulling at the small black leather bag that was slung across Austin's suede coat. "Why didn't you call? Where have you been?"

Austin was looking at Susan, his eyes shimmering with warmth and something else Louis couldn't immediately decipher. Affection for Susan or surprise that she didn't return his embrace as warmly as he had given it?

Benjamin finally drew his father's attention downward, reluctantly away from Susan.

"Want to see my telescope? I got all the planets, too, and that bus you sent me from England and—"

Austin flashed a grin, patting Benjamin's head. "In a minute, Ben. Your mother and I need to talk first."

Austin looked at Louis, then back at Susan. "Sorry to break up your evening, Susan. I would've called except I found myself in town kind of suddenly, and I knew you wouldn't mind if I just dropped by."

Susan took a step back. "I do mind."

"For his sake, I meant," Austin said, nodding to Benjamin.

Benjamin was stroking Austin's suede coat, oblivious to the tension.

Susan set her jaw. "Of course not," she said tightly.

Austin looked back at Louis. "I'm sure you understand, mister . . . ?"

"Kincaid. Louis Kincaid." Louis looked at Susan. "I think I should go so—"

Susan touched his arm. "No, stay."

"I don't think—"

Her fingers tightened around his wrist and she pulled him quickly into the kitchen, out of sight and earshot of Ben and Austin.

"Louis," she whispered. "Please stay."

Louis leaned close to her. "Do you know how awkward this is for me?"

"Yes, yes. And I'm sorry. But I don't want him thinking he can walk back into our lives without even so much as a phone call first. It's been that way every time. Every couple of years, he just shows up and tries to treat me like we're still married. He touches me and stares at me in ways—"

"Just tell him to hit the road."

"But he does it *in front* of Ben. It's like he dares me to cause a scene."

Louis was silent, listening to Austin and Benjamin tussle playfully in the living room.

"I tolerate him for Ben," Susan said softly. "I can do this by myself. I've done it before, but I'm asking you to help me this time."

Louis knew what was happening. She wanted Austin to think she had another man in her life. A part of him understood, but a part of him was also pissed. They had been friends these last eighteen months, but not close enough for her to have earned the right to use him like this.

Susan was looking up at him, waiting.

Damn . . .

She was a public defender. She handled liars, cheaters, and murderers every day. But this was different. This wasn't the woman talking; this was the mother.

Louis nodded. "All right."

Susan led him back to the living room. Austin was putting his fedora on Benjamin's head and they both looked up.

"So, what's the plan?" he asked, standing and adjusting the bag that hung across his chest. "Pick a restaurant, my treat."

"We're eating in," Susan said, "the four of us."

Austin's eyes moved from Louis to Susan. "All right. As long as you're not making spaghetti. You know I can't handle all those spices you put in it."

"They're having steak," Benjamin said. "I'm having a hamburger."

"I'm sure Ben would love it if you had what he was having," Susan said.

Austin smiled, sensing the slight. "Sure. The last thing I want to be is a burden. A burger will be just fine." He started toward the front door.

"Daddy?" Benjamin called. "Where are you going?"

"I'll be right back," Austin said. "I'm just going to get my overnight bag."

"You're staying the night?" Benjamin cried. "You're really staying this time? Wow! Can I help? Mom, can I help get Daddy's stuff?"

Louis glanced at Susan. She was staring lasers at Austin, who seemed only amused.

"Go ahead," Susan said.

"Here's the keys, Benny," Austin said, tossing them to Benjamin. He caught them and ran out the front door, still wearing Austin's hat. Austin looked back at Susan.

"I suppose I'm to sleep where he sleeps as well?" Austin asked.

"You're lucky you're not sleeping in the garage," Susan said. "How dare you do this to me with no notice."

Austin tilted his head toward Louis. "In the past, you never seemed to need notice."

Susan grabbed a candle off the mantel and poised to throw it at him. But Austin simply flashed her another smile.

"I better go help Ben," he said, going out the door.

Louis had never seen the dining room table set for dinner before. Susan used it for her desk, and it was always heaped with court files, law books, and her open briefcase, with one corner taken up by Benjamin's schoolbooks. Tonight, however, she had set it with cheery blue and yellow place mats, a couple of candles, and a small grocery store bouquet of flowers. It made him feel good that she had gone to such trouble for him. It made him feel pissed that Austin had showed up to spoil it all.

He glanced at the man standing across the table. But he wasn't about to let the bastard know it.

Susan came out of the kitchen with a fourth place mat and silverware for Austin but didn't set out a glass for wine. Austin's eyes went to the bottle of burgundy on the table.

"I don't suppose you have a glass for me, do you?" he asked.

Susan glowered at him and went into the kitchen. She returned with a Flintstones juice glass, plunking it down in front of Austin's plate. She went back in the kitchen.

"She never did have enough glasses," Austin said, as he helped himself to the wine.

Louis didn't have a chance to answer before Susan returned carrying the plates. She looked up at Louis and Austin. "Well, let's eat," she said.

Austin sat across from Louis, Susan on his right, Benjamin on his left. Susan ate in stony silence. Louis did the same. Austin was barely touching his food, his eyes drifting between Susan and Louis. Benjamin was talking nonstop, monopolizing the conversation.

"Daddy, are you home for good now?"

Austin picked at his mashed potatoes. "No, I'm afraid not. I have to head back to Australia soon."

"Australia? That's where they have kangaroos, right?"

Austin smiled at Benjamin. "And koala bears."

"Cool."

"I thought you were in England," Susan said.

"I was for a while, but business took me to Australia and we've set up our offices there. We've been there about a year now, and a couple months ago, we set up an office in Miami. That's why I'm here, to check on my partner and see how things are going." He gave Benjamin a smile. "I played hooky today to come over and see you, sport. Had to sneak away without telling anyone."

"I won't tell," Benjamin said.

Susan was silent, stabbing her steak.

"So, what do you do, Austin?" Louis asked. He didn't really want to know, but the tension was getting to him.

Austin glanced at him. "I'm in imports." He reached in his pocket and pulled out a business card, holding it out.

Louis hesitated, then took it. He gave it a quick glance out of courtesy then put it in his pocket.

"What line of work are you in?" Austin asked him.

"I'm a private investigator," Louis said.

Austin smiled. Or smirked. Louis couldn't tell. "Really? Is that how you two met? Defending someone accused of some horrendous crime?"

"As a matter of fact, yeah," Louis said.

"Louis is a great private eye, Daddy," Benjamin said. "He caught a serial killer and everything. He used to be a cop, too."

"I suppose law enforcement is an honorable enough profession," Austin said. "But you have to wonder about defense work. Must be tough on the conscience, I would think."

Susan was staring at Austin. Louis suspected she had heard this before.

"What's a conscience, Ma?"

Susan turned to Benjamin. "That's the part of your brain that tells you when to do the right thing."

"Does everyone have a conscience?" Benjamin asked.

"No," Susan said, looking at Austin.

Austin held her eyes for a moment, then went back to pushing his mashed potatoes around on his plate.

"What do you import, Austin?" Louis asked.

"Collectibles and antiques from Indonesia, among other things. It requires a lot of travel, unfortunately, and of course, handling the native people isn't entirely pleasant, but you deal with it."

"Are you rich, Daddy?" Ben asked.

Austin hesitated. Louis knew Susan had once described Austin to Benjamin as "cash poor," probably because he seldom sent any child support, and it was an easy explanation for an eleven-year-old boy to accept. But Louis suspected Austin had more money than he let on. At least enough to wear suede coats, Italian slacks, and a gold Rolex and to travel with a Vuitton duffel. Okay, maybe the Rolex and duffel were fake, but that big black BMW parked in the drive wasn't, rental or not.

Louis's eyes dropped to the small black Vuitton bag that Austin had slung across the back of the chair. And what kind of a man carried a purse, for crissakes?

Austin picked up his burger with both hands. Louis focused on his long fingers. Shit, the guy even had manicured nails.

"Your son asked you a question, Austin," Susan said.

Austin took a bite of the burger and set it down. He gave Benjamin a smile. "Sometimes I'm rich and sometimes I'm not."

Susan let out a snort.

"It's an up-and-down business," Austin said, looking at her. "But right now, it's up. That's one reason I came by."

Austin reached back and pulled something out of the black bag. He held out a bill to Benjamin.

"Merry Christmas, Benny."

"A hundred dollars!" Benjamin yelled. "Is that real? Is that for me?"

"Yup."

Benjamin sprang from his chair and threw his arms around Austin's neck. Austin patted Benjamin's back, but was looking at Susan.

For what? Louis wondered. To see if the gesture had impressed her? From the look on her face, it pissed her off.

"Christmas was three weeks ago. You missed it," Susan said.

She pushed away from the table and rose, picking up her plate. She snatched up Austin's plate and went into the kitchen. Louis heard the clatter of dishes in the sink.

"Ben, why don't you go put your money in your room?" Louis said.

"Yeah, good idea." Benjamin disappeared down the hallway.

Louis debated what to do. Go in to the kitchen? Disappear with Benjamin and let these two slug it out? Or knock Austin on the seat of his nice Italian pants?

Austin reached back for his purse. He pulled out a big fat cigar and a lighter. He was about to light the thing when Susan came back to the table. Her eyes were flashing as she looked down at Austin.

"Get out," she said, her voice low.

"Okay, I won't light it," Austin said with a smile.

"I don't care about the damn cigar. I just want you out. Now. I'll tell him you had to leave suddenly. Just like you always do."

"Baby, you don't mean that. It's only money and it made him happy."

Austin stood up and went toward her, arms spread. "Look, maybe I come on too strong sometimes, but I'm just trying to make things up to you."

"You're pathetic," Susan hissed.

Austin reached for her, slipping his hand around her waist.

Louis stood up. This was enough. He was out of here.

Suddenly, Susan drew back and slapped Austin. Austin touched his face, then stepped backward just as Benjamin came back in the room. He was holding a *Star Wars* piggy bank.

His eyes moved slowly from his father to Susan. "Are you two fighting again?" he asked softly.

Susan wiped her face. "No, Ben. We're okay."

Austin's pained expression changed quickly back to a smile. He still had the cigar in his hand. He slipped off the paper ring and held it out to Benjamin. "Want to wear Daddy's ring?"

Ben stared at the ring for a second then took it, slipping it on his index finger. Louis could see the label. It was a Macanuda cigar. Expensive.

"What do you say we go for ice cream?" Austin asked Ben.

"He hasn't finished his hamburger," Susan said.

"Who needs burgers when you can have Fudge Ripple? Is that little ice cream store still over on McGregor?"

"Yeah, and they have blue bubble gum ice cream now," Benjamin said. He looked at Susan. "Can we go, Ma? Huh? Can we go?"

Austin didn't wait for an answer. He carried Benjamin from the room, setting him on the sofa to help him with his shoes.

Louis watched Susan. Her eyes brimmed with tears and she was shaking.

"I'll have him back in an hour," Austin called out, slipping on his coat.

Louis waited until he heard the front door close, then he went to Susan. She closed her eyes and leaned forward into his arms.

CHAPTER 4

Friday, January 15

A cold front was on the way. Louis could feel it, feel the subtle change in the night air. One moment it had been a sigh of a breeze, coming soft and warm from the gulf. Then a pause—almost like an inhalation—before the wind shifted. The auger-shell chimes on the porch were doing their click-clack bone dance and the temperature was beginning to fall.

Louis got up and went inside. He returned with a sweat-shirt and a Heineken and sat back down in the wicker chair. Issy jumped up into his lap and began kneading his stomach.

Louis took a long drink of the beer, his eyes out on the black waters of the gulf as he absently stroked the cat's head.

Shit, it was all screwed up.

Three days had passed since that night at Susan's. He had called once, but she seemed distracted, distant. Louis had heard Austin and Benjamin laughing in the background. He had hesitated, then just come out and asked her if Austin was still staying at the house. She said he was, but that it was only so Benjamin could have time with him. Louis had cut the conversation short and hung up.

Then, earlier tonight, Susan had called him back.

"He's leaving tonight," she said. "He's going back to Australia."

There had been an awkward pause on her end.

"He wants us to go with him," Susan said.

"What did you tell him?" Louis asked. It had been a struggle to keep his voice neutral.

"Tell him? I told him no, of course."

Of course?

"What about Benjamin?"

Another long pause. "I haven't told him yet. He'll want to go. What son wouldn't want to be with his father and go play with real koala bears?"

Louis said nothing.

"It's going to be hard on Ben," Susan said. "It's always hard, but he's old enough now to know things. Like the fact his mom and dad are never getting back together. Like his dad won't . . . can't . . . be there all the time."

Louis heard the pain in her voice but still said nothing.

"Louis? Are you there?"

"What do you want from me, Susan?"

"I don't know. I . . ." She let out a long breath. "Could you come over?"

"What for?"

"Austin is going to ask me again to come with him. And he'll do it in front of Ben this time. I know he will. If you're here, maybe he won't. Maybe Ben won't get upset. Maybe . . . shit, I don't know what I'm saying."

Louis let out a sigh.

"Louis, Austin will do whatever he needs to do to get what he wants. That's the way he is. This time he wants Benjamin. He doesn't care if he hurts me to get him." She paused again. "Would you come over, please?"

"I don't think that would be a good idea, Susan," he said.

Silence. "You're right," she said softly. "I shouldn't have asked." And she hung up.

Louis took another drink of beer, his other hand light on Issy's back as he looked out over the gulf waters. Maybe he should have told her he would come over. What would it have cost him? An hour of his time? A little discomfort? Why had he said no? Pride? Or was it just not wanting to get into the damn messiness of it all?

The phone rang. Louis ignored it, afraid it was Susan again, or afraid it wasn't. He wasn't even sure.

After ten rings, the phone went quiet. He finished the beer. The wind picked up, sending the auger-shell wind chime rattling and letting loose a rain of leaves from the sea grapes trees. Louis watched the leaves swirl on the sand. January in South Florida and it felt almost like fall in Michigan.

The phone started ringing again. He counted the rings. Ten, eleven, twelve. She wasn't going to give up this time.

He lifted Issy to the floor and rose, going into the bedroom. He snatched up the receiver.

"Look, Susan—"

"Try again, Rocky."

"Mel?" Louis switched on the lamp and sat down on the edge of the bed. "Hey, when did you get back?"

"This morning."

"How'd it go?"

"Not great."

Louis could hear a squeak and he imagined Mel Landeta folding his lanky body into the old Eames chair in his apartment. He waited, knowing it always took Mel a moment or two to get comfortable.

"So what did the doctor say, exactly?" Louis asked.

"He told me to take some vitamin A."

"What?"

"You heard me. Vitamin A. They think it might slow things down. So I will be seventy when I go blind instead of sixty-five."

Louis didn't say anything. Mel Landeta was his friend, although Louis wasn't even sure that was the right word for it. How did a man get to be twenty-eight years old and never have a real male friend? He knew the answer. It was the same reason he didn't want to go over and help Susan tonight. Friendship was messy. It required putting yourself out there.

Mel had retinitis pigmentosa. He was forty-five with no family, an ex-cop living on disability. He was slowly going blind. Friendship didn't get much messier than that.

"So you going to take the vitamins?" Louis asked.

"Why not? Vitamin A is supposed to help you get woodies. I may not *see* who I'm screwing but at least she'll be happy when I'm done."

Louis laughed. He knew Mel hadn't had a serious woman in his life for years. Neither had he, for that matter.

"So how'd the big date go?" Mel asked.

"It didn't."

"What, did she back out on you?"

"Worse, her ex showed up."

Mel let out a low chuckle. Louis didn't say anything. He didn't really want to talk about it, or maybe he did and just didn't know how. Mel had come over for dinner the night before his appointment with the eye specialist in Miami. Louis had opened up some about Susan, finding comfort in the fact that Mel couldn't see how his expression changed whenever he mentioned Susan Outlaw. Which was stupid because he knew Mel could hear more in a voice than most people saw in a face.

Louis heard the click of a lighter and the sound of Mel inhaling his cigarette.

"So you gonna tell me what happened?" Mel asked.

"Nothing to tell. We all had dinner together. It was all very civilized."

"Until you lunged across the meatloaf and choked the guy."

"We had steaks."

Another pause. The wind was picking up. The front door slammed shut. Issy came running in.

"So what you going do now, Rocky?" Mel asked.

"I don't know," Louis said, watching the cat.

"You want me to slip her a note in homeroom for you?"

"Fuck you."

Mel laughed. "Sorry."

Louis was quiet, his eyes on Issy. The cat was stretched out on the terrazzo floor at his feet, meowing and twitching.

"The ex is going back to Australia," Louis said. "He asked Susan and Ben to go with him."

"And?"

"She's going to tell him no."

"Going to?"

"He's leaving tonight." Louis was watching the cat as it pawed at his feet. "Susan asked me to come over and be there."

"Just be there?"

"Moral support."

"What, she afraid of him or something?"

"Not exactly. But he's . . ." Louis shifted the phone to his other ear. "He's her ex. They've got a history together."

It was quiet on the other end of the line.

"Good-looking guy?" Mel asked finally.

"Shit, I don't know. I guess."

"Money? Charm? Taller than you?"

"I don't need this, Landeta."

"So you going over there or not?" Mel asked.

"I told her no."

"Big mistake, Rocky."

"Why? Why the hell should I go over there?"

"Defend your turf. Mark your territory. Make your claim. To show her you care, for crissake. Shit, no wonder you never have a date."

"I have dates." Louis stared at Issy. The cat was acting really strange now, writhing on the floor and meowing loudly.

"What the fuck is that noise?" Mel asked.

"My cat."

"Sounds like you're strangling it."

Louis rose off the bed, watching the cat. "She's in heat. It's annoying."

Mel laughed. "Get her a boy cat."

"Forget that, man. I don't want kittens."

"Then you better get her fixed."

Issy let out a wail like a crying baby.

"The thing's going nuts. I'll take her in first thing tomorrow," Louis said.

"What about tonight?" Mel asked.

Louis sat back down on the bed. "So you think I should go over there?"

"Yup. Show her you care. Women like men who do that. You're already in her head, Rocky. Now you got to get in her heart."

Louis was quiet.

"If you don't go, you're going to end up in worse shape than that cat," Mel said. "I need some sleep. I'll talk to you later."

Mel hung up. Louis put the receiver back in the cradle and leaned back against the headboard. The bedroom had turned cold now, the wind whistling between the jalousies. Louis watched Issy on the floor. She stopped her writhing long enough to look up at him.

"I know how you feel," he muttered.

He rose suddenly and went to the closet. He grabbed a jacket, slipped on some old loafers and snatched up his car keys. With a last look at Issy, he left the bedroom.

Susan was glad to see him. At least it seemed like it from the relieved expression on her face as she opened the door.

"Come in," she said, holding open the screen door. Louis followed her into the living room. It was warm after the chill of the outside. There was a fire going in the hearth and the TV was on, the volume turned low. The lumpy blue sofa was covered with case files and Susan's briefcase was propped open on the coffee table next to an empty wineglass.

Susan was wearing old jeans with a rip at the knee, a

baggy red sweater, and bright pink socks. She started to tidy up the mess on the sofa.

"Sorry, I was working," she said. "I've got a prelim Monday morning. She picked up the wineglass and paused. "I'm drinking pinot. You want some?"

"You got a beer?"

She nodded and went to the kitchen. Louis followed. He noticed the house seemed awfully quiet.

"Where's Ben and Austin?" he asked.

"They're not back yet," Susan said, taking a Heineken from the refrigerator. "Austin said they were going to lunch at McDonald's, then over to Lakes Park. Ben likes to ride the train there. They probably stopped for ice cream." She opened the beer and held it out to Louis.

Louis saw her eyes stray to the clock on the wall. She let out a sigh and refilled her wineglass. When she looked back at Louis, her eyes were dark with worry.

She picked up the wineglass and left the kitchen; Louis followed her back to the living room. She was sitting on the sofa, staring at the television, elbows on knees, her hands clasping the wineglass. The guy on the TV was talking now about the cold front, standing in front of a big map marked with huge crescents of white moving down from the north toward the Florida peninsula.

"Are they late?" Louis asked.

"Yes . . . well, no," Susan said. "Austin told me he has to leave here no later than five-thirty. He has a plane to catch in Miami and it leaves at ten. I saw his ticket. He had tickets for me and Ben, too."

"He bought tickets before he asked you to go?"

"That's how he is. He just does things without asking."

Louis glanced at his watch. It was almost six. He knew it was at least a two-and-a-half hour drive to Miami. He sat down next to Susan, pushing aside a pile of legal briefs.

"He'll bring him back," he said.

Susan shook her head slowly. "You don't know him."

Louis nodded to the suede coat and hat laying on a chair by the door. "He left his coat and hat."

"He said it was going to rain and he didn't want to get it ruined," she said absently.

"He wouldn't leave his precious suede coat here, Susan."

She set the glass down sharply on the coffee table and jumped up, going to the window and pulling back the curtain.

Louis stifled a sigh and turned back toward the television. The type above the talking head said "Body Found in Glades." With a glance back at Susan, Louis dug the remote out of the cushions and turned up the sound.

"Broward County deputies are investigating the discovery of a body found yesterday at a rest stop off Alligator Alley just inside the county line. The unidentified woman was most likely the victim of a sexual assault."

Louis glanced back at Susan. She was still staring out at the street. He went back to the news.

"The victim is a black woman in her late twenties, about five feet five, one hundred and fifteen pounds. Police are asking anyone who might know the woman to please contact the Broward County Sheriff's Department."

There was a photograph on the screen now. It was of the victim's face, probably taken on the autopsy table. Her dark hair pulled back away from her round face. But she didn't look black, Louis thought with a slight flash of annoyance. The woman looked Hawaiian . . . Polynesian, maybe.

"It's ten after," Susan said.

Louis looked at her. Her mouth was drawn tight and her eyes teary.

"You want me to go look for him?" Louis asked.

She hesitated, then nodded.

Louis turned off the television and stood up. "Where's the McDonald's and the ice cream place?"

"I can show you."

"No, you stay here. You need to be here when they get home."

Susan nodded and gave him directions to the McDonald's and ice cream place. Louis started to the door, catching a glimpse of a small framed photograph of Benjamin on the mantel. He picked it up.

"Can I take this?" he asked.

"What for?"

"To show it around."

Susan's face sagged, and it suddenly occurred to him what she must be feeling, what it must feel like to have someone ask if they can take a picture of your missing kid. He had done it before in the child custody cases he had worked. But he had never realized how much hope could be pinned to a small photograph.

"Susan, I'm sure they're fine," he said. "They probably just lost track of time."

"Call me every time you stop."

Louis nodded and walked out, Benjamin's photo in his hand.

CHAPTER 5

As Louis swung into the McDonald's, his heart dropped at the sight of three Lee County school buses parked in the lot. The place was packed. He drove around the back of the building, looking for Austin's BMW, but saw nothing. Finally he parked, grabbed the photo of Benjamin off the passenger seat, and went inside.

The place was noisy, filled with the laughter of the teenagers. Louis elbowed his way to the front of the line and pushed Benjamin's picture forward. The teenage cashier glanced up at him.

"You need to wait your turn, Mister."

"No," Louis said sharply. "I'm a cop and this kid is missing. I need to know if you saw him in the last few hours."

"I've only been here since six. You need to ask Jason."

"Which one is he?"

She tilted her head toward the back and let out a yell. A skinny young man came forward. Louis leaned over the counter and held out the photo. "I need to know if you saw this kid earlier this afternoon. He's missing."

The young man looked confused. "Man, we're busy in here. I don't know."

"Think." Louis said. The noise died suddenly, and Louis

saw the other employees staring at him. He swung the picture in front of them.

"Anyone seen this kid today?" Louis asked loudly. "Anyone?"

"He was here just before four," a young girl behind the counter said as she moved forward. "He had a Happy Meal and a Sprite. He wanted a shake but his father told him he'd have ice cream later, so he could wait."

Louis left, pushing open the glass doors and stopping on the sidewalk. He could see the sign for the ice cream place just across the convenience store parking lot. He walked to it.

Queenie's Ice Cream was empty, except for a brunette woman behind the freezers. She was rinsing scoopers in a sink and looked up as he came in. "Got a special on sundaes. Only a dollar-ninety-nine."

Louis held up the photo. "I'm looking for this kid. Was he in earlier?"

Her eyes widened. "What's happened to him?"

"Have you seen him?"

The woman's eyes stayed on the photograph of Benjamin. "Yes, he was here earlier with his father." She looked up at Louis. "At least I thought it was his father. He *seemed* like a father."

"What time did you see him?"

"Four or a little after. They both had fudge ripple in a cup."

"Do you know where they went?" Louis asked.

"I think they were headed to Lakes Park," the woman said. "I heard the father—sorry—the man say something about the little train and he said he wanted to tell him something very important. Oh my, I had no idea."

"Lakes Park . . . where is it?"

"It's a couple miles from here on Gladiolus Road." She gave Louis directions and he left, jogging back to the car. He jerked the Mustang into reverse, peeling out onto Summerlin Road. It took less than ten minutes to get to the park entrance.

Inside, he slammed to a stop in front of a wooden sign that read PARK HOURS 8 A.M.–6 P.M. There was a phone booth, and he thought about calling Susan, but he wanted to look here first, just in case.

He climbed out, scanned the few cars left in the lot, but didn't see the black BMW. He saw a map of the park and hurried over to it. The place was huge, almost three hundred acres of nature trails, swimming spots, picnic areas, and playgrounds. Louis looked frantically around at the trees.

He spotted the miniature train on the map and ran back to the Mustang. He drove along, forcing himself to go slow, keeping an eye out for the black BMW. But it was after closing now, and everyone had left. Rounding a curve, he saw a lake, shimmering under the reddening sunset. Ahead was a sign for the train. He pulled into the lot and jumped out.

He trotted to the already shuttered ticket booth. The little train sat empty beyond the turnstile. His eyes came to rest on a trash can, and he spotted an ice cream cup with the distinctive Queenie's pink lettering.

Louis swiveled, scanning the lot, the trees, the nearby playground.

Nothing. No one.

Man, why was he even still here? Why was he even looking when he knew they were probably halfway across the state? Shit, he should've called the cops right away. He was wasting time.

As he hurried back to the car, a pay phone caught his eye. He needed to call Susan now. Maybe they were back. Maybe everything was all right.

Susan answered before the second ring. "Did you find them?"

He took a deep breath. "They were everywhere you said, but there's no sign of them now."

"I'm calling the Sheriff."

"No, call Dan Wainwright," Louis said. "He's your chief out there and he can be there quicker. Use my name. He'll come himself."

Louis hung up and glanced around the parking lot. His gut was in a knot, but it wasn't the cold hard fear that came with the thought that a loved one was in danger. It was anger. Anger that a man could put an ex-wife and mother through this. Anger that a man could put his own son through anything like this. Anger at his own inability to stop it or even see it coming.

Louis glanced at the clock on Susan's mantle. It was ten minutes to seven. His eyes drifted back to Dan Wainwright. He was standing in front of Susan, his cap tilted back on his head, a notebook in his hand. Wainwright was in uniform, his towering, bulky body seeming to fill Susan's small living room. Louis had watched Wainwright at work before, always marveling at the chief's calmness. Maybe it was the older man's quiet authority, composure born of decades of FBI work and years of just plain living that Louis didn't have. The coolness combined with his sheer size and mane of white hair gave Wainwright a gravity that somehow conveyed a sense that things would be all right.

But Susan wasn't buying any of it. Louis could see that in her face as she poured out the day's events to Wainwright.

Louis went to look out the window, then came back to stand for a moment beside Susan. He went back to stand at the window, looking out at the darkness.

Wainwright watched Louis's pacing out of the corner of his eye. "Mrs. Outlaw, where was your husband staying while he was in town?" he asked. "Have you tried calling there?"

"He was staying here," she said.

Wainwright's eyes flicked to Louis.

Susan saw the look. "I know how that sounds, but it was for Benjamin's sake."

"I understand." Wainwright closed his notebook and took a deep breath. "I'm sorry to tell you this, but I'm afraid all we got here is a petty custody battle."

"Petty?" Susan said. "Petty?"

"You're a lawyer, Mrs. Outlaw," Wainwright said. "You know how these things are. He's the boy's father."

"I've had custody of him for the last five years with barely a word from the asshole. Doesn't that mean anything?"

"What do you have on paper?" Wainwright asked.

"What?"

"What's in your divorce papers regarding custody?"

Susan stared at him, her body tight. "We're not divorced."

Louis's eyes shot to Susan. Her eyes were steady on Wainwright, but Louis sensed she could feel his stare.

"We have a separation agreement," she added.

Wainwright looked at Louis, raising a brow. "I suppose that's something. Does it say anything about custody?"

She shook her head. "Just that he's supposed to pay child support and has to call before he shows up."

"And you've held him to that agreement?" Wainwright asked.

She shook her head again.

Wainwright cleared his throat. "What do you want me to do, Mrs. Outlaw?"

"Dan, can't you call Miami and see if they can intercept him at the airport?" Louis asked.

"I can try but I doubt they'll lift a finger, Louis," Wainwright said. "There's no crime here."

"No crime," Susan said, turning away.

"Wait," Louis said. "He can't take a child to Australia without a passport."

Susan spun back to face them. "That won't stop him. Austin's the kind of man who knows people. He's not above getting Benjamin a passport illegally. And there are plenty of people in Miami who would do it. Believe me, I know. I defended one once."

The room fell silent again. Louis looked at the clock. Almost seven.

"Mrs. Outlaw," Wainwright said. "I'm sure he'll call you

when he gets to wherever he's headed. He probably just wants to scare you."

"He doesn't want to just scare me," she said. "He wants me to go back with him and he's using Ben to make me come. Don't you understand?"

"Did he ask you before he left? To go back with him?" Wainwright asked.

She nodded. "He said we'd have a new life, that he had money now. That he was sorry for everything. I don't know what gave him the idea I'd even consider it."

"You sure?"

Susan's eyes narrowed. "Sure about what?"

"That you didn't give him any ideas about a reconciliation?"

She stared at Wainwright, her eyes livid. "What exactly are you asking me?" she said.

"Susan—" Louis said.

"No, I want an answer. Are you accusing me of sleeping with him?"

Wainwright didn't flinch. "I was only suggesting that sometimes urges can be impulsive between people who have an emotional history and what starts out to be a quickie for old time's sake can sometimes be misconstrued."

Susan pointed to the door. "Get out of my house."

Louis came forward. "Susan—"

She spun, her eyes silencing him.

Wainwright sighed, slipped on his cap, and started toward the door. "I'll call Miami and I'll let you know if it does any good." Wainwright stopped at the door. "Good night, Mrs. Outlaw."

She didn't reply, her arms crossed over her chest. The door closed. The clock chimed and Louis looked up. Seven straight up.

"I need to get going," he said.

"You're leaving?" Susan asked.

"For Miami. I've got less than 3 hours to catch that plane."

"I'm going with you."

"No. What if we're wrong? What if he is just trying to scare you and shows up back here?"

"You know he won't come back here. I'm going with you."

Louis shook his head. "You need to stay here on the chance that something else has happened, like an accident or something. I'll call you when I get there. I promise."

She looked at him, a wave of anger in her eyes at being left out.

"We've got to be a team here, Susan. You need to stay."

"Wait," she said, disappearing. She came back from the bedroom with a pager, and slapped it in his hand. "I'll page you if I hear anything. And *only* if I hear anything."

Louis turned it on and slipped it into his pocket. "What airline were the tickets for?"

She frowned. "I didn't actually see the tickets. He told me they were for Sydney. Wait . . . wait, I remember him telling Ben something about koala bears on the airplane."

"Qantas, that's their mascot," Louis said. "Okay, I'll call as soon as I can."

He opened the door and looked back at her. The yellow porch light glimmered in her dark, teary eyes.

"He's fine, Susan. He's with his father."

She put her arms around Louis's neck and gave him a quick hug. "That's what I'm afraid of," she whispered.

CHAPTER 6

Chaos. That was Louis's first thought was as he went through the glass doors of Miami International Airport. A swift-flowing stream of people dragging suitcases. Screaming babies. Burning neon advertising duty-free booze and perfume. And a Babel of languages he couldn't understand.

His second thought: no way was he going to be able to find Austin and Benjamin in this mess. If they were even here.

Louis pushed his way through the crowd, his eyes scanning the signs above the ticket counters. Aerolinas Argentinas. Sol Air. Iberia. Varig.

He trotted on, dodging the luggage carts and the women pushing strollers. Alitalia. KLM. Martinair. Copa. Edelweiss Air.

He caught a glimpse of a clock as he ran past the El Al counter. It was nine-fifty-five.

Aeromar. Copa. TACA. Cayman Airways. Mexicana.

Damn it! Where the hell was Qantas?

He spotted a guy wearing a badge on a string around his neck and ran to him.

"Which way to the Qantas counter?" Louis asked.

The man just stared at him.

"Qantas! Where is it?" Louis demanded.

The man muttered something in Spanish and walked away.

Shit! Louis looked around. The human river eddied around him and there wasn't an official-looking person in sight. He spotted another guy in what looked like a porter's vest. He was running some weird giant turntable that spun Saran Wrap cocoons around luggage.

"Hey," Louis said, raising his voice. "Where's Qantas, man?"

The sweating man did not look up as he jerked a giant piece of Samsonite onto the turntable. He pointed left.

Louis looked. He had raced right by it. He ran to the counter, pulling out the photo of Benjamin. There was one agent, an older woman tapping away at her computer.

"Excuse me," Louis said.

"One moment, young man."

He slapped the photo of Benjamin down on the counter. "This boy might have been abducted. I need to know if he is on one of your flights."

She looked up. "Abducted?"

"He was with a man, a black man about six foot. His name is Austin Outlaw. He has a ticket for your flight to Sydney tonight. Could you check, please?"

The woman's blue eyes blinked and she punched a few buttons on her computer. "Yes, here he is. Austin Outlaw." She looked up at Louis. "There are also reservations for a woman and a child."

Louis could see what the old woman was thinking— mom, dad, and son. Sounded like a vacation, not an abduction.

Louis glanced at his watch. The flight had left. "Did they get on the flight?"

"Oh, I'm afraid I can't tell you—"

"This is official police business."

The woman's blue eyes narrowed. "You don't look like a policeman. Show me your badge."

Louis stared at the woman. She didn't blink.

"Look," he said quietly. "I'm a private investigator and the boy's mother is back in Fort Myers worried sick." He paused. "You got any kids?"

Now the woman blinked. "Four grandkids," she said. "How do I know you're telling the truth? How do I know the three of them didn't all just go off together?"

Louis pointed at her computer screen. "Look and see if Susan Outlaw got on that plane. You don't have to tell me anything. Just look."

She hesitated then punched a couple buttons. Louis watched her expression carefully. Her brows knitted slightly and she looked up.

"She didn't check in, did she," Louis said.

The woman still said nothing.

"That should tell you I'm not lying," Louis said. "Just tell me, please. Did the boy get on that plane?"

Louis waited but the woman wasn't going to say anything more. He started away from the counter.

"Young man?"

Louis looked back.

"Neither of them did. The man or the boy," the woman said.

Louis hurried away. He realized he had left the beeper in the car. For all he knew, Austin had dropped Benjamin off back home and gone on his merry way. He had to call Susan.

She picked up on the first ring. "Did you find them?" she asked.

That wasn't good. "No."

"Louis, oh God." Her voice was trembling. "Are they—"

"He never got on the plane."

Louis heard her let out a long breath.

"He hasn't called?" Louis asked.

"No, no, nothing! I swear if I see him again I will kill him for this!"

"Susan, calm down."

"No, I won't calm down! How can you even tell me that?"

Louis rubbed the bridge of his nose. There was a long silence on Susan's end.

"I'm sorry," she said quietly. "It's just . . . I'm going crazy sitting here, Louis."

"I know." His eyes swept over the crowd, almost like he expected to see Austin and Benjamin emerge from it. But he knew they weren't here. He wondered now if Austin had even left Fort Myers. What the hell kind of game was Austin playing?

"I'm heading back, Susan. There's nothing to do here."

"What if he changed his ticket? What if he took Ben somewhere else because he couldn't get a passport?" she asked.

Louis could almost imagine what sort of scenarios were running through her head now.

"There's no way I can find him if he did, Susan," Louis said. "I got lucky at Qantas. No one's going to tell me anything. I'm not a cop. There's nothing else I can do here."

Susan said nothing.

"I'll see you in a couple hours," Louis said. "We'll figure out something then."

A long pause. He could tell she was crying but trying not to let him hear it. Then she said softly, "All right," and hung up.

With a final scan of the crowd, Louis headed for the exit. Outside, he paused, shocked by the cold night air. The temperature had dropped a good ten degrees. The newly arrived people standing in the taxi lines were shivering in shorts and bare arms, expressions of mild shock on their faces. No one ever expected cold weather in Miami. No one ever planned on it.

In the Mustang, he quickly started the engine and flipped on the heater. He sat with his hands pressed between his knees for warmth. A musty burning smell filled the car, signaling the old heater kicking on, but then it went cold. He switched it off.

Damn, what now? What the hell could he possibly do to

help Susan, other than turn this over to Wainwright and then
sit there and hold her hand? His anger was heating up with
the car, anger at Austin Outlaw and at his own sense of im-
potence.

You don't look like a policeman. Show me your badge.

Three years since he had worn one. He had learned to live
with it, even finding some sense of satisfaction in hanging
his P.I. license on the wall. But Benjamin was missing and
Susan needed his help. Help he had no power to give her.

He reached down and with a quick jerk, slammed the
gear shift into reverse. He stopped, his eyes focusing on a
wad of paper on the floor of the passenger side. Austin's
business card. He had tossed it there the first night out of
disgust.

He picked it up and pressed it open. AUSTIN OUTLAW,
PACIFIC IMPORTS. And a Miami address on Southwest Eighth
Street. His eyes went to the beeper on the seat.

If Austin was still in Miami, there was a chance he might
have gone to his office. But there was no sense in giving
Susan false hope—or more reason to be upset. He would go
check out the office first and then call her back. He popped
open the glove box and rooted around for a map. All he had
was the beat-up state map he used when he had a case outside of the Fort Myers area, which wasn't very often. In the
three years he had lived in Florida, he hadn't even been to
the East Coast.

He turned the map over. There was a small inset of Greater
Miami-Dade that showed the airport. From there he was able
to trace a rough route to Southwest Eighth Street. Louis
tossed the map aside, stuck the business card up in the visor,
and headed out of the parking lot.

As he turned off Le Jeune Road onto Eighth Street, Louis
caught sight of a blinking sign on a bank. It was 10:32. And
52 degrees. It had been a balmy 70 degrees at noon. He
wondered if Benjamin had a jacket.

Louis strained to see the street numbers in the dark. A
feeling of dread was starting to pit in his stomach and he

didn't even try to ignore it. He had learned to trust his instincts, especially when he was in the dark. And right now, his instincts were telling him that something had gone wrong.

All the signs were in Spanish, which only increased his growing anxiety. Dentista. Paradise International Envios a Cuba. Carga Immigracion. He was heading into unknown territory in more ways than one.

The cars ahead had stopped. Nothing was moving; the street was blocked. And now the guy in the Volkswagen ahead was getting out of his car. Louis laid on the horn. Then he saw it—the sweep of blue and red lights ahead. Something tightened in his stomach. He was only a block away from the address on Austin's card. He pulled into a parking lot, got out, and started sprinting toward the lights.

He pushed through the crowd and came to a stop at the yellow tape. It was stretched across the parking lot of a plain two-story stucco building. Downstairs was a unisex hair salon, a restaurant, and an income tax place. And upstairs, a clot of Miami-Dade cops standing at an open door. The sign painted on the window said PACIFIC IMPORTS.

There was an ambulance in the lot with its back door open, but there was no one inside. Louis looked back at the building, his eyes scanning the scene for a uniform close enough to talk to.

Then a man emerged backward from the doorway of Pacific Imports. He was pulling a gurney with a body on it, but the body was in a black bag, zipped closed. Louis moved closer and saw the back of a black uniform. He edged down the tape and tapped the cop on the shoulder.

"What's happened here?" Louis asked.

The officer glanced back at him, then looked away.

Louis tapped the cop again. The cop ignored him.

"Hey, listen," Louis said, "I need some answers here."

The cop spun around. "Back off."

Louis ripped his ID badge from his pocket and held it out. "I'm looking for a missing kid. He might be in that building.

Just tell me who's in that body bag and if there's a kid upstairs."

The cop's eyes dropped to the ID card, then rose to Louis's face.

"Please," Louis said.

The cop hesitated. The gurney was being wheeled to a van labeled Dade County Morgue.

"All I know is that the dead guy is a black dude, about thirty-five or forty. He was sliced up pretty good. Someone said he owned the joint."

Louis felt his chest draw tight as his eyes shot to the window of Pacific Imports. "I need to talk to a detective," he said.

The cop shook his head. "They're busy."

Louis stared at the cop as he turned away, his eyes focused at the back of his head. Then he stepped back quietly and moved a few feet away. The van was pulling out of the lot. Louis watched it head up Eighth Street. He spotted a man in dark pants and a plaid sports coat. On his belt was a gun, cuffs, and a gold shield.

Louis ducked under the crime scene tape and walked toward him. He saw a uniform heading toward him and sped up, drawing out his ID card again as he walked.

The detective saw him coming.

"Detective," Louis said quickly, reaching him. "I'm a P.I. pursuing an ex who might have kidnaped his own son from the mother. I—"

The uniformed officer's hand clamped down on Louis's arm. Louis jerked away. The officer reached for him again.

"The man I'm chasing, that's his office—" Louis said, pointing toward Pacific Imports as the uniform pulled at him. "And he had the kid with him."

The officer gave Louis a jerk backward and Louis broke free again, planting himself in front of the detective.

"The kid is only eleven," Louis said.

This time when the cop came back at him, the detective held up a hand to hold him off.

"What's the name of the guy you're chasing?" the detective asked.

"Outlaw. Austin Outlaw."

"What's he look like?"

Louis drew another breath, his eyes flicking up to the windows. "Black male, six-foot, about 170 pounds . . . dark skinned, wavy hair. Wears expensive clothes . . . Rolex."

"Sounds like our victim."

Jesus.

"Was there a kid upstairs?" Louis asked.

Someone came up behind them. "Tom, we probably got another body."

Louis strained to hear what they were saying but they dropped their voices and turned away.

Louis looked up at the open door of Pacific Imports, his chest so tight he couldn't breathe. The uniform had gone back to crowd control, and Louis just stood there, his eyes locked on the office.

"Hey, P.I." the detective called from the bottom of the steps.

Louis hurried to him.

"You can identify the kid, right?"

Louis nodded.

"Come on then. Walk on the paper and don't touch the walls."

Louis followed him up the stairs. He could hear the dull slap of his shoes on the concrete steps, but everything else seemed muted. He couldn't seem to think, to predict, to even visualize what he might see upstairs. Everything was dark, cold, and close and for a moment he felt like he was blacking out. But he knew he wasn't. He had turned it all off—the fear, the dread and the images. Something had kicked back in, a coolness he learned a long time ago.

He walked blindly behind the two men, who led him into a reception area, down a hall, and to a small room—more like a closet—off the main office. Two men were standing over a carved wood chest that looked like a cheap import people put at the foot of their bed. It was no more than three feet long and two feet wide and sat about five inches off the ground on short wooden legs.

There was a small padlock on the front that one of the men was working on getting unlocked. Under the chest, dripping from the bottom, was a widening pool of blood.

The detective glanced at Louis. "You sure you want to see this?"

Louis nodded again, afraid to speak.

The lock gave way and the cop on his knees looked up at them. The detective with Louis reached down and opened the trunk.

Blood. Skin. White skin. Blond hair, matted with blood.

Jesus. Jesus.

It wasn't Benjamin. It was a woman. A tiny woman, her body crammed inside the chest, her face, hair, arms covered in blood. So much blood she looked as if she were floating in it.

Louis felt his chest shudder with a long breath and he stepped back.

"You know this woman?" someone asked.

"What?"

Louder. "Do you know this woman?"

"No, no."

"All right, thanks. You can go."

Louis drew his eyes off the woman and looked around the room. "Was there a kid? A small boy about eleven? Did anyone see a boy?"

The cops shook their heads.

"Go wait outside," someone said.

Louis turned, trying to clear his head. Benjamin must have been here. He had to have been. But what the hell had happened?

"Take a hike, P.I. You're done here," the detective in the plaid coat hollered.

Louis left, pausing in the outer office.

His eyes swept over the room. He had seen none of this

on the way in. He'd been too focused on what they were going to find in the back, but now . . .

There were papers scattered everywhere and the desk chair was overturned on the floor. The headrest and surrounding carpet were stained black with pools of blood. The beige file cabinets were streaked with bloody prints and splatter. Louis stared at the white wall over the desk. There was a long arc of blood, the tail splaying high on the wall.

He recognized the pattern. He had seen it once before. He knew Austin's throat had been cut and the long red arc was spray from the artery.

"You done looking, sport?" the detective asked.

Louis didn't answer him, heading out into the night. He could feel the cold air rush against his sweating face as he hurried down the steps and for a minute he thought he might be sick.

He stopped at the bottom, drawing in a breath, the neon of nearby stores a bright blur against the red and blue lights.

He heard the detective come up behind him.

"Hey, P.I., in case you were wondering," the detective said. "We just ID'd the victim. His name was Wallace Sorrell."

"Sorrell?"

"Yeah." The detective pulled out a notebook and started writing something. "What's *your* name?"

"Louis Kincaid."

"Where's your office?"

Louis was staring up at the open door of Pacific Imports. It wasn't Austin. He wasn't dead. Then where the hell was he? And where was Ben?

"Hey, I asked you a question, P.I."

Louis looked back at the detective. "What?"

"Where's your office?"

"Captiva. It's near Fort Myers."

"Yeah, yeah, I know where Captiva is. They got enough over there on that little island to keep you busy?"

Louis ignored the question. He was looking back up at the office windows.

"What's the kid's name?" the detective asked.

"Benjamin Outlaw. He's eleven. They left Fort Myers about three or four hours ago. Maybe longer."

"Description?"

Louis gave him one, but his mind was already kicking back into gear, eager to ask his own questions.

The detective took down Susan's name and address, and the description of Austin's rental car, then slapped his notebook shut.

"Thanks. We'll be in touch."

"Hey," Louis said. "This Sorrell guy, who is he?"

"He and your deadbeat dad were partners in that import business. The woman in the chest was probably the secretary."

"What did they import?"

The detective started to answer him, but stopped. "Uh-uh. No way. You need to take that crappy little P.I. license back to paradise and do your investigating over there. It ain't no good here."

"It's good all over Florida," Louis snapped.

The detective snickered. "Miami ain't Florida."

Louis didn't move.

"Go home, P.I.," the detective said. He walked away.

CHAPTER 7

Louis stared at the phone. He couldn't bring himself to pick up the receiver. He didn't want to tell Susan that he hadn't found Benjamin. He didn't want to tell her what he had seen at Pacific Imports.

He glanced at the television. The first thing he had done after he checked into a room at the Airport Days Inn was to switch on the TV and scan the channels for news of the Pacific Import murders. But there had been nothing so far. Apparently, two slashed bodies wasn't big news in Miami.

He looked at his watch. The eleven o'clock news was coming on. He had to call Susan and get this over with.

She picked up on the second ring.

"Susan, it's Louis."

"Louis? Where are you?"

"I'm still in Miami."

"Miami? Why?"

Louis rubbed the bridge of his nose. "No word yet? No calls?" he asked.

"No . . . no. I would have beeped you." He could hear a breathy exhaustion in her voice, like she had cried hard and had nothing left. "Louis, why are you still in Miami?"

He took a deep breath. "Something's happened," he began slowly. "At Austin's business office."

"Oh no, oh God . . ."

"Susan, wait. It's okay. It's not Ben. I didn't find him. Not yet."

She was breathing hard. He could imagine her, sitting alone in the small dark kitchen at the yellow Formica table. He wanted suddenly to be there with her, to hold her.

"Austin's business partner is dead," he said. "He was murdered."

"Murdered? What? How?"

"I don't know. I was over at the office but the cops won't talk to me." He glanced at the television. The news was on. "Susan, I'm going to stay here, see what I can find out."

"Where are you? I can be there in—"

"No, you stay there. If Ben comes home, you've got to be there."

She was talking, but not making sense, just a torrent of words coming out, a babble, like a crazy person talking to herself. She *was* crazy . . . crazy with fear and worry.

"Susan, stop. Calm down," Louis said firmly.

Her voice dwindled to a small sob.

"There's something else."

"God, what?"

"Whoever killed the partner might be after Austin."

She was silent but he could hear her heavy breaths.

"They might know about you," he said. "And they might figure he'll go back there."

"Here?"

"I'm calling Dan Wainwright and having him send an officer."

"To sit at the curb?"

"To sit in the house."

"In my living room?"

"Yes."

"I don't want a cop in my house all night."

He closed his eyes briefly. "Susan, if you saw what I saw

tonight, you'd want him in your bedroom. Trust me on this, please."

He heard her choke back a sob, then her voice came back in a whisper. "Okay."

"Try to stay calm. I promise you, I'll find Benjamin."

"I know," she said. "I know you will."

Louis waited a few seconds until he heard the click of her phone. Then he pushed down the button with his finger, waited for a dial tone, and called Wainwright.

Louis gave him a quick rundown on what he had seen in Austin's office. Wainwright agreed to go to Susan's himself. Louis thanked him and hung up.

Louis glanced at the TV. The newscast had started and Louis saw the letters below the anchors: "Double Murder in Little Havana." He picked up the remote and turned up the volume. But after a minute listening, he knew there was nothing in the report that he didn't already know. The woman in the chest was, in fact, the office secretary, and police were estimating the deaths happened sometime earlier in the day.

Louis leaned back against the headboard, the remote slack in his hand as he stared at the screen. The newscast had moved on to a report about the cold front with film of farmers in west Dade covering tomatoes with netting. But Louis didn't see it. He was seeing that slash of red on the white walls, seeing that woman's bloody body bent into a fetal curl of death.

He rubbed his face. His gut was telling him Austin was dead. And Benjamin was, too. Whoever had done this was cold-blooded enough to kill a secretary who just happened to be in the wrong place at the wrong time. They wouldn't stop at a boy.

Louis closed his eyes.

Ignore it . . . ignore your gut feeling for once.

And replace it with what? Hope? Faith? Whatever it was that was keeping Susan going right now?

Louis pushed himself up off the bed and went into the

bathroom. He flicked on the light and stared at himself in the cold light of the white-tiled cubicle. He ran the water, splashed some on his face, and went back to the bed.

He switched off the television and sat on the edge of the bed. In the sudden quiet, the outside sounds filtered in to him. The tire-hum of the nearby freeway ramp, the muted screech of a jet taking off overhead, the clatter of the ice machine, and a babble of Spanish out in the hallway.

How in the hell was he going to do this? He didn't even have a map of Miami let alone a badge. He stared at the phone. But it was either find a way or head for home, tail tucked between his legs, just like that detective said.

Louis picked up the receiver and dialed a Fort Myers phone number. It rang eleven times.

"Mel, it's me, Louis."

"What? Louis? Shit, what time is it?"

"Just after eleven."

"Morning or night?"

"Night. Mel, I need your help."

"Just a second."

Louis heard the clank of the phone and then the click of a lighter. He waited until Mel came back on line.

"Okay, what's up," Mel said, exhaling.

"I need your help. I'm in Miami and—"

"Miami? What the hell you doing over there?"

"I'll tell you later. You still got any pull with Miami-Dade PD?"

"Why?"

"I'm looking for a lost kid and need help getting information." Louis filled Mel in on everything that had happened. Mel was quiet for a moment.

"Shit, Louis," he said. "You know I didn't leave there under the best of circumstances." He paused. "How do you know the kid isn't already dead?"

"I don't," Louis said.

Mel exhaled more smoke into the phone. Louis could almost see him, sitting there in the dark of his apartment, remembering what it was like to work a case.

"You want me to come over there?" Mel asked finally.

Louis tried not to hesitate. "Not yet. Let me try to work it alone."

Mel coughed. "Okay. I'll make a call. I got this friend on the force, Joe Frye."

"I appreciate it, Mel."

Two hours later, the temperature had plunged to 40 degrees. Louis shivered as he got out of his car, wrapping his arms across his chest as he looked at the nondescript wooden building facing him. It didn't look like a restaurant. It was more of a low-slung shack set down among some rundown buildings strung along a poorly lit narrow street. But this is where Mel had told him to meet Joe Frye. The detective was just coming off swing shift and agreed to meet him.

The restaurant was called Big Fish, but Louis didn't see any sign. He could certainly smell fish, though, a dank smell that hung in the cold, still air, mixing with diesel fumes and river funk. He went up to the door and went in.

A bar on the left with rattan stools and a small dining area to the right. There were French doors that opened out onto a deck, but tonight they were shut against the cold. The place was empty, just a guy behind the bar putting glasses in a dishwasher.

He looked up at Louis. "We stopped serving at eleven."

"I'm looking for Joe Frye. Is he here?" Louis said.

"Joe?" The bartender smiled. He cocked a head to the French doors. "Sure. Outside."

It was dark out on the deck, the inky Miami River reflecting the gaudy green and purple lights of a nearby office building. Louis saw the glow of a cigarette and then a dark form sitting in a chair, long legs propped up on the railing.

"Detective Frye?" he said, going forward. "I'm Louis Kincaid."

The legs came down and Joe Frye stood up. Louis caught the dull shine of a black leather jacket as the detective stepped into the light coming from inside the restaurant.

Joe Frye was tall, with hair pulled back in a ponytail and a face all angles and lines. Slender, lanky, with just enough curves to tell Louis that Joe Frye was a woman.

"So," Joe Frye said. "How do you know Mel?"

Louis had a sudden flash of Mel, sitting in his apartment, laughing his ass off.

"He's a friend," Louis said.

She stared at him, the shadows playing across her face like black fog. A flash of a pale eye, and the fine cut of a white cheekbone.

"A good friend?" she asked.

"The best I got," Louis said.

She came forward, passing by him, moving to a wooden table. She slid her hip on the edge, looking out at the river.

"How's he doing?" she asked.

Louis wasn't sure how much she knew about Mel's blindness, and he hesitated. She saw it.

"I know he's got RP," she said. "He told me before he left here."

"He gets by. He can still see some."

She was sitting fully in the yellow light of the restaurant now, her eyes still on Louis's face. She was looking at him in a way that was oddly familiar but he couldn't place just who had stared at him like that before.

She looked down, picking a piece of lint off her dark pants. "So, who are you chasing here in Miami and why?" she asked.

Louis pulled the photo of Benjamin from his pocket and came to her, holding it out.

"His father took him. We thought he was heading to Australia but he never got on the plane."

She took the picture, holding it up to the light before she looked back at Louis. "Mel didn't tell me this was just a custody case."

"It's not," Louis said. "The boy's father was partners with the guy who got sliced up in the Little Havana double-homicide today."

She looked at him with new interest and then down at the photo again. "When's the last time you heard from the father?"

"This afternoon. He was visiting his ex-wife in Fort Myers, took the kid for ice cream and never came back."

Louis felt the cold wind come up behind them, and he shivered slightly, stuffing his hands in the pockets of his jacket.

"What kind of business did the father and his partner run?" she asked.

"Imports."

She almost smiled. "Imports. What, drugs? Exotic animals?"

"The father said it was furniture, chests, lamps, you know."

"People don't execute lamp importers."

"I didn't see anything in the office that would indicate what they imported."

"You were there?"

Louis nodded.

"What did the scene look like?"

Louis drew a breath. "Blood everywhere. It looked like they cut the partner's throat while he was still at his desk. I'm figuring the secretary was cut up, but still alive when they put her into a chest, given all the blood on the floor."

"Was the place ransacked?"

"Yeah, drawers open, papers on the floor."

"Sounds like drugs to me," Joe said, handing Benjamin's photo back.

"The mother's a lawyer," Louis said. "I don't think she had any idea her ex was into anything like this."

"And you?" Joe asked. "Where do you fit in?"

"I'm a private eye, that's all," Louis said. "I was trying to track the father down before he left the country."

Joe eyed him for a moment and he knew she heard the lie in his answer, just as she had seen the hesitation when she asked about Mel.

She slipped off the table, her long body reminding Louis of how his cat, Issy, moved when she rubbed up against the furniture.

"So, what do you want from me?" Joe asked.

"I need to know where to go from here. I need to know what happened there and what you guys think the killers were looking for."

She was silent, shaking her head slightly.

He started to say something, then just held up a hand. "Forget it. Sorry to bother you," he said.

She let him get almost to the restaurant door before she spoke. "I'll help you."

He stopped, turning to face her. A second or two passed; the only sound was the lapping of the river against the pilings.

"Where are you staying?" she asked.

"Days Inn near the airport."

"I'll do some checking. Get back to you."

"What do I do?"

"If you don't hear from me by morning, go canvas the neighborhood around the office. Find out what these guys really imported and who their enemies were. I'll get what I can from the inside."

Louis nodded. "Yeah, okay."

"You thought about the mother? She might be in danger, too."

"I got a cop there."

"Good." Joe said. She glanced at the photo in Louis's hand. "I'll check the morgue, too, for unidentified bodies."

The lights from inside the restaurant went out. Louis turned and started to leave.

"Hey," she said. "I wouldn't normally say this to a guy, but I'm going to say it to you."

"What?" Louis asked.

"Be careful. These guys are sick fuckers, Kincaid. As mean as they get."

"I know," he said.

She was just sitting there, hands thrust in her leather jacket.

"I appreciate you doing this," Louis said.

"Hell, I haven't done anything crazy since Mel left. He almost got me killed once."

Louis almost smiled. "Yeah, me, too."

She turned away. Louis just stood there, watching her silhouette in the dark. She had her face tipped toward the cold wind.

"Good night," he said.

She turned back to him, gave a small nod, and looked away, back out at the black river.

CHAPTER 8

He didn't realize he had fallen asleep until he heard the jarring ring of the hotel phone. He was on his stomach, still dressed in his shirt and jeans, his shoes still on his feet. He grabbed the phone, struggling to sit up.

"Susan," he said. "Have they—"

"It's me, Joe Frye."

He pulled himself all the way up, squinting at his watch. Four-thirty A.M.

"Yeah," Louis said, running a hand over his face. "What's happened?"

"You need to come down to the morgue."

"Oh, no," he whispered.

"I got an unidentified black juvenile, about ten or eleven. He was found in a drainage ditch out near Opalocka."

Louis was silent.

"I should've taken the picture," Joe said. "I could've done this for you. Sorry."

"It's . . . okay. Give me directions."

Louis scribbled them on a hotel pad, and pulled himself off the bed. He walked numbly to the bathroom and splashed some cold water on his face. Grabbing a towel, he wiped his face and leaned on the counter, head down.

Jesus. He didn't know if he could do this. But he knew there was no one else. He straightened, drew in a steadying breath, and left the room.

The early morning was cold and dark, filled with sounds he didn't really hear. His body was tight, every muscle on fire, yet he felt strangely numb inside, like some weird force was at work keeping the fear shoved way down deep where he couldn't feel it.

It had rained and the streets were slick and dark, the damp night air misty with the eerie orange glow of the street lights.

She was waiting for him outside the morgue. It was a big, ugly building, the concrete sides stained with Spanish graffiti. She was wearing jeans and the leather jacket again, this time with a gray wool scarf wrapped around her neck. In the harsh light, he could see her face for the first time—angular, hooded light gray eyes, with a spray of fine lines that hinted at her age as somewhere in her midthirties.

"You look frozen," she said.

He shook his head. "I'm fine."

She turned and led him inside.

Their footsteps echoed in the long, sterile hallway. Everything seemed oddly white and clean, so different from the outside. He glanced up at a clock on the wall. The numbers were big and black, the face of the clock bright white. Like it was made that way so people didn't mistake what time it was when they made the long walk down the hall.

They walked. More halls. More lights. More clocks.

Finally, she paused in front of a large window. The vinyl drape behind it was closed. He knew she was waiting for him to tell her he was ready. That's how it went. They always waited so you could prepare yourself. If that was even possible.

He gave Joe a small nod. She tapped on the glass and the curtain scraped open.

Louis's eyes moved over the boy in one quick sweep. He saw ragged black hair, full lips, and chubby dark brown arms.

His breath came out in a rush. "It's not him. It's not Benjamin."

Joe motioned to the man and the curtain closed. Louis turned away, leaning on one arm against the cool tile wall.

He felt her hand on his back.

"Okay, we're out of here," she said.

They walked in silence back out into the hallway. Joe took her car keys out of the pocket of her leather jacket and started away. Louis paused, wiping a hand over his face. It came away wet. He didn't realize he had been sweating.

Joe turned back. "You okay?"

"Yeah, yeah," he said. He was looking around the hallway, like he didn't know where to go next. Joe saw it and came back to him.

"I found out a couple of things," she said.

Louis focused on her. "What?"

"Wallace Sorrell had three broken fingers."

She was trying to take his mind off the boy back there behind the curtain by talking about the case. He felt a surge of gratitude.

"They wanted something from him before they killed him," she said.

"Did the office have a safe?" Louis asked.

"Yes, but it was still closed and locked. Had more than two thousands bucks in it."

"Find any drugs?"

"Not yet. Narcotics is on it."

"I don't think Austin Outlaw was a drug dealer. There's something else going on here," Louis said, crossing his arms.

"Then what did they want?"

"Information. Something only Sorrell knew."

"Like what?"

"Like where something or someone was."

"Like your friend Austin."

"He's not my friend," Louis said quickly.

Joe's hooded gray eyes were steady on Louis. "So, you going back to Fort Myers?"

"Yeah, Susan is . . ." His voice trailed off as he shook his head. "I don't know. I have to . . . I need to do something."

Joe hesitated then stuck the car keys back in her jacket.

"Let's go," she said, nodding in the opposite direction.

"Where?"

"We might as well go take a look at Wallace Sorrell while we're here."

Joe led him to a small office, where a thin man in a lab coat sat at a desk, an Egg McMuffin in his hand. He looked up as Joe approached the open door.

"Hey, it's Joe Friday," the man said. "What you doing here so early, Detective?"

"Helping a friend do an ID," Joe said. "You got a guy named Sorrell in the freezer?"

"The dude cut up on Eighth Street?"

"Yeah. We need to see him."

"Right now?"

"Come on, Lenny, you owe me."

The diener reluctantly set his McMuffin down and got up. "A man can't get any peace around here."

Louis and Joe followed him back down the hall to a heavy door. Lenny yanked it open and they stepped into the cold, musty air of the refrigeration unit. There were six gurneys. Louis could see the gray-pink flesh of the bodies through the heavy plastic. Except for one that was dark. Lenny went to it and unzipped the bag.

"He's all yours. The doc won't get to him till later this morning," he said.

Joe Frye stared at the body. Louis watched her face. Not one muscle moved. He came forward.

Other than the blood splatters, Walter Sorrell's face didn't have a mark on it. But his throat had been cut so deeply Louis could see a glint of vertebra.

"They didn't beat him," Louis said.

"Didn't have to. Look," Joe said, her eyes traveling down the corpse's torso.

Louis looked at Walter Sorrell's forearms. The front of the skin on his left arm had been slit open from wrist to the crook of the elbow. The skin was gone, sliced off in ragged strips. The same incision had been made on the right arm, but the skin was still there, peeled back in flaps.

"My breakfast is getting cold," Lenny said behind him. "Zip him back up when you're done, okay?"

Louis heard the door of the refrigeration unit open and bang shut. He took his eyes off the body and up to Joe. She was staring at the skinned arm.

"Whoever did this took their sweet time," she said.

"Torture," Louis said.

Her eyes came up to meet his and she nodded. "See the bruises on his wrists. He was tied. Probably to his chair. That's where they found most of the blood. The question is, did he tell them what they wanted to know."

"What about the secretary? Does she have the cutting pattern on her?"

Joe shook her head slowly. "No, I read the report. They slashed her throat. Not another mark on her." She bent closer to the body and stared at the flaps of skin.

"It looks like the knife was very sharp, but there is little skill involved here," she said softly. "It's sloppy."

Louis was quiet for a moment and Joe looked up. "What are you thinking?"

"They're after Austin," Louis said.

"How do you know?"

"I just remembered something he said. He told Ben he was playing hooky from work. He didn't tell his partner he was going to Fort Myers. Maybe Sorrell couldn't tell them where Austin was no matter what they did to him."

"But secretaries always know where their bosses are," Joe said.

Louis stared at her across the body. "Maybe she hid at

first and heard what happened to Sorrell. And when they found her, she told them."

They were both quiet. Louis turned up the collar of his jacket against the cold of the freezer and started toward the door. Joe zipped up the body bag and came out into the hall, where Louis was waiting.

Louis rubbed a hand over his bristly face. He leaned back against the cold white tiles and let out a tired sigh.

"I don't know where to go next," he said.

"Sometimes there's nowhere to go," she said. "At least for the moment. If you want to hang around until tomorrow, you can help canvas the area around the office. See who saw what."

Louis glanced up at the clock. It was five-thirty-five. No way could he make it back home across Alligator Alley without falling asleep. And he wanted to stay. He wanted to know more. He wanted to be the one to find Benjamin, if he was here.

He nodded slowly. "All right," he said.

He followed Joe back outside, still shivering from the cool air in the morgue.

"You remember how to get back to your hotel?" she asked.

Louis glanced to his right, seeing in the foggy distance the fuzzy headlights that dotted the freeway. Shit. He had no idea. But he wasn't about to tell her that.

"You take a wrong turn down here, you're a dead man before dawn," she said.

He looked at her.

"My apartment is only a few miles. Come with me. Grab a few hours sleep and I'll take you back to Eighth Street in the morning."

He glanced at his car.

"It'll be safe here. The employees start showing up at six."

"You got any food?" Louis asked.

She laughed softly. "Food *and* a couch."

He climbed in her red Bronco, the cold rippling through him. She saw it and turned on the heater.

"Damn, it's cold," he said.

"It snowed here once—1977," Joe said. "I came out that morning and there was friggin' snow on my windshield." She put the car into reverse. "Thought I left that shit behind when I left Ohio."

She swung the car onto the empty road and accelerated so quickly that Louis was pressed back against the seat. He took a moment to close his eyes, but his mind was awake, alive with images of what he had seen today. He pushed them away, but now he was seeing Susan, sitting on her sofa, phone in hand, eyes reddened. He flashed onto another woman, a faceless mother somewhere who was crying for the boy back in the freezer.

"I need to call the mother," Louis said.

"Not a problem," Joe said, turning in to an apartment complex.

She led him up some stairs, pausing outside a heavy door that read: 3C. She opened the deadbolt first, then the lock above the doorknob, and shoved the door open with her hip.

He followed her inside. There was a light on in the corner. It was a small apartment, with a kitchen separated from the living room by a bar and a sliding glass door that opened onto a small balcony. He could see a sleek ten-speed bike out on the balcony.

He heard her snap shut the two locks, then she moved by him, slipping off her scarf, followed by her jacket. She dropped both on a chair, heading to the kitchen. She was wearing a thin gray shirt with short sleeves. Her skin was pale and Louis could see a small tattoo on her upper arm. It was a lizard.

A calico cat appeared in the hall, let out a cry, then followed her to the kitchen, jumping up on the counter. She cupped its face in her hands to rub noses with it. She was talking to the cat like it was a baby.

She reached for the bag of cat food and shook it. Another cat strolled out, and the room filled with hungry cries as she fed them.

"Two?" Louis asked.

"I used to have seven."

She flicked on the coffee and opened a cupboard, bringing down two mugs. From the refrigerator, she took out two containers and set them on the counter.

Louis took off his jacket and came forward, picking up one of the containers she had set out. Dannon blueberry yogurt. This was food?

He heard her laugh and looked up.

"You should see the look on your face," she said.

"I'm sorry. I guess I was expecting eggs or . . . something."

She hesitated, her hand on her hip. "I got leftover pizza."

"That'll work."

She withdrew a pizza box from the refrigerator, nodding toward the phone. "Call the mother. The coffee will take a few minutes."

Louis called Susan. She was hoarse, but calm. She told him Dan Wainwright had sent two cops and they were in the living room watching some old movie. She told him she had slept a few hours, but he didn't believe her. He didn't say much, just listened. He didn't tell her where he was, or where he had just come from. There was no reason to.

When he hung up, he took a breath and turned back to Joe. She handed him a plate of pizza.

"She okay?"

Louis nodded, taking the plate to the sofa. The first few bites were gobbled down, but as he picked up the second piece, he started looking around the living room.

His eyes were drawn to two photographs sitting on a bookshelf near the TV. Two uniforms. He recognized the black one as Miami-Dade. But the other was blue . . . with a skirt.

He rose and walked to it, chewing the pizza. The woman

in the black uniform was a younger Joe. He guessed the older woman was her mother. They could have been twins, except for the hairstyles and uniforms. The mother's uniform looked like something a stewardess might wear, complete with a little hat. But there was a badge on her jacket.

Joe came up behind him.

"Your mother?" Louis asked.

"Yes. She was a cop in Cleveland. She was my inspiration, but things were pretty sucky for women back then."

"Not the best, even now," Louis said.

"You got that right."

His eyes caught sight of a small plant on the shelf. It was brown and withered.

"You need to throw that thing away," he said. "It looks dead."

She reached past him to get the plant. She held it, picking at the brittle leaves. "I used to have a slew of plants. Filled up that whole wall."

"What happened to them?"

"I got promoted," she said.

She went back into the kitchen and tossed the plant in the trash. "I had no time after that. No time to cook, take care of my cats, or water plants. I got stuck once on a four-day stakeout and when I got home, they were all dead."

"The cats or the plants?" Louis asked.

"You're not a cat person or you wouldn't make jokes like that."

"Actually, I have a cat."

He frowned and Joe saw it. "What's the matter?"

"I forgot to tell someone to look after her."

"Cats can take care of themselves. She'll be okay for one day."

"She's in heat."

"You better get her spayed."

"That's what Mel said."

"Like Mel knows about cats."

Louis walked to the kitchen, setting his plate in the sink. "I think Mel knows about a lot of things people don't think he knows about."

The coffee was done brewing and he poured himself a cup, glancing around for the sugar. A gigantic orange cat was watching him from the counter.

"Where's your sugar?" he asked.

"Sorry, I don't use sugar," Joe said, disappearing into the bedroom.

Louis stared at the black liquid in the cup, then drank it, grimacing. He dumped it in the sink. He went back to the living room, sinking into the sofa. He rubbed his face, then rested his forehead in his palms. He had been sitting a few minutes when a pillow hit him in the shoulder.

"We'll head to Eighth Street around nine, when the businesses open," she said.

Louis looked at her, then at the pillow. There was a yellow blanket folded across the arm of the sofa.

"Yeah, okay," Louis said.

She disappeared and Louis heard a door close.

Louis remained sitting, his eyes drifting to the photo of Joe with her mother, across the dark TV, finally coming to rest on the sliding glass door. He rose and walked to it. He could see the lights of downtown Miami, back dropped by the weak pink glow of dawn.

"Louis. Go to bed."

He turned. She was standing by the sofa. Her hair was down around her shoulders, her face in the shadows.

"It's hard to do nothing," he said.

"There's nothing you can do right now except sleep."

"It doesn't seem right to sleep."

She was quiet for a moment. "This isn't just any kid, is it?"

He looked back out the glass door. "He's pretty special."

"You have a relationship with the mother?" she asked.

He glanced back at her, surprised by the question.

"I'm only asking so I know how close you are to this," she said, coming toward him. "You're a liability to me if you're emotionally involved. You know that."

"I can handle it."

"Hope you're right."

She was standing there in the middle of the room, holding a cat, and wearing a long, baggy T-shirt that came to her knees. Her face was scrubbed, her feet bare.

She didn't look like a cop right now. But she was. She had all the power and he knew there was nothing he could do in Miami without her.

"Don't leave me out of this," he said.

She looked at him for a moment, then started back to the bedroom, the calico cat in her arms. "I'll wake you at eight-thirty. Get some sleep."

He heard the bedroom door close and he turned to the sofa, dropping into it. He wedged off his sneakers, and propped the pillow in the corner, pulling the blanket up over him.

He had been lying there a few minutes when the orange tabby jumped on his legs. His first instinct was to push it away, but before he could, it settled in the crook behind his knees. It felt strangely familiar. Strangely comforting. He let it stay.

CHAPTER 9

Saturday, January 16

Joe gave him an old sweatshirt to wear. It was a faded orange color with a snarling cartoon dog head on it underscored with the words CLEVELAND BROWNS DAWG POUND.

It was ugly but it was clean and warm, and Louis was glad to have it on under his jacket as he headed back out to Eighth Street the next morning.

The sun was out but the temperature was still hovering around forty-five. Louis parked the Mustang and walked to Pacific Imports. The scene was still cordoned off with yellow tape and there were a couple of Miami-Dade squad cars blocking the parking lot. The two uniforms were standing around drinking 7-Eleven coffees, and in their heavy parkas, the fake-fur collars pulled up, they looked like kids bundled up in snowsuits going out to play.

Louis glanced around. There were a fair number of people out on the street, considering the cold. But all he could hear around him was Spanish, a babble that was as intimidating as the foreign signs. He stood there, looking for some place to start.

A small park sat catty-corner to Pacific Imports. There

was a red-tile roof pavilion enclosed in heavy iron bars, but beyond the gate, Louis could see men sitting at concrete tables. As he drew closer, he could hear a muted clicking sound.

The old men playing dominos at the tables did not look up as he came in the gate, but Louis could feel their eyes on him, watching him furtively. One younger man, lounging near a tree smoking a cigarette, stared openly as Louis tried to ask questions.

"Excuse me . . ."

Click-clack-click-clack.

"I need to talk to someone—"

"No habla inqles."

Clack-clack-click.

Finally, he gave up, driven out of the park by the cigar smoke and the stare of the young man.

He had no luck at any of the businesses he tried. Everyone seemed to be looking at him with weirdly strained expressions, like he was a plague carrier or worse. When he went into a hair salon, the lone woman backed away from him, gripping the scissors she had been using and muttering something in Spanish. She had the same look on her face that everyone did.

He knew the look—fear of a strange young black man. He knew one of the words she said, too.

"Vete."

He had heard it before from the Mexican workers back in Immokalee. *Vete . . . go away.*

Back out on the street, he stood on the corner, trying to figure out what in the hell to do next.

He looked at his watch. Joe said to meet him at Pacific Imports at ten. He had only a couple minutes to wait.

As he stood there, trying to warm up in the sun, his eyes drifted back across the street. There was an old man and a girl sitting at a table in front of the café directly across from Pacific Imports. They had not been there when Louis had gone in to question the owner. The little girl was looking at Louis. He tried a small smile.

She didn't smile back, but at least she wasn't looking at him the way the others had. He went over to the café.

"Hello," he said.

The old man was wearing heavy dark sunglasses and an old brown jacket. A cane rested against his chair. His claw-hand was wrapped around a tiny cup of mud black coffee, a Spanish newspaper was folded in his lap. He looked away from Louis, ignoring him. But the girl was staring at Louis's sweatshirt.

"Is that a dog or a bear?" she asked, pointing.

Louis glanced down at the emblem. "A dog, I think."

"He looks mad."

"I think he's supposed to look that way."

She was looking right into Louis's eyes now. At least she didn't look scared of him.

"I was wondering if you could help me," he said. "I have some questions—"

"Celia," the old man said sharply, *"No hables el Negro."*

The girl glanced at Louis and then said to the old man, *"Esta bien, abuelo. Esta perdido y le hace salta directiones."*

The old man gave a grunt and grabbed his cane, pulling it closer. The girl looked back at Louis. She was about twelve or thirteen, pretty, with her dark hair pulled back in a pony-tail and tiny gold hoops in her ears. She still didn't smile at Louis—he had a feeling there would be hell to pay from Grandpa if she did—but her brown eyes were friendly. It was the first warm look he had gotten since he arrived in Miami.

"I don't want to get you in trouble," Louis said.

"It's okay. I told Grandpa you were just asking me for directions. Are you lost?"

"No." Louis pointed across the street. "I'm trying to find out some information about what happened over there yesterday."

"Some people were killed," she said.

"Yes, I know. I'm helping the police find out who did it."

She tilted her head, as if looking at him in a new light.

"Do you live around here?" Louis asked.

"Yes, around the corner," she said, pointing.

"Did you see anything strange here yesterday? Anything at all?"

She shook her head. "I was in school. But Grandpa was here," she said. "He is always here. He comes here every morning to drink his coffee and read *La Verdad.*"

Louis looked at the old man, who was just staring straight ahead, his eyes hidden behind the dark glasses.

"Can he see okay?" Louis asked the girl.

"Oh, sure. He had cataract surgery last year."

Louis turned and roughly aligned himself with the old man's sight line. The old man had a direct bead on the lot, stairway, and front door of Pacific Imports.

"Could you ask him some questions for me?" Louis asked the girl.

She hesitated. "I don't think he will answer."

"Why not?"

She fidgeted in her seat. "He doesn't like black people."

Louis's eyes went to the old man's face. But he was still staring straight ahead, mouth set in a hard line.

"Could you try, please?" he asked the girl.

"Maybe he will talk to you if I tell him you are a policeman."

Louis hesitated. "Okay."

She spoke softly to her grandfather. The old man still would not look at Louis, but at least his grip on the cane lessened some.

"Okay," the girl said. "What do you want to know?"

"Ask him if he saw anything strange yesterday."

The girl touched the old man's arm. *"Abuelo, vistes algo raro ayer?"*

"Ese negro esta muerto," he spat out. *"Se lo merecia!"*

The girl glanced at Louis then back at her grandfather.

She began to speak to him softly but firmly. The old man listened and then began to speak again, pointing toward Pacific Imports. The girl leaned close to listen, then looked up at Louis.

"He said there is usually only one black man who works up there, but a couple days ago, another black man came."

"What day was that?"

She asked him and looked back at Louis. "The other man came here on Monday in a black BMW."

"He's sure it was a black BMW?" Louis asked.

The girl nodded. "Grandpa loves cars. He is sure. He says he saw the second black man leave the next day. He had a suitcase in the trunk. He didn't come back."

"How does he know?"

The girl shrugged. "Grandpa sits here all day. He doesn't like to be home because my baby brother cries a lot."

Louis ran a hand over his face. That meant Austin made an appearance at his office five days ago, left for Fort Myers a day later, and hadn't been seen back here since.

"Ask him if he ever saw a boy with the man," Louis said. "A black boy."

The girl translated and turned back. "No, just the two men."

"Ask him if he saw anyone go in who looked . . ." Louis hesitated. "Who looked strange."

The girl frowned and spoke in Spanish again to her grandfather.

"He saw . . ." she sighed. "He says he saw *dos Yankis*—two white men—go up there yesterday after lunch. Someone shut the blinds and then soon after, the white men came back out."

"Why did your grandfather think that was strange?"

"They were wearing gloves."

"Gloves? It's cold. Lots of people are wearing gloves."

"Yes," the girl said, "but Grandpa says the men put on their gloves *before* they went into the office."

Louis hesitated, wondering where to go next. "Is there anything else?" he asked. "Can he remember what kind of car they had?"

She asked and turned back to Louis. "He says it was a big, old blue Cadillac, with dark windows, you know, tinted? He says it looked like a car a drug dealer would drive."

"Anything else? Anything at all?" Louis asked the girl.

She spoke again to her grandfather. She looked up at Louis and shook her head.

"No, I'm sorry."

The old man started speaking again, pointing toward the parking lot across the street. He seemed to be upset about something.

The girl looked contrite when she looked back at Louis. "I'm sorry," she said. "He gets mad sometimes about things. Men broke into our home and stole some things once and now we have bars on the windows. Grandpa isn't mad at you. He's just mad at everyone."

The old man said something under his breath, pointing again at the lot. Louis heard the word *Yankis* again.

"What did he say?" Louis asked.

"He says he thought the *Yankis* had come to steal that car over there."

Louis looked to where the girl was pointing. There was one car in the lot of Pacific Imports beside the two police cruisers. It was an old Chevy Bel Air, red and black, and restored to its pristine 1953 condition.

The old man was talking again, but his tone had changed. He was pointing toward the old car, speaking softly, reverently.

"Grandpa said he had a car like that back in Cuba, only his was blue," the girl told Louis.

The old man muttered something.

"What?" Louis asked the girl.

She blushed. "He called the man a bad word. He said he hated seeing him touch that beautiful car."

Louis's eyes shot back to the Chevy. Fingerprints? Damn, could they get that lucky? He turned back to the girl.

"Thank you very much," he said. "And thank your grand-father for me."

This time the girl smiled.

Louis jogged back across the street, stopping at the tape that stretched across the lot. He was considering approaching the two uniforms when he saw Joe's red Bronco pull up. She got out and came toward him, her shoulders hunched in the leather jacket, her hands stuffed in the pockets of her black jeans. She was wearing huge tortoise-shell sunglasses that covered a good part of her face. Her hair was back in its ponytail.

"Sorry I'm late," she said. "I was over at the station getting an update."

"No word on Austin Outlaw, I take it?" Louis asked.

"No, but we checked all the flights out of MIA last night and he wasn't on any of them. Checked Fort Lauderdale, too, just in case. Nothing. The BMW was due to be turned into Avis last night. No sign of it."

Louis let out a sigh, shaking his head.

"So, you find anything?" she asked.

"Would you believe fingerprints?"

She stared at him. "Prints? Where?"

Louis nodded toward the café across the street. "Some old guy over there saw two guys go up to Pacific Imports." Louis pointed to the Bel Air. "And before they went up, one of them was looking in that car over there."

"Damn," Joe said softly. "Can we get that lucky?"

"I don't think the car has been moved," Louis said. "It has a For Sale sign in the window."

A faint smile tipped Joe's lips and she ducked under the yellow tape. Louis followed.

One of the uniforms was leaning against the back fender of the Bel Air.

"Harvey, move your ass," Joe said.

The cop looked up at her. "Why? Nothing going on down here, detective."

"No, I mean, move your ass off the car. We need to dust it."

The officer straightened, looking at the Chevy. Louis waited as Joe filled him in, and then as Joe went upstairs to the Pacific Imports office. She spoke for a moment with a guy in a brown sports coat, who looked down at Louis. Louis recognized him as the detective he had approached on the first day, the one who had told him to go back home to Captiva. The guy looked like he was giving Joe a hard time.

After a moment, he went back inside the office and a crime unit tech came out. Joe led the tech down to the Chevy and then she came back to Louis.

"The old man said he saw their car," Louis told her. "It was an old blue Cadillac, big, with dark tinted windows."

Joe nodded in approval. "We'll put out an APB for it. Good work. It's hard to get people around here to talk sometimes."

"I think it was the Dawg sweatshirt," Louis said.

"What?"

"Nothing." Louis was quiet, looking up at the windows of Pacific Imports. The detective in the brown sports coat was standing outside, staring down at them.

"I hope I didn't cause you any problems here," Louis said.

"Problems?" Joe said.

"With that detective," Louis said nodding upward.

"Who? Kemper? Don't worry about him."

"Well, I know how cops can be. They don't like outsiders interfering with their case."

"Well, it's not his case now. It's mine."

Louis couldn't hide his surprise. Joe gave him a half-smile.

"I know what you're thinking—how the hell did she get this big juicy case?" she said. She was watching the tech starting in on the Chevy Bel Air. "Things are different here," she said. "Guys like Kemper don't care much about Eighth Street or little dead black boys."

She let out a sigh and then looked back at Louis. "I could use a caffeine fix. Come on, I'll buy you a cafecito."

Louis glanced quickly at his watch. He had managed to ignore the guilt he was feeling about being away from Susan. He had been able to justify staying in Miami by reasoning that maybe Austin and Benjamin were still here. But his gut was telling him that Austin had never left Fort Myers. And that was where he needed to be right now.

"I can't," Louis said. "I really need to get back to Fort Myers."

Joe hesitated, then nodded. "Yeah, okay, I understand. But I need a favor before you leave."

"Sure. Anything."

"I need you to come to the office and fill out a statement for me," Joe said. She paused just a beat. "Come on. You can call the mother from there."

CHAPTER 10

The City of Miami Police Department was housed in a large modern building in Overtown, a neighborhood of gray municipal buildings and rundown apartments the colors of a heat-bleached sunset. In the distance, Louis could see the gleaming high rises of Biscayne Boulevard and the steel skeleton of a new basketball arena going up. After the close smells and sights of Little Havana, this area had an oddly desolate feeling to it. A chain-link fence surrounding a vacant weed-choked lot. Wide streets with no people though it was high noon. And above, a monorail whispering by, its sleek cars empty. It felt like a city in some sci-fi movie where a mutant bug wipes out the population but leaves everything running.

Louis followed Joe into the spacious lobby. His shoes echoed on the tile walls and floors. All the signs were in English and Spanish. The uniform behind the large circular information desk gave Joe a nod as she led Louis past.

They took the elevator to the second floor, and Louis followed Joe through a door that said CRIMES AGAINST PERSONS UNIT. He had been looking for something that said HOMICIDE.

His first impression was noise: the warbles and rings of

phones, the banging of metal file drawers, a hacking cough, a low laugh. Then sight: gray metal desks, towers of paper, flickering green computer screens under the mean glare of florescent. And finally, smell: cigarettes, greasy take-out chicken, and a faint odor of sweat.

Joe got pulled aside into a discussion with another detective. Louis stood at the door, transfixed.

So this is it.

His eyes focused on a white erasable board that covered one entire wall. He knew it was the homicide case board. Every station had one. He scanned the headings atop each column: Victim. Date. Location. Investigator. Status. Weapon. Motive. Suspects. ME. It was all there—in black and red ink.

The board was over twenty feet long and six feet high. There were sixty-three open cases. The double-murder on Eighth Street was third to last. Two more since last night.

"Louis! Over here."

Joe was beckoning from a desk in the corner. He went over to her, aware of the subtle shift of eyes following him. Joe was the only woman and he was the only black man, except for a guy dressed in an orange Dade County jumpsuit sitting at a desk giving a statement.

Her desk was near the windows. Through the streaked glass, he could see the cars whizzing by on I-95. Joe's phone was ringing.

"Have a seat," Joe said, grabbing the phone.

While he waited for her to finish the call, Louis scanned the room again, trying not to look like he was staring.

He had worn a badge before. He had worn a uniform, and had once, in his rookie year, even assisted a detective on a domestic shooting death. But that had been back in Ann Arbor, a small force in a college town where the four-by-four-foot homicide case board never filled up. After that, he had worked in even smaller departments, places that weren't big enough to have case boards or make distinctions between plain tin badges and gold ones.

Louis's eyes swept the room. Four, five, six. He could count six gold badges here right now. Seven . . . he had forgotten Joe.

He looked at her, focusing on the heavy gold badge that hung on her belt.

Joe hung up the phone. "Okay, come on," she said, "I want you to meet my boss."

Louis followed Joe across the office. Some of the men looked up at Joe's face, their eyes dropping to her ass as she passed. Then they would glance up at Louis curiously. He knew they thought he was a boyfriend or something. And he tried to decipher the look. Envious? Protective? Or disapproving?

At a corner office with the plate MAJOR ANDERSON on the door, Joe knocked, then went in. The man behind the desk looked up. He was built like the bulldog on Louis's sweatshirt, with a silver-blond brush cut and gray-green eyes in a ruddy, tanned face.

"Major, this is—" Joe started.

"Louis Kincaid," the man said, standing and extending his hand.

Louis shook it. "You know me?"

"I know *of* you."

Louis glanced at Joe. She looked confused.

"I'm Major Anderson," he said. "Kevin Anderson. Have a seat. It's a pleasure to meet you."

Anderson began to rifle through a stack of magazines on his credenza. "I just read about you a few weeks ago in *Criminal Pursuits Magazine,*" he said. "It was on the Paint It Black killer, the guy you caught a few years back."

Louis could see Joe out of the corner of his eye but she was still just standing near the door, her arms crossed.

Anderson looked at her. "Joette, go grab us some coffee, would you?"

She didn't move.

"Don't give me that look. You're closest."

She disappeared.

Anderson finally gave up trying to find the magazine and sat down at his desk. "The article said you refused to be interviewed. How come?"

"I don't like reporters," Louis said.

"They can make or break your career," Anderson said. "And making a name for yourself is the only way you're going to make any money doing what you do. You're only what? Twenty-five, twenty-six?"

"Twenty-eight," Louis said. "And I do okay. I do better than okay."

Joe came back and handed Louis a Styrofoam cup and some sugar packets. She set Anderson's cup on his desk, then leaned against the doorjamb.

Anderson was sitting back in his chair, just looking at Louis over the steeple of his fingers. Louis took a drink of coffee. It was awful but at least it was hot.

"The article said you used to be a cop," Anderson said.

He needed to nip this in bud; he wasn't about to explain why he had quit and he had a feeling the article had pretty much told the whole story anyway.

"Major, I know how you guys feel about P.I.s—"

Anderson stopped him with a raised hand. "Most of the guys. Not all. Not me, that's for sure. I have no problem with you. I respect what you've done, and I hear the guys on the West Coast think you're okay, too. Hell, anyone who can put a serial killer and goddamn slimy ass lawyer in jail is okay in my book."

Louis glanced up at Joe. She took the cue and stepped forward. "Louis is here looking for a missing kid. The kid's father is connected to one of the victims on Eighth Street."

Anderson never looked at her. "Think your kid's in Miami?"

"I did, but now I'm not so sure."

"So you're heading home?"

Louis nodded.

"Well, I'll have Joette keep you up on things." Anderson finally looked at her. "Let me know if you need her to check on anything for you."

Anderson stood up and stuck out his hand. Louis rose and shook it.

"Tell Mel Landeta I said hello," Anderson said.

"I will."

Louis picked up his coffee and followed Joe out. She closed the office door and looked at him, her head cocked.

"Criminal Pursuits Magazine?" she asked. "I didn't know I was in the presence of a greatness."

She wasn't smiling but Louis could see the amusement in her narrow eyes.

"Is Joette your real name?" he asked.

She nodded. "I've told him not to call me that. I think if he ever called me Joe, he'd have to start picturing me having balls instead of boobs."

Louis smiled.

She looked off toward the window. "Let's go do the report and get you out of here."

Louis followed her back to the desk. He glanced at his watch as he sat down. It was almost two P.M. He'd been gone twenty hours. It felt like a month. He stared at the form, pen poised, then he looked at the phone.

"Dial nine to get a line out."

He looked up at Joe. "Thanks."

Joe left him alone. He dialed Susan's number. It rang five times, six. He sat there, hand to his brow, listening to the empty ring. Finally, someone picked up.

"Hello."

A man's voice.

"Who's this?" Louis demanded.

"Who's *this?*"

"Louis Kincaid. What the hell—?"

"Hold on." The sound of the phone being muffled and then the man was back. "Sorry, sir. I was just checking. This is Officer Jewell, Sereno PD."

"Where's Susan?"

"I think she's asleep, sir. She's right over on the sofa there. Should I go get her?"

"No, no . . . don't wake her. Just tell her I called and am coming home."

"Will do, sir."

Louis hung up and sat there, staring at the phone. Then he pulled the form over and began filling it out. He was signing his name when Joe came back.

He rose quickly. "I've got to go."

She nodded. "Yeah, yeah . . . of course you do." She paused. "Come on, I'll walk you out."

"No, that's not necessary." Louis hesitated, then held out his hand.

Joe stared at it for only a second then took it. Her hand was warm, her grip was firm, then it softened. Louis held it for a second longer then let go, taking a step back.

"My phone's there on the form," Louis said.

"I'll call you the minute we get anything."

Louis nodded and started away quickly. He knew Joe Frye was watching him but he didn't look back.

It was raining, a stinging cold rain, by the time he hit the toll booth at Alligator Alley. The sky was low and putty colored over the dull green carpet of the wetlands bordering the road that cut across the state to the West Coast. The wipers on the Mustang needed replacing; they made a *drone-scrape drone-scrape* sound as they moved across his field of vision.

The road was a straight gray ribbon, barely visible now in the quickening dusk and downpour. He switched on the headlights, then the high beams.

Drone-scrape. Drone-scrape. Drone-scrape.

He was thinking about Ben. Was he out in this rain somewhere? Was he with Austin? Was he still alive?

Drone-scrape. Drone-scrape.

He was thinking of Susan. How in the hell was he going to face her?

He was thinking of Joe Frye and Miami and the homicide department. No, Crimes Against People Unit. Thinking about the electric buzz of that big dirty room and that big white board with life and death spelled out in red and black erasable ink.

Drone-scrape. Drone-scrape.

He was out in the Everglades now, passing into the Corkscrew Swamp. The rain was letting up. Almost home.

The buzz of the beeper on the passenger seat made him start. He snatched it up, keeping one eye on the road. He squinted at the number. It wasn't Susan's, and for a second he didn't recognize it. Then his heart skipped a beat. It was Sheriff Wainwright's personal line.

"Shit," he whispered, tossing the beeper aside.

He pushed the Mustang over eighty. He almost didn't see the sign for the rest stop until it was too late. He braked hard and swerved in. It was a small turnout with picnic tables, but Louis let out a breath when he saw the pay phone.

He left the car running and sprinted to the phone. They patched him through to Wainwright in a squad car.

"Dan. Louis."

"We found Outlaw's car," Wainwright said. "It's at Lakes Park."

"Lakes Park? I looked. I didn't see it there. Benjamin . . . did you find Benjamin?"

"The car's in the lake, Louis."

"What?"

"I just got the call. We're on our way there now with a retrieval crew. I wanted to get you first."

Louis couldn't move, couldn't breathe.

"Louis?"

"Yeah, yeah, I'm here."

Louis closed his eyes, tilting his face up to the cold rain. He pulled in a deep breath. "I'm on my way."

CHAPTER 11

It had stopped raining and was almost dark by the time Louis swung the Mustang into the park entrance. Two squad cars were at the gate, their bubble lights splattering red and blue on the wall of trees. Louis rolled down his window but the deputy standing in the road recognized him and waved him through.

He fought the impulse to barrel in, easing off the gas as he entered the park. In the distance, between the thick trunks of the oaks, he could see more flashing blue strobes.

He jerked the car to a stop and got out, his eyes scanning the clearing.

There were picnic tables and benches to his right, back dropped by trees and brush. The silhouette of a playground and a children's train loomed against the darkening sky. To his left was the lake, shimmering black under the glow of the portable lights on the shore.

Sitting on the edge of the water was a wrecker, its gears grinding as the tow chain wound slowly against the metal pulley. The trunk of the black BMW broke the surface of the water first. The sound of rushing water filled the cold air.

Louis hurried toward the water, paused only a second at the edge, then stepped into the lake.

"Kincaid!"

He didn't stop, trudging through the knee-deep water toward the car. A deputy rushed to stop him and Louis moved to push him aside, but someone else caught his arms.

"Kincaid. Stop." It was Dan Wainwright.

Louis pulled his arm away and continued toward the car. By the time he reached it, it was fully exposed, the black finish streaked with muddy water, the windows too deeply tinted for Louis to see inside. He reached for the door, but Wainwright grabbed his arm, this time holding tight.

"Wait till it's on ground for God's sake, Louis."

Louis stopped, drawing back. Wainwright let go of him, and the two of them followed the car to the grass. The wrecker began to lower the BMW to the ground.

They waited.

Across the roof of the car, Louis could see the tight faces of a half-dozen cops. Most were Fort Myers officers in navy blue uniforms and heavy dark jackets. Behind them were three Lee County sheriff's deputies, wrapped in fur-collared green jackets. Louis's eyes settled on the Fort Myers's chief of police, Al Horton. Horton's face was stiff and red, his eyes teary from the wind.

When the pulley stopped grinding, Horton stepped forward, and looked up, meeting Louis's eyes. He gave Louis a subtle shake of his head, a warning to stay back, stay calm.

Louis held his breath, his eyes dropping to the dark windows of the BMW.

With gloved hands, Horton opened the driver's side door. Water rushed out, and to Louis's shock, the dome light came on.

Louis edged closer. The leather seats were puddled and muddy. And they were empty.

"Al," Louis said. "The trunk."

Horton looked around for the trunk switch, found it and Louis heard the trunk pop open. He stepped between the rear bumper and the wrecker, meeting Horton at the rear of the car. Horton looked at him again, then lifted the trunk with the tip of his finger.

Shapes. Big dark shapes.

A flashlight clicked on behind them.

It was luggage. Just suitcases sitting in a pool of water. Nothing else.

Louis turned away, walking up the grassy slope. He realized he hadn't been breathing and he drew in a cold breath. It hurt.

Just suitcases.

He ran a hand over his face. His nose was cold, and his feet were beginning to freeze, too. He shouldn't have gone in the water. He shouldn't have gotten wet. He shouldn't have even left Fort Myers.

He looked to his left, down the narrow jogging path that stretched into the tunnel of trees.

"Don't even think it," Wainwright said from behind him.

Louis looked back at Wainwright. He was scraping the mud off the soles of his shoes.

"He still might be alive out here somewhere."

Wainwright stopped scuffing and looked up at Louis. The blue strobes from the police cars pulsated in his eyes, but Louis could clearly see the compassion.

"I don't think he is," Wainwright said. "But we'll search again in the morning."

"But he might be laying somewhere back there. He might—"

"Listen to me," Wainwright said. "We walked the whole park this afternoon. Me, Horton, and a dozen other cops. If Benjamin had been here, we would've found him then. Or he would've found us."

Louis crossed his arms, burying his frozen hands in his armpits.

"Louis, they're not here."

"Then where the hell are they?"

Wainwright glanced back at the car, then to the ground. "I think they're dead."

Louis swung his hand toward the car. "If they wanted him dead, they would've left him in the car," Louis said. "They've taken him. I know it."

"For what? They didn't want the boy, they wanted the ex-husband."

Louis shook his head. "Maybe they needed something from Austin, information of some kind. Maybe they had to take him somewhere to get it. And maybe Benjamin is leverage. What better way to get someone to cooperate than to threaten their kid in front of them?"

Wainwright nodded slowly. "Okay. Maybe. So what happens then?"

"What do you mean?" Louis asked.

"What happens after Outlaw tells them what they want to know?"

Louis was silent, his eyes focused on the trees over Wainwright's shoulder.

"Then what happens, Louis?"

They both die.

Louis felt Wainwright's hand on his back and he stepped away from it, feeling a shiver run through him.

Wainwright went on, his voice clear, but gentle in the darkness. "This is probably a drug double cross of some kind and these guys are most likely back in Miami or even South America by now. They're hired guns, Louis. Outlaw got himself in some shit and the boy is collateral damage."

Louis faced Wainwright. "How the hell do you expect me to tell Susan her son is collateral damage?"

Wainwright met his eyes. "As easy as you can, Louis."

Louis looked at the ground. The bloodied images of yesterday came surging back, but now Benjamin's small face was in his head, too. And Louis's imagination was forming pictures of Benjamin's small body, broken and dumped somewhere, his cries unheard.

Adults. They knew. They knew that bad people did bad things. They knew what killing and torture and death were, and if they were abducted, they knew there was probably no way out unless they could save themselves. Because they understood that cops were just human and that there were no superheroes.

But kids.

How long did it take before they realized no one was coming for them?

Louis felt Wainwright's hand on his back and he stepped away from it. He looked down the jogging path. "I think I'll walk the lake once. One time. I won't step off the path."

"Louis, there are over thirty cops here. Half of them on their own time."

Louis didn't reply.

"They're here to walk the lake. They're here to search. If there's anything to find, they'll find it."

"Damn it, I have to do *something*."

Wainwright put a firm hand on the back of Louis's neck. "You need to be with Susan. Now get the hell out of here."

CHAPTER 12

Louis eased the car to a stop in the sandy driveway of his cottage, and turned off the engine. It was dark, except for a soft yellow glow coming from a nearby cabin. The rustle of the rain-driven wind in the palms drowned out the usual rhythmic rush of waves from the gulf.

He had decided to come home first before going to Susan's. The first reason was to get his gun. He had left yesterday expecting to be gone only an hour or so, and had left the Glock at home. He had felt naked the last twenty-four hours, especially after seeing the crime scene in Miami.

But the second reason he had gone out of his way to come home was pathetic. He wanted to postpone—if even for an hour—telling Susan that her son might be at the bottom of the lake.

He shivered. The cold had saturated his body, numbing his feet and toes, and he was still wearing the same clothes he had left home in a day before, except for the sweatshirt Joe had given him. He sat for just a moment longer, then pushed open the car door and walked slowly to his cottage.

Flipping open the screen door, he reached for the knob on the inner door. It was locked and as he dug for his keys, he paused. He usually left the door unlocked.

Louis turned and peered into the deep shadows of the yard. Then he stepped to the window and looked inside. It was too dark to see anything. But he was so tired, maybe he was wrong about locking up.

He unlocked the door and stepped inside, turning on the living room light. It was just as messy as he had left it—the newspaper scattered on the sofa, an empty Heineken bottle and a plate with bread crumbs on the counter.

Stripping off the Cleveland Browns sweatshirt, he sat down in the nearest chair. He pulled off his wet sneakers and socks, tossing them aside. His toes were dark red and tingling.

He rose and went to the refrigerator, getting a beer. He went into the bedroom, taking long pulls from the Heineken as he walked. As he hit the bathroom switch, he paused again in the doorway.

Where was Issy? She hadn't eaten. She should have been at his feet the moment she heard the door.

He heard a bump and spun around, his hand automatically going for the Glock on his belt until he realized it was in his nightstand drawer. The bedroom was dark, full of shadows cast by the weak bathroom light. His eyes moved slowly around the room.

"Who's there?" he called.

A soft scraping, like a body sliding against a wall. Louis set down the beer and moved slowly toward the nightstand. He pulled open the drawer groping for the gun. It wasn't there.

Shit.

His eyes strained into the dark near the dresser. A figure was huddled there in the corner.

"Kincaid?"

He knew that voice.

A man moved slowly from the shadows. Louis froze when he saw his Glock in the man's trembling hands.

"Outlaw?" Louis asked. "Austin Outlaw?"

The man came into the thin light from the bathroom, the gun aimed at Louis. "Yeah, yeah, it's me."

For a second, Louis could only stare at him in shock. Then the question flashed in his head. "Where's Benjamin?"

Austin blinked. "Ben?"

"Where the hell is Benjamin?" Louis asked again.

"He's not with Susan?" Austin asked.

"What? Fuck no, he's not with Susan," Louis said. "Where the hell is he?"

Austin didn't answer, running a hand over his face. Louis stepped forward and jerked the gun from Austin's hand.

"Where's Ben?"

"I don't . . . I don't know."

"You don't—?"

Louis turned and clicked on the lamp near the bedroom door. The light was bright, and Austin brought up a hand to shield his eyes.

"Ben is missing," Louis said. "He's *been* missing for twenty-four hours. We figured you two were together."

Austin's eyes widened, then his shoulders slumped and he covered his face with his hands.

Louis stuffed the gun in his jeans and came to Austin, jerking him out of the corner. Austin's yellow polo shirt was streaked with dirt and he had bits of dried leaves and twigs in his hair. Austin gave out a sharp cry of pain, grabbing at a towel he was holding against his thigh.

"What the hell happened?" Louis asked. "How did you lose him?"

"We were at the park, getting ready to leave. I got out of the car to throw away the ice cream cups," Austin said slowly. "That's when I heard the shot zing by my ear. When I turned around, that's when I got hit with the second shot." Austin motioned toward his leg, wrapped with a bloody towel.

"Where was Ben?" Louis demanded.

"In the car. It was a good thirty feet away."

"What did you do?"

"I jumped in the bushes."

Louis could only stare at him.

"I heard this guy coming after me," Austin went on. "So I crawled deeper into the trees. And then I ran."

"You *ran?* You ran and left Ben there? How could you just leave him there?"

"I thought I saw him get out of the car and run away. And besides, what else was I supposed to do?" Austin snapped. "I didn't have a gun. I didn't even know who was shooting at me. I figured whoever it was, they were after me. I didn't think they'd even bother with Ben. He's just a kid."

"What the hell did you think happened to him?"

"I figured he made it home. He's a smart kid," Austin said.

"But you didn't even call to make sure!"

"I did call!" Austin shouted. "I swear I called twice and a man answered. He wouldn't let me talk to her. So I just hung up."

"You hung up? Why didn't you tell the guy who you were?"

"How the hell did I know who was there? I thought it might be the guy who shot at me."

"Are you crazy? How could you just assume that?"

"I figured if Ben hadn't made it home, I would've heard something. When I got here, I watched the TV . . ."

"Watched TV?" Louis said.

"Calm down, man," Austin said, his eyes going to the Glock. Austin wiped a trembling hand over his sweaty face and his eyes slid back to Louis. "I thought Ben would be okay."

Louis stared at him hard. "You should've gone back."

"I *did* go back," Austin said. "I waited. When it was dark I went back. When I saw that my car was empty, that's when I figured Ben got away, found a phone, and called home. That's what Susan always told him to do."

"Why the hell didn't you call the cops?"

Austin hesitated, then took a another step away from Louis. Louis grabbed his arm, pulling him back. Austin yanked away, squaring his feet.

"Stop jerking on me. I'm wounded!"

"You sonofabitch," Louis hissed, stabbing at Austin's chest. "You're wanted for something, aren't you? You were protecting your own ass. Who wants you dead?"

"I don't know."

Louis started to raise his hand and Austin stepped back.

"I don't know, goddamn it! I swear I don't know!"

Louis turned away from him. He didn't understand any of this. He didn't understand what Austin was doing here, who he was running from, or how he could have left Ben. Nothing was making sense.

He drew a breath and looked back at Austin. "Have you been here this whole time?"

Austin nodded, the muscles in his jaw twitching.

"Why did you come here?"

Austin hesitated, looking up at him. His dark eyes looked like pools of oil, wet and thick. "I didn't know who they were or what the hell they wanted. I didn't want to lead them back to Susan's." Austin shook his head. "I had about forty bucks on me, so I spent it on a cab to come over here. I didn't know where else to go."

"But why here?" Louis pressed.

"Shit, man," Austin said. "All Benjamin could talk about was you. How you lived on Captiva at some place called Branson's on the Beach, how you were such a big shot private eye who could catch anybody." Austin's eyes bore into Louis. "I figured maybe you could help me."

Louis turned and walked back to the living room. He ran an arm across his brow, then looked down at the phone.

Call Susan? No. She needed to hear this in person.

Wainwright.

He dialed Chief Wainwright's number and waited until they got him patched through. Louis could hear the rain and the wind and knew Wainwright was still at the park.

"Chief, I need you to meet me back at Susan's."

"Can't. Not for a while. We're just wrapping this up and just got a call on a missing delivery guy. What's up?"

"Austin Outlaw is at my place. He's been hiding out."

"Holy shit. What from?"

"Someone took a shot at him," Louis said.

"And the kid?"

"Still missing."

Silence.

"What should I do with him?" Louis asked. "You want him at the station?"

"No . . . no. Taking him anywhere exposes him. Let me think. Can we keep him there for a few hours?"

Louis glanced back at Austin. He was sitting on the bed and had taken off the towel to examine his wound.

"I need to get back to Susan's," Louis said. "I haven't even told her about the car yet. Can you send someone to watch him?"

"In a couple of hours I can."

"Good." Louis hung up and walked back to the bedroom, stopping in front of Austin.

"Your partner . . . Sorrell. He's dead. And so is your secretary. They were killed yesterday."

Austin didn't look up. "I know. I saw it on the news."

"Jesus Christ, it didn't occur to you *then* that we were looking for you?"

"All it gave was the place and the names. They didn't say anything about me. Or Ben being missing."

Louis wanted to belt him. "I don't believe you don't know what this is about," he said. "Two people are dead and your son is gone."

Austin shook his head, quiet.

"Talk to me!" Louis shouted.

"I don't know anything!"

"Fuck you." Louis walked to the bathroom and set his gun on the sink. He pulled off his T-shirt and unsnapped his jeans. When he looked back into the bedroom, Austin had stood up and was looking around.

"Don't leave," Louis said.

"Where the fuck you think I'm going to go?"

Louis watched Austin for a moment. *No. No way was he screwing this up.*

Louis came back out and pulled open the nightstand drawer. He grabbed a pair of handcuffs and snapped one on Austin's wrist. Austin tried to pull away, but Louis jerked him back and had the other cuff around the wood slat in the footboard before Austin could react.

"I need something for my leg!" Austin called after him.

Louis headed back to the bathroom. He jerked open the medicine cabinet, and pulled out some gauze and tape. Grabbing a clean towel he went back to the door and tossed them on the bed. Without looking at Austin, he went back and got into the shower.

The hot water burned and he leaned into it, his head down, his eyes closed. He wanted to lose himself in the heat and steam, to stop the aching coldness for just a few minutes.

His head shot up.

Sonofabitch.

He pushed back the curtain and grabbed a towel. Wrapping it around his waist, he went quickly back to the bedroom.

Austin looked up from bandaging his leg.

"You lying fucking coward," Louis said.

"What?"

"You never went back to your car," Louis said. "It was gone. They shoved in the lake."

Austin stood up, the chain between the cuffs tight. "Christ, Kincaid, if they took him, it was already too late," he said. "Don't you get it? I couldn't have saved him."

"You didn't even try."

Austin just stood there. Louis turned in disgust and went back in the bathroom. He stood in front of the fogged mirror, staring at his own blurred reflection. But he was seeing Benjamin's face, seeing it and wondering what he was thinking as he watched his father run. And wondering what he was thinking when his father didn't come back.

CHAPTER 13

A cop wearing the black uniform of the Sereno Key Police Department opened the front door after peering at Louis through the small window. Louis didn't recognize the guy, but the cop seemed to know Louis and swung open the door to let him in.

His brass name tag read: A. Jewell. "Evening sir. Chief said you'd be coming around."

The living room was quiet, with only one lamp lit, and the television was turned to *Police Story*. Jewell picked up the remote and muted the TV.

"Anything going on, Officer?" Louis asked.

The cop shook his head. "Nothing, sir." He held up a notebook. "I've been keeping a log of neighborhood activity. But it looks like just the normal comings and goings."

Louis nodded. "Did you take a couple of calls from a man earlier today?"

"Yeah, two. He asked for Ms. Outlaw, but wouldn't give his name," Jewell said, flipping a page. "Since then, it's been just the chief. He calls to check in every hour on the hour."

Louis shivered. The house was freezing cold. "Where's Susan?" he asked, looking toward the kitchen. He could smell coffee brewing.

"In the bedroom," Jewell said. He saw Louis's eyes go to the sandwich and Coke can sitting on the coffee table.

"The lady said to help myself," Jewell said.

Louis nodded and went down the hallway. The bedroom door was ajar and he knocked lightly. There was no answer so he pushed it open. The bedside light was on, the blankets and sheets pushed down, but Susan wasn't there.

Louis poked his head in the bathroom. Not there either.

"Susan?" he called out.

He went to Benjamin's door. It was closed.

"Susan?"

He opened it. The room was dark except for a glowing nightlight by the side of Ben's bed. She was sitting on the lower bunk, wedged in the corner, her head down, a Star Wars comforter pulled up over her knees. She said nothing as she looked up; her eyes asked the question.

He realized at that moment that she knew nothing about everything he had seen in the last twenty-four hours, and suddenly he wasn't sure where to start.

"Louis?"

"We haven't found him yet," Louis said.

She put her head back down.

Louis sat down on the bed's edge, ducking his head under the upper bunk. She pushed away the comforter. She was wearing old gray sweatpants and a baggy black sweater. Her hair was a mess, her feet bare.

"I was in the kitchen and I heard the cop's radio," she said. "I heard something about a car in the park. He wouldn't tell me what was happening."

"They found Austin's car in the lake," Louis said. "There was no one inside. When I left the park, I went home and—"

"You've been gone since yesterday," she snapped. "You've called like one time and then you find the car and you go *home* before you bother to tell me anything?"

He took her shoulders, holding firm. "Listen to me."

She was silent.

"Austin is alive. He was hiding at my house."

"He's what? What did he do with Benjamin?"

Louis quickly recounted Austin's pathetic story and with every word, Susan's body grew more rigid. By the time he got to the part where Austin took a taxi to Captiva, she was pushing him away, crawling off the bed.

"I'll kill him," she said, her hands balled into fists. "I swear I will."

"Susan, I wanted to kill him, too, but that won't help anything. You've got to stay calm."

She turned and left the room. Louis scrambled to follow her. He found her in her bedroom, throwing things from the top of the closet. He went to reach for her arm and she spun toward him, a nickel-plated revolver in her hand. He snatched it from her, stepping back.

"Stop this. Now."

She glared at him, then her shoulders slumped and she wiped at the strands of black hair that hung in her face. "I'm sorry. I'm sorry."

He wrapped an arm around her shoulders, leading her out into the living room.

"Put this away somewhere," Louis said, handing the revolver off to Jewell.

He sat Susan down on the couch and went to get her a cup of coffee. He spied a bottle of wine and brought her a glass instead.

He placed the glass in her hands and urged her to take a drink. Her face twisted slightly at the first taste, but she took another, then another.

Finally, she set the glass on the coffee table and wrapped her arms around her belly. "What is happening here, Louis?" she asked softly. "Who would take Benjamin?"

He sat down next to her and took her hand. "Chief Wainwright is on his way over. Maybe we can figure this out."

She closed her eyes. "I hate him with every ounce of my soul," she whispered.

Louis pulled her to him and she fell against him. Her breaths were ragged, her muscles tight. The phone rang and he felt her jump.

Officer Jewell moved to answer it, but Louis waved him off and went to the phone, grabbing the receiver.

"Yeah?"

"Outlaw? Is that you Austin Outlaw?"

Louis hesitated. "Yeah. Who's this?"

The phone went dead. Louis hung it up slowly. It was one of them. He knew it. Anyone else who knew Austin was in Fort Myers was dead. But what was the point in calling? They hadn't demanded anything. They had only wanted to know if Austin was here.

"Louis, who was it?"

Louis looked at Susan standing at the kitchen door. Jewell was right behind her. He motioned slowly toward the floor.

"Get down," he said quietly.

Jewell immediately took Susan's arm and sat her down on the floor.

"Stay here," Louis said.

"Louis, what—?"

"Susan, just stay here. Please."

Louis crept back into the living room, turning off the television and the table lamp. Jewell was right behind him. They sat down on the carpet, backs against the couch.

"Sir, who was on the phone?" Jewell asked.

"One of them."

"What'd he want?"

"I don't know. He thought I was Outlaw."

Louis looked across the dark house to Susan. She was still sitting just inside the kitchen, a hand pressed to her mouth, her eyes locked on Louis. In the quiet, Louis could hear the hum of the refrigerator. And faintly, the hiss of tires on the wet street outside.

Louis scrambled across the carpet and rose slowly, flattening himself against the wall. He peered out a crack in the drapes. A car's red taillights were disappearing around the corner. Other than that, the street was quiet, most houses dark. He looked back at Jewell.

"Jewell, you said you got two calls today from a man. Are you sure there were only two?" he asked quietly.

"I swear, just two and it sounded like the same guy."

Louis knew those calls were from Austin, if he was telling the truth that he had called here.

"What about yesterday?" he asked.

"None."

"Then this is the first time they've called here."

"Louis?" Susan called out.

"Stay there, Susan."

"Louis, what the hell is going on?"

"Susan, please. I have to think."

Louis's mind was whirring. It had been twenty-eight hours since Austin got away in the park. If they wanted something from him, why did they wait so long to make contact?

"Jewell, you're positive no one else has called?" Louis asked.

"I told him to tell people not to call, Louis," Susan said before Jewell could answer. "I wanted to keep the phone clear for Ben to call."

"Like I said, sir, it's just been the chief," Jewell said.

"Then why the hell did they wait until tonight to call?" Louis said, almost to himself.

"You said they think you're Austin Outlaw," Jewell said. "Maybe they saw you come in tonight."

"Austin and Louis don't look at all alike," Susan said.

"Excuse me, ma'am." Jewell said gently. "I don't mean to be rude or anything but to some white guys, most black guys look a lot alike, especially if they're the same height and build. Plus it's dark and it's been raining hard. Easy mistake to make."

Louis stared at Jewell. Then he looked at Susan. Even in the dark, he could see something new in her eyes. Something crowding there with the fury over Austin and the overwhelming pain over Benjamin. She was looking around her own home, the place she had so carefully made into a place of safety and light, and now she was seeing the shadows and feeling the cold creeping in from the outside.

Damn it. He had done exactly what he was trying not to do by leaving Austin at his place. He had led the killers right back here.

And he had made himself—and Susan—a target.

Louis wanted to go to her. But he stayed at the window, looking out at the empty street, his hand resting on the butt of the Glock in his belt.

CHAPTER 14

The pizza box was warm against his palm, even with the glove on. His heart was beating fast, and he tried not to look nervous, tried not to look around the neighborhood as he waited on the porch for someone to answer the door.

He knocked again. He heard the lock click and an old wrinkled face appeared in the doorway. He was trying to remember his instructions.

Stay cool. Be friendly and she'll let you in.

"Pizza, ma'am," he said, giving her a smile.

"We didn't order a pizza."

He motioned toward the paper stuck to the top of the box, then looked at the house numbers above the door. "This is the address I got."

Her tiny brown eyes peered at him. "But we . . ."

"Well, shoot," he said, easing closer to her, a foot now inside the door. "I'm in big trouble. This is my second mistake this week. Can I use your phone?"

She hesitated, her eyes moving to the Toyota parked in the drive. A bright magnetic Pepe's Pizza sign sat on the roof.

He edged further inside the door, feeling the screen against his back. "Please, Ma'am. I'll be fired if I don't get this right this time."

The old woman moved back. Adam Vargas stepped all the way into the house and closed the heavy door behind him. She turned to show him the way to the kitchen.

Don't take too long. Do it fast.

Vargas followed the old woman to a bar that separated the dining room from the kitchen. He set the pizza box on the bar. Reaching under his denim jacket, he drew out his knife. She was turning to hand the receiver to him when he cut her, drawing the knife quickly across the sagging skin of her throat.

She didn't utter a word. Just looked at him with those little brown eyes and dropped to the floor, falling against the bar, knocking the pizza box to the floor.

"Ida?"

Vargas's head shot up.

An old man. He was standing in the small kitchen at an open door leading to the garage. His eyes dropped to his wife's body on the floor. To the pool of red blood spreading across the white linoleum.

Damn it.

Then the old man reached for a kitchen drawer, but Vargas was there, hand to the old man's throat, bending him backward over the kitchen table. The man's hands came up at him. Vargas slit his throat, feeling blood spray across his own face.

Damn it.

He let go of the man, and wiped a sleeve across his face. Time to get out of here. He started back to the front door, then stopped.

The clicker. The goddamn garage clicker. Byron would've killed him if he had forgotten it.

Vargas walked back through the kitchen, pausing at the door leading to the garage. It was dark, but with the light from the kitchen, he could see a big white Buick. But there was still enough space to park the Toyota.

He jerked open the Buick's door and poked his head in, looking for the garage door opener. *Nothing. Shit.* He popped the glove box and rifled through the neat stack of maps. *Where the hell did they keep the damn clicker?*

He was about to give up when he had a thought and flipped down the visor. There it was. He grabbed it and started back toward the kitchen. He stopped, looking up at the overhead light. A long string hung from the fixture.

He wondered if the light would go on when the door opener was activated. He hit the button. The door started to move, but the light didn't go on. Good.

He hit the button again and the door stopped a foot above the ground.

He left the house, slowing his steps when he hit the porch, trying to look cool, like Byron had told him.

Climbing back into the Toyota, he drew a deep breath before he started the car. Byron Ellis was in the backseat, hunched down.

"Did you get the clicker?"

Vargas held it up.

"Back out slowly."

Vargas backed down the drive and drove slowly away from the old people's house, past Susan Outlaw's house, rounding a curve at the end of the street. Then he stopped the car again, near a rise of bushes, and rolled down the window.

He reached up and pulled the magnetic pizza sign from the roof, tossing it on the seat. He let out a breath, looking down at the dead body of the pizza delivery guy squashed to the floor on the passenger side.

He rolled the window back up against the cold. The car was ripe with the smell of pizza and it made his stomach roll with hunger. "How long do we wait here?" he asked.

Byron Ellis sat up. Vargas could see his face in the rearview mirror.

"I don't know. A few more minutes."

"Man, it worked, just like you said it would," Vargas said. "You knew we might have to come back and you were checking things out for a good place, right?"

"Yeah, right, Adam. Now be quiet."

Vargas looked again in the rearview mirror. "Did I do okay?"

"Are the old people dead?"

"Yeah."

"Then you did okay."

They sat for a few more minutes.

"Okay, let's go back," Ellis said. "Easy like, but quick. Turn the headlights out and hit the clicker for the garage as soon as you round the corner."

Vargas turned the Toyota around and drove back to the old people's house. It was easy to disappear quickly inside the dark garage.

They walked back through the kitchen. Ellis stopped and looked at the old man spread out on the table.

"Jesus, Adam, you made a mess."

Vargas frowned. "It's the only way I know how."

Ellis glanced at him. "Forget it. It's okay."

Ellis walked around the old woman and leaned over the sink, looking out the window to the backyard. Then he disappeared into the living room, turning off all the lights.

Vargas pulled his knife back out of its sheath and walked to the sink. He was careful to step around the table, careful not to step in the wide pool of blood that had covered most of the linoleum in the tiny kitchen. He looked down at the old woman, curled there on the floor. He didn't even remember slicing her. Her husband, yes, he remembered doing that. But the woman . . . funny, he didn't remember how she had died.

Vargas paused at the sink and turned on the faucet, laying his knife on the counter.

You made a mess.

Mess? Death was supposed to be messy. It wasn't supposed to be quiet and neat, like having your wrinkled old heart just shrivel up and stop in your sleep one night. If you were going to die, better to go out fighting.

Like cops. Hell, they went out every day knowing they

might have to fight for their lives. That actually gave him some respect for them.

Far more than he gave that coward Austin Outlaw. The bastard ran. Deserted his own kid. He was the kind who would slip away quietly, like from a drug overdose, a disease, or maybe even suicide. That man needed to understand what a death of glory was.

He took off his gloves and held his hands under the warm stream for a few moments. He squinted at his fingers.

Blood . . . how did he get blood on them? He glanced at the black gloves he had tossed on the counter. There was a tear in the palm, sliced completely through.

Damn it.

They were fifty-five dollar gloves, a "getting out" gift from Byron. Gloves were important. In *Shane,* the Black Angel always put on his black gloves before he killed someone.

He'd have to keep these for now. It was too damn hard to find good gloves in Florida.

Vargas picked up the knife and held it under the running water. He washed it until the water was clear again, then picking up a sponge, he wiped down the knife's thick, curved blade. He was careful to get all the blood out of the place where the steel met the wood hilt. When he was finished, he started to turn off the water then stopped. No prints, Byron had said.

He spotted a dish towel. It had a border of blue ducks; it matched the blue ducks marching across the wallpaper and he had a vision of the old woman standing in Wal-Mart, carefully matching up all the kitchen accessories. Getting her ducks in order.

He used the towel to turn off the water then to wipe the knife dry. He put the knife back in the sheath on his belt, careful not to touch the counter with his bare hands.

"Byron, I ruined my gloves. I cut them," he said, coming back into the living room. "I'm sorry."

"Don't worry about it." Ellis glanced back. "Did you touch anything in there?"

Vargas shook his head.

"Where's your gloves? I told you to keep your damn gloves on."

Vargas slipped the gloves back on. "Are you mad at me?"

"No, of course not. Why would I be mad?"

"If I hadn't fucked up out there in Alligator Alley . . ."

"That was my fault. I should've gone with you."

"And if I hadn't missed Outlaw at the park."

"My fault, too. I shoulda taken the shot. I know you're lousy with guns."

"But if we'd gotten him at the park—"

"Shut up, Adam. It's done."

Ellis peered silently out the window, watching Susan's house. Vargas turned and walked to the back of the house. He wanted to see if the old man had a nice set of leather gloves. Not likely. You didn't need them much here. But then again, lots of these old geezers came from up north and some kept gloves around for the trip home.

He went to the first bedroom and turned on the light. He blinked, staring at the room.

Cowboys.

They were everywhere. Cowboys dancing across the wall. And more, on the old chenille bedspread twirling lassos, and there on the lampshade riding bucking broncos around the bulb, and there on the curtains . . . hundreds of cowboy hats.

He stood staring at it all, thinking about his own room back in the trailer. This should've been his room.

He wanted to stay there and just look at them for a while longer, but he had to find some gloves. He pulled open the dresser and rummaged through the clothes. Nothing. He gazed around, his eyes finally going to the open closet. Just a bunch of old clothes and some blankets on the shelf. But there were a couple of old Hush Puppies shoe boxes up there, too. He pulled the first one down and took off the top. Baseball cards. He tossed it on the bed and got the second box down, flipping off the lid.

He let out a slow breath.

The box was full of plastic cowboys, Indians, and horses. They were old and there were maybe a hundred of them crammed in the box.

Vargas pulled out a little figure wearing a hat and fringed chaps. He knew who it was. And he was proud he knew.

"Byron," Vargas called. "C'mere."

"What?"

"You gotta see this."

"Well, bring it out here."

Vargas paused, grabbed a handful of the figures, and stuffed them in his pocket, tossing the shoe box on the bed. He went back to the living room, carrying the figure.

"Look at this. It's Gene Autry."

"Who?"

"Gene Autry."

"Oh yeah," Ellis said without looking back. "He was that guy who got the medal in World War II or something."

Vargas stared at him. "Nah, that was Audie Murphy. Gene Autry was a famous cowboy. What's the matter with you, you didn't have a TV when you were a kid?"

Ellis ignored him, his eyes intent on the street.

Vargas held the plastic cowboy up, trying to see it better in the darkness.

"Hey, come over here and watch the house," Ellis said.

"Why? Where you going?"

"I want to get rid of these damn bodies," he said. "It's bad enough we gotta sit here and wait for fuck knows how long till Outlaw shows up. I ain't living in blood until then."

"Where are you going to put them?" Vargas asked.

"In the trunk of the Buick," Ellis said, heading to the kitchen. "It's cold enough out there they shouldn't start to stink for days."

Ellis disappeared. Vargas set the Gene Autry figure on the windowsill, tilting his head to look at it. He began to sing softly as he looked back out at the house across the street.

"Back in the saddle again . . . I'm back in—"

He stopped suddenly.

A white car was coming down the street. It slowed and pulled into Susan Outlaw's driveway, parking behind the old Mercedes. Vargas peered into the dark, watching as a man got out of the car. He hurried through the rain and up to the porch. In the few seconds he paused under the porch light, Vargas got a look at him—tall, black.

Shit. It was Outlaw.

Vargas looked toward the kitchen then back at the house. A cop opened the front door and Outlaw slipped inside.

Vargas let the blind go. Hell, he had only seen Outlaw a few times. On Friday, when they had first driven down this street, they had seen Outlaw from pretty far away putting suitcases in his trunk and when they realized he was leaving, they had decided to wait and get him when he drove back to Miami. But then he had put the damn kid in the car and they had to rethink everything.

And he had seen Outlaw again at the park, but it had been getting dark and then when they shot at him, he had run.

This guy was the same height . . . and he looked black . . .

Vargas looked back out at the street. Damn. It had to be Outlaw, or why would the cops let him in? He wasn't wearing a uniform or anything.

Shit, if that was Outlaw, then maybe they could make their move tonight. Maybe later, about three in the morning, when the cop outside was drifting off to sleep out of boredom and the cop inside had settled down in front of the TV. Maybe they could get in and kill the bastard while he slept right next to his wife.

Vargas could hear Ellis dragging the second body into the garage.

And maybe if *he* was the one who came up with the plan this time he could impress Byron, and make up for screwing things up in the park.

But first, he had to make sure it was Outlaw in the house.

His eyes drifted toward the kitchen but he didn't want to leave the window to make the call. That's when he saw a second phone on a small stand near the hall leading to the bedrooms. He went and picked it up, stretching the cord to take the phone as close to the window as he could. He knelt at the window, reached in his jeans pocket, and unfolded a slip of paper with a phone number on it. He dialed it and a man answered.

"Outlaw? Is that you, Austin Outlaw?"

"Yeah. Who's this?"

Vargas hung up, setting the phone on the floor. Yeah. *Yeah.*

He cracked the blind, watching. Suddenly, the lights in the house went out and he couldn't see it anymore.

Something was wrong. Shit . . . what the hell was going on?

Ellis came back in, wiping his gloved hands on his jeans. "What a fucking mess," he muttered.

Vargas stood up, moving away from the window. He stepped past Ellis, through the kitchen doorway. He had to have a minute to think this out, figure out the next move.

"Where you going?" Ellis asked.

"I'm hungry. There's another pizza in the car. I'm going to get it."

The garage was dark, and he tripped over something, cursing softly. He felt his way around the white Buick, and the string from the overhead light hit him in the face. He jerked the light on, and stood still, trying to sort things out, trying to figure out why the lights had gone out in Outlaw's house all of a sudden. Maybe he should have told Byron about Outlaw right from the start.

He started back inside the house, remembered the pizza, and went to the Toyota. He yanked opened the front door and grabbed the vinyl pizza warmer. Setting it on the hood, he took out the box and shut the Toyota's door. Turning off the garage light, he took the pizza back to the kitchen.

Ellis was still standing at the front window, the phone in his hand. He was staring at Vargas.

"Adam, who did you call?"

Vargas set the pizza box on the counter.

"Who the fuck did you call?" Ellis asked again.

Vargas hesitated. "Outlaw. He's in the house. I saw him go in. I called to make sure and he answered."

Ellis stepped toward him. "You shouldn't have called!"

"Why the hell not?"

"Jesus fucking Christ, Adam, think!"

Vargas stared up at him.

"We lost Austin twenty-four hours ago and we wait until *now* to call?" Ellis said. "Why the hell would we wait that long? Don't you think that is the first thing they are asking themselves?"

"So what if they are?"

Ellis slammed the phone down on a table. "You gave us away, man! They *know* now you saw him go in that house. That means they *know* we can see that house right this minute! Why the hell do you think they turned the lights off?"

Ellis went back to the window, cracked the blind, and looked back at the street. "Fuck, man, in about two minutes, this whole street is going to be filled with fucking cops."

Vargas just stood there, his blue eyes tearing up. *Fuck. Damn it. Fuck. Fuck.*

Ellis let the blind go. "Come on, we're getting out of here."

"How?" Vargas asked. "We're on a damn island. One way in, one way out. How we going to get that pizza car back to your car and then get over the causeway?"

Ellis hesitated. "We'll have to leave my car because we're not taking the pizza car anywhere. Or the old folks' car. We're taking their boat."

"What?"

"This house is on a canal, Adam," Ellis said. "I saw it the other day. I saw the boat, too."

Ellis was looking around the living room. "You sure you didn't touch anything without your gloves on?"

Vargas was silent, his head down.

"Adam!"

Vargas looked up.

"Did you touch anything in here without gloves?"

Vargas shook his head slowly. "I'm sorry," he said quietly.

Ellis stared at him for a long time. "Go out back and get in the damn boat. I'll be right there."

Vargas nodded and left the house through the back door. He walked to the small dock and waited, folding his arms over his chest. He felt a few drops of rain on his neck and he started to shiver.

CHAPTER 15

The only light in the kitchen came from a single candle on the table. Louis could barely see Susan's face, but he could see the flicker of the flame reflected in her dark eyes, eyes that were singed with an anger he knew was meant for Austin.

"We need to get you out of here," Louis said.

"No," she said softly.

"We can't protect you here," Louis said. "They might be right across the street."

"And so might Benjamin," Susan said.

"Then what do you want me to do?"

Susan didn't blink. "Go get them."

Louis shook his head. "We need to wait for the Chief, and I doubt he'll go busting into all the houses up and down the street tonight."

"Why not?" Susan said. "If they're close, then Ben is close. Why won't you go look for him?"

"It's not that easy, Susan. There are fourteen houses on this street, a half-dozen acres of brush at the end, and a canal on the other side. They could be sitting in a boat in the mangroves over there, for all we know."

"Excuse me, sir."

Louis and Susan both looked up at Jewell. Louis hadn't even realized he had been standing there in the doorway, listening.

"Sir, it's thirty-nine degrees outside," Jewell said. "My bet is that they're still inside somewhere."

Louis ignored him, leaning across the table to Susan. "Look, we'll search the houses when Wainwright can get some more officers here, but you need to leave now."

Susan shook her head.

Louis looked up at Jewell. "Chief say how long he'd be?"

"Another hour or so. Now he's got an accident on the causeway. He's in traffic."

"This is crazy," Susan said. "We're sitting here in the dark, held hostage by a couple of madmen we can't even see, and the only person who can do anything about it is tied up in traffic."

"Look, if I knew where to look I'd go myself," Louis said. "But I can't go blindly charging into these houses, Susan."

She looked away from him. Louis stood up and moved to the counter to pour himself another cup of coffee.

He knew he shouldn't snap at her like that, but he couldn't work a miracle here. What she was asking was crazy and dangerous. And stupid.

"Sir, can I say something?" Jewell asked.

Louis sat down with his coffee. "Go ahead."

"I think we could narrow our search if we took a look at the possibilities."

"What do you mean?"

Jewell opened his notebook. "This afternoon, Ms. Outlaw gave me the names, ages, and descriptions of all the neighbors she knew. We could go over the list and determine which ones might be more vulnerable than others and check those houses first."

"Let me see that," Louis said.

Jewell handed Louis the notebook. Louis scanned the rundown: a young married couple in the pink house, two guys directly across the street, three more younger couples, a single attorney, two elderly couples, and a vacant green house three doors down on the opposite side of the street.

Louis stood up, motioning Jewell to follow him. When he reached for the front door, Jewell caught his arm.

"Are you going out there to see which houses had a view of you when you were coming in?" Jewell asked.

Louis nodded.

"If you don't mind, sir, you might let me do that. They might shoot at you."

Louis hesitated, then stepped aside, letting Jewell go out onto the porch. Louis spoke to him through a crack in the door.

"Can you see the empty green house from here?"

"Yes, sir. Clear view."

"Okay, what about that one with the blue shutters? It belongs to an old couple."

"No, sir. Bushes and trees obstruct their view."

Louis marked it off.

"What about the other old couple . . . five houses down on the other side. Pink flamingos in the yard."

"It'd take good eyes but, yes, you can see it good enough."

Louis walked him through several more, then Jewell came back inside.

"The empty house is our best shot," Louis said.

"What's our next best guess?" Jewell asked.

"The house with elderly folks in it, at the end of the road, with the flamingos," Louis said. He could feel Susan's eyes on him and he turned to her.

"So now you know where to start," she said.

"I'm not going out there alone, Susan."

"I'll go with you," Jewell said.

"No, then *she's* alone."

Susan glanced up at the bookshelf where Jewell had placed her revolver. But then she sank onto the sofa, her hands clasped.

"Jewell," Louis said, "call the Chief and tell him about the empty house."

Jewell moved away and Louis stayed at the curtain, his

eyes traveling up and down the quiet street. The street was almost dark and in the glow of the street lights, the raindrops looked like falling glitter in the cold night air.

The street seemed frozen. Lifeless.

He heard Jewell come back to the door. "Chief says he'll get some backup from the Sheriff and be here as soon as he can. He's bringing someone to tap the phone."

Louis nodded. "What else did you write in that book?"

"What do you mean?"

"Tell me what these people were doing, when they left, who came over."

Louis could hear Jewell flipping through his notebook, and saw his penlight click on.

"The guys both work day shift. They got home tonight around six. I saw the red-haired lady walk her dog, the guy next door to her was in his garage for a while today."

Louis was listening but his gaze remained on the quiet street. There was nothing moving. Only three lights on the whole street.

Jewell was still talking. "The red-haired lady picked up her newspaper at four, the old folks with the flamingos got a pizza about thirty minutes ago, the guys had a visitor at seven—they seemed to know him—and the red-haired lady came out again—"

"Wait," Louis said. He was remembering the phone call he had made to Wainwright at the cottage. Wainwright had said he was delayed because he was wrapping up a call on a missing delivery guy.

Louis turned to Jewell. "Who got the pizza?"

"The old folks with the flamingos."

"Did you see the pizza man *leave* the house?"

"Sure. He walked to the door, and walked out a few minutes later."

"Anything else happen at the house after that?"

Jewell looked back at his book. "Yeah, about ten minutes later someone came home in a dark compact car, used the garage opener, and pulled inside."

"Did the dark compact look anything like the pizza delivery car?"

Jewell looked down again, then up at Louis. "I don't remember, sir. I just noticed the pizza sign lit up on top of the car, not the make or model."

"What was the name of the pizza company?"

"Pepe's."

Louis looked back at Susan. "Get me their number."

"It's Ben's favorite. I have it memorized," she said, going to the kitchen.

She brought him the phone, the number already dialed. But there was no answer. Louis looked up at the clock. They were closed.

"Jewell, you guys have a missing delivery man," Louis said. "Call in and see where he worked."

Jewell radioed the station. Louis heard the response. Pepe's Pizza.

"It's not the empty house," Louis said. "It's the old folks at the end of the street. It has to be."

Louis repositioned himself to get a better look at the flamingo house. He could barely see the house from here. There were no lights in the front windows and no cars in the drive. The garage door was closed.

If they were in there, there was a good chance Ben was, too. But what did they want? What were they waiting for? And why had they announced their presence with a phone call?

"Sir, what are we going to do? Call for more units?"

Louis shook his head. "I don't want half-a-dozen sirens screaming down this street. If these guys had the balls to call, they might think they're safe and I don't want them running."

"So what do we do? Wait?" Jewell asked.

"No, you don't wait. You go," Susan said, coming forward. "Damn it, Louis, if *you* don't go, I will."

He ignored her. "Jewell, get us some backup but have

them park on another block and walk in under cover. And tell them to get Wainwright on the phone *now*."

Susan was at his arm. "That will take too long!"

He took her by the shoulders and started to walk her back to the sofa, but she twisted away from him.

"Stop treating me like a child!" she said.

"Then stop being crazy, for crissakes," Louis said. "You want to get me killed? *And* your son?"

She stiffened, drawing back her shoulders. Her lips quivered a little, but she was no where near crying. She hated him right now and he knew it. Hated him for not somehow being able to prevent all this from happening. Hated him for being cautious. For being human.

"If it was *your* son, you wouldn't wait," she said.

He could only look at her, afraid if he said anything, he would regret it. Neither of them moved.

"Sir?"

Louis didn't look at Jewell, his eyes locked on Susan. Finally, she turned away, going to the kitchen. He watched her take hold of a chair and lean into it, her head down.

"Sir?"

"What?" Louis said.

"The garage light went on at the flamingo house."

Louis went back to the window. The garage door was closed but he could see light through the little windows. Then the light went out.

They were leaving. Damn it. Damn it to hell.

He turned and grabbed the revolver off the bookshelf. Susan was coming back into the room and he held the gun out to her.

"Take this and go sit in the closet," Louis said. "Shoot anyone who won't identify himself."

CHAPTER 16

Louis was crouched outside the old couple's house. It had stopped raining, but the ground and bushes were wet and he could feel the chilling dampness seeping into his clothing. It was dark and the streetlights were a dull glow in the misty air.

He heard Jewell breathing softly behind him. "You want the back or front?" Louis whispered.

Jewell pointed to the front door.

"Give me about two minutes," Louis said.

Jewell nodded, and Louis crept away, staying in the bushes until he reached a wood fence. He pulled up the metal latch. It let out a squeak, and he stopped, listening. Nothing.

He went in the gate, crouching against the house, easing his way around the corner. He could make out the shape of a lawn chair, a small patio, and a barbeque. He pulled his Glock up in front of him and drew in a breath, holding it.

For a moment, it was quiet. No crickets. No wind. No nothing.

Then he heard it. A soft putter in the distance.

His eyes snapped to the darkness of the backyard. The smell was faint, but he knew what it was—brackish water and gas fumes. And he knew what was back behind the house—a canal. He stared hard into the blackness. Slowly, the shape of a small dock came into focus.

A boat. That's what he had heard. A boat moving quietly and quickly away.

Damn it. Damn it.

Louis squinted beyond the dock. He could just make out the ripples in the inky canal water and beyond that, the black fringe of mangroves. They were gone, hidden now in the narrow, twisting channels of the mangroves. It had to be them. No one else would be out on that canal this late, in this cold.

He looked back at the house. He knew he still needed to go in. And he knew he needed to go in, gun drawn, in case he was wrong.

Louis retraced his steps to the back door. The door was unlocked and he pushed it open, peering around the door-jamb. The house was dark, but he had the sense that he was in the kitchen. He slipped inside, his eyes jumping from corner to corner, his ears alert for the slightest sound.

He took a step, and his shoe skidded and he went down, trying to catch himself on a table. His elbow crashed against a chair and he was on his ass, sitting in something wet.

He grabbed the table edge and scrambled to his feet, jerking the gun back and forth. But he saw no one, nothing. He worked his way forward, to the living room. It was dark, too, and he reached out, hoping to find a light switch. He felt nothing along the wall.

The front door crashed open and Louis swung his gun toward the sound. A blur filled the foyer then vanished into a short hall. He hoped to hell it was Jewell.

"Jewell," Louis hissed.

Jewell's voice came back. "The place clear?"

"Can't find a damn light."

A light went on in the short hall. Louis headed toward it, and saw Jewell moving cautiously to the first bedroom. Louis followed him and slipped past to the second bedroom. The light switch was right near the door and he flicked it on.

The bedroom was small, the closet open. It looked untouched except for a ripple in the chenille bedspread where someone might have sat down. On the bed were a couple of boxes, the contents dumped. But no people, living or dead.

He heard Jewell out in the hall and left the bedroom to follow him. He knew where Jewell was headed. The last place they needed to look was the garage. Louis realized he had probably missed the door coming through the kitchen.

Jewell had a flashlight, and Louis could see it dancing over the kitchen walls as he came up behind him. Jewell found a switch and reached around the corner and turned it on.

"Sweet mother of God," Jewell whispered.

Louis came up next to him.

The white linoleum was streaked in red. What had been a large thick pool was smeared in all directions with a trail heading to the garage.

Oh, Jesus. That's what he had slipped in. Blood.

The edge of the table and the white doorjamb had bright smears of crimson fingerprints.

Louis looked down at his hand. He had wiped the stickiness from the kitchen floor on his jeans when he had stood up, but he hadn't gotten it all. His palm was tinted red, the creases and lines like tiny bloody rivers in his skin.

Jewell was moving toward the garage. Louis followed, the bloody dampness in his jeans thickening with every step.

The garage door was closed and Jewell used his shoulder to push it open. They were met with a rush of cold air. Jewell's flashlight swept over two vehicles.

Louis walked in, and pulled the string on the light.

Two cars. One was a pristine white Buick. The other was a Toyota with pockets of rust. A red vinyl pizza warmer sat on the hood of the Toyota, empty.

They approached the Toyota on opposite sides. On the front seat was a magnetic rooftop Pepe's Pizza sign. The driver's seat, the front window, and dashboard were smeared with blood.

Someone was huddled on the floor of the front passenger

seat. Red and green shirt. Dark hair. Louis knew it was the pizza delivery man.

"Jeeze," Jewell whispered.

Louis turned. Jewell had popped the trunk of the Buick and was staring inside. Louis went to him.

The old man was on top of the woman. His pasty white skin and thin gray hair were streaked with blood. He lay on his back, his milky eyes open, his head dropping back over the shoulder of his wife. The gash in his neck gaped open, the tissue sliced as clean as fresh butcher meat.

Louis stepped back, running an arm over his face. He drew in a cold breath, let it out, then drew in another. He forced himself to look again into the trunk. He could see the woman's bony legs under her husband. He could see the rolled edges of her knee-high stockings. But he couldn't see under her, to the trunk's bottom.

"Sir," Jewell said, "the back of your jeans are covered in blood. Are you wounded?"

Louis shook his head, his eyes fixed on the bodies as another thought came to him. A horrible thought. "We need to see if Benjamin is under these bodies."

"We shouldn't touch them."

"I know that, but I need to make sure."

Jewell hesitated, then looked around. He spotted garden gloves on the wall and grabbed them, holding them out to Louis.

Jewell reached in and carefully lifted the ankles of the old man, placing them gently toward the rear of the trunk, getting most of the weight off the woman.

Louis pulled on the gloves. Then he placed his hands on the old woman, shifting her gently to get a look underneath her. The vinyl was dark and sticky, and Louis gave the body a soft push to see further. Nothing.

Thank God . . .

Jewell let out a loud breath, then tried to cover it by glancing around the garage. "Guess we better check the Toyota trunk," he said.

They moved back to the rear of the Toyota. Louis was surprised to see the trunk ajar. He used his gun barrel to lift it open.

It was empty, littered with soda cans, old clothing, and a small spare tire. Wires hung disconnected from the tail lights, and there was a small rust hole in the bottom panel.

Jewell came up next to him. "How did they get away without us seeing them?"

"There's a canal out back," Louis said. "They took a boat. I heard it when I was coming around the house."

Jewell clicked on his radio and Louis turned, heading back in the house. He left the garden gloves on and walked back through the kitchen toward the living room. He found the light this time and turned it on. His eyes moved over the room.

Window blinds, slightly crooked, the edge caught against the sill.

A phone on an end table, turned not toward the easy chair but toward the same window.

A pizza box overturned on the beige carpet and a path of bloody footprints, probably his own. Two dirty round imprints in the carpet under the window, like someone with muddy pants had knelt there.

Louis moved carefully to the window and lifted the blind with the tip of his gloved finger. The lights were still out at Susan's but he could see the outline of her house against the trees. He could also see his Mustang sitting in the driveway.

He started to turn away, wondering why the hell these guys had taken a chance like this, what had been their plan, when something on the window sill caught his eyes.

It was a tiny plastic cowboy, a gun in his outstretched hand. It looked old, the kind of toy kids played with in the late fifties or early sixties, before Star Wars action figures and cars that turned into robots.

And it was out of place.

Louis looked around, looked at the blue duck wallpaper in the kitchen, the worn Barcalounger, the collection of framed family photographs clustered around the vase of silk flowers on the crocheted doily. The old couple had been well into their seventies. Their house was immaculate, the table edges free of fingerprints, the picture frames filled with the faces of the couple and their son and grandchildren. But there were no children living here now.

So where did this toy cowboy come from?

Louis turned and went back to the second bedroom. Nothing seemed disturbed except for the two shoe boxes on the bed.

One held baseball cards, old and probably valuable, but left untouched. The other contained dozens more of the little plastic figurines—Indians, cowboys, horses.

What were the killers doing in here? Looking for money or valuables? Louis moved back to the living room and looked again at the small figure on the sill. Had they given it to Ben, thinking he would like it or maybe even to stop him from crying? And had Ben left it for them? Was he trying to leave clues?

Louis went into the kitchen and carefully pulled open drawers until he found some Ziplocs. He picked up the cowboy with a finger between the chaps and dropped it in the bag.

Man, Kincaid, you're stretching this. This is probably nothing.

Louis glanced at the garage door, hearing Jewell talking to Chief Wainwright on the radio. Jewell clicked off as he came in from the garage.

"What's that?" Jewell asked.

Louis put the baggie in his pocket. "I don't know. Maybe a shred of hope."

CHAPTER 17

They were gathered back in Susan's living room. It was cramped and close, the overheated room filled with the smells of wet wool, burnt coffee, and fatigue. Chief Wainwright was stationed near the fireplace, flanked by two Sereno cops wearing black rain slickers. A third cop in the green uniform of the Lee County Sheriff's Department stood nearby, talking to Wainwright. Jewell had gone back to his usual spot at the door. He hadn't removed his soaked windbreaker and his blond hair was plastered to his head.

From his position on the sofa, Louis watched the young cop's face. Jewell was trying hard to look stoic and untouched by the scenes he had seen in the old couple's house. He wasn't old enough to quite have the look down yet.

Jewell caught Louis's eye, held it for a moment. It occurred to Louis that the young cop had been here since this afternoon, probably working the third shift that normally ran until midnight.

"Jewell," Louis said softly.

"Yes, sir?"

"You need some rest. Go home."

"I'd rather stay here, sir."

There was something in Jewell's eyes that told Louis not to press it. Maybe it was just a sense of propriety, but Jewell wanted, *needed,* to stay. Louis understood. Jewell had been with Susan since this whole thing started, shared her home, seen her at her worse. He understood that odd sense of immediate family these sort of situations created.

Louis gave Jewell a tired half-smile. The young cop went back to looking out the small window in the door.

Wainwright's voice was a drone in the background and Louis let his head drop back on the sofa. He was dog tired but still alert. The living room curtains were closed and the spots of red and blue lights moving across them looked almost festive in contrast to the dimness of the living room. Louis had counted ten cop cars outside the last time he looked. There were only five cops on all of the Sereno Key force, so he knew Wainwright had called in help from the sheriff's office and from Chief Horton over in Fort Myers. For all his FBI experience, Wainwright knew he couldn't handle this one alone. There were too many bodies now. And Ben was still missing.

Louis could hear other voices coming from the hallway. It was the tech crew, dusting Ben's room so they had his fingerprints. The clock on the mantel chimed once. Louis looked at it, then at Wainwright. Like everyone else, Louis was waiting for him to take the lead.

Wainwright was holding up the Ziploc with the plastic cowboy in it. "Gene Autry," he said softly. "I had one of these when I was a kid. I don't think this means anything."

"It was out of place," Louis said.

Wainwright's blue eyes stayed on Louis, and Louis could read the sympathy there. But that's all there was. The Chief thought Ben was dead. Louis looked at the other faces. They all did.

Wainwright gave the Ziploc to one of his men, said something under his breath, and the cop left. Louis knew a second tech crew was dusting the old couple's house and that as soon as Gene Autry made it back to the lab, they would dust him, too. And if anything matched what they were lifting from Ben's room, they would know he was still alive.

If . . .

Susan came in from the kitchen, carrying a tray. She set the tray down on the coffee table. "I'm sorry," she said. "All I have is peanut butter and jelly."

She moved away, going to stand at the kitchen doorway.

The cops all looked at each other then at Wainwright. He gave a small nod. One of the cops picked up a sandwich and began to eat. The others didn't move. They were new, part of the second team sent to Susan's house.

There was a light knock on the door. Jewell opened the door. A man in a wet windbreaker came in carrying a black case. He and Wainwright exchanged a few words.

"Ma'am?" Wainwright said.

Susan looked up.

"Is that phone in the kitchen the only one?"

She nodded.

Wainwright nodded to his man and he moved past Susan with his case to set up the tap. Wainwright saw Louis watching him.

"We might get another call," he said.

"Why?" Susan asked.

"They called once," Wainwright said. "They might call again."

Susan didn't reply, slipping away down the hall. Louis pushed off the sofa and followed her. She was standing at the open door to Ben's room, watching the techs. He could almost read her mind, understand what she was thinking. Ben was gone, vanished, and now here were these strangers, tapping her phone, moving around her son's room, leaving black smudges on the windowsills, the furniture, and everything Ben had touched. It was like being touched by something ugly and dark, and he knew that no matter what the outcome of this, those marks would never really go away.

"Susan."

She turned but didn't even look at him. She went across the hall and into her own room. She crawled onto the bed, burying her face in the pillow. Louis came in to sit on the edge of the bed. He touched her hair.

"Susan."

It took a moment, but she finally turned to look up at him. Her eyes were dry, empty.

"He's just a little kid," she said.

"I know."

"He's just this little skinny kid." There was a catch in her voice.

"He's smart, Susan."

She shook her head slowly. "No, no, you don't get it. They pick on him. At school, they tease him . . . he isn't . . ."

She put her face into the pillow.

"Susan, listen to me. Ben is smart. He knows how to use his brain. He is smart in a way most kids his age aren't."

She didn't move.

Louis hesitated, then got up and left the room. He went into Ben's room. The techs were gone. Louis went to the closet, and rummaged through some boxes and clothes in the corner. He found what he was looking for and came back to Susan.

"Susan, look at this."

She turned to face him and frowned slightly when he held out a book. Her frown increased when she saw the title: *In the Presence of Evil: Mass Murderers and Serial Killers.*

"Where did you get this?" she asked, sitting up.

"In Ben's closet."

She took it from Louis and opened it.

"He showed it to me once," Louis said. "When I first met you, that night you were working on the Cade case and you asked me to babysit? He showed me this."

Susan was quiet, turning the pages, looking at the lurid pictures. Finally she closed the book and looked up at Louis.

"Ben is okay," Louis said.

Susan's eyes filled with tears as she clutched the book.

Finally, the tears fell, silently down her drawn face. He thought for a moment she was going to lay back and bury herself in the pillow, but she didn't. She leaned into him, her forehead on his shoulder.

"Louis."

Susan's head came up and Louis turned to see Wainwright in the bedroom doorway.

"Sorry," Wainwright said. "But we might have their car."

"What car?" Susan asked.

Wainwright hesitated, like he didn't have the time or inclination to explain to her.

"What car?" she repeated.

"It looks like they picked up the pizza guy here on Sereno Key," Wainwright said. "Then they drove *his* car to the old folks' house. But they had to get over to this island somehow. We figured they left a vehicle over here somewhere so I had the guys look. We think we got it at a Circle K near the causeway."

Louis started to get up, but suddenly he could feel Susan's hand heavy on his arm. He knew he should stay. He knew he needed to be here and sit with her until she fell asleep or cried herself out.

She took her hand from his arm and placed it on his shoulder, giving him a gentle push.

"Go," she said. "I'll be all right."

Louis stood up and left the bedroom.

The car sat in the shadows behind the Circle K, its dark blue finish glistening in the weak glow of a old floodlight. It was a Cadillac El Dorado from the early seventies, long and sleek, with a faded black vinyl top. The thin strip of decorative chrome was gone, and the hood ornament had been snapped off.

Louis walked to the driver's side and hit the interior with a flashlight. A second light came from Wainwright on the passenger side.

The car was empty. Louis tried the door and it opened with a groan. The dashboard and seats were cracked, brittle from decades of baking under the Florida sun. The floorboards were covered in dried mud and newspapers.

Louis leaned over the seat and swept his light slowly over the back. He was looking for something that told him Ben had been in this car. It wouldn't have been hard to scratch some letters in the old vinyl or to leave a button, or something that would give them . . . what, a lead? Hope?

But he saw nothing.

"Louis, is there a trunk switch?"

Louis brought the light back to the front steering wheel.

"I don't see one."

Louis withdrew from the car and flicked off the flashlight, sticking it under his arm as he walked back to the trunk. He stuck his hands in his pockets and waited while Wainwright dispatched an officer to get a crowbar.

"They tell me the car is registered to a Byron J. Ellis, of Fort Myers," Wainwright said, coming over to Louis.

"What's his history?"

"Sixteen years for manslaughter up at Raiford, and a couple of GTA's. He's been out about eighteen months, last known address was Fort Myers."

"No Miami connection?"

"Not that we can see off his sheet."

"Susan ever deal with him?"

"No. He was convicted down in Collier County."

The officer appeared with the crowbar and Louis and Wainwright stepped aside.

"How far away was the pizza guy's last delivery?"

"Couple of blocks from the old folks' place."

A sharp wind suddenly blew through, shaking loose the raindrops from a palm tree. A drop hit Louis on the back of his neck and trickled under his collar, sending a current of shivers down his back.

"Got it, Chief."

They turned back to the car and Louis found himself easing up, letting Wainwright go ahead. It occurred to him that this was yet another place he had to look, another corner, another room, another trunk. Each time something inside him pulled tight, like a steel brace that would somehow keep him upright if he saw what he most feared to see. He had to force himself to walk over to the open trunk this time.

Wainwright turned and looked back at him, his face a pale mask in the dim light.

"It's empty, Louis."

Louis felt the relief pass through him like the damp wind, and he quickened his step, flicking on his flashlight. The light danced over the inside, but there was nothing to see except junk. Louis's flashlight beam paused at the inside of the rear bumper, where the taillight wires came through to the trunk. The tiny wires had been pulled out of their holes, leaving the right tail light unworkable. The wires of the Toyota had been pulled out, too.

"Chief, look."

Wainwright's beam stayed on the wires for a moment, then disappeared. "You think the kid did that?"

Louis looked at the other taillight. The wires were intact. He stood upright, running an arm across his face.

"The wires on the pizza guy's car were pulled out. Too big a coincidence. I think Ben did it."

"Why would he do that?"

"Remember a couple years back, that guy who was held in a trunk and used the wires to get the attention of the cops? It was all over the news."

"Yeah, I remember. But you're not going to convince me an eleven-year-old boy would. And even if he had seen it on TV, he'd never think to try it."

"Ben would."

Wainwright turned away, gave some instructions to his men, and looked back at Louis.

"I know that Mrs. Outlaw has to have her hope, Louis. People in her situation don't have anything else. But you should know better. You know what kind of people we're dealing with here."

Louis didn't want to hear this. Wainwright put a hand on his shoulder, but Louis shrugged it off, turning toward Wainwright's cruiser. He climbed back inside. Wainwright got in and they drove back to Susan's in silence.

Louis stopped inside the front door to pick up the overnight bag he had brought from his cottage. Two new cops were there and they didn't even look up at him. Jewell, still at his post at the door, gave Louis a slight nod as he went down the hall.

In the bathroom, he changed into worn sweats and a pair of old socks. Going to Susan's room, he paused at the door. Susan was curled on the bed and looked to be asleep, but she was still wearing her clothes.

He went in, leaving the door ajar so he could hear anything outside. He turned off the light. Slowly, carefully, he eased down onto the bed next to Susan, sitting up against the headboard.

The bedroom was dark but in the slender shaft of light coming in from the hallway, he could see the open door of Ben's room across the hallway.

Susan stirred and turned toward him. He sat still, not moving. The rain had started up again, coming now with a hard cold wind that seeped in through the panes of the jalousie windows. Susan shivered next to him but didn't wake up.

Louis got up and went to the window, giving the crank a hard twist. No use. The glass slats of the old window were as tight as they would get.

He crawled back under the comforter, easing close to Susan. For several minutes, he just sat there, trying to get warm. But he couldn't. And he finally knew that the cold came not from the outside but from somewhere deep inside.

There was something oddly, terribly, familiar about it. It had been a different dark bedroom, a different cold wind, a different place. But the feeling was the same, the feeling that he was alone and no one was coming to help him. He was eight again, alone in a bed in the dark in a strange house listening to the Michigan winter wind outside the window. He couldn't even remember which foster home it had been, or even the face of the man who was supposed to take care of him.

He had lain in bed, shivering and crying, waiting for someone to come and turn on the light, to bring him another blanket. No one came.

Louis pulled the comforter up over his chest.

Ah, Ben, be brave. Be brave and believe.

It was another hour before he finally fell asleep.

CHAPTER 18

Sunday, January 17

Benjamin sat on the bed, legs crossed, his back against the wall. They were in a motel room, somewhere far away from Sereno Key. They had come here last night, late, and they had hustled him inside under a blanket. He knew they were afraid someone would see him.

When they had gotten inside, he had curled up in a ball against the wall in the corner of the second bed, fighting tears, not wanting to let these guys hear him cry again. If he did, the blond man would get mad again. He couldn't stand crying, he said.

Ben had expected the blond man to eventually throw him off the bed, taking it for himself. But he hadn't. Ben had awoken in the same spot, the thin spread thrown over him, a pillow squeezed against his chest.

The blond man, the one called Adam, was standing at the window. He was still wearing that same red T-shirt he had on yesterday, and those gloves he never took off, even when he ate. His skin was white, too white for someone in Florida, but he had muscles. The other guy, Byron, was in the bathroom. He was older than Adam and Ben wondered if he was the blond guy's father because he bossed the blond guy around a lot, but still talked nice to him like a father would.

But they didn't look too much alike. Byron was darker. He had tattoos all over him and they were ugly, except for the bird on his back. It looked like the eagle on the dollar bill.

Byron had just gotten out of bed and was in the bathroom now. Ben could hear him making gross noises behind the thin wall.

Ben tried to figure how long he'd been with the men. Friday night he barely remembered. It had all started in the park, when he saw them shoot at Daddy and then suddenly they had him, dragging him away from Daddy's car and putting him in the trunk of another car. That's when he had pulled out the taillight wires, but it hadn't done any good. No cops pulled them over.

Then he had fallen asleep, and wasn't sure how long it was before he heard the car tires going over the metal things on the Sereno Key causeway. He knew it was the only causeway with metal things and he thought he was going home, but he wasn't.

Instead he had been taken from that trunk to another trunk that smelled like pizza. He had pulled the taillight wires out there, too. But again, no one seemed to notice.

He had stayed in that trunk until the man named Byron let him out and walked him through the blue and white kitchen that he knew belonged to Mr. and Mrs. McAllister, the old people who lived down the street.

He had seen blood on the McAllisters' white floor and he had almost stepped in it and then Byron had put a hand to his eyes like Ma did when people on TV got shot up or were getting naked and Byron had said "Don't look at that stuff, kid."

But he had looked. Even though he didn't want to.

The blood . . . he didn't want to step in it. But he knew now he *should* have. That way he would've left a footprint and maybe his Daddy would have found it and known he was there.

He had to let them know he was still alive. If he didn't, they would stop looking for him. And he didn't want them to stop looking.

The bathroom door opened and Byron came out. He wasn't wearing a shirt and his skin was wet. Byron opened a box of donuts sitting on the other bed and looked inside.

Adam turned from the window. "You decide what we're going to do now?"

Byron picked a donut from the box. "I'm thinking on it."

Ben inched forward on the bed. He really wanted a donut but he was scared to ask. He was so hungry.

"Sir?" Ben said softly.

Byron looked at Ben over his shoulder.

"Can I have a donut, please?" Ben asked.

"Finally hungry enough to talk, huh?" Byron said. He tossed him the box.

Ben picked out a glazed donut. It was getting hard but he ate it anyway, his eyes watching Adam as he moved to the center of the small room. Adam was watching TV now, too, his hand resting on the tip of the knife in his belt. The knife Ben figured he had killed the McAllisters with. The knife that caused all the blood on the kitchen floor.

It didn't look like any knife he had ever seen, a short blade with a place to put your fingers, like brass knuckles. Adam liked to bring the knife out sometimes and feel it. Sometimes he cleaned his fingernails with it but it didn't look like it did much good.

"You done thinking yet?" Adam asked.

"Yeah," Byron said. "I got a new plan. This is what we do. We call them back and get Outlaw on the phone. We tell him this is a regular kidnapping and we want the hundred grand in exchange for the kid. Then we split for good."

"For good? You mean never come back?"

"I'm tired, Adam. I'm tired of all the shit and I just want some peace."

"In Aruba?"

"Hundred grand would go a long way in Aruba."

Ben watched as the blond guy got up and walked a small circle in front of the TV before he turned back. "I don't want to stay in Aruba the rest of my life, Byron. And I don't want to be a wanted man for the rest of my life either. I'd like to come back here one day. I have family here."

"That old man doesn't give a shit about you."

"Uncle Leo's been good to me."

"Good? What kind of asshole tells you if you don't straighten up, he'll leave you out where the boars can eat you?"

Byron got up and put a hand on Adam's shoulder. "After this is over, we won't need him anymore. *You* won't need him anymore. Trust me. It will be all right."

"But what if Outlaw doesn't come? Don't they usually send some cop to deliver ransoms?"

"We tell him *he* has to come. We make him drive all the way out here somewhere so the cops can't follow him without being seen by us. When he hands over the money we shoot him."

Ben looked up at the two men. Tears welled up in his eyes.

Kill his daddy?

He felt his body go tight and his chest suddenly seemed filled with something hard and sharp. He wiped the tears away with both arms, smearing the glaze from the donut across his cheek. His eyes caught a glimpse of the knife.

Don't cry. Don't cry.

"What do we do with the kid?" Adam asked.

"We take him with us and leave him there."

"Leave him alive? What if they find him? He'll tell them everything. He'll tell them who we are. We have to kill him, Byron."

"I've told you this before, Adam, guys that hurt kids are scum, and we're better than that. There are some things you don't kill."

Ben pressed himself against the wall. He didn't know what was happening. They were going to kill his daddy and then just leave him somewhere? He'd seen what it looked like out here on the way to the motel. There was nothing but swamp and he had seen a sign about boar hunting and he didn't want to be out there by himself. What if no one ever found him? What if they didn't even try?

Ben's eyes dropped to his hands. The black and gold cigar ring was still on his finger and he started spinning it nervously.

He pulled the paper ring off his finger, his heart pounding. He knew what he'd do. He'd leave the ring as a clue, just like he did the car wires. If they found the ring here, then they would keep looking. They wouldn't let him die out there with the boars.

Ben slipped the paper cigar ring under the pillow, drawing his hand back out slowly. He laid his head quietly down on the pillow, his eyes on the flying bird tattooed on Byron's back.

He wished he could fly like the bird. He wished he could fly home.

CHAPTER 19

Somewhere in his brain Louis heard the door open, the gentle click of a lock, and the wheeze of the screen. Voices drifted in with the cold air and he turned slowly on his back.

A slow ache made its way through his lower back, then moved to his shoulders. He laid still, for a moment staying in that warm, mindless place between sleep and consciousness, not wanting to move or think. Then suddenly his mind jumped back.

Back to the blood-soaked kitchen. A trunk full of bodies. And Benjamin.

His heart quickened and he opened his eyes. He looked first at the nightstand. His Glock was still there, and the small clock read eight forty-five.

Then he turned and looked at Susan, still sleeping next to him. She was facing him, her eyes squeezed tight as if staying asleep was an effort. The comforter was tucked under her chin, and her hair was spiked around the powder blue pillow. Even in sleep, she didn't look peaceful.

He moved gently, easing out from under the comforter, and swung his feet to the hard wood floor. He picked up the gun and started out to the living room. He stopped in the bedroom doorway, just inside the short hall.

In the center of the living room stood Joe Frye, her black

leather jacket slick with rain, her light brown hair dark and damp. Her gold badge hung from her neck on a chain. She was standing next to Jewell. She was as tall as he was, but despite her slenderness, she looked more commanding than he ever would.

"Joe," Louis said.

Her gray eyes jumped to him, moving quickly over his rumpled sweats, stockinged feet, and the gun in his hand. Her eyes flicked behind him and Louis knew she could see into the bedroom, see Susan in the bed.

Joe's eyes came back to him. "Sorry to show up like this, but this was the only address I had besides yours," she said.

"It's okay," Louis said, coming toward her. "What's happened?"

"Nothing as far as Benjamin is concerned, but we have a suspect."

"Who?"

"A man named Byron Ellis," Joe said, holding out a manila file. "We got him from his prints on that old Chevy Bel Air outside Outlaw's office. He's an ex-con out of Raiford."

"Yeah, I know. We got the name early this morning," Louis said.

Joe looked confused. Louis filled her in on everything that had happened, the pizza guy's murder, the carnage at the old people's house, Ellis's suspected getaway by canal.

"Was he alone?" she asked.

"We don't know," Louis said. "I doubt it."

Louis moved to the sofa, setting the Glock on the coffee table. He opened the manila folder and looked at the black and white photograph of Byron Ellis. He had expected to see the typical mug shot, empty or defiant eyes, and a sneer. But Ellis's eyes had a spark of humor, the head tilted slightly to the side, his lips tipped in a faint smile. His face was pockmarked, the lines along his mouth and around his eyes were deeply scored into his dark, leathered skin.

The statistics said Ellis was forty-five, but despite the smile, Louis suspected it had been a hard forty-five years.

His record was as Wainwright had stated the night before, a smattering of grand theft auto, burglaries, and finally the manslaughter charge that sent him to Raiford.

"What's happened?"

Louis's head snapped to Susan, standing in the bedroom doorway, her robe pulled tight. He started to stand up but Joe was quicker. She moved to Susan and took her hand, covering it with both of her own.

"I'm so sorry."

Susan looked confused.

"I'm Detective Joe Frye, Miami PD."

"What are you doing here?" Susan asked, pulling her hands away.

Louis came forward. "Joe's handling the homicides in Miami," he said.

"But what are you doing here now?" Susan asked, her voice starting to tremble.

"We have no news on Benjamin," Joe said quickly. "I'm sorry, I should've told you that right off. But we do have a suspect."

"You know who took Benjamin?"

"We know one of them," Joe said.

Susan's eyes dropped to the file folder in Louis's hand. She held out her hand and he gave it to her. She looked at it for a long time, flipping through the pages.

"Do you know him?" Joe asked Susan.

She looked up. "No, why?"

"Louis told me you were an attorney here. Ellis was convicted in Collier County, but has had trouble here as well. I was wondering if you ever had any legal dealings with him or heard the name?"

"No, I've never heard the name or seen this man." Susan handed the folder back to Joe and let out a tired sigh. "I'm sorry," she said. "Can I get you cup of coffee?"

Joe smiled. "I'd like that."

Susan disappeared into the kitchen. Joe started to take off her jacket and Louis helped her, hanging it on a coat tree near the front door. When he looked back, she was looking through Ellis's file, her fingertip at her lips.

She was wearing faded black jeans and a black turtleneck sweater. The jeans were slightly baggy on her long legs, drawn in around her small waist by a heavy black belt with a silver buckle. Her sweater fit her like a swimmer's wet-suit, taut across her breasts and broad shoulders. She wore no jewelry except for a large gold man's watch, hanging loose on her slender wrist.

"Sir," Officer Jewell said, nodding toward the door. "Chief's here."

Jewell held the door open, and Chief Wainwright hustled through it, throwing off water like a dog. He had a piece of paper in one hand and with the other, he started to unzip his jacket. His hand paused halfway down, his eyes fixed on Joe. But Louis knew it wasn't the black turtleneck tight over her breasts as much as the gold shield that hung against them.

"Who are you?" Wainwright asked.

Joe's shoulders straightened and she came forward, hand out. Wainwright did not take it. She kept it out long enough to make sure both Louis and Jewell noticed, then withdrew it, wrapping her long fingers along the edge of the folder.

"Detective Frye, Miami PD."

"And you're here why?"

Louis thought about intervening, but was sure Joe wouldn't want him to. Or even need him to.

"Chasing a suspect," Joe said. "Same one as you, one Byron Ellis."

Wainwright did a lousy job of hiding his surprise that Joe already knew the name.

Joe didn't wait. "Can I see last night's scene?" she asked.

Wainwright turned. "Nope, 'fraid not."

"Why not?"

"It's not finished being processed."

"Can I see Ellis's car?"

"It's not finished being processed either."

Joe drew back, a little muscle twitching in her jaw. She inhaled thinly. "Is there anything I can see, Chief?"

"Your way home," Wainwright said.

Joe took another breath, the gold shield rising and falling against her sweater.

Susan came from the kitchen, carrying a tray of coffee cups. She walked with a stiffness Louis had come to recognize as anger, and he suddenly realized just how insane and cruel this conversation must have seemed to her. He wanted to apologize for both of them, but Susan spoke first.

"Detective Frye isn't going home," Susan said. "She came all the way over here to give us a name. And that's more than any of you have managed to get."

Wainwright's face reddened as Susan handed him a cup of coffee. "Mrs. Outlaw, we had the name. We had the name last night."

Susan didn't seem to care. She passed out the rest of the coffee mugs, then sat down on the sofa.

Joe waited a moment, then went and sat next to Susan, taking her mug of coffee. Wainwright was talking in a low voice to Jewell. Louis walked to Joe, but didn't sit down.

"We have something else, too," Louis said. "Austin Outlaw's alive. He was hiding."

Joe almost choked on her coffee. She wiped her lips with her fingers, then looked up at Louis.

"But the boy wasn't with him?"

Louis shook his head.

"Where is Austin now?" Joe asked.

Wainwright looked at his watch. "They'll be moving him from the hospital about now."

"To where?"

"The jail. For his own safety."

Joe set her coffee mug on the table and looked at Wainwright. "Why not bring him back here?" she asked.

"And get him killed?" Wainwright asked.

"No," Joe said, drawing out the word. "I think your six thousand cops out there could probably keep that from happening. That wasn't what I had in mind."

"Then what did you have in mind?" Wainwright asked.

"I think we need to talk to him."

Wainwright set his cup on the mantel and pointed some-where in the direction of the Sereno Key jail. "We spent half the damn night talking to him. The man knows nothing. At least nothing he's willing to tell."

"I'd still like to talk to him."

"About what?"

"His *business,* Chief. Don't you think that might just have something to do with all this?"

Louis was watching Susan. She was listening intently, her arms crossed, her face like stone.

"We know he runs a shitty-ass import business," Wain-wright said.

"It's *what* he imports, Chief," Joe said.

Wainwright wasn't going to bite again. This time he waited, watching her. Joe glanced at Susan as if checking to see if she was ready to hear more.

"Your husband didn't import lamps and baskets," Joe said to Susan. "He imported people."

"What?" Louis said.

"Pacific Imports is an agency that brings workers in from Micronesia. They contract with various kinds of companies to supply them labor. The companies pay for transportation over here and for setting up the workers in housing in ex-change for them remaining in their employment for a speci-fied length of time."

Susan stared at Joe, her eyes snapping. "I knew he was low," she said in a hard whisper, "but I didn't think even he was capable of something like this."

"It's perfectly legal," Joe said.

"So was slavery," Louis said.

With a quick shove off the sofa, Susan stood up. She walked slowly to the front window. Louis thought about going to her, but there was something in the stiffness of her back that kept him where he was.

Wainwright took a breath deep enough to strain his but-tons. "So what do you think is going on here?"

"You asking *me*?" Joe said.

"Yeah, I'm asking you."

"I think Austin Outlaw was supposed to bring something different this trip, something someone wanted very much," Joe said. "And either he failed to deliver it or double-crossed his buyer somehow."

"Drugs?" Louis asked.

"That's my guess," Joe said.

"Austin wouldn't do drugs," Susan said softly.

She sounded like a parent in denial whose kid had just been hauled off to detention. She must have sensed they didn't believe her, because she came toward them.

"His brother died of drugs at fifteen," she said, looking from Joe to Louis. "He just wouldn't do that."

Joe stood up. "Well, they want something from him." She looked to Wainwright. "I'd like to ask him a few questions."

"We got people who can talk to him, Miss Frye," Wainwright said. "Why don't you give Officer Jewell here what you have on this Pacific Imports and—"

"I don't think so," Joe said calmly. "I think we can both talk to him, don't you?"

Wainwright's voice was just as calm. "We got a missing kid and a triple homicide here. Every agency in the county is on this case. Thanks for your offer, but I think we can handle it."

Joe looked down at the coffee table and shook her head. "Dear God, save me from the penis wars."

Louis was close enough to hear it. Wainwright didn't appear to. He headed back toward the door, his radio crackling. Louis heard something about an address, but his gaze was on Susan. She was staring at Wainwright, incredulous at his refusal to accept Joe's help.

Louis was disgusted, too, but now was not the time to take a stand. They had all had a rough forty-eight hours, and Susan was barely holding it together. A blowout here would only make matters worse.

Louis watched as Susan walked over to Joe. She leaned close and whispered something.

"We got a possible address on Byron Ellis," Wainwright said, taking his jacket back from Jewell. He slipped it on and faced Joe and Susan.

"It was a pleasure, Miss Frye," Wainwright said. "I'm sorry I couldn't accommodate you this trip. Maybe next time."

Joe moved away from Susan, coming toward the door.

"Chief, I have a double homicide of my own back in Miami. I have every reason to believe Austin Outlaw may know something about it."

"So?"

"If you don't allow me access now, I'll get a material witness order and take Outlaw back to Miami."

Wainwright's eyes shot to Susan, then back to Joe, who was now in his face.

"I'll fight it," he said.

"And more people will die while you try," Joe said.

Wainwright's brows came down hard over his eyes, and for several seconds he stood perfectly still. Then he turned, waving his hand.

"All right, for crissakes. Go have your talk."

Wainwright zipped up his jacket and left. Only Jewell putting out a hand prevented the door from slamming.

Joe reached for her jacket. "Anyone coming with me to the jail?"

"Give me a minute," Susan said, disappearing into the hallway.

Louis looked at Joe, hoping she would say something to put Susan off, delay the inevitable explosion between Susan and Austin, but Joe didn't seem concerned.

"Joe, letting her see Austin right now is not a good idea," Louis said.

Her eyes swung to Louis quickly. "She's desperate for information, Louis. This man *lost* her son. She has every right to confront him."

"I just want to—"

"Protect her?"

"Maybe."

"What makes you think she needs you to protect her? Or even wants you to?"

The bedroom door opened and Susan reappeared. She was wearing jeans, an old red sweater, and was struggling to get her arms in a black jacket. Her hair was still frayed but pulled back with a red scrunchie, and her face was scrubbed. She seemed different. Her movements were quicker, sharper. Her jaw was set, and her eyes had a spark of . . . what? Anger? Determination? Purpose?

She stopped in front of Joe and Louis, pulling up the zipper on the jacket. "Let's go."

Joe stepped back to let her pass. Susan went outside and Louis leaned back into the room to look at the bookshelves near the TV.

"What are you looking for?" Joe asked.

"Making sure Susan didn't take her gun with her," Louis said.

"Is it still there?"

"Yeah."

Joe gave him a wry smile. "Seems like it's Austin you should be thinking about protecting. Not her."

CHAPTER 20

The interview room was very small, not really meant to hold three people. It smelled of sweat with an undernote of something foul, as if the desperation of the legions of losers who had sat in here had somehow permeated the drab green wall paint.

Joe and Susan had taken the chairs at the metal table. Louis wedged himself near the door. None of them had spoken since the cop had put them in here, telling them that the jail staff was in the middle of a medical emergency with another prisoner and it would be a while before Austin was available.

Available. Like they needed an appointment to see the weasel.

Louis raised the Styrofoam cup to his lips and took a drink of the stale coffee. He felt the urge to pace but there wasn't enough room. There was only the table, two chairs, and a mirror on the interior wall, one-way glass, Louis knew. A small speaker was mounted on the wall near the door.

Joe had pulled her notebook out and was asking Susan questions. When had she last seen Austin before this visit? How much did she know about his import business? Did she know his Miami partner?

Susan sat stiff in her chair, hands folded, intent on answering Joe's questions. She shifted now and then, her emotions jumping between frustration and anger as she realized
she knew so little about her ex-husband. Sometimes she
would look away from Joe, struggling for answers, for some
tiny shred of information about her past, a past that might
somehow shed light on the horrible present.

Joe glanced up at Louis, then closed her notebook, sitting
back in her chair. She stretched a long leg out to the side and
draped her arm over the back of the chair.

"Tell me what he was like thirteen years ago," Joe said to
Susan.

Susan's eyes flicked up to Louis, then she looked away,
pushing her hair from her face. "What does that have to do
with anything?"

"Maybe nothing," Joe said. "But it might trigger a memory. Maybe there's something he wrote or said, something he
put in a letter or postcard."

Susan's shoulders seemed to relax, and she drew in a long
breath as she took her first step back.

"We met at a New Year's Eve party in nineteen seventy-
five," she said in a near whisper. "I was almost twenty. He
was twenty-five."

Joe was quiet, letting Susan fill the pause.

"He wore this beautiful black suit and gold cuff links, and
he had a tiny diamond earring in one ear." Susan looked up
at Joe. "I had never dated a man who wore an earring before.
I thought men who wore earrings were all . . ."

Susan fell silent.

"Gay?" Joe asked.

Susan gave her a small smile but it quickly disappeared
as she nodded.

"Now *cops* wear earrings in their off time," Joe said.

"Not many," Louis said.

Joe placed her long fingers over Susan's clasped hands.
"The suit got you, huh?"

Susan sighed. "I guess so. I fell for a suit. That and his . . ."

his personality. He was everything I wasn't. He had this sparkle about him that I think people hoped would rub off on them." She paused, pulling her hands from Joe's and dropping them to her lap. "I guess that's what I hoped, too."

Louis wanted to look away from them, but there was nothing to stare at but the green walls.

Girl talk. A strange moment of female intimacy that Louis didn't understand or didn't even want to know about. Somewhere in his brain he flashed on an image of his older sister, Yolanda, and her best friend whose name escaped him, a large girl with stiff, pointy braids and bright red lipstick. It was summer, on a porch, and they were talking about Nate Broosher. Louis was six years old, hiding just inside the screen door.

He so fine . . .

What's so fine about him?

Girl, those lips. What else is there to like?

Why you like those big ass lips?

Yeah, theys big, but they do make for some good kissin'.

Louis had shrunk away into the house, flushed with a feeling he didn't understand.

Susan gave out a bitter little laugh in response to something Joe asked. Louis glanced at the door but he knew he would have to knock to signal an officer and that would disrupt their conversation more than his staying.

"We all have an Austin in our past, Susan," Joe said.

Susan nodded. "He bought me my first chateaubriand, my first dozen roses, and my first diamond," she said, glancing at her bare fingers.

"How long before you got married?"

"Five months."

"Did you know what kind of business he was in back then?"

"Some kind of land investments. He made some decent money off some local developments. Construction here was booming and he bought some apartments and condos that he sold off for a huge profit."

"Anything shady about them?"

"Not that I could see."

"So you two were doing okay, then?"

Susan's face wrinkled. "*He* was doing okay. I was work-ing as a legal secretary and wanted to quit and go back to school, but he kept saying he needed to reinvest our money for our future. We ended up pawning my diamond for some Christmas presents one year. It wasn't long after I learned he was blowing it on other investments. Bad investments."

"Like what?"

"He never said exactly. Nothing was working for us then. I should've seen it coming, but I didn't."

Louis was looking at Susan but she was staring at the table, like she didn't really want anyone to see how gullible she had been.

Susan looked up suddenly at Joe. "It wasn't all bad," she said. "Parts of it were still good, you know? We had this crazy sense that the world turned just for us. We had this idea that, that . . ." Her voice trailed off and she shrugged.

"What happened?"

Susan went to take a drink of her coffee, but saw the Styrofoam cup was empty. She held it for a few seconds, then set it down.

"I got pregnant."

"How'd Austin feel about that?"

Susan's smile had a hint of bitterness. "He was happy. He went out and maxed out the credit card on baby stuff we couldn't afford and even started painting the extra bedroom for a nursery."

"But?"

"Three months later he was gone, and there were all these paint cans left in the room. He was off on an overseas busi-ness venture he couldn't pass up. I was so sick with morning sickness I couldn't work, and I . . . I . . ." Susan started shak-ing her head, anger setting in. "I had to go on public assis-tance. I had to use food stamps."

Louis crossed his arms, his head down.

Joe let Susan's anger pass before she spoke. "Did he come back for Ben's birth?"

Susan nodded. "Stayed three weeks. I thought Benjamin would make a father out of him, keep him home where he should be. But then one afternoon, he handed me five hundred dollars and said he had to go again."

"How long after did you try to divorce him?"

It was a minute before Susan could answer. "It took me about five years to save up the money. When I served him with the papers, he flew all the way back from Hong Kong. Begged me to try again. I told him I'd try again if he would stay in the States with Ben and me."

"Did he?"

"He stayed three months. I got up Easter Sunday and found a basket on the kitchen counter that he left for Ben and a card for me." Susan paused, took a breath, then went on. "The card said, *I will never be who you want me to be.* He took the divorce papers with him and disappeared. I just let it go. It costs money to find someone."

"After that," Joe said, "it was just birthday cards and Christmas presents?"

"When he remembered. I think he's been back twice since."

"Has anyone ever called your home looking for him? Creditors? Businessmen?"

"Not in years."

The door opened and a uniformed officer stuck his head in. "You the people waiting for Austin Outlaw?"

Joe nodded.

The door opened wider, and Austin slowly came in. The first thing that caught Louis's eyes was Austin's gold Rolex and neck chain. They were a stark contrast to his ripped trousers and the white Gatorland T-shirt that stretched tight across his chest and arms. Louis guessed the cops had given him the shirt from the jail lost and found, but he had to wonder where Austin got the Luster-Curl that glinted off his black hair.

164 P.J. Parrish

The door closed behind Austin, and he stood stiffly, his dark eyes moving from Louis, to Joe, and to Susan, where they rested for several seconds. Louis tried to see something in his eyes. A hint of regret? Humility? Confusion? To his shock, he thought he saw a spark of indignation.

Susan rose and walked to him, paused a second, then raised her hand. He made no move to stop her, and her palm hit his cheek with a smack.

"You bastard," she hissed.

Louis tightened, his instincts telling him Austin might strike back and if he did, Louis knew he'd kill him. But Austin hadn't moved.

"Are you done, woman?" Austin asked.

She answered him by slipping back into her chair and looking away.

Austin pulled his gaze from Susan and looked at Louis. "Have you found Benjamin yet?"

"No."

Joe rose and gave Louis a discreet nod. He followed her out, pulling the door closed behind him. For a moment, they just watched through the window as Austin stood by the door, head bowed, and Susan sat at the table, glaring up at him.

Joe flipped the speaker on.

"I'm not being nosy," she said to Louis. "I want to hear what he tells her about Ben."

"You don't have to explain to me," Louis said, watching Austin and Susan through the glass.

Susan didn't say anything right away. Austin looked at the empty chair, but did not sit down. The two of them and their silence seemed to fill the tiny room.

"I guess they left us in here so you could beat up on me some more, so go ahead," Austin said. "Take your best shot."

Susan was silent.

"Come on," Austin said. "Rip me a new one, just like your boyfriend did last night. Make this look like it's all my fault."

Susan's eyes lasered up to Austin, but she didn't come out of the chair. "It *is* your fault," she hissed. "You've done something to cause this. What is it this time?"

He curled his lip in disgust. "I just came to visit my wife and son."

"I'm not your wife."

He shrugged, looking around the room. His eyes stopped on the mirrored glass and Louis knew Austin knew they were being watched.

"How could you just let them take him?" Susan asked.

Austin rolled his eyes. Susan repeated the question, louder this time. Austin let out a tired breath and began to speak.

Louis and Joe listened as he went through the same pathetic story about throwing away the ice cream cups, but he didn't add the part—the lie—where he said he went back for Benjamin. He stopped after he said he hid in the bushes for a while, his gaze flicking again toward the one-way mirror.

"You are unbelievable," Susan said.

"What do you want me to do now, Susan?" Austin asked.

"I want you to tell the cops the truth. I want you to tell them what this is all about."

"I can't," he said.

"Can't or won't?" she snapped.

Austin leaned on the table. "*Can't.* Because I don't *know*." He slammed a hand on the table and spun away. "Damn it, why doesn't anyone believe that?"

"Because you lie when you breathe, Austin. Your whole life is a lie."

He spun to face her. "Everyone lies. You lie. Cops lie and even bet Kincaid lies."

Susan stood up. Louis reached for the doorknob, but Joe caught his arm.

"Wait."

"Joe—"

"Wait."

"This isn't about you or Louis," Susan said. "It's about

Benjamin. My God, Austin, what is wrong with you? Your son is gone!"

"A son I barely know thanks to you!"

Louis grabbed the doorknob. This time it wasn't to prevent a fight; it was to start one with the bastard. Joe quickly stepped in front of him.

"Louis! Cool off."

Louis spun away, his back to the glass. He could still hear their words, filtered through the small speaker.

"I told myself I wanted to come here to ask you what happened," Susan said, her voice calm. "I wanted to look in your eyes when you answered me. But I shouldn't have bothered."

Austin crossed his arms, his gaze steady on her face.

"Because there's nothing in there to look at," Susan said. "No husband. No father. No man."

"You want a *man,* Susan?" Austin said, his voice rising. "You want me to do something to help find Ben? Okay, how about this. I'll walk out of here right now, even though I got two killers after me, and I'll go back to the house with you."

"What are you talking about?"

"They want me, right? They shot at me once," he said, pointing to his chest. "I'll give them the chance again. Then maybe when they kill me, they'll give Ben back."

Susan stared at him.

"Is that what you want? You want me dead? Will that make you happy?" Austin yelled.

Susan looked away.

Joe flicked off the speaker and the voices were gone. She came up behind Louis.

"I want to go in and ask him a few questions. Why don't you go get a cup of coffee or something."

"I've had enough."

"Enough coffee or bullshit?" Joe asked.

Louis didn't answer. He was watching Susan and Austin, their voices muted now, but the hatred was enough to fog the glass.

A uniform came toward them down the hall. He handed

Louis a folded piece of paper. He opened it, Joe reading over his shoulder.

> *Sir: I have received four phone calls in the last two hours. Once they asked for Austin. The other 3 times they just hung up. I think someone should be here to take the next call.*
>
> *—Officer A. Jewell*

"You've got to get back," Joe said.

Louis nodded, sticking the note in his pocket.

"Take Susan with you," Joe said. "She's had enough, too."

Louis looked back through the glass. Susan was sitting, elbows on table, head in hands. Austin was just standing there, head bowed. Both of them looked spent, trapped.

"I'll stay here and question him," Joe said.

"No," Louis said, watching Austin. "Let's take him back with us."

Joe's eyes flicked to Louis. She didn't need to say a thing, but Louis knew she was thinking the same thing he was. That they probably had a better chance of getting information out of Austin back at Susan's, and that her house, out on that island and surrounded by cops from three jurisdictions, was probably safer than the damn Sereno Key jail at this point. But if Austin was in fact the target, they were risking his life.

He looked in Joe's steady gray eyes and saw a part of himself reflected back, the part that didn't play by all the rules when something had to get done.

Joe gave a small nod and opened the door. Susan looked up as they came in.

"Susan, we have to get back to your house," Joe said gently. "They've made contact."

Susan was out of the chair and through the door without even looking at Austin. Joe gave Louis a look and followed Susan.

Austin was slumped against the wall, arms folded over

the Gatorland T-shirt. Louis could see a vein twitching in his forehead.

"Come on," Louis said.

Austin looked up. "Where?"

"Back to Susan's," Louis said. "We're granting your wish. You're going to get a chance to play hero."

CHAPTER 21

Austin sat at the far end of the kitchen table. He had discarded the Gatorland T-shirt for a knit shirt and khaki pants that one of the Sereno Key officers had purchased for him at Kmart. It had taken Austin's last few dollars. Louis had watched with a small stab of satisfaction as Wainwright took the slender black alligator wallet from Austin's hand, dug inside and handed the bills to the waiting officer. The cheap shirt was a garish pink and the khakis were too short.

All Austin's other clothing had been confiscated as part of the evidence from the trunk of the BMW when it was pulled from the lake. The clothes sat in Austin's soggy three-piece Vuitton luggage in the Sereno Key evidence room. Except for the butterscotch trench coat, scarf, and fedora, which hadn't been moved from the coat rack near the door.

Louis focused on Austin's fingers holding a glass of water. There was a faint rim of dirt under his nails. About the only thing left of the suave Austin Outlaw now was the Rolex.

Louis glanced up at the wall clock. It was near six. The killers had not called back.

The hours had dragged by in a gnawing silence as they all tried to stay out of each other's way. It was useless. The house was too small. The rain was too relentless. The cops' hovering presence too oppressive. Wainwright and his men in the living room. Seven cruisers outside. And a block away, TV vans now.

Louis's eyes drifted to the refrigerator. There was a drawing on it, something Ben had done. Dinosaurs . . . but not the green monsters that most kids drew. These were carefully drawn replicas of a T rex and a brontosaurus with a volcano simmering in the background.

Louis closed his eyes. It was so quiet he could hear the clock ticking. Not a normal quiet. The terrible quiet of a kid not being there.

The sound of water running made him open his eyes. Joe had come in and was at the sink, rinsing dishes. She caught his eye as she came over to gather up the mostly untouched cartons of Chinese takeout.

Louis looked across the table at Susan. She was picking at an orange, peeling away the rind with her fingernail. It reminded Louis of the way Mel Landeta ate lemons. It reminded Louis that he needed to call him. He hadn't spoken to him since Friday afternoon. Just forty-eight hours ago.

"It's getting dark," Austin said suddenly.

Susan's fingers stopped for a second on the orange rind.

Austin looked at his Rolex then at Louis. "They aren't calling. They've given up."

"No, they haven't."

They all looked up at Joe.

"That's what they're waiting for—dark." She looked directly at Susan. "They'll call."

Austin let out an anxious breath and leaned back in the chair. The kitchen fell quiet again. Louis could hear Wainwright out in the living room, his voice a low drone as he filled in one of the deputies just coming on shift.

Louis's gaze drifted back to Joe. He was thinking about how she managed to get Susan to talk about Austin in less than five minutes. He had known Susan for almost two years and never knew how she felt about black suits, earrings, Easter, or anything else.

But he did understand now why Susan wasn't willing to let Austin slip so easily back into Benjamin's life.

We all have an Austin in our past, Susan. He wondered what had happened to Joe's Austin.

The phone rang.

Susan jumped. Joe turned. Wainwright was at the kitchen door, signaling Louis to pick up the wall phone.

Louis grabbed it. "Yeah."

"Austin Outlaw?"

"Yeah."

A pause.

"This is really Outlaw?"

"I said it was. Who is this?"

"What's your kid's middle name?"

Louis looked at Susan. "Why the hell do you want to know his middle name?"

"What the fuck is it?"

She was mouthing something but Louis didn't catch it.

"Who the hell is this?"

Susan grabbed a paper napkin, scribbled on it, and shoved it in front of him.

"Answer me, asshole."

"Thomas. His middle name is Thomas."

Another pause. The sound of a diesel engine. A truck.

"Talk to me," Louis said.

"That took too long."

"Stop the games," Louis said. "What do you want?"

"A hundred thousand dollars."

"A hundred thousand dollars?" Louis repeated for the others.

"Yeah. Your kid not worth that much to you?"

"Of course he is," Louis said. "Let me talk to him."

A short laugh. "Sorry. He isn't exactly available right now."

"How do I know he's alive?"

Another pause.

"You just gotta have faith, my friend."

"Faith in a man who kills for the fun of it?" Louis asked.

The next pause was so long Louis thought maybe he had hung up. But he was still hearing traffic.

"Okay. When and where?" Louis asked.

"I'm going to call back thirty minutes from now. I want you to get one of those mobile phones and give me the number when I call back."

"Where am I supposed to get a mobile phone in a half-hour?" Louis asked.

"Ask one of those cops standing there. I bet they got one."

Louis looked up at Wainwright, who gave him a small nod.

"Okay, what happens after I get this phone?"

"You, the phone, and the money are going for a drive. I'll call you along the way and give you directions."

"Look, I need some guarantees here."

"The kid's alive and will stay alive if you do what you're told. That's the only guarantee you're going to get."

"Wait a minute," Louis said, still trying to buy time. "It's Sunday. All my cash is tied up in the business and the cops locked all that down as soon as you murdered my partner. I can't raise that much in a few minutes."

"Don't lie to me again."

The line went dead. Louis replaced the receiver.

Susan, Austin, and Joe waited quietly for a recap and Louis gave it to them, word for word as close he remembered it.

Wainwright spoke first. "I would've bet my career this wasn't a kidnaping for ransom."

Susan looked up at Wainwright. "Me, too, but now that it is, we can deal with it. If they want money, then Ben is still alive. We give them the money and they let him go."

"Mrs. Outlaw," Wainwright said. "You're a lawyer, you know—"

Susan jumped up. "Yes, I know. I know the odds are against it. But it's something!"

"Wait a minute, guys," Joe said. "We got other problems here. First, we got FBI issues."

"No," Susan said. "I don't want them. I don't want any more cops. We'll just pay it."

Austin's gaze slipped to Susan and Wainwright. When he looked back, he found Louis staring at him. He looked away, bringing the glass of water up to his lips. When he took a drink, the water trickled down his chin and he wiped it away with the back of his hand.

"Susan, Susan. Hold up. Listen," Joe said. "Do you even *have* that kind of money?" She motioned toward Austin. "Do either of you?"

Susan collapsed in her chair. "We need time," she said. "God, we need more time."

Louis was still watching Austin. Someone had just offered to give him back his son for money and he was just sitting there silent.

Don't lie to me again. Don't lie to me again.

They knew he had cash. Was it just because of the designer clothes, the Rolex, and the BMW? Or did they know something more? And if Austin had that much cash, where the hell was it?

Louis had seen Austin's black alligator wallet earlier in the day. He had seen his luggage in the trunk of the BMW. What he hadn't seen was that damn Vuitton purse Austin had at dinner that first night, the purse he had gone into to dig out that hundred dollar bill for Ben.

It had to be here in the house somewhere. Louis turned in his chair, his eyes sweeping over the house. They stopped on the closed door to Ben's bedroom.

He was remembering what Susan told Austin that first night: *You can stay but you'll sleep in Ben's room.*

Austin suddenly stood up. "Excuse me," he said, starting to the back of the house. For a moment, Louis suspected he might actually be going to Ben's room. But Austin went straight down the hall for the bathroom. Louis got up and followed.

When Austin moved to close the bathroom door, Louis stuck his hand against it, shoving it back open. He slipped inside the small bathroom, closing the door.

"What the fuck?" Austin said.

Louis grabbed the collar of Austin's shirt and slammed him up against the tile wall.

"You sorry sonofabitch," Louis said. "Where's the money?"

"What money?"

Louis clenched the shirt tighter. "The money these guys know you have."

Austin swallowed hard, his breath quickening.

"Where is it?" Louis hissed.

Austin tried to struggle out of Louis's grasp. Louis brought a fist up in front of his face. "Where is it, damn it?"

"All right, all right. It's in Ben's room. I hid it in an old backpack under his bed."

Louis pulled him closer, wanting to slam him harder into the tile. Instead he slung him to the side. Austin tumbled into the tub, grabbing at the shower curtain and pulling the rod and curtain down with him.

"Jesus, man," Louis said. "How do you live with yourself?"

Austin looked up at him, his eyes teary. "You don't understand."

"I understand you don't give a damn about your son."

"He's already dead!"

Louis drew back, but held his hand in the air, unable to hit him. He was pathetic. A sorry, pathetic coward.

Louis dropped his arm and jerked open the door. "Go get the money and give it to Susan. Now."

Austin struggled to get up. He pulled at his shirt and tried to even out his breaths, but it wasn't working. Louis gave him a shove out the door.

He stayed in the bathroom and waited, hearing the door to Ben's room squeak. A few seconds later, he watched as Austin emerged with the black purse and headed to the kitchen.

Louis turned and picked up the shower rod. It was spring

loaded and would easily go back up. Thank God. He didn't want to have to explain any of this to Susan. He stood on the toilet and started to wedge it back into place.

"How did you know?"

Louis turned to see Joe in the doorway. He went back to working the pole tight between the walls.

"He had a purse the first day I met him," Louis said. "I haven't seen it since. How much did he have?"

"He says it's a hundred grand less about six hundred. All one hundred dollar bills."

Louis had the pole in place and jumped down. "Does she know I had to force him into it?"

"I don't think she's had time to figure it out." Joe paused. "Helluva good call."

"Yeah, well, maybe I know a weasel when I see one."

"You speak from experience?"

Louis looked at her. The light was bright in the bathroom, accentuating the fine lines around her mouth. Her lipstick was faded, leaving only a thin red line around the edge of her lips. Under her right eye he could see a faint smudge of mascara that looked almost like a tear had caused it.

"Yeah, I do," Louis said, turning to smooth the shower curtain back down into place.

"Father?"

Louis nodded.

"Is that why you hate him so much?"

"No," Louis said. "Austin disgusts me because he's a coward."

Joe waited, and Louis knew she was allowing him to fill the silence like she always did when she was trying to get someone to open up. And he didn't want to let her in. Not this far. Not this soon. But the words came anyway.

"He never went back," Louis said. "He never went back to get Ben in the park. And what do you think that kid was thinking? How do you think he must have felt when no one came?"

For a few seconds, neither of them moved. Joe's hand started to come up, maybe to touch him, maybe not, he wasn't sure. But she paused in midair, then brought it to her head, raking back her hair. She glanced at the big watch dangling on her wrist.

"C'mon, Wainwright wants to talk to you."

Louis followed Joe back to the kitchen. Before he even reached the kitchen door, he heard Susan's voice, tight, angry.

"How can you even *ask* who's going to deliver the money?" she said, her face in Austin's. "*You're* delivering it!"

"Mrs. Outlaw," Wainwright started. "I'm not sure we should deliver anything to these guys. This whole ransom thing could be a ruse just to lure your husband out there to kill him."

"What if it isn't? What if you're wrong?"

"I can't stop any of you from making this delivery," Wainwright said. "But sending an untrained civilian out there is only going to get him or the boy killed."

"Maybe we should ask the man himself," Joe said. "What about it, Mr. Outlaw? You still want to be a hero?"

The kitchen fell quiet as Austin's gaze shot to her. His lips parted, but nothing was coming out, and Louis could see the humiliation in his eyes.

"I'll go," Louis said.

Susan looked at him, stunned. "No, they'll know. Your hair is shorter, your skin is lighter, your features . . ." Her voice fell to a whisper. "It won't work."

Louis turned and left the kitchen.

"Susan," Joe said. "They mistook Louis for Austin once."

"That was in a porch light," Susan said. "In the rain, from five houses away. They also saw Austin in the park in broad daylight—"

Susan stopped suddenly, her eyes flicking up to the kitchen doorway.

"Oh my God . . ." she whispered.

Louis stood in the door wearing the butterscotch coat, black scarf, and fedora.

"I'll go," Louis said again.

CHAPTER 22

They wired him.

Louis stood in the kitchen, bare-chested, arms outstretched. Joe was taping the thin wire to his back, smoothing it against his skin with the tips of her fingers. Then he felt her clip the recorder to the back of his belt, next to his holster. In front of him, Wainwright was securing the wire to his chest, running it over his shoulder.

Less than thirty minutes ago, the killer had placed a second phone call. After Louis had given him the number to the mobile phone, he had been given instructions.

Come alone in a regular car. No cop cars. No helicopters. No questions.

Wainwright had been the one to suggest the wire. At first Louis wondered why. Kidnappers didn't usually exchange pleasantries during a drop. In fact, they were seldom seen at all. But this didn't feel like an ordinary kidnapping for ransom, and if these guys wanted something besides money, then maybe there was a chance for some discussion.

"How does this work?" Louis asked.

"You'll have to turn on the recorder yourself," Wainwright said. "Feel for the switch."

Joe's hand directed his to the record button at the small of his back. He turned it on and off a couple times.

"Try not to move around if they're talking to you," Wainwright said. "We won't be able to hear them."

Susan came to the kitchen doorway, arms crossed. "Why isn't he transmitting to a receiver?" she asked. "Why can't you listen to what is happening?"

Joe glanced at her. "He'll probably get out of range of any standard receiver. We'd never be able to pick him up if we can't stay close."

"Then why record at all?" Susan asked.

"To get solid evidence," Joe said. "If they're dumb enough to talk to him."

Louis met Wainwright's eyes. There was another reason, he knew. If he got killed out there tonight, and the killers just left him there as they had all their victims so far, at least the cops could listen to his murder afterward.

Louis looked into Susan's eyes and he suspected she somehow had come to the same conclusion herself. She turned away, heading toward the bedroom.

Wainwright held out a bulletproof vest. "You know we can't protect you under these conditions," he said softly.

He looked eighty years old right now, his white hair limp and uncombed, fatigue and fear clouding the blue eyes. Wainwright was ex-FBI, and like Joe, he was willing to invent new rules when the game got tough. He had once killed a child abuser in cold blood. But he knew risking Louis's life was beyond any boundaries.

Louis took the vest and strapped it on. He grabbed a long-sleeved T-shirt off the chair and pulled it on. He saw Jewell coming toward him with Austin's fedora and butterscotch coat.

"Wait," Susan said, coming back from her bedroom. She walked to Louis, holding a small purple bag.

"Sit down, please," she said.

Louis started to protest, but then she unzipped the bag and pulled out a small bottle of dark brown make-up. He realized she wanted to darken his skin. Austin's face was dark brown, his own more the color of sand. She was halfway between, a rich medium brown.

Louis sat down and she poured a few drops of makeup on her fingers, and rubbed it onto his face. His eyes flicked up to Joe, halfway expecting to see a smile, but he didn't. She was watching intently.

He closed his eyes, listening to Susan's shortened breaths, smelling the faintly medicinal scent of the makeup, feeling the desperation in her touch.

"Susan, please hurry," he whispered.

He felt her paint something on his eye brows, then she backed away, looking at him.

"That's as dark as you're going to get, I'm afraid," Susan said.

He stood up and Jewell held out the hat and coat. He pulled on the coat and walked to the mirror near the door to put on the hat.

His hands stopped midway as his reflection came into view. The thought was bizarre, so out of place for the moment, but *Jesus . . . he looked like his mother.*

"Thought you might need these, too," Jewell said.

Jewell was holding a pair of night vision glasses in his hand.

"Good idea," Louis said, throwing the strap over his shoulder.

"Chief," someone called from the door. "Phone's installed in Mr. Kincaid's car."

"You know how to use one of those phones?" Joe asked.

"How hard can they be?" Louis asked.

"It can get complicated. Especially when you've got other things on your mind."

"I'll figure it out. Can you trace the caller?"

"Yes, but it takes a long time," Joe said. "Especially if they're using a mobile phone, too. Our systems haven't caught up to the technology."

"Can you tell where *I* am from it?" Louis asked.

"Only generally and that's if you have a signal."

"There's a chance I won't have one?"

Joe nodded. "Yes, if they take you too far out of the city, which we're pretty sure they'll do."

Wainwright held out a police radio. "Take this. It's on the sheriff's office frequency. They have the widest range. As long as you stay in or around the county, they'll be able to pick you up on this. But don't use it unless everything goes to shit. They might have one just like it."

"I don't know if I agree with that, Chief," Joe said. "Use your secure frequency. Let Louis tell us where he's headed."

"If they got one of these, then they can listen to anything," Wainwright said. "They're smart."

"Ellis is a high school dropout," Joe said.

Louis grabbed the radio from Wainwright and stuck it inside his coat. "Stop. Both of you."

The room fell quiet. Louis saw Susan watching them. She was leaning against the wall, the sleeves of her red sweater hanging down over her hands. She looked exhausted, scared. And grateful.

"Louis," Wainwright said, "I'm asking you one more time to wait for the bureau. I can have them here in an hour."

Louis looked up at the clock on the mantel. It was 10:11 P.M. He had to be at the corner of Main and Seventeenth in nineteen minutes. "We don't have time. Where's the money?"

Jewell thrust out Austin's purse. Louis took it and went to Susan.

"I promise you," he whispered, "if it's possible, I'll bring him home."

She put her arms around his shoulders and pulled him close, holding him tight for only a few seconds. Then she drew back.

"Be careful," she said hoarsely.

Louis's gaze moved to Austin, who was waiting near the front door. He had the urge to say something, but now wasn't the time. And what was the point? Everyone here knew Austin should be the one heading out into the night to make the trade for his son.

"Louis," Wainwright said suddenly. "I want you to take someone with you."

"I can't. They said alone."

"In the trunk, Louis. Or the back. I want someone there if the shit hits the fan."

Louis glanced around the room. His eyes stopped on Jewell.

"You game?"

"Yes, sir."

Wainwright nodded. Jewell hustled into his coat and started toward Ben's room to gather his things. Louis walked out the door.

The street was dark, all street lights and porch lights turned off at police request. The cops had cleared the area of extra patrol cars and reporters. The street was empty, eerie in the mist.

Louis stood on the porch while Jewell crept to the driver's side of the Mustang.

"Louis."

He turned to see Joe behind him.

"I didn't want to say it inside but I think Chief Wainwright is right. This isn't a normal kidnapping."

"I know."

"Take this," she said, holding out a small gun, snug in an ankle holster.

"I already have two," Louis said. "Mine and Susan's."

"You can never have enough."

Louis took the gun, taking one last look up and down the street. He walked to the car.

Jewell slipped in the backseat as Louis got in. He told Jewell he could pull down the backseats and crawl into the trunk if and when he needed to. Jewell didn't reply but Louis could hear him messing with the seats as he started the car and backed out of the driveway.

A few miles down the road, he saw headlights in the rearview mirror and he knew it was cops, and that they would follow him as long as they could. A few blocks after that, those lights disappeared, replaced by two more. It went on like that as Louis crossed the causeway onto the mainland and reached Main and Seventeenth. Then all the headlights disappeared, but Louis knew the cops were still close.

He parked away from the street lights, and turned off the headlights. He looked up at a clock on a nearby bank. He was two minutes early.

Louis pulled the goggles from his pocket and held them to his eyes. He turned toward a street light. The lens filled with a sharp greenish glow and he pulled them quickly away.

"You're not supposed to look at the street lights with them, sir. They're for total darkness," Jewell said quietly from somewhere in the back.

Louis put them back on the seat. Another minute passed. Louis glanced at the phone, then picked it up. A light went on. He put it back in the cradle.

The clock on the bank now read 11:32.

"Sir," Jewell whispered from the back.

"Hmm."

"Do you have any heat in this car?"

Louis rested his elbow on the window, his hand over his mouth. "Sorry. It's dead."

"Going to be a long cold night," Jewell said softly.

CHAPTER 23

They were far from Fort Myers now, long ago leaving behind the strip-mall neon of 41 South, moving down past Naples, making the turn eastward where the road took on its old Indian name of Tamiami Trail. They had lost their police tail miles ago, the cops backing off when Louis steered the Mustang onto a deserted stretch of highway. They were moving away from civilization now and heading into the vast empty gut of the Everglades. Louis had seen a sign for Collier Seminole State Park, so he had a vague sense of where they were. Somewhere way south, where the bottom of the state spread out into the islands of Florida Bay like a tattered flag. Where the reassuring lights of the pretty, pricey retirement towns blinked out. Where the night sky grew huge and dark and the only thing between you and the end of the world were a few fishing outposts and thousands of mangrove islands.

The calls on the mobile phone had been coming in at varying intervals. Sometimes the voice would direct him to make a turn at a certain landmark. Other times, the order would be to just pull off the road and wait until the next contact.

That was what was going on now. Louis had pulled off

the road and the Mustang was idling. They were somewhere southeast of a town called Belle Meade. Tamiami Trail was rain-slick and deserted, not a headlight or landmark.

The drone of the wipers was interrupted by the phone.

"Keep going till you hit 29. Go north till you see a sign for the James Memorial Scenic Drive. Take it to the end and turn left. Go five-tenths of a mile and go left. Go to the dead end and wait." The phone went dead.

Louis felt Jewell stirring in the backseat and heard the rustle of his map.

"Where we going, Jewell?" he asked.

"We're heading into something called the Fakahatchee Strand State Preserve, sir. The scenic drive looks like the only road in and no other out." There was a pause. "No wait. I'm wrong, sir. It looks like there's one other road coming out—Miller Boulevard. Tell the chief to wait where Miller Boulevard comes back out onto Tamiami."

Louis called Wainwright to tell him the directions.

"We're gonna have to back off, Louis, or they'll know you have a dozen cops on your ass," Wainwright said. He clicked off.

A couple miles later, Louis saw the turn for 29 and headed north. It was still raining, light but constant, and the Mustang's headlights were two flat beams penetrating the misty darkness of the two-lane road. The only sound was the beating of the rain and the drone-scrape of the wipers. Louis spotted a sign for James Memorial Scenic Drive and turned. He could make out a scattering of small houses and trailers but they soon fell away. After they passed a gravel quarry, the road turned narrow and rough and then there was nothing.

He picked up the phone and hit a button to dial. No signal.

The Mustang hit a teeth-jarring pothole, then another that almost jolted the wheel out of his hands. Louis jerked the wheel back and slowed.

"Shit. You okay, Jewell?"

"Yes, sir."

Darkness. No lights behind or above. Louis flicked on the high beams. A grotesque tunnel of arching trees came to life in the light. Louis had to struggle to keep the Mustang in the middle of the narrowing road.

Miles more. Then, something ahead. A wall of trees. They were at the end of the scenic drive. Louis slowed and turned left. The road got worse. He couldn't chance taking the Mustang over 20 mph.

"Jewell, you better get down," Louis said.

Jewell wedged his body down behind the seats. But Louis watched the odometer. At exactly five-tenths of a mile, there was another road. No signs, just another narrower gravel path leading into the darkness.

He turned and crept forward. The high beams picked up a yellow metal sign. CAUTION. ROAD DEAD ENDS AT CANAL. NO WAY OUT.

The Mustang crawled along. The road ended. Louis shoved the gearshift into park. He sat back, letting loose his grip on the wheel. The rain beat a tattoo on the Mustang's cloth top. Steam rose off the engine, curling into the weak beams of the headlights, floating on the light until it was washed away by the rain.

Louis rolled down his window, but he saw nothing. He started to roll it back up and stopped.

Two small white lights moving in the distance. They seemed high off the ground. Truck lights, maybe. But he didn't see any road. Hell, there could be five roads out there right now and he wouldn't see them.

"They're here, Jewell."

There was no sound from the back. But Louis could feel the press of Jewell's body through the seat.

Louis reached down to make sure Joe's ankle holster was secure. He patted his side for Susan's revolver. The Glock was on the passenger seat.

The headlights were coming right at the driver's side door, growing larger and bouncing like the vehicle was coming over rough ground. The lights grew brighter with each second. Louis put a hand to his eyes as the sound of an engine pricked his ears. He was sure now it was a truck, maybe one of those souped-up monster trucks.

The grind of a four-wheel drive and then the lights stopped about thirty feet from Louis's door.

Louis jerked the Mustang in reverse and tried to back up, intending to bring the Mustang headlight-to-headlight with the truck to even out the visibility, but he was stuck. The rear tires spun, kicking up mud.

The truck's engine roared loudly as a warning, lurching forward and stopping. Louis shoved the Mustang back into park.

Jesus, he was a sitting duck here, lit up like a Christmas tree.

He heard a door slam above the truck's engine, and a man's voice that was lost in the wind.

Louis drew a thin breath, his chest was tight. His heart felt like it had stopped. He glanced down at the Glock laying on the passenger seat.

He picked up the night vision glasses and looked out the window, hoping to hell they couldn't see exactly what he was doing. There was a glare, but he could see a man standing by the driver's side who looked a helluva lot like Byron Ellis.

"Get out!" the man shouted.

Louis set the glasses down and picked up his Glock. He moved across the front seats and out the passenger side, holding the Glock down at his side behind the folds of the coat. He knew the shift in weight would alert Jewell to where he would be.

He reached beneath the coat and flipped the switch on the tape recorder. Then he crouched, the Mustang between him and the idling truck. The headlights of the truck were so high, the beams shot over the top of the Mustang, stretching deep into the darkness behind him. The man outside the truck turned on a flashlight and moved it over the Mustang windows.

"Where's the boy?" Louis shouted.

"Take off the hat. Let me see your face."

"Where's Benjamin?"

"Take off the fucking hat and stand up."

Louis tossed the hat and rose slowly over the roof of the car. He squinted into the glaring misty rain but could see nothing. He heard a different voice, but it was hard to make out. The other man answered, but it was inaudible to Louis.

"Come around the car, Outlaw."

"No. Show me the boy," Louis said.

"We'll take you to him."

"No."

Again, the second voice. Louder this time, but still muted. Agitated. Angry. But still Louis could not tell what he was saying. Were they arguing?

Footsteps. Sucking sounds in the mud. The flashlight beam was moving.

Louis raised his Glock, bracing his arms on the roof.

"Stop. Stay where you are," Louis said.

"You shoot me, the boy dies."

Metallic sounds. More sloshing through the mud. Louis felt the Mustang jiggle, Jewell moving inside.

"I got the money. Just give me the boy," Louis yelled.

The beam of the flashlight was still. The second voice: "What the fuck are we waiting for?"

"Shut up. Get the money, Outlaw."

Louis reached into the front seat and grabbed Austin's purse. He held it up for them to see.

"Show me Benjamin."

"Put the money in front of your car, in the headlights. And don't throw it. You throw it, we kill the kid."

Damn it. They were trying to draw him out. This had nothing to do with the money.

"I see the boy first," Louis said.

Louis felt the Mustang move and saw Jewell in the back-seat. He made a discreet motion for him to stay down.

It was quiet for a few moments and all Louis could hear

was the soft sprinkle of raindrops across the fabric roof of the Mustang. And he heard the next few words clearly.

"Get the kid," the man said.

Footsteps going back toward the truck. A creak of something opening that didn't sound like a truck door but something smaller, followed by the bang of a lid slamming on a box or a metal chest. *Dear God, what had they been keeping him in?*

Footsteps coming back.

The flashlight swung left.

Ben was crouched in the mud, his small body washed with white light. He was dirty, his jacket and jeans mud-caked, and his glasses crooked on his nose. He had duct tape across his mouth. The man was clutching the shoulder of Ben's open jacket.

Oh, Jesus.

As much as he had hoped for this, Louis hadn't expected it. Ben was alive.

"Take the money to the front of your car and set it down."

Louis knew he couldn't shoot blind. And he couldn't depend on Jewell getting a clean shot if he missed.

"Put the fucking money in front of the car!"

Damn it. If he stepped out there now, he was dead. Everyone was dead. Unless he could get them to release Ben first. Then, even if they did take a shot at him, maybe Jewell could somehow get Ben out of here.

"Maybe *this* will make him part with his money," the second man said. A glint of silver appeared at Ben's throat.

Benjamin tried to struggle but the man clamped him against his hip, the knife under his chin.

"All right!" Louis shouted.

He moved toward the front of the car, the bag in one hand, his gun in the other, his body tense, braced for a shot he prayed would hit the vest.

The one man had the flashlight, and the other held Benjamin. Louis was playing the odds that there wasn't a gun trained on him at the moment. He moved into the Mustang's headlights and dropped the bag on the ground.

An explosion shattered the air, and he felt a sledgehammer to his chest, spinning him to his right. His Glock went off in reaction, jarring loose from his hand. A second bullet hit him high in the back, sending him reeling against the car. He fell against the Mustang's headlights, unable to get his breath, his legs crumbling under him. He dropped to the mud, fighting to get out of the light, back around the tire, but he couldn't move, couldn't even draw a breath.

"Go see if he's dead!"

Glass shattered and more shots rang out, this time coming from inside the Mustang. Jewell.

Susan's gun. Under the coat.

But he couldn't get his hand inside, couldn't find the grip of the .38, still couldn't get a breath.

Bullets riddled the door of the Mustang and Louis ducked into the mud, crawling behind the front tire. He pulled in as deep as breath as he could stand, and wrenched Joe's gun from the ankle holster.

A roar of noise. Splattering mud. Then quiet.

He craned his neck to look up, blinking at the darkness. The truck was gone. And so was Ben.

Louis dropped his head, pain surging through him. His eyes brimmed with hot tears, his hand circled so tight around Joe's gun his knuckles were white.

Damn it. Damn it.

So close. They had been so damn close.

He heard heavy breaths. And someone running.

Louis's head shot up, the gun pointed at whatever was coming at him.

"Sir?"

Louis ran a sleeve across his face and tried to stand up. When he couldn't, Jewell put an arm under him and helped him. Louis leaned against the car, hand to his chest, his head spinning. He felt Jewell's hand on his arm, steadying him.

"They're gone," Jewell said. "I chased them on foot as far as I could but I got in some mud, then just swamp. They got away . . . I don't know." Jewell took a deep breath. "I don't know how, maybe some access road."

"Ben?" Louis whispered.

"Gone, sir."

Louis closed his eyes.

"Sir, you okay?"

Louis nodded, wincing.

"You had to do it," Jewell said.

"I should've handled it another way. I should've . . . done something else . . . I should've . . ."

"There was nothing else you could do," Jewell said, pointing to Austin's purse on the ground. "The money was our only leverage and they didn't even really want it. They wanted you."

Louis shook his head, the pain in his chest engulfing him. "Not me," he coughed. "Outlaw. They wanted Outlaw."

CHAPTER 24

It took a long time to get the Mustang out of the mud and even longer to find their way out of the preserve. Jewell's map was no help because every turn in the dark maze seemed to lead to another canal. Some of the roads were so overgrown with brush they had to back out, moving slowly to avoid the stands of dark swampy water on each side.

Jewell was driving now and with every dead end, Louis could feel the young cop's frustration building, feel his sense of impotency. It was a full two hours before they found the scenic drive, and another hour before they made it back to the gravel quarry and homes. Back on Tamiami Trail, there were no cop cars waiting for them. Miller Boulevard had turned out to be just another rutted path dead-ending in a gaping pool of black water.

At East Naples, Louis finally got a signal on the phone. He gave Wainwright the news of their failure. During the rest of the drive back, Louis remained quiet, the throbbing in his chest growing stronger with every mile.

It was after four A.M. when Susan and Joe met him inside the door. Louis paused, holding Susan's teary gaze as long as he could.

"I'm so sorry," he whispered.

Susan wrapped her arms around him. It hurt, but he held her awkwardly in an half-embrace, fighting not to fall against her. When she finally pulled back, she wiped her face, trying to hold it together.

"Do you need anything? Are you okay?"

"I'm fine," he said.

The next few minutes were a blur. He had a vague sense of Wainwright asking questions, of Joe's pale face watching him. Susan was pacing, demanding to hear the tape. Austin was slumped on the sofa. He didn't even look up at Louis.

Louis tried to peel off the suede coat without pulling at his chest muscles, but he couldn't. Joe was there, reaching up to help him, her eyes dropping to the bullet hole in his T-shirt.

He started to lift the shirt over his head, but couldn't do that either. His eyes swept the room, at Jewell and the two other cops standing at the door, at Joe watching him. And at Wainwright, sitting at the kitchen table with Susan. The tape was playing now, and Louis could hear his own voice, tinny and strained.

"Where's the boy?"

Suddenly, the Kevlar vest was heavy on his aching chest. He went through the kitchen without stopping. Wainwright looked up but Susan didn't, too intent on the tape. Louis pushed open the door to the Florida room just off the kitchen.

Louis looked for a light but couldn't find a switch. He knew Susan didn't use the room much; he had been out here only once to help Ben with a flat tire on his bike. It was just a catchall junk room filled with boxes and a few pieces of mismatched lawn furniture. Some of the glass slats in the jalousie windows were missing. There were puddles on the old tile floor.

Slowly, he crossed his arms and grabbed the bottom of the T-shirt. He tried to pull it up but the pain was unbearable and he had no strength. He gritted his teeth and tried again.

He heard the scrape of the door but didn't turn around.

"Here, let me help."

Joe was behind him. He didn't try to stop her as she gently pulled the shirt up his back and over his head. She was careful as she peeled back the Velcro tabs and took the heavy vest off him, tossing it to the floor. She carefully removed the wire.

"You should go to the hospital," she said.

He shook his head, fighting the dizziness.

"Stay here. I'll be right back."

He waited alone, feeling the cold air flow across his bare chest.

In another hour or two, it would be sunrise. Monday morning. Three mornings ago he had awakened in his cottage, antsy to come to this house, eager to pick up where he and Susan had left off before Austin showed up. By sunset, he was in Miami, looking at corpses.

And now. He spotted Ben's bike leaning against the far wall. Now he was feeling like if he spent one more night in this house, he would go crazy.

Louis heard the door squeak and Joe returned, coming up behind him. He jumped at the gentle press of something icy against his shoulder blade.

"Easy, easy," Joe whispered.

He stood perfectly still, letting her hold the Ziploc full of ice on his back. The cold breeze swirled around him and he could feel the faint tickle of her hair on his bare skin.

"Jewell said you took two shots," she said.

"I got hit in the chest first."

She came around and looked at the bruise spreading over his chest. She pressed the Ziploc against his upper chest, her other hand holding his back. He could feel the tingle of the ice and the warmth of her hand all at once. He felt his nipple grow hard, saw her face so close, smelled the musk of rain, earth, and her.

She was standing inches away and he couldn't bring himself to look into her eyes. When he finally did, he saw—what?

Permission.

He held her eyes for a second longer. He reached up and covered her hand with his and gently pushed her hand away.

Joe stepped back. She reached down, picked up his shirt, and held it out to him. He took it and slowly worked it back over his head by himself.

Joe had gone to sit down in one of the lawn chairs. When he sat down in the other one, she reached over to a table and picked up a juice glass, holding it out to him.

"What's that?" Louis asked.

"Brandy. I brought it out for you."

"Susan doesn't keep brandy in the house."

"Wainwright mentioned you could use a drink and he sent someone to get some."

Louis took a drink. Cheap stuff, but it would do.

Joe was looking at him. He half expected her to say something about him beating himself up over his failure to get Benjamin, but then he knew she wouldn't.

Louis took another drink, staring out into the darkness of the small yard. He couldn't see the palm trees, but he could hear the fronds rustling like taffeta.

"I watched a father shoot his own son once," Joe said.

Louis glanced at her. All he could see was her profile outlined by the light coming from the kitchen window.

"We were in a hostage standoff situation and we had managed to get the father out of the house and onto the lawn, but he was holding his five year old in his arm, a gun at the kid's head. We couldn't get a clean shot."

"You got him to the lawn. You were almost there," Louis said.

Joe shook her head. "He started to lay the gun down, but then he just pulled the trigger. Almost wasn't good enough."

Louis brought the glass to his lips and took a drink. After the burning in his throat subsided, he spoke. "How'd you deal with it?"

She sat back in the chair, the glass dangling in her hand. "Once I realized I couldn't get rid of the memory, I decided to live with it. I keep a photo of the kid in my wallet. Whenever I need to, I take it out and look at it."

"Can I see it?"

She put down her glass and reached into the back of her jeans for a thin billfold. She pulled a photo from behind her Miami PD identification card and handed it to him.

Louis held it up to the light of the kitchen window. He was a tiny child, looking closer to three years old than five. His shaggy light hair was in his eyes, and he wore a crooked grin.

Louis handed it back.

"I talk to him sometimes," she said.

Louis didn't want to tell her he'd talked to skulls and graves, so he said nothing.

She brought her legs up to her chest, wrapping them with her arms, curling into a ball, stretching her baggy gray sweater down over her knees, pulling the sleeves down to cover her hands. It was like she was trying to make herself safe and warm, but she was too tall and the chair was too small. She sat there in a tight ball, chin on knees, staring out into the dark yard. Louis was looking again at her profile, sharply outlined in the stark kitchen light. The strands of hair unloosed from her ponytail did nothing to soften the angles of her face; the darkness did little to hide the fatigue in her eyes. He realized she probably hadn't had any more sleep than he had in the last forty-eight hours. He wanted to reach over and brush the hair back from her face.

He wanted . . .

He wanted her to wrap herself around him, pulling him close. He wanted to hide, somewhere inside her. He wanted to feel safe and warm. He wanted to make her feel that way, too. He took another drink of brandy instead.

"I should go see how Susan's doing," he said.

"I heard her go into the shower. I think she's still there."

"Still?"

"Women do that."

"Do what?"

"Cry in the shower. It's easier that way. No one can hear you and the water feels good, like someone holding you."

Louis rolled the glass between his hands.

"I better go," she said, standing.

"Where?"

"I saw a motel up near the town center. I need some sleep." She shook her head slightly as her eyes went to the kitchen. "I can't sleep here."

Louis reached into his pocket. He held out his keys. "Take these. Go stay at my place. I'm staying here." He gave her some quick directions to his cottage on Captiva.

She hesitated, then took the keys. She brushed her hair back, holding it off her face as she looked at him.

"So where do we go from here?" she asked.

"I don't know," Louis said.

She gave him a small smile.

"Get some sleep," Louis said.

"You, too." She turned and was gone.

Louis heard her speaking to Wainwright. Then it was quiet. A little while later, the light went off in the kitchen.

Letting out a long breath, he finished off the last drop of brandy and set the glass down on the tile. He dropped his head back against the wall. It was just before dawn and a heavy gray light was starting to take over the blackness. Gray like her sweater and eyes.

He ran his hand over his unshaven chin and it dropped heavily down to his T-shirt, resting on the hole over his heart.

CHAPTER 25

Monday, January 18

It was morning but the kitchen was full of shadows, the overhead florescent light weak and flickering. They could hear the steady patter of another day's rain against the windows, but all the bad jokes about it had stopped long ago.

Chief Wainwright sat at the small yellow table, an empty coffee mug and a plate of untouched toast in front of him. His white hair was wet, combed back away from his lined face. Bags of flesh hung under his eyes, seeming to pull down his face.

Austin was seated on Wainwright's right. He wore the same clothes he had been in last night, the khakis and pink shirt. Louis knew he had slept in them, if he had slept at all.

Susan was standing at the sink, her back to the window. She wore a white chenille robe, her hair pulled back with a white scrunchie. Her face was etched with a deep, unwavering pain, but her eyes held a look of renewed determination.

Louis hadn't spoken to her last night. By the time he had come in from the Florida room, she had been asleep. He had closed her door and stretched out on the sofa, but the pain in his chest had made sleep difficult.

"I wanted to talk to all of you before I left this morning," Wainwright said. "I think I have a plan but before I put it in motion, I wanted to make sure we are all on the same page."

The kitchen was quiet as they waited for Wainwright to go on.

"I think we all know now that this was never about the money," Wainwright said. "They were after Outlaw, plain and simple." His eyes drifted to Austin. "I wish I knew why."

Austin shifted in his chair and when no one spoke, he glanced around quickly, then crossed his arms over his chest.

"I told you I don't know," he said tightly. "I borrowed the money from the business and the only person who might be pissed about that is Wallace Sorrell and he's dead now, isn't he?"

Susan glared at him. "You *stole* the money."

Austin's eyes slid to her. "Whatever. But unless Wallace was into things I don't know about and that money was owed to someone else, I got nothing for you guys. Nothing."

"As usual," Susan said.

"Mrs. Outlaw, please," Wainwright said. "Just listen to me for a minute. So far, we've been waiting on them to communicate with us and after last night, I don't think they're going to call us with another ransom demand since now they know that *we know* all they ever wanted was Outlaw."

"Then let's give him to them," Susan said.

"Ma'am," Wainwright said, a hint of impatience in his voice. "You know we can't do that. We can't trade your husband for your son."

Susan's mouth opened to respond, but she closed it quickly, biting back her words. Louis was pretty sure it was damn close to *"Why not?"*

Wainwright stood up. "All right. Here's the plan."

He took a breath, and stuck his hands in the pockets of his uniform pants. "We're going to release the story to the media that we've had a kidnapping, a ransom demand, and that the victim's father, one Austin Outlaw, was killed making the ransom drop."

Susan's head snapped up but Wainwright held her silent with an open hand.

"We need to draw a reaction here," Wainwright said. "Because if we don't, there's a good chance they'll come after him again, and in the process kill more innocent people. Or they'll decide to wait until we call off all the dogs."

"You'd call this whole thing off?" Susan asked.

"After a while, we'd have no choice," Wainwright said. "With no contact, eventually the threat disappears. The police can't protect your ex-husband forever."

"Who cares about protecting him?" she asked, throwing her hand toward Austin. "What about finding Benjamin?"

"Let me finish," Wainwright said. "When we announce that Outlaw is dead, the kidnappers will believe their mission has been completed. Then, one of two things will happen."

Wainwright's voice tightened. "They'll either release their hostage or dispose of him."

Susan let out a half-scream, half-growl and tried to stand up, but her chair banged against the wall behind her, sandwiching her between the chair and the table.

"You're crazy!" she said.

Wainwright put a hand up again, but Susan ignored it. "I say we do just the opposite," she said. "We tell them Austin is alive and if they want him bad enough, they'll try again. They'll come to us and we . . . we can—"

"Do what, ma'am? Sit in your house for God knows how long and wait for these two guys to come bursting through the door?"

Susan leaned on the table. "No. If they think Austin is still alive, we buy time. Time to find them." She grabbed Byron Ellis's file from the table. "We have a suspect. If you give him a reason to bail out, we'll never find him or Ben."

"We've got two different agencies crawling this side of the state for him right now. We're out of time."

"No we're not!" Susan yelled. "Benjamin is alive. Louis saw him just hours ago!"

"That's part of the point, damn it," Wainwright said.

Susan was rigid, her eyes narrowed at Wainwright. "I don't understand."

"Looking back, I think these guys grabbed Ben at the park figuring that eventually your husband would think it was safe and return to get his kid."

"But he *didn't,*" Susan said.

"No, so they took Ben with them. I think the ransom-kidnapping thing was an afterthought, a way to make good use of their unexpected package. I'm not sure they ever really wanted to kill the boy. I think they intended to release him last night after they killed Outlaw."

"They would have released Ben with me laying there dead?" Austin asked.

Wainwright nodded. "I think so. They were betting we'd eventually find the boy."

"No, this won't work," Susan said, shaking her head. "It won't matter if they think Austin is dead. They will kill Ben anyway. Ben can identify them."

"We'll cover that," Wainwright said. "We release Ellis's name and mug shot, announce he's our suspect. Then the identification issue becomes moot. We take away their reason to kill Ben."

Susan slowly sank back into her seat, her eyes locked on Wainwright. She wanted desperately to believe him, believe that what he was proposing would work, believe that what he was saying was true—that they wouldn't kill Ben.

Louis's eyes went to Wainwright. A few days ago the chief had been sure Benjamin was dead. Had he really changed his mind, or was he grasping at something else, something closer to faith? That was an even stranger concept. Faith that a couple of psychos would stop short of killing a child when they had sliced up everyone else in their path. Faith that somehow this could still work out okay.

"That is the plan," Wainwright said. "I need you all to go along with it. Once it's announced, you'll get questions, phone calls. Promise me you won't talk to the media. Especially you, Mrs. Outlaw."

Susan looked up at Wainwright, then turned to Louis, a question in her eyes.

She wanted—needed—to know what he thought. As a defense attorney she had a learned distrust of cops, but she had grown to respect Louis and he knew that if he told her this was the right way to play it, then she would agree, even if reluctantly. And he knew that if Wainwright was wrong, he himself would also carry the blame.

He wasn't sure if Wainwright's plan was brilliant or stupid, but something about it made some kind of weird sense. Why had they even brought Benjamin to the drop if they hadn't intended to let him go?

"Louis?" Susan asked.

He met her eyes.

"I think it's better than just sitting here and waiting to see what they do," he said. "At least this way, we're in control."

She dropped her head, her clasped hands resting on the table. "All right," she whispered.

Wainwright gathered up his things and left the kitchen. Susan watched him go, then pulled Byron Ellis's file to her and started reading. Austin got up and muttered something as he headed to the Florida room. Louis watched him, framed by the small window behind Susan, as he sunk into a chair. A moment later, Louis smelled the pungent odor of his cigar.

Louis rose and went to the living room. He pulled on a jacket and went outside, pausing on the front porch. Through the drizzle, he could see the taillights of Wainwright's car as it pulled away. A Sereno Key cruiser still sat at the curb, an officer inside. Half a block away, Louis watched a couple of Lee County Sheriff's Crime Scene investigators in slick yellow raincoats working the crime scene at the old people's house. Another county car sat at the end of the street.

In Susan's driveway he saw another man, squatting next

to the open passenger door of his Mustang. He wore a rain-coat that had LEE COUNTY CSI stenciled on the back. Louis walked to the driver's side, his eyes moving over the muddy car.

The side window was shattered, a few shards of glass still stuck in the rubber molding. Small crystals of glass shimmered in the rain water that had puddled in the backseat.

He saw a rip in the cloth top where a bullet had passed, and he touched the frayed edge, seeing again how Jewell was positioned in the backseat, knowing how close this bullet must have come.

There were two more bullet holes in the door panel and one more near the front of the car that had creased the metal just over the left headlight.

"Looks like a nine millimeter."

The man's voice startled him and Louis looked back over the roof of the car.

"What?" Louis said.

The crime scene investigator was holding a bullet in gloved fingers. "I said it looks like a nine millimeter. Same as the ones in the vest."

Louis nodded absently, then looked back at the car. "How long before you can release the car?"

"I don't know. Maybe in the morning."

Louis glanced down the street, anxious to get out of there. He had no idea what would happen when Wainwright's announcement hit the news. But he sensed that time was running out, one way or the other, and Wainwright was right about one thing. They couldn't wait for Ellis and his partner to make the next move.

It was time to go looking for them.

Louis's eyes were drawn back to the Mustang's shattered window. The tech was packing up and noticed him.

"You need a ride somewhere?"

Louis shook his head. "No thanks. I got someone I can call."

CHAPTER 26

"Things look different in the daylight."

Joe glanced over at Louis and then back at the road. They were in her red Bronco, retracing the route Louis and Jewell had taken to the drop site the night before.

"This is the way they took you in," Joe said.

"I know. Things just look different," Louis said.

Joe didn't respond as she headed the truck north onto 29. Louis watched for landmarks, anything that gave him a sense of where he was. Maybe it had been the damn rain or more likely his own anxiety over the drop, but he realized now he had hardly paid attention to where he and Jewell had gone. Not that there was much around here to see. Tamiami Trail cut a clean concrete slash through the wilderness of the Fakahatchee Strand State Preserve. They had passed a sign for a place called Carnestown but there was no town there that he could see. Where the hell was the damn "scenic drive"?

He was just about to tell Joe to stop and turn around, that they had missed the turn, when he saw a small sign that said COPELAND. And then another marking James Memorial Scenic Drive.

"This is it. Pull in here," Louis said.

They rounded a bend and a scattering of houses came into view. A small old ranch-style place here, a beat-up mobile home there. No sidewalks, no neat landscaping, but lots of trucks in dirt driveways and dogs in the yards pulling on their chains.

"Somewhere up here we turned right. And I remember seeing a quarry or something," Louis said.

The road turned from asphalt to gravel and soon they saw the quarry. A guy in a dump truck stared at them as they drove past. The road narrowed and turned rutty, the trees arched over them as all the meager signs of civilization fell away.

Joe had to slow down to avoid the watery potholes. Louis grimaced with each bump, the bruises on his chest radiating pain despite the Tylenol Joe had given him earlier.

He eyed the landscape bordering the road. Above, black cypress trees rising tall and bare until they branched out to grab the gray sky. Below, still stands of inky water punctuated with cypress stumps sharp as thrusting arrowheads. Spiny air plants and pale ghost orchids clinging to the trees, giant ferns moving in the wind like billowing green blankets. And everywhere, a strange oppressive feel, like if you stood still for too long in this place, the plants and moss and trees would consume you.

The road ended. Louis repeated to Joe the directions he had been given last night. A few minutes later, he saw the yellow metal sign. CAUTION. ROAD DEAD ENDS AT CANAL. NO WAY OUT. And beyond that, the dark shapes of vehicles. A cruiser. A van.

As they drew closer, Louis realized the vehicles were from law enforcement. A cruiser from Collier County, an FDLE crime scene investigation van. Joe pulled to a stop and cut the engine. They got out.

Louis scanned the landscape. It looked nothing like what they had just driven through. This was flat, with high dry grass that moved like wheat in the brisk cold wind. Far off, he could see a few trees thrusting up through the grassland.

There were some investigators working the scene, marking shell casings and tracks. Crime scene tape sagged between two bushes and they didn't cross it.

"This the right place?" Joe asked.

Louis nodded, pointing to the deep ruts in the mud beyond the tape. "That's where I got stuck. There's a shell casing out there, too."

"They'll find it," she said. One of the investigators was walking toward them and Joe went over to talk with him.

Louis was silent, staring out at the grassland. He knew this is where he had come, knew this is where he had stood, where Benjamin had stood. But it had no feel now of the terror of last night. It was empty. Empty of houses, people, and any reason for anyone to have been there in the first place.

Joe walked up next to him. "What are you thinking?"

"I'm thinking there are no roads except the one we came in on." He pointed north. "They came at my Mustang perpendicular from that direction. How the hell did they get their truck in here?"

"All-terrain vehicle?" Joe asked.

Louis nodded. "But this place is like a maze with all these canals. They knew exactly where to take us. They knew exactly how to get out. They knew we wouldn't be able to follow them."

"Byron Ellis's last known address was Fort Myers but his sheet says he was born and raised in Gary, Indiana. Not many swamps in Gary."

"So his buddy is local," Louis said.

Joe looked out at the landscape. "Think you can find your way back to Copeland?"

Louis could see a taunt in her smile and gave her one of his own. "Come on, let's go."

Back in Copeland, they parked the Bronco and started walking. The town was just a collection of houses, no stores or central core. They started with the nearest house, showing Byron Ellis's mug to anyone who would open the door. Few would. And no one recognized Ellis or remembered seeing his car, the old blue El Dorado. They approached the last house. There was a faded sign stuck in the yard. It read: HANK'S GUIDE SERVICE. YEAR-ROUND WILD BOAR HUNTING $150 INC. FREE CLEANING AND QUARTERING.

Joe nudged Louis and nodded toward the sagging carport. "Swamp buggy," she said.

Louis looked at the weird machine. It was like a giant souped-up go-kart, with huge tires supporting an open chassis with seats on top. The tire treads were caked with mud.

They went up and knocked. It was a couple of minutes before the door scraped open. A scrawny old man with sun-seared skin peered out at them. He was shirtless, a pair of dirty jeans hanging on his thin hips. His eyes flicked from Joe to Louis and stayed there. Louis had the feeling there weren't many strangers in Copeland. And even fewer black men.

"What you want?" the man said.

Joe stepped forward and showed her badge. The man's eyes bugged. "We're looking for this man," Joe said, holding out the picture of Ellis. "Can you help us?"

The guy tore his eyes off Joe's face to glance at the photo. "Nah, don't know him."

Joe pocketed the photo. "Okay, thanks."

Louis could feel the man's eyes following them as they walked back to the Bronco.

"Even if he knew Ellis, he wouldn't tell us," he said.

Joe turned to look at him over the hood of the truck.

"It's the small-town thing," Louis said. "We aren't going to get anything here."

Joe looked around at the motley collection of houses and trailers. "I know. But I can't shake the feeling Ellis has some connection here." She let out a sigh. "Let's get out of here."

Back at the intersection of 29, Joe turned left and headed north. Louis knew she was heading to pick up Alligator Alley for a quicker shot back to Fort Myers. He settled into the seat, trying to find a comfortable posture to ease his aching chest. Joe turned on the wipers. The droning sound was lulling and he leaned back into the headrest. The road was smooth and empty except for a few eighteen wheelers. There was nothing to break the green monotony and he was about to close his eyes when a flash of a sign caught his eye. He sat up, twisting around to look.

"Joe, turn around," he said.

"What?"

"I saw a motel back there. Turn around."

Joe found a turnoff and headed the Bronco back south. She slowed as they approached a sign for the Haven Motel. It was the standard block of rooms, lined up to face the highway with an office at the far end. Some time ago, maybe in the sixties, it could have been the kind of place a tired family might pull into when they had driven one mile too far on their vacation road trip. A plain concrete building but with clean sheets and a Coke machine outside. Now, however, the yellow paint was peeling, the screening on the doors was flapping in the wind, and some of the rooms didn't have numbers anymore.

As Louis got out of the Bronco he looked up at the neon sign. The name of the place was really HEAVEN MOTEL—the E was burned out.

A man was standing at the office door looking at them as they approached.

"Wonder where he keeps Mrs. Bates," Joe said, pulling out her badge. "Excuse me, sir, Miami Police. We're looking for someone and wondered if you would take a look at a picture."

The man's little pig eyes narrowed, although Louis wasn't sure whether it was because Joe was a woman, a cop, or from Miami.

"Have you seen this man?" Joe asked, holding out the photo.

The man didn't answer. But Louis was sure he saw something flick across the guy's eyes. He stepped forward.

"We're looking for a missing boy," he said. "This man abducted him."

The man rubbed his stubbled chin. "Yeah. Okay. He checked in yesterday, real early."

"Did he have a boy with him?" Louis pressed.

"Didn't see one. Only him. But it was raining hard so I didn't look outside."

"When did he leave?" Joe asked.

"He didn't. Paid me for two nights up front."

Joe glanced at Louis. "He's still here?"

The man waved to the lot. "Well, his car is gone. Probably out getting something to eat. When he got here, he asked me where he could get some food. Ain't much around here but I told him he could go down to—"

"The key," Louis interrupted. "We need the key to his room."

The man took a step back from Louis. "Is it legal for me to just give you a key?"

Louis held out his hand. "It's your motel, isn't it?"

"Okay, okay." He disappeared into the office and came out a moment later. Louis and Joe followed him down the line of doors to the end. The man stopped at number seven. The numeral hung upside down; the drapes were closed. Louis could hear sounds inside— canned laughter. The television was on.

The man unlocked the door. Louis pushed his way into the room, gun drawn.

The overhead light was on. The television was blaring. Twin beds, one with the covers and sheets in a tangle, the other untouched except for a pillow crammed in the corner. Plastic bags, beer cans, pretzels on the floor, a box of donuts on the dresser.

"Ben!" Louis called out.

Nothing. No one. He spun to the closed bathroom door and didn't hesitate. He jerked it open. White tile. Towels on the floor. Louis tore back the plastic shower curtain.

When he came back out, Joe was standing in the middle of the room, shaking her head. "They're gone, Louis."

Louis turned, his head bowed, hands on his hips, his

breathing coming hard from his aching chest. Then he reared back and kicked a trash can. It went flying into a lamp, sending it crashing to the floor.

The motel owner was hovering in the doorway and looked at Joe. "You cops are paying for that busted lamp."

Joe ignored him, moving to Louis. "They must have seen the news," she said, nodding to the TV. "Ellis must have seen his mug on TV and they split."

"In a big hurry from the looks of it," Louis said.

"Hey, you gonna pay for that lamp?"

Joe turned back to the motel owner. She let out an impatient breath and went outside, taking the man with her. After a few words, he left. When Joe came back into the room, Louis was moving slowly around the room. He carefully lifted a blanket, pulled open the dresser drawers. He knelt to look under the bed.

"What are you looking for?" Joe asked.

He stood up. "Some sign that he was here."

Joe suppressed a sigh. Louis moved to the bed in the corner, picking up the corner of the pillow.

"Louis, you shouldn't touch—"

Louis paused, his eyes lasering in on a small ring of paper that had been under the pillow. He bent over and carefully used his pinky finger to pick it up. He turned, holding it out to Joe.

"What is it?" she asked.

"A cigar ring," Louis said. "Austin gave it to Ben."

Joe came forward. "Ellis could have left it."

"No. See this label? Macanudo. That's what Austin smokes. It's expensive. Ellis wouldn't smoke this."

Louis was quiet for a moment, staring at the little paper ring. "He left it on purpose," he said.

"What do you mean?" Joe asked.

"Ben. He left this here on purpose. He's trying to tell us something. He's trying to tell us he's still alive."

Joe was quiet.

"You agree with Wainwright, don't you," he said.

"What do you mean?"

"You think I'm grasping at straws."

Joe hesitated, then smiled slightly. "Not straws. At cigar rings maybe."

Louis turned away, looking around the motel room. The room was cold; the trail was cold. Another door opened, another dead end.

"Come on," Joe said. "If we leave now, we can make it up there by dinner."

"Where?" Louis asked.

"Raiford. I was thinking that maybe Ellis hooked up with his partner while he was in prison. Maybe someone will talk. Maybe we can get a lead."

Louis could see in her eyes that she knew it was a long shot and he had a feeling she had suggested it just so they had an excuse not to go back to Susan's and just sit there. But he didn't care.

He slipped the cigar ring into his pocket. "Let's go," he said.

CHAPTER 27

It took five and a half hours to drive up to Raiford, and they arrived just as the warden was leaving. He balked at the idea of an impromptu visit by a private eye and an out-of-town cop. But when Joe threw the weight of a missing child and the Miami PD at him he relented. They had a meeting at nine A.M. tomorrow with Ellis's longtime former cell mate, Yancy Rowen.

But for now, there was nothing to do but wait.

They stopped at a restaurant a couple miles east of the prison for an early dinner. Louis had immediately gone to the pay phone and called Susan for an update, hoping against hope that something had broke in the case. Maybe the killers had called back, or Wainwright had a lead on Ellis, or even the most extreme hope that Ben had been found. But there was nothing. When he told Susan that he and Joe were at Raiford to track down Ellis's past, Susan had told him to be careful, and had added, "Thank Detective Frye for me, too."

They ordered dinner, then Joe went to call Miami and check in with her department. As he waited for her, Louis sipped his coffee, looking around the small restaurant. It was a crowded log-cabin place attached to a motel called THE

LAST STOP. He wondered how many relatives had spent the final minutes of a loved one's life inside one of the tiny rooms.

He rubbed the back of his neck. He was stiff from the long drive, his chest still aching. And he was tired from too little sleep, too much coffee, and the constant chill in his bones.

He glanced down at Byron Ellis's file on the table. They had spent the drive up going over it, reworking what few clues they had, trying to put themselves in the minds of Ellis, his unknown partner, and even Austin Outlaw. But they had come up with nothing.

The waitress brought their food. Louis stared at his burnt rib-eye. He had ordered medium rare but he was too hungry and too tired to send it back. He picked up his knife and fork and tried to cut it.

Joe slid back into the booth across from him, pulling Ellis's file toward her. "Listen, I had a thought," she said.

Louis didn't look up as he sawed the rib-eye. His brain was slowly shutting down, and a part of him just didn't want to talk about this anymore. It had nothing to do with the need to find Benjamin. It was the futility of the day, the closed doors in Copeland, the constant rehashing of the information in Ellis's folder, and the silence of Susan's telephone.

He suddenly realized Joe had said nothing more and he looked at her. She was pouring ketchup onto her fries.

"What was your thought?" he asked.

"Never mind. Sometimes things get distorted when you look too long at them. We'll talk about it in the morning."

He took another bite, wondering if she had seen the weariness in his eyes. His gaze drifted to the fogged window. The temperature this far north was a good 20 degrees colder than back at home, making everything feel even worse. He wiped his sleeve on the glass. Beyond the blur, he could see the string of doors for THE LAST STOP motel. He counted sixteen. There was one car in the gravel parking lot.

"Louis, can I ask you something?"

His eyes moved back to Joe's face quickly. That question usually meant something more personal was coming, something that would require he open a door to a place inside him to answer, a place *she* wanted or needed to go in order to get to know him better. He didn't open those doors for many people and wasn't sure he wanted to now.

A quick image of Mel Landeta flashed in his head, followed by his words *you sure like living on your little island, don't you?* Mel had said that to him after repeated attempts on Mel's part to gain Louis's friendship. Louis had eventually let Mel on his island, both literally and figuratively. Now he would easily call Mel a friend.

Joe was still waiting for an answer.

"Sure," Louis said. "Go ahead."

"Are you happy doing what you're doing?"

That wasn't what he thought she was going to ask. He hesitated. "I'd be happier if this steak was edible."

"I mean the work you're doing and where you're doing it."

He didn't want to go into all this. "Yeah, I like it fine."

Joe sat back, swirling a fry in ketchup. She didn't seem to feel the need to ask more, but now he was curious.

"Why do you ask?"

She bit off the tip of the fry. "Major Anderson asked about you."

"Your boss?"

She nodded.

Louis waited for her to say more, and when she didn't, he took a bite of the steak, stalling, trying not to seem too interested. She continued to eat her fries, one by one, biting off the tips, then dipping them in the ketchup.

"What did he say?" Louis asked.

"Just wanted to know how you were doing," she said, shrugging. "Asked me what I thought of you."

"Why did he want to know?"

She finally stopped nibbling at the fries and leaned forward. "The department is under pressure to diversify. They're making progress at the patrol level, but the upper ranks are still a bunch of stale, pale males."

He knew where she was going with this. He pushed his plate aside and leaned toward her.

"Now, he didn't even come close to any kind of a firm job offer," Joe went on, "but I know him and I know how he thinks. He's already done some homework on you and he wouldn't ask my opinion if he wasn't considering something further down the road."

"But not entry level."

"I'm just guessing, but I think he'd want to keep you for himself."

"Homicide?" Louis asked.

"Crimes Against Persons."

Louis was quiet.

"Are you interested?" she asked.

"I have things to take care of first," Louis said. "But yes, I think I am."

Joe ate a couple more fries, then wiped her mouth with a napkin. "I think we should go snag some rooms," she said.

Louis glanced at her half-eaten burger. "You're not finished."

She shrugged. "You look beat. I can get this wrapped up to go." Before he could object, she motioned to the waitress.

Louis waited for her outside under the awning, hands in his pockets. She came up next to him and they headed across the lot toward the motel office, heads ducked into the wind.

"Here, take this." She handed him the wrapped burger. "I'll get our bags; you go on in."

Louis nodded and went into the office, a bell tinkling above his head. It was warm and stuffy inside, and a gnarled little man looked up from behind the counter. He set aside his newspaper and wobbled over, laying his veined hands on the counter.

"I take cash only. Up front."

Louis pulled his wallet from his back pocket. "No problem."

"Rooms are twenty-five fifty, plus tax."

Louis grabbed the pen off the counter and started filling in the card. The bell tinkled again and he felt a rush of cold air at his back. Joe came up to the desk, carrying their overnight bags. The man's little brown eyes zipped to her, suddenly alive with interest.

"You got dinner. I'll get this," Louis said to Joe.

The man's eyes went from Louis to Joe and back to Louis. "You two together?" he asked.

Louis looked up, the pen paused over the card. "That a problem?"

The man held Louis's gaze for a moment, his whiskered jaw clamped shut. Then he grabbed a room key from the cubbyholes behind him and slapped it on the counter.

"We need two," Louis said.

The old man glanced at Joe then turned and plucked a second key from the cubbyholes, setting it on the desk. Joe came forward and picked it up.

"Thanks," she said. "How's the heat in the rooms?"

Louis was amazed to see her giving the man a smile. And even more amazed to see the old geezer smile back.

"Not too good, ma'am," the man said. "Old and rusty like me."

"Awful cold up here," Joe said.

"Yup," the man said. "Happens every few years. The orange growers hate it. Call it a killing rain. But it ain't never been this bad."

Joe nodded and hoisted her bag, turning to the door. Louis followed. It had started to rain again, and as they hurried across the lot, he looked up. The rain glinted in the floodlights like tiny knives slicing through the darkness.

CHAPTER 28

Adam Vargas settled back into the cracked seats of the black '71 Camaro. He had parked his car across the street from the Lee County Sheriff's office so he could watch the cops going in and out the glass doors. He hadn't wanted to use his own car for this; he didn't want it to end up impounded like they had done with Bryon's car. But there had been no choice, so they had been forced to backtrack to East Naples to pick up the Camaro. Like Byron said, they couldn't keep stealing new cars.

Vargas chewed at his cuticles as he stared at the parade of uniforms. Things had gotten fucked up again.

They still weren't sure Outlaw was dead. Hell, now they weren't even sure that *had been* Outlaw last night. The TV said he was dead, but Byron said they couldn't trust it, that they had to be sure this time.

So now Byron had a new plan. A way to find out for sure.

Vargas turned on the wipers to clear the drizzle, his eyes watching the cops. They seemed to travel in pairs. He needed a guy by himself and he was getting tired of waiting.

For once in your life, Adam, be patient. Don't kill the first cop you see and don't take a cop from Sereno Key. It's a

small department. They know each other. Get one from the
county sheriff. They got lots of them.

Vargas looked up at the darkening sky. The heavy clouds
were lead-colored, but the rain had turned misty, hovering in
the air like gray wet ghosts. He knew it was only five P.M. but
it was almost dark. That would probably be better anyway,
doing this after dark.

A tall guy came out, pausing to zip up his dark green jacket.
Good . . . he was the right size. His hair was dark, clipped short,
high above his ears. He walked with long strides, arms bent,
eyes jumping around the parking lot. Vargas sat up in the
seat, watching as the cop put on black leather gloves.

The cop climbed into a marked cruiser and drove out of
the lot, turning east. Vargas followed.

The cop didn't seem to be in a hurry, barely doing the
speed limit. Vargas could tail him easily, the cruiser's bubble
lights visible even in traffic.

Vargas followed him for over an hour. He watched the
cop make a traffic stop, cruise through McDonald's for a
burger, stop and chat with a guy in another cruiser, and finally pull into one of those huge convenience store plazas
with a Pizza Hut counter inside and fifteen gas pumps outside. Vargas pulled in after him and watched as the cop disappeared toward the back of the store.

Piss-stop. Perfect.

Vargas got out, and pulled his T-shirt over his belt, covering the sheath of the knife. He hurried through the misty rain
into the store and back to the restrooms. He pushed on the
door with his shoulder, afraid it might be a one-person bathroom and the door would be locked. But it swung open. And
it had a latch-type lock on the inside that he could flip closed.

It was a big john with bright florescent lights and hospital-
white tile floors. The porcelain urinals and sinks gleamed
from a fresh rub-down of Formula 409. The stalls were painted
aqua blue, the handles as polished as rich people's silverware.

As Vargas let the door wheeze close, the cop turned to look at him over his shoulder. Vargas gave him a friendly nod. As the cop turned away, Vargas coughed, watching to see if the cop looked his way. When he didn't, Vargas hacked again, using the sound to cover the click as he used his elbow to lock the door.

You can't slit his throat, Adam. You'll mess up the uniform. Use this. It has a knot in the middle. Come up from behind and get this on his throat right in the middle. You'll have to jerk it real good.

Vargas put his hand in his pocket and drew out a small cord that Byron had cut from the drapes at the motel. He unzipped his pants with the other hand as he approached the urinals so the cop would hear the sound he was expecting to hear. The cop was shaking himself off when the cord went around his neck, and Vargas could feel it catch in the folds of skin as the cop's chin instinctively came down toward his chest.

Vargas gave the cord a quick snap, drawing it tight.

The cop started to struggle, one hand raking at the cord around his neck, the other grappling for the gun on his belt. The cop managed to grab the grip and was fighting to free the gun from the holster.

Vargas slammed him sideways into the stall partition, smashing the right side of his body against the wall. He heard a clatter of metal and saw the gun skitter across the tile.

Vargas jerked the cord again, pulling it so tight he could feel the loop getting smaller as it cut deeper and deeper into the cop's neck. The cop was weakening, his sputtering starting to fade to gasping whispers. Vargas gave him one last shove forward, ramming his head into the top of the urinal.

The cop's head hit with a fleshy thud and he crumbled to the floor, the upper part of his body supported only by the cord still in Vargas's hands.

Vargas dropped the cord and leaned against the sink, drawing deep breaths.

Jesus. Motherfucking asshole wouldn't die.

The door rattled. He had to hurry.

Vargas dragged the cop to the last stall and flopped him down. Pulling off his own jeans and T-shirt, he bent and started stripping the cop. He was dead weight, and damp and fleshy, and nothing was coming off easily. Vargas broke a lace trying to get the shoes off.

Damn it. Damn it. He was going to blow this. He knew it.

He worked quickly to re-dress himself, his fingers shaking as he buttoned the dark green uniform shirt.

The door rattled again.

Vargas zipped and hooked the pants, hoisting up the utility belt and pulling it tight across his belly to buckle it. He was surprised it was so heavy, even without the gun.

The gun.

Vargas dropped to his knees and searched the tile floor. He spotted the gun in the first stall and quickly retrieved it, careful not to touch the stall wall.

When he stood, he caught sight of himself in the mirror.

Shit . . .

The green shirt stretched tight across his chest, and the gold star gleamed under the florescent lights. The gun belt was snug on his hips, the stripe down the pants perfectly aligned.

It fit. It fit . . . perfect.

Vargas took a step back, staring at himself in the mirror, a smile creeping onto his face. He spread his feet, and cocked his hand over the gun. With a jerk, he moved to draw the gun. But it sat too high on his belt. The barrel caught in the holster as he tried to whip it out and the gun almost spun out of his hand.

Damn it.

He'd have to lower the belt so it rested more on his hip.

Another rattle of the door.

Vargas hurried back to the cop, and wedged his own sneakers onto the man's feet. He almost touched the door handle but stopped in time, grabbed a wad of toilet paper and used it to lock the stall door. He crawled out underneath on his elbows. Grabbing the green nylon Lee County Sheriff's Department parka, he threw it on, and stuffed his T-shirt and jeans inside before zipping it.

Using his forearm, he flipped up the door lock. A guy was waiting outside, his knees kind of squeezed together. But he took a respectful step back, seeing the uniform. Vargas didn't acknowledge him, walking from the store.

Outside, he reached into the jacket pocket and retrieved the cop's black gloves, pulling them on as he walked.

He walked slowly, holding himself tall. Tall and perfect.

Perfect. This was fucking perfect. Byron would be proud. He had done good so far . . . didn't leave a print, didn't make a sound.

Perfect. All he needed now was a hat.

When he reached the cruiser, he paused for a moment, admiring it, then pulled the door open. He stared at the radio, at all the lights and gadgets and buttons and things. And the big locked-down shotgun between the seats. He eased into the driver's seat.

He started the car, and sat there for a moment, hands resting on the wheel. His eyes went to the brimmed hat sitting on the passenger seat.

He picked it up and put it on. He sat higher in the seat to look at himself in the rearview mirror. He smiled.

It wasn't *exactly* a cowboy hat, but it would do.

He was inside the door. He couldn't believe how easy it was. The asshole outside hadn't given him a second look. The cop inside had even opened the door for him. His name tag read A. JEWELL. Vargas figured him to be about his own age, maybe twenty-three or twenty-four. He had fair, scrubbed skin, short blond hair, a shaved neck, and lots of ear showing. A rookie.

"The sheriff asked you to stop by?" Jewell asked.

Vargas smiled as he took off his hat. "Yeah, wanted to know if you guys needed anything. I had a few extra minutes."

"I could use a hot meal. We've been living on soup, peanut butter, and coffee."

"I'll stand watch if you want to run and get something."

Jewell looked toward the back bedrooms, then shook his head. "No, I better not. I need to stay here."

Vargas shrugged. "No problem."

Jewell's eyes lingered on him a few more seconds.

The gloves. He's looking at the gloves. No, the gun belt is too low. Shit.

Jewell finally wandered into the kitchen. Vargas came deeper into the living room and looked around, edging toward the hallway. One of the bedroom doors was open and inside he could see a black woman. She was folding towels and stacking them on the bed. She had to be the mother. She didn't look very happy.

She looked up and saw him, and Vargas tensed, his heart jumping at the thought she might somehow know he wasn't a cop, or somehow know through some weird maternal thing that he was the man who had taken her child. Her brown eyes remained on him for a moment and he gave her a nervous smile. She didn't return the smile, but instead reached out and softly closed the door.

Vargas set the hat down on the table near the front door and went to the kitchen. There was a weird black contraption hooked to the phone, a bulletproof vest hanging on a chair, and a tape recorder on the kitchen table. Next to the recorder was an empty coffee cup and a manila folder. Paper clipped to the front of the folder was a black and white photo of Byron Ellis.

Jewell was pouring himself a cup of coffee. For a second Vargas thought about shooting him but knew the cop outside, the woman, and anyone else in the house, would hear the shot. Plus he wasn't sure how quick he could get that damn gun out of that dipshit holster. Especially with gloves on.

"Where is everyone?" Vargas asked.

Jewell didn't look up as he added sugar. "The Chief is back at the station, Detective Frye is staying out on Captiva at Mr. Kincaid's place. And I'm not sure where Mr. Kincaid is."

Vargas turned away. He wasn't sure who any of those people were, but he did know that Jewell didn't mention Outlaw. Outlaw was either in the morgue or in this house.

He moved back to the hall, glancing behind him. The second bedroom door was cracked, and Vargas placed a gloved hand against it, pushing it open gently.

There was someone on the lower bunk bed, a nightlight illuminating his dark brown face and curly black hair. His hands were under his head, and he was snoring softly. *This* was Outlaw. He could see it now. This was the guy they had first seen in the park. How the hell could he have mistaken that other guy for this asshole?

Vargas's hand moved to the knife hidden under his jacket and he wondered if he could do it now. But then he heard Byron ragging on him again.

Don't try anything in the house unless you are sure you can get away. Don't be a fucking cowboy, Adam. I need you to come back safe.

If he did Outlaw now, he would have only a few seconds to get out of the house and back across the causeway. He'd have to do the woman and the cop, too.

"What are you doing?"

Vargas spun around and he found himself face to face with Jewell. His hand almost came out with the knife. But Jewell stepped back quickly, too far for Vargas to get a quick swing. Jewell's hand was resting on the butt of his gun, and his holster snap was undone.

Vargas brought his hand from his jacket, empty. "Just looking."

Jewell was staring at Vargas's chest and it took Vargas a second to realize the sheriff's jacket was open far enough to reveal the gold star, name badge and everything else on the shirt.

"Lt. Zompa," Jewell said, a new hint of respect in his voice. "I'm sorry. But we should leave the man alone. He was up most of the night."

"Right," Vargas said. "No problem."

Jewell turned his back and started back into the living room. Vargas's hand went into his jacket again.

Another door opened. "What the hell are you doing?"

Vargas turned to see the woman.

"It's bad enough I have to have all of you in my house day and night," Susan said, glaring at Vargas. "But you don't have to keep looking in my son's room like it was some kind of freak show."

She put out her hand and gave Vargas a shove. He stumbled, surprised the woman would even touch him. She pushed him again.

"Go do whatever it is you do here outside. I'm sick of all of you!"

Vargas hesitated.

"You'd better go, sir," Jewell said.

Without a word, Vargas turned, grabbed the hat off the table, and left. He was in the car and down the street before he realized how hard his heart was pounding.

That bitch. Damn it. Damn it. Damn it. He had been so close. He had almost done it. But he knew what Byron would say. Almost wasn't good enough. Almost was never good enough.

His eyes dropped to the clock on the dashboard. He calculated how long he'd been gone overall. Less than thirty-five minutes. How long did it take before cops started wondering why some dead cop in the john wasn't answering his radio?

Vargas made the causeway, cruising through, the Sereno Key cop in the parked cruiser giving him a wave. He hit the traffic of Fort Myers and took Cleveland Avenue back to the convenience store. He slowed a few blocks south of the store, looking for some sign that the dead cop had been found. But he saw none.

He pulled into a mall, parking the cruiser between a van and a motor home as far away from Cleveland Avenue as he could. He got out of the cruiser and locked it, his T-shirt and jeans stuffed inside the hat he carried under his arm. He walked quickly across the parking lot, over to Winkler. He went around the back of a deli and disappeared behind some Dumpsters. Except for the gloves, he stripped again, the wind biting at his skin as he struggled back into his jeans and T-shirt. He put the cop's gun in the waistband of his pants.

He looked at the hat.

He wanted to keep it but if there was some kind of setup back at the convenience store, he'd be busted big time walking back to his Camaro carrying this. He couldn't risk it.

He wrapped the hat inside the uniform shirt and placed it gently on top of the trash in the Dumpster. He'd come back for it later.

CHAPTER 29

Tuesday morning, January 19

Louis and Joe emptied their pockets into plastic trays and handed over their guns and IDs to a tight-faced correctional officer. He studied the IDs, checked a long list of names, then handed them back. They were searched, first patted down, then with a wand. Another officer flipped through Joe's manila folder, then handed it back to her without a word.

Louis followed Joe to a second building and they were searched again by officers as stonelike as the structure itself. Another short walk down a narrow hall, not deep into the prison at all. The correctional officer opened a door and they went inside a small room.

It was plain and damp, only a table and two chairs. The metal table was secured to the concrete floor with bolts.

They heard Yancy Rowen coming before they saw him. A steady rhythm of clanging chains and shuffling feet.

Two corrections officers moved him in through the doorway. Yancy Rowen was a tall man, thin but heavily muscled, his arms hanging from the sleeves of the blue prison smock like thick lengths of knotted black rope. There was a heavy chain around his waist that fed into a black lock box. A second chain went down to the cuffs around his ankles. His hands were cuffed to the box, so he couldn't move his arms more than a few inches.

Rowen's face was long, with a wide jutting chin at the bottom and a smoothly shaved scalp at the top. His lips turned down at the corners and his hooded eyes were set deep into the sockets. Under his left eye was a small tattoo of a teardrop.

His gaze shifted from Louis to Joe and came back to Louis. They didn't leave Louis's face as a guard locked the handcuffs to a metal loop embedded in the small table. The other guard was working on locking the ankle cuffs to one of the table's legs.

Joe waited until both the officers had retreated to their posts flanking the door. She had a copy of Rowen's record and she set it down on the table between them.

Louis had read Rowen's sheet already. A short history that began with grand theft motor vehicle and ended with a series of armed robberies committed with his older brother where a man was shot and killed. Louis remembered that Byron Ellis had been a car thief, too.

"Mr. Rowen, my name is Detective Frye. Miami Police Department," Joe said, slipping into a chair.

Rowen's eyes drifted over to her face. "What you want from me?" he asked.

"Help."

"What kind of help?"

"Information about Byron Ellis."

Rowen just stared at her. Joe kept her eyes and voice steady.

"Ellis has partnered up with someone that we think he might have met inside. It's important we identify this other man."

Rowen's stare grew colder. Joe held it for a few more seconds, then sat back in her chair. She glanced at Louis.

"Ellis has abducted a boy," Louis said.

Rowen's eyes swung slowly back to Louis. "Boy? How old?"

"Eleven," Louis said.

Rowan gave a small snort. He tried to slump in the chair, but the wrist loops held him in place.

"We need to find Ellis," Joe said. "We need to find the man he's with."

Rowen didn't move. But Louis could see a vein pulsing in his neck.

Joe flipped through Rowen's papers. "You have a parole hearing coming up in six months. How about we tell the board you helped us save a boy's life?"

Rowen's lips tipped into a smile.

"Mr. Rowen?" Joe said.

The smile faded. "Didn't know him," he muttered.

"You were his cell mate for five years," Joe said.

"Didn't know him."

Joe pursed her lips. "Five years living together in a room the size of a closet and you didn't know him?"

Rowen didn't look up as he shook his head slowly. "It's not good to get too close to people in here."

Louis was watching Rowen carefully, watching that throbbing vein, watching his eyes not meeting Joe's, watching him pulling against the table cuffs like he wanted to get away.

"Mr. Rowen," Joe went on, "Ellis got out eighteen months ago. Who did he know here in Florida he might have hooked up with?"

Louis focused on Rowen's arms as he pulled against the cuff. His arms were straining hard now, the muscles jumping out in high relief. Both arms were covered with tattoos. His left arm was an elaborate tableau showing a nude African woman with Medusa-snake hair standing atop a tombstone, surrounded by skulls breathing fire. There were hands clasped in prayer and a cross on his right forearm amid some elaborate swirls, a BE MINE on his hand and above the elbow, a ferocious snake that coiled up around his bicep and disappeared into his sleeve.

The snake was jumping now as Rowen flexed his arm against the metal loop.

"Mr. Rowen," Joe said, raising her voice slightly.

Rowen looked at her with a jerk of his head. His eyes were bulged, and he leaned closer to Joe, speaking through clenched teeth. "I said I didn't know Ellis. I don't know his new boy either." Rowen looked back at the officers by the door. "Get me out of here."

The guards didn't move. Joe stood up, the metal scrape of her chair echoing in the room. She looked at the officers.

"We're done here. Thank you."

Louis rose and they left the room, the door clanking shut behind them. They were silent as they were escorted back to the secured check-in area, where they picked up their guns and turned in their visitor badges.

They didn't speak again until they were outside. Joe stopped to zip up her leather coat, Louis to pull up the collar of his jacket. The wind coming across the parking lot cut into them, sending the metal halyards on the nearby flagpole clanking like a frantically tolling bell.

"That was a waste of time," Louis said.

Joe didn't say anything as they hurried to the Bronco. Joe started it up and flipped on the heat. They sat waiting for the truck to warm up.

"Did you notice his tattoos?" Joe asked.

"Yeah, the snake woman was real cute," Louis said.

"They were very well done," Joe said. "Not your usual quick-prick job with a needle and broken Bic. These were done with a gun."

"Gun?" Louis said.

She nodded. "The cons make tattoo guns out of slot car motors, hollowed out pens, batteries, and guitar strings. It's a big deal to get a real tat."

"Tat?"

"Tat, tac, ink. That's what they call them. They're very important to the inmate's sense of self or belonging. An expert could probably analyze that snake woman and tell you more about him than a shrink could."

"What's the teardrop for?" Louis asked.

"They signify kills . . . murders."

"Like notches in a belt?"

Joe nodded, picking up Ellis's folder from the backseat. She flipped through the pages.

"You looking to see what tattoos Ellis had?" Louis asked.

She nodded. "Here it is: crosses, a naked woman, and a flying bird. No snakes or teardrops."

"What are you looking for?"

"Some sign in the tats that Ellis, Rowen, and our unknown perp traveled in the same circles or gang. But I'm seeing nothing."

"But that listing of Ellis's tattoos wouldn't necessarily include anything he got while in prison, right?" Louis said.

"True."

Louis propped an elbow on the door of the Bronco and looked out at the flat, gray landscape. They had come here hoping that an embittered inmate might actually say something to help them. It had been a long shot at best. Rowen was hollow and cold, his shell scarred with crude artistry only he understood. The man didn't seem to care about Ellis, a small boy, or freedom. He didn't care about a damn thing.

"Where to now?" Louis asked.

Joe shoved the truck into gear. "Might as well go home."

CHAPTER 30

The moment Louis walked back into Susan's living room he knew something was wrong. Wainwright and Jewell were standing shoulder to shoulder, watching the television. They didn't even look at Louis.

"What's wrong?" Louis asked.

"Dead cop," Wainwright said. "They found him about an hour ago in a convenience store over on Cleveland."

Louis dropped his overnight bag on the floor and went over to the television. It was around three but the local news had broken into the soap operas, and the type below the talking head said WINK-TV EXCLUSIVE. There was a head shot of a dark-haired man wearing the green uniform of the Lee County Sheriff's Department.

Joe came in, dropping her bag. "What's going on?" she asked.

Louis held up a hand. Joe's eyes went to the television.

"The deputy has been identified as Lieutenant Jack Zompa," the anchorwoman read. "Police say the deputy was strangled and left in a restroom before being discovered, partially clothed, late last night by a custodian. Police will not confirm reports that the deputy's uniform and gun may have been stolen. Sheriff Mobley could not be reached for comment."

"Did you know him?" Joe asked Louis.

Louis shook his head, his eyes still on the TV. Zompa looked to be in his late thirties, with a full dark mustache and the steady-eyed gaze typical of police personnel file photos.

"I knew him. Good cop," Wainwright said. "No wife or kids."

"Thank God for that at least," Joe whispered, her eyes not leaving the television.

Wainwright moved away, shaking his head. Louis started to take off his jacket and noticed Jewell. He was standing there, ramrod straight, his eyes intent on the television, his mouth hanging slightly agape.

Louis had a pretty good idea what Jewell was thinking, what he was feeling. The kid was young enough that he might not have had someone close to him die. And even though he didn't know the dead cop, any dead cop was like a death in the family.

He was trying to think of something to say when it struck him that there was something else there in Jewell's eyes, something that looked more personal—something awfully close to horror.

"Jewell," Louis said.

He didn't take his eyes off the TV.

"Jewell, what's wrong?"

The young cop's blue eyes finally moved to Louis. "He was here," he said.

Louis glanced back at the TV. "Who? Zompa?"

Jewell shook his head, like he was trying desperately to figure something out. "Yes . . . no. I mean, a deputy came here yesterday. His name tag said Lieutenant Zompa." Jewell nodded toward the television. "But it wasn't him."

Louis came over to him. "What do you mean?"

Jewell's expression was turning sick. "It wasn't that guy on TV. It was another guy, blond . . ."

"When, Jewell?"

"Yesterday . . . last night, around six or six-thirty. I remember because it was dinnertime and I was getting hungry."

Now Joe had joined Louis at Jewell's side. "What did he say, what did he do?" she asked.

"I don't—" Jewell ran a hand over his face. "He just . . . he just came in and sort of looked around. And then he left."

Louis knew Wainwright had come up behind him but he kept his attention focused on Jewell. "Nothing else? Just looked around?" Louis pressed.

Jewell shook his head. "He went back toward the bedrooms, and I saw him looking in the little boy's room. Mr. Outlaw was in there sleeping and I told Lieutenant Zompa— the man, I mean—to let him sleep. And then I remember Ms. Outlaw, she came out and started yelling at him."

Louis could feel Wainwright's breath hot on his neck. Louis hoped Wainwright would stay quiet long enough to get as much information out of Jewell as possible.

"What else?" Louis asked calmly.

Jewell's face had gone pale and he was sweating. "I thought something was wrong . . . something about him was wrong." He looked up suddenly at Louis. "His gun belt . . . it didn't fit right. It was too big for him or something, and his gun was hanging down too low."

Wainwright pushed forward. "What did you do?"

Jewell stared at him. "Sir?"

"What did you *do*?"

Jewell blinked twice. "Nothing, sir," he said softly.

"Nothing," Wainwright said from between clenched teeth. "How could you do nothing? Didn't you question him? Didn't you ask him what he was *doing* here? Couldn't you *tell* he wasn't a cop?"

"Chief," Louis said quietly.

Wainwright ignored him. "Jesus H Christ! A fucking homicidal maniac walks right in, takes a nice long look around, and you do nothing?"

A redness had started at Jewell's neck and was creeping up, flooding his face with shame and humiliation. He was trying hard not to look away from Wainwright.

Finally Wainwright broke away with a dismissive wave of disgust. "I gotta call Mobley." He started to the kitchen and stopped to look back at Jewell.

"You stay right here."

Jewell's eyes skittered to Louis and then he quickly looked away. He turned and went to stand at the door.

Joe muted the TV and tossed the remote on the sofa. "I could use a drink," she said softly. She disappeared into the kitchen.

Louis looked at Jewell. For a moment, he wanted to tell him he understood, that he himself had once let a killer slip away. But he knew there was nothing he could say that could make Jewell feel better. Jewell had to find his own way out of this.

Louis started off to the kitchen, hoping Joe had left him something from that bottle of cheap brandy.

The house was filled again with cops, and now the dark green sheriff's office uniforms dominated the plain blacks of Wainwright's Sereno Key force. Three SO detectives were wandering around the house, in and out of the bedrooms. Two more SO uniforms were standing guard by the door. A crime scene tech had been brought in, but when Jewell told them the intruder had worn gloves, there was little for the tech to do. There was little for any of them to do.

Except the sketch artist. She was sitting at the kitchen table with Jewell, working her pad and pencil as Jewell quietly gave a description.

There was no place to sit, and it was too cold to go outside, so Louis finally had found a place in the hallway where he could stand and be out of the way. From his vantage point, he could see Sheriff Lance Mobley and Wainwright in the kitchen near Jewell and the artist. Wainwright was not a small man, but now he looked dwarfed by Mobley. Louis could hear their voices growing louder as Mobley ripped into Wainwright for everything from the chief's failure to establish a secure perimeter to his oversight of not keeping a clearance list of who was allowed in the house. Jewell was just sitting there, the angry words flying over his head, trying not to listen, trying to keep focused on the sketch artist.

Louis shook his head in disgust. He had to get away from this. He rose, went quickly through the kitchen and pushed open the door to the Florida room.

The cold air felt good after the stuffiness and chaos inside. He paused to pull in a deep breath.

He saw someone sitting on one of the lawn chairs in the far shadows of the porch. He knew it wasn't Joe. She had left to go check in with her own department.

"Susan?"

She didn't answer. He went over to her. She was curled into a ball, a blanket wrapped around her. She didn't look up at him.

Louis pulled over the other lawn chair and sat down in front of her.

"Susan," he said, reaching out.

They were too far away from the kitchen window for him to see her face clearly, but he could see the hard set of her jaw, the rigidity in her body that could only come from shock at this point. All these people in her house again, all these uniforms, and they weren't here for Ben now. They were here because of a dead cop.

"Susan, listen to me," Louis said. "I know what you're thinking. But this is still about Ben."

Susan looked up at him for the first time.

"What's going on in there right now will help the case, help us find Ben."

Susan stared at him. "You don't get it," she said quietly.

Louis had his hand on her arm. He could feel her body shaking through the blanket.

Her eyes were intense on his. "You don't get it," she said. "I touched him. He was in here and I *touched* him."

She brought up a hand to her mouth, closing her eyes, as if she were trying not to be sick. Mobley's voice carried out to them, angry and cold. Susan shut her eyes tight and pulled back, away from Louis's hand.

He knew what she was thinking. *It's their fault this monster got in. They can't protect me. They can't bring back my son. Neither can you.*

"I'm going in," Susan said suddenly, throwing off the blanket.

"I'll leave you alone," Louis said.

"No, I need to do something." She stood up, looking toward the kitchen. "Maybe I can help with the sketch."

She left Louis sitting alone on the porch.

CHAPTER 31

Wednesday, January 20

Adam Vargas set the last of the little plastic cowboys on the windowsill and looked at them. They all had different poses. Some with lassos. Some with guns. There was one with bowed legs that was meant to sit on a horse and it couldn't stand up by itself, but he had set it there anyway, laying it on its back. He'd have to get him a horse.

He heard footsteps and turned to see Ellis coming down the hall, bare chested, his jeans low on his waist. He had slept late, like he always did.

Ellis went into the kitchenette of the single-wide trailer, and opened the Styrofoam cooler, bending to peer inside.

Vargas could see the bird tattoo on his back, wings spread, beak tilted up toward a sun. There was a naked woman on his left arm and that stupid one on his hand, but Vargas liked the bird best. The bird meant something—escaping, flying to a better place, Aruba.

Vargas looked down at the smooth white skin of his own arms, holding them out in front. His whole body was like that, pale, almost hairless, unmarked by the black ink of prison artists. Just the way Byron liked it.

"Are we out of Pepsi?" Ellis asked.

"Sorry."

Ellis grabbed a can of beer instead and leaned on the short bar that separated the kitchenette from the living room. He was shivering.

"You look like shit," Vargas said. "You feeling okay?"

"I'm tired. I'm tired of running. I'm tired of this shit-hole place. I'm tired of the cold. I'm just tired, Adam."

Vargas was quiet. He spotted a sweatshirt draped on a chair and went to get it, holding it out to Ellis.

"I'm sorry I screwed it up," he said. "I'm sorry I couldn't finish it while I was in there."

Ellis gave him a weary look. "You did good. You found out what we needed to know." He took the sweatshirt and pulled it on.

"Yeah, but now what?" Vargas asked. "We can't get back in there and Outlaw sure as hell ain't coming out any time soon. What we going to do now, Byron?"

Ellis came around the bar and sank into a tilted three-legged chair, one of the few pieces of furniture left in the trailer. "I don't know," he said.

Vargas was quiet. He never heard him say that. He always knew what to do. He watched Ellis, watched him staring at the wall. Vargas knew he was thinking about getting warm on some beach on Aruba. Thinking maybe that they were never going to be able to fly off to the sun.

Vargas went back to the windowsill, bending the broken blinds to look out through the dirty window at the gray day. He picked up one of the cowboys, rubbing it gently with his thumb. "Hey, By?"

Ellis glanced at him. "What?"

"I was just thinking."

Ellis waited patiently.

"I was thinking, you know, about on the TV yesterday at the motel when they said Outlaw was dead?"

Ellis nodded slowly.

"Well, you and me know that ain't true. But I bet Uncle Leo doesn't."

Ellis just stared at him for a second, thinking. "What are you saying?"

Vargas shrugged. "Just that Uncle Leo doesn't know we didn't get the job done and that maybe he doesn't need to."

Ellis sat forward. "You'd lie to your uncle about something like that? You'd take his money knowing you hadn't done the job?"

Vargas hesitated, staring at the little cowboy. He'd never lied to Uncle Leo before, but things were different now. Everything was fucked up. They had killed too many people, the cops had Byron's name and they were on the run, having to hide out in this shit-hole abandoned trailer with no food, no heat, no electric. If they didn't do something quick, they were never going to get out of this.

Vargas looked at Ellis. "Yeah, I'd lie to him."

Ellis didn't say anything and for several minutes, they just sat there, listening to the rattle of loose aluminum on the roof.

Finally, Ellis rose and paced slowly around the tiny room. "You'd have to go there alone," he said softly, turning back toward Vargas.

"I know."

"You'd have to go today."

"I know."

"And once we leave, you'll never be able to come back," Ellis said.

Vargas set the cowboy in the window. "I know that, too."

Again, they were quiet.

"Okay," Ellis said, nodding. "Okay. Let's do it. Let's do it now."

Vargas stood up and started toward the back of the trailer for his jacket and keys. He stopped and turned back.

"Are you sure about this?" Vargas asked.

"It was your idea, Adam. And it's a good idea."

Vargas shifted from one foot to another.

"Look, there's no other way," Ellis said. "Don't worry about Leo. He's got money, Adam. Guys with money can get out of things. And maybe if the cops go after him, he'll be so busy trying to get out of this mess, he'll leave us alone."

Vargas stared at his shoes.

"What's the matter now?" Ellis pressed.

"I don't know. Maybe we should just tell Uncle Leo we blew it. Maybe I shouldn't lie to him. I owe him a lot."

"You owe him? Jesus, Adam, what did he ever give you?"

"He took me in."

"Adam, you grew up alone, watching movies. That's not how family treats family, don't you understand?"

Vargas was staring at the thread-bare green shag carpet. He had heard this before; they had argued about this before.

Ellis put a hand behind Vargas's neck and pulled him close, chest against chest, cheek against cheek. Byron's fingers were icy against his neck.

"You can do this, Adam. I know you can do this."

Vargas leaned into him. Ellis's arms were around him, strong, like that first night in Raiford. He'd been terrified then but it had been all right. He was terrified now. But he knew it would be all right this time, too.

"Okay," Vargas whispered.

"Good boy," Ellis said. "Tomorrow at this time, we'll be sitting on a beach somewhere."

"How are we going to get out?" Vargas asked.

"We'll head straight to Everglades City. We can get a boat down there. When you got money, you can get anything you want."

Vargas went to the small bedroom to get his jacket, grabbing it off the doorknob. He started to leave, but stopped. His eyes moving slowly across the tiny room. There was no furniture left, except for the mattress they had dragged in from the other bedroom. Just the mattress and that small broken headboard.

Vargas's eyes locked on the broken headboard.

They had come here late last night, after they had seen

the TV report. That had been his idea, too, because he had known the trailer was empty from other times he had snuck back. Times when he wanted to remember things that happened before Uncle Leo. Before Raiford. Before Byron.

But he had never been back inside until now.

As his eyes wandered over the thin bleached paneling, the dirty green shag rug, and the broken headboard, he thought about the cowboy bedroom at the old people's house.

There had been no cowboys here. No good guys. There had been shadows and shame. Footsteps in the hall. The creak of the bedroom door. And his stepfather's drunken grunts as Adam's small hands worked to satisfy him.

And if you tell anybody I'll hang you on a hook just like them hogs.

But it stopped one hot day when Vargas was twelve. His mother was gone and he had been alone in the trailer with his stepfather. It was the first time he had come at him in the daytime. It was the first time he told him to drop his pants.

Vargas's eyes came back to the broken headboard.

He had been bent over his own bed, his jeans at his knees, his stepfather's thick fingers digging into his hips. The knife was in a sheath, hanging on a belt that was looped over the headboard. It was a boar skinning knife his stepfather had given to him only a week before. He was planning to take him out the next day to learn how to use it. *Gonna teach you how to be a man, kid, gonna teach you how to kill.*

The knife had gone into his stepfather's belly so smoothly at first Vargas hadn't been sure he actually stabbed him. So he twisted it before he pulled it out. And when he still didn't fall, he had slit his throat.

Vargas's gaze moved from the headboard to the window and the land beyond.

He had buried him out there somewhere. After he used the knife to practice the skinning his stepfather had so badly wanted him to learn.

When Mama asked about the big stain in the carpet, he

told her what he had done. She wiped his tears and said, "Some things just need killing." And she'd been right.

"Adam," Ellis called. "What the hell's taking you so long?"

Vargas turned and left the bedroom. Ellis was standing at the kitchen counter.

"Be careful," Ellis said.

"It's just Uncle Leo."

Byron was standing there in the empty room, shivering. "Like I said, be careful."

CHAPTER 32

It was only a photocopy, but it was clear and detailed. The man's hair was light, just long enough to part and comb. His boyish mouth tipped up at the edges and his eyes held a playfulness that would have been out of place in a police sketch, except for the fact that the artist had been trying to capture what Jewell had struggled to describe as friendliness.

But as Louis looked at the sketch now, he didn't see friendliness. He saw the same look his cat had when she had cornered a bird.

Joe was driving the Bronco. Under her leather jacket, she wore a cinnamon-colored sweater. Her hair was yanked back in a messy ponytail and her cheeks were brushed with a hint of pink that Louis knew had to have come from the wind. She had abandoned makeup days ago.

Louis looked back at the road. The sky was a blend of grays and purples, clawlike clouds scratching their way over the scrub lands. He wasn't sure why they were going back to Copeland. Even with a sketch of a new suspect, a man they believed to be from this area, they would likely be met with more closed doors. But it was better than sitting back at Susan's, waiting while Wainwright, the sheriff, and now the state guys waged their battle of power and blame.

Joe slowed as they made the turn off 29 into Copeland.

"Did you tell the chief we were coming back out here?" she asked.

"Nope."

"Probably just as well."

Joe parked the Bronco near a trio of trailers and they got out. Even with the wind, it was incredibly quiet out here. Louis remembered hearing somewhere that Copeland had once been a thriving town, built on cypress logging. Now it seemed lifeless and forgotten.

"Geesh," Joe said. "You'd think there'd be a store or something out here. How do these people survive?"

Louis didn't know and didn't care. He folded the sketch and followed Joe to the first trailer, waiting while she knocked. There was no answer, even though they could see movement beyond the blue curtain. No one answered at the second trailer, and at the third trailer, the old man they had talked to on their first trip didn't recognize the sketch.

They walked on, across the asphalt street to a cluster of Kleenex-box houses. Rusted bicycles, dented trash cans, and old furniture cluttered the yards. A child's face peered at them from behind a cracked window. Joe tried that house first.

Louis waited out near the gate while she talked to the owner, a middle-aged guy with a ragged beard, bulbous eyes, and baggy blue jeans. His eyes stayed on the sketch a long time, but when he looked up at Joe, he was shaking his head. It was the same at the other houses they tried.

They came to the house at the end of the street, this time Louis taking the lead up the plywood porch. Joe waited at the bottom, her gaze moving out across the landscape.

"We didn't hit that place over there the first time," she said, pointing.

Louis followed her finger to a rusted green and white trailer listing in waist-high weeds. It was set apart from the others at the far end of the street. "It looks abandoned," Louis said, knocking on the door of the house.

The aluminum door opened and a woman peered out. She

was old, her face leathered and lined, her eyes strangely un-
focused. She wore a man's cardigan over her nightgown.

"Who's there?" she asked.

"My name is Kincaid and we're police officers," he said,
lying for simplicity. "We're looking for a man."

"Who'd you say you are?"

"Police officers. We're looking for a man. Can you take a
look at this picture—"

"I can't take a look at anything. I'm blind. Go away."

She started to close the door, but Louis put up a hand.
"Ma'am, that trailer at the end of the street . . . anyone living
there?"

"The green one? Nah. Ain't nobody been there for years."
She slammed the door.

Back in the Bronco, Joe started to turn around so they
could head back to 29.

"Wait," Louis said." Let's check that abandoned trailer out
while we're here."

Joe pulled the Bronco up and killed the engine. They
trudged through the weeds up to the trailer. The rusted mailbox had fallen off its post and was laying in the weeds. Louis
kicked it over. It read: Raif & Janice Fletcher. Joe had gone
on ahead and had mounted a couple cement blocks that
served as steps. As she pounded on the door, Louis went to
the side of the trailer, straining to see in the high window. It
was covered with aluminum foil.

Joe was still pounding on the door. Louis leaned against
the side of the trailer waiting, his eyes wandering out over
Copeland's streets. He felt the trailer shift, but he knew it
was more likely from the wind rather than from the weight
of someone moving around inside.

"It's empty," Joe called out. "Let's get out of here."

She jumped off the cement blocks and started back
through the weeds to the Bronco. Louis looked back at the
front window of the trailer, half-expecting to see some curious face peering back at him through the blinds. There was
no face.

But there was something else. A flash of color that had caught his eye. On the inside of the front window, on the narrow sill in front of the broken blind, stood four small plastic figurines.

He stepped closer. Cowboys.

Louis felt a kick in his gut. His instincts were telling him it hadn't been the wind that had moved the trailer. Someone was inside, someone now watching them. He suddenly had a feeling that if he didn't keep walking, they could be shot where they stood.

Joe had paused by the mailbox.

"Joe," Louis said, "get in the truck."

She didn't question him.

"Drive," he said, once inside.

She put the truck in gear. "What did you see?" she asked.

"Toy cowboys," Louis said. "Just like the one in the old people's house. Find a place to pull in, some place we can't be seen from the trailer."

She headed back to the main road. She stopped the Bronco behind an empty cinder block building and turned to face him.

"That Gene Autry cowboy in the McAllister place? Ben didn't leave it," Louis said, jabbing a finger at the sketch. "*He* did."

Louis crushed the sketch up and rolled down the window. He threw the wadded sketch out. He sat there for a moment, hand at his brow, staring at the green and white trailer.

"We need to call this in," Joe said. "My radio is no good here. How far back was that pay phone?"

"Ben could be in there. I'm not leaving," Louis said tightly.

"Then I will. I can run back to it in a few minutes."

"They'll see you."

"We can't just sit here. We have no choice."

She rummaged in her console for change and got out, sprinting away from the car.

A sudden *varoom-varoom* split the silence, the clamor of an unmuffled car engine. Louis's head shot up.

He looked out the open window of the Bronco in time to see a spray of gravel and dirt coming from around the back of the green and white trailer. Then what looked like a Jeep with no top and huge tires took off down the road, moving away from them fast.

"Joe!" Louis shouted out the window. But she was already running back to the Bronco.

She jumped in, slammed the Bronco into drive, and took off, flattening Louis against the passenger seat.

CHAPTER 33

The swamp buggy was about a hundred yards ahead, careening down the road, its heavy tires spitting gravel and dirt. Suddenly, it straightened and shot off, heading down the scenic drive toward the quarry.

Joe punched the accelerator.

Louis could see there was only one man in the open front seat of the buggy. Dark hair. Had to be Ellis.

"There's no other way out," he said.

"And no way he can outrun us in that thing."

They were gaining on the buggy. Suddenly, the Bronco took a hard jolt and Louis threw out a hand to brace himself against the dash.

"Shit!" Joe said.

The hard-packed gravel was gone, the road turning rough and rutted, pitted from the hard rains. Louis caught sight of a sign marking the entrance of the Fakahatchee Strand. The Bronco hit a deep hole and Joe had to jerk the wheel hard to keep it on the narrowing road. Louis felt the shock penetrate the still tender bruise on his chest.

Joe was silent, gripping the wheel, trying to steer the Bronco around the holes and ruts, keeping it from spinning off into the cypress trees and swamps bordering the road. Louis gritted his teeth at every swerve and jolt.

The Bronco bounced into a deep hole, sending up a spray of mud. The windshield went opaque brown.

"Damn it!" Joe yelled. She had to ease off as she flipped on the wipers. It was a couple of seconds before the washers cleared enough for them to see again.

The buggy was pulling away. With its giant tires and open, windowless carriage, it now had the advantage. Joe hit the gas heavy again, but with every bone-jarring slam, she had to back off.

"You're losing him!" Louis yelled, squinting through the mud-smeared windshield.

"I know, damn it!"

Suddenly, there was a spin of mud ahead of them. The buggy had come to a stop. A second later, it took a sharp veer to the left.

"It's the turn south," Louis said. "I remember it from the drop. There's a stretch of good road ahead. Keep with him."

Joe followed, hitting the turn at a reckless speed, but then maneuvering out of a spin. A few seconds later, Louis felt the road smooth out some and the Bronco's tires found their grip. The swamp buggy was maybe fifty yards ahead now, and the Bronco was closing in.

Louis pulled his Glock out of his holster and looked down for a split second as he chambered a round.

"Shit!" Joe yelled.

Louis looked up to see the buggy disappear off the road.

"He went into the fucking trees!" Joe hit the gas and the Bronco bounced up to the spot where the buggy had gone off the road. Joe slammed on the brakes, throwing Louis into the dashboard. The Bronco spun to a stop at the edge of the brush.

Louis couldn't see anything through the muddy windows. He pushed open the door and jumped out, gun raised.

Nothing. Just a stand of squat palms and reeds and two

deep tracks running off through the mud into the far brush. He could hear the growl of the buggy moving away.

Joe was at his side, gun drawn, breath coming hard and fast. She saw the tracks and swung back to Louis.

"We'll never make it in there! Shit! He's—"

"Joe, quiet!" Louis ordered.

She stared at him.

"Turn off the Bronco!"

"What?"

"Just do it! Now!"

She ran back and switched off the engine.

Louis raised the Glock slightly, turning his head.

Joe came up, gun raised.

"Wait. Listen," Louis said.

Joe didn't move. Louis strained to hear.

"What?" she said.

"No engine." He was staring into the brush in the direction of the tire tracks. "I swear I heard something, like water, like a splash."

He darted into the trees, his feet hitting hard mud, the broken trees and branches scraping at his ankles. With each step, the ground grew more soggy, and he could feel water seeping into his shoes.

He smelled gasoline. A thin cloud of steam rose from beyond the bushes ahead of him. He moved closer, feeling water swirl up around his ankles, then to his knees. He parted the bushes cautiously.

The buggy was nose-down in the inky black water, the back wheels still spinning slowly. He couldn't see the seats, couldn't see the man. But he could see the metal box on the back of the buggy, locked with a pad lock.

On the other side of the buggy he heard movement. A thrashing in the water. Branches snapping. His eyes swung back to the locked box.

He heard panting behind him. He knew it was Joe.

"Go, go," she said. "I'll check out the buggy."

Louis moved around the buggy, mud sucking at his shoes. The water was cold and black, with sharp, broken cypress stumps breaking the surface like spikes.

He heard a groan and another splash and he swung the Glock to his left. He saw the man, trudging through the water, arms flailing for balance.

Louis tried to run, but couldn't. The water pulled at his thighs, his shoes stuck in the mucky bottom. His chest felt ready to explode. But he was getting closer; he could hear the man gasping for breath.

"Stop!" Louis yelled.

The man glanced over his shoulder but kept going.

Louis got his first good look at him. He was covered with mud but Louis could tell it was Byron Ellis.

Louis pushed through the water, almost close enough to take him down. Ellis came to a stop, and started to look back again as Louis lunged at him, wrapping his arms around Ellis's shoulders.

They crashed sideways into the water. Ellis started throwing wild punches and it was all Louis could do to hold his head above water and keep hold of Ellis's shirt. Louis tried to hit him with the butt of the Glock, but the water muted the blow.

A fist landed, hard and solid, into Louis's chest, sending an explosion of pain through his upper body so strong he stumbled backward, grabbing his right shoulder. He couldn't backpedal quick enough to keep his balance.

The muddy water rushed over his face. And for a second, he was under, Ellis a blur coming back to him.

As his head came out of the water, he saw Ellis's arm stretch out at him, saw something black glistening in his hand.

A gun.

Louis tried to bring his Glock from under the water, but it was heavy, caked with mud.

A shot cracked above his head. Then another.

It took Louis a second to realize it was not Ellis who was shooting. The shots had come from somewhere else.

Louis turned and saw Joe standing a few feet away, knee-deep in water, her gun leveled.

Ellis let out a moan and staggered, falling face first into the water. Louis struggled to his feet and stumbled to him, turning him over.

Ellis's eyes were open and moving, but he was limp, his hands empty. Louis grabbed him under the arms and started dragging him to dry ground.

Don't you die on me, sucker. Not yet. Not yet!

Louis collapsed onto the dirt, letting go of Ellis as he tried to catch his breath. Ellis was just laying there, his shoulders and head resting against a cypress stump.

"Louis!" Joe called out.

"Ben! Was he in the buggy?" Louis yelled back to her.

"No. The box was empty."

Louis grabbed Ellis's shirt. "Where is he?"

Ellis moaned, his eyes just a blank stare. He was dying. Louis could see it in his eyes.

"Where's Benjamin?" Louis shouted, shaking him. "Talk to me you son of a bitch! Where's Benjamin?"

Ellis eyes moved from Louis to Joe, now standing over Louis's shoulder. Ellis shut his eyes. His breath was coming raspy and wet. The wound in his chest was oozing blood.

"Answer me!" Louis shouted.

Ellis opened his eyes. "He's dead," he wheezed.

With a cry, Louis flung Ellis into the mud. Ellis sputtered, struggled to sit up, but fell back against the tree.

Louis got to his feet, wiping his face. Joe was just a blur in front of him. His chest burned and he couldn't seem to pull in a full breath.

Ellis coughed. "You killed him," he said.

Louis turned back.

"What?"

Ellis grimaced and looked up at Louis.

"You . . . you cops. The night you brought the money."

Louis dropped down next to Ellis in the mud. "What are you talking about?"

Ellis spat out blood. "We didn't kill the kid. You did. You cops shot him. We took him out of there but he died later."

Louis went numb, his mind racing backward.

Setting Austin's purse down in the dirt.

The first shot hitting him in the chest, spinning him around. Then his own gun going off, jarred from his hand by the recoil. And a second shot slamming into his back. Then Jewell spraying the darkness with his bullets.

Louis grabbed Ellis's shirt, shaking him. "Where did you leave him?"

Ellis didn't answer.

"Where did you leave his body?" Louis yelled.

Joe was suddenly next to him, trying to get his attention, her hands on his chest.

"Louis, he's dead," she said.

Louis looked down at Ellis's mud-streaked face and empty brown eyes. He felt Joe's hands on his, gently prying his fingers off Ellis's shirt. He finally sat back, his breath coming in hard, painful spurts.

Joe knelt next to him in the mud. He felt her arms come around him. He buried his head in her shoulder.

CHAPTER 34

They had gone back in guns drawn, but Louis had known the trailer would be empty.

He had walked the narrow hall, pushed in the paper-thin bedroom doors and jerked open closets, but there had been no one there. Then he had started upending the few pieces of furniture, looking for that one little thing he was sure Ben would leave. A shoe string. A toy. A small dirty hand print placed deliberately on a wall.

Nothing.

Joe finally had to drag him outside, forcing him to sit in the Bronco and wait until the cops showed up. She had tried to tell him he shouldn't believe a thing Byron Ellis said. He was a criminal, a killer who had nothing to lose by lying.

But Louis had turned away in anger. Not at her, but at the idea—the thought—that Ellis might be telling the truth.

For the last hour, he had been sitting in the Bronco, rewinding that night over and over in his head, trying to remember if he had heard Ben's voice after the shots rang out, trying to remember seeing him fall, trying to remember anything that would prove Ellis wrong.

The cigar ring in the motel. He was sure Ben had left it. But when? The drop had been Sunday night. If the ring had been left on Monday, that meant Ben had been alive after the drop. But if it had been left on Sunday . . .

Louis shut his eyes.

"Nice mess you made in there."

Louis looked up to see Chief Wainwright standing at the passenger window. There was a fleet of cop cars behind him from both Lee and Collier counties.

"What were you looking for in that trailer?" Wainwright asked.

"Something Ben might have left," Louis said.

Wainwright let out a sigh.

Louis could tell Wainwright still wasn't buying this trail of clues thing. But he didn't care.

Wainwright glanced at the trailer. "You find anything?"

Louis shook his head.

"Collier County is pissed, you know that."

"We had to go inside," Louis said. "You know that."

Wainwright nodded. "But you didn't have to contaminate the scene."

Louis didn't reply. He didn't care about that either.

Wainwright glanced down the scenic drive, where they had followed Ellis to the swamp. "Detective Frye told me what Ellis said, that you might've shot the kid," he said.

Louis watched the activity around the trailer. Sheriff Mobley and a man Louis guessed to be the Collier County sheriff were having words near the door. Someone was stringing crime scene tape. A tech pulled open the rear doors of the CSI van and hauled out a large black box.

"You don't believe him, do you?" Wainwright asked.

Louis looked at him. He wanted to say *hell no, I don't believe him. He's a lying ex-con who kills for the fun of it.* But he couldn't. A part of him couldn't get the possibility out of his head because it made some kind of weird sense. Wainwright had said it. *I'm not sure they ever wanted to kill Ben. I think they intended to kill Outlaw, take the money, and release him.*

And Louis had agreed with him.

"Did they find anything out at the drop scene?" Louis asked. "Can they account for all the shots?"

Wainwright looked away, then back. "No. We pulled two of theirs out of your car, and found one of Jewell's in a stump. That leaves one of yours and three of Jewell's unaccounted for."

There was another noise, something coming from overhead, a *whoop-whoop* noise Louis instantly recognized. He opened the door against Wainwright's chest and got out, looking up.

It was a helicopter, white with a big red seven on the side. A Fort Myers TV news chopper.

"Damn it," Louis said.

"What?" Wainwright said.

"Susan," Louis said. "What did you tell her?"

"I haven't told her anything. I was at the station when Frye called."

"I need to get back," Louis said. "Susan can't see this on TV. Where's Joe?"

"Never mind Joe." Wainwright pointed to his cruiser. "I can get you back quicker. Let's go."

Louis opened the door to Susan's house and went inside, followed by Wainwright. Susan, Jewell, and Austin were standing in the middle of the room, eyes locked on the TV. A female reporter was standing at the turnoff into Copeland, the police cars and the trailer far in the background.

Jewell looked over at them. Wainwright motioned for Jewell to follow him back outside. The young man locked eyes with Louis for a moment, then walked past him out the door.

Susan was looking at Louis, one hand closed over the other against her chest. Her eyes flickered between confusion and fear.

He went to her, taking her shoulders.

She pulled away from him. "What's happened? They said one of the suspects is dead."

"He is. It was Byron Ellis. Joe had to shoot him."

She waited, silent, looking up at him.

"We found Ellis in a trailer out near a preserve, but Ben wasn't there with him."

"What about the other man?" Susan asked.

Louis shook his head.

"Did you find anything else? Was there any sign he was—"

"Susan," Louis said. "Sit down. Please."

She didn't move.

"You, too, Austin," Louis said. Austin knew what was coming. Louis could see it in his face.

Austin reached out and put a hand on Susan's shoulder, gently directing her to the sofa. She sat down, rigid, her hands clasped, her knees pressed together.

Louis picked up the remote and switched off the TV. He sat down on the coffee table so he was level with them. They waited, Austin's hand sliding over to cover Susan's. She didn't seem to notice. She was staring at Louis, her eyes glistening with questions.

"Before Ellis died," Louis said. "He . . ."

The words caught in his throat and he looked away, feeling his chest tighten. He could hear Susan's quickened breathing, smell the lingering smoke of Austin's last cigar.

Louis forced himself to look at them. Austin's hand was clenched over Susan's and they were both leaning forward.

The words came out in a hoarse whisper. "Ellis said Ben is dead."

Susan let out a wounded cry, jerking her hands away from Austin, drawing them to her chest. Tears spilled down her cheeks as she clenched her eyes shut.

Louis started to reach out for her, but Austin's hand was there, on her shoulder, on her arm, on her face wiping her tears.

Louis waited. Susan's sobs were the only sound in the room. Finally, he touched Austin's arm and nodded toward the door.

"I need to talk to you," he said quietly.

Austin looked confused, but started to move away from Susan. She grabbed Louis's wrist.

"What *else*?" she asked.

"Susan, let me handle this," Austin said.

Susan tightened her grip. "What else is there? What were you going to tell him that I couldn't hear?"

Louis looked down at her. "You'll probably hear a report about this later on tonight and I wanted you to hear it from me first."

She stood up, her fingers still curled around his wrist.

"Ellis said something else, too," Louis said. He could hear himself say it, but it didn't sound like him. The words came hollow and flat. "He said Ben was shot the night we tried to deliver the money. By one of us."

A second passed.

"Us?" she whispered. "Us? You mean . . . ?"

Then, slowly, she shook her head. She let out another cry, this one from deep inside, a low gutteral sound that came from rage. She jerked her hand from his wrist and pushed him away.

"No," she cried. "No, No. Not this way! Not by you!"

She came at him, pushing him backward, her hands pounding against his chest, her cries now like a wounded animal.

"Get out!" she cried.

"Susan—" Austin said.

"Get out! Get out now! All of you!"

Louis tried to catch her flailing arms, but she tore from his grasp, spinning away. Austin grabbed her so she wouldn't fall. She fought him, until he wrapped his arms around her so tight she couldn't move. He was holding her up as she sobbed.

Austin looked at Louis over Susan's head. "Go," he said.

Louis turned and opened the door, stepping out onto the porch. He closed the door behind him.

The street was dark and quiet. It was sprinkling, small, light drops that pinged on the cars and windows. Crime scene tape flapped in the breeze at the old folks' house across the street. A lone Sereno Key cruiser was still parked at the curb. Wainwright's cruiser was parked in front of the house next door. The chief was sitting in the driver's seat, head back. Louis knew he was waiting to give him a ride home.

Louis saw someone standing off to the side, in the driveway near Susan's old Mercedes. It was Jewell. He was just standing there, looking back at Susan's front door. His black Garrison cap was beaded with rain, the brim shadowing his eyes.

Louis went to him.

Jewell looked up. His face was wet, his eyes red-rimmed and weary.

"How you doing?" Louis asked.

Jewell's voice trembled. "Fine, sir."

"Look . . ." Louis began.

"Sir, can I say something?" Jewell interrupted.

Louis nodded.

"It wasn't you," he said. "Your shot went into the dirt. It had to have been me."

Jewell's blue eyes never wavered from Louis's face, and his mouth was drawn tight into a line that quivered at the edges.

Louis put a hand on his shoulder, over the Sereno Key patch on his sleeve.

"Thank you, Jewell," Louis said.

Jewell glanced at Wainwright's cruiser sitting at the curb, waiting for Louis. "The chief has relieved me of duty."

"Then go home," Louis said.

"I can't, sir. I can't—"

"Jewell, go home."

Jewell hesitated then nodded. "Yes, sir."

Louis watched him walk down the block and get in his cruiser. A moment later, it disappeared down the dark street. With a final look back at Susan's door, Louis started toward Wainwright's car.

CHAPTER 35

It was near nine by the time Wainwright dropped him off at the cottage. Wainwright had told him Collier County wanted him back first thing tomorrow to do his statements. But for now, the only thing Louis wanted was to be alone.

He trudged up the sandy drive to the screened-in porch. He fumbled for his keys, unlocked the front door, and went in.

Tossing the keys on the bar, he stood in the dark for a moment. He could smell the dank stink of the swamp rising up from his clothes but he didn't care. He could feel the steady throb of pain in his chest but he didn't care about that either.

He went to the refrigerator and opened the door. The light made a slash through the dark kitchen. Louis stood there, leaning on the refrigerator door, staring blankly at the nearly empty metal shelves.

Something soft touched his leg. He looked down. Issy was sitting there, looking up at him. He blinked, trying to remember the last day he had been home, the last time he had fed the cat. Sunday? Saturday? He shut his eyes, dropping his head.

"I fed her."

Louis looked up.

Joe was standing there, just on the other side of the bar. There was a blue towel wrapped around her head and she was wearing a robe. His robe.

"When'd you get back?" he asked.

"About a half-hour ago. Collier County sheriff kept me pretty busy for a while."

She came forward out of the shadows. "You told Susan?" she asked.

Louis nodded slowly. He looked back at the inside of the refrigerator, decided he didn't really want a beer, and shut the door. A moment later, the lamp in the living room came on and Joe straightened, looking at him from across the room. Her face was shiny and red from the heat of her shower. He could see questions in her eyes, and he was grateful she wouldn't ask them right now.

"I need a shower," he said quietly.

She nodded, reaching for the towel around her head. "Give me a minute and I'll get out of your way."

Joe disappeared into the bedroom, shutting the door. Louis sank down on the sofa, his head falling back against the cushions, closing his eyes. He had no idea how much time had passed when he heard her return. She was wearing a huge T-shirt and clutching a blanket. Her hair was wet, combed back from her face, accentuating the angles.

Louis got up, wincing slightly. "I'll be right back," he said.

"Do you want something to eat? I can—"

He held up a hand and walked slowly into the bedroom. He closed the door and stood there a moment, looking around. Her suitcase was open on the floor, clothing spilling out. Her mud-stained black jeans and cinnamon sweater lay in a small heap in a corner. Her leather coat was hanging on the knob of the closet.

The bedspread was pulled up, like she had hastily tried to straighten things up. Louis went into the bathroom.

Strange things on the sink. A plastic leopard-print toiletry bag. A bottle of Tylenol. A big round hairbrush. A pink plastic razor. A blue Secret deodorant. A spray bottle of something green. He picked up the bottle, looking at it. Jean Nate After Bath Mist.

He brought it up to his nose. It smelled like a man's cologne. But softer, creamier.

He set the bottle down and stripped quickly, getting into the shower. He turned on the water. It was cool but he didn't even notice it, and he just stood there under the hard spray, eyes shut, waiting until it turned warm.

Hot water now. Slowly, very slowly, his muscles unknotted, his body relaxed, his mind let go. He just stood there, head bowed, arms braced against the walls, letting the water wash over him. The hot water was almost gone by the time he finally grabbed the soap and washed himself.

Switching the shower off, he got out and went back into the bedroom, toweling himself off. He hadn't noticed it the first time he came into the bedroom, but now he saw his robe there on the end of the bed where she had left it.

He tossed the towel aside and picked up the robe. He started to put it on but then he paused.

She was there. Her smell was there in his robe. That man-woman creamy smell from the green bottle. And something else that was just her.

He put on the robe and went out to the living room. Issy was curled up on the sofa but Joe wasn't there. The front door was open, letting in the cold. Louis went out onto the porch.

Joe looked up at him from her place on the wicker chair. She was bundled in the blanket, her hands wrapped around a coffee mug.

"Where'd you find the coffee?" he asked.

"Didn't. It's brandy."

She was looking up at him. "I don't drink much," she said. "But I found this in your kitchen and thought it might help. I can't . . ."

She looked away. "I can't . . . get warm," she said softly.

He went over to her, gently pulling her up from the chair,

wrapping his arms around her. He could feel her shivering through the blanket. He could feel her wet hair against his cheek.

Something broke inside him, flooding him with need. A need to touch and be touched. A need for something good, something clean and something warm.

She drew her head back and he could see her eyes, teary in the cold. See her lips, still quivering.

He brought his hands up and cupped her face, kissing her, gently at first, then more deeply as he felt her body respond to his. She tasted warm, her lips sweet with brandy.

The blanket fell off her shoulders as his lips moved down her neck, over her collarbone and back up again, to her cheek, her eyes, and her mouth. His hands found her body under the T-shirt. Smooth, warm curves he wanted to explore forever.

Her hands were inside his robe, over his shoulders, on his back, pulling him closer, and harder against her.

"Louis—" she whispered.

He covered her mouth with his and leaned into her, pushing her backward, his hands trying to work the T-shirt higher up on her body, over her head so he could see all of her. Touch all of her. *Have* all of her.

"Louis—"

"Don't talk."

"Louis," she said.

He drew back, and realized he had wedged her against the wall and the wicker chair.

"Inside," she whispered.

"No," he said. He grabbed the blanket that had slipped to the chair and spread it on the floor of the porch. When he looked back at her, she was pulling the T-shirt over her head. She dropped the T-shirt to the floor and lay down on the blanket.

He couldn't see her clearly in the dark. He undressed quickly and knelt on the blanket. She pulled him down, into her arms. Cold skin against his own cold skin. Then the warmth as she wrapped the blanket over them both.

CHAPTER 36

After he left the trailer, Vargas had stopped at the convenience store near Carnestown to call Uncle Leo. He tried the refinery first, where Uncle Leo's office was. Some secretary had told him Uncle Leo was off for the week, taking care of some personal business.

He had found that funny. Personal business. Strange way of saying *I've got to hire somebody to kill somebody for me.*

When Vargas called the house in Naples, he told a maid that he needed to speak to his uncle.

"Tell him it's his nephew and that it's an emergency."

She told him Uncle Leo would be home in an hour and to call back. He drove on to Naples, finally pulling into a convenience store to call back. This time the maid said he could come to the house, but not until eight P.M.

Two hours to kill. It wouldn't be good to show up at Uncle Leo's early. So he went into the store, bought a chili dog and an orange soda and ate them as he thumbed through some car magazines. Finally, the punk clerk got mad and told him to get out.

He went back to the Camaro and stuck in a Marty Robbins tape. He slumped down in the seat, listening to Marty singing "Rich Man, Rich Man." A small knot was forming in his gut.

Part of it was plain old fear—fear that this wasn't going to work out, that he and Byron would never get away. But he also felt a twinge of anticipation. He hadn't been to Uncle Leo's house in a long time . . . eight years.

He had lived there for a while once. After his mom died when he was thirteen, some social worker came to the trailer, helped him pack his bag, and then took him on a long drive. He remembered being led up to a huge white house on the water and into a big room. That was the first time he had met Uncle Leo.

"I'm your mother's brother," he said. "You'll stay here now."

He could still remember the nice room he had in a far corner of the house. Remember eating his dinners with the old housekeeper in the kitchen, and spending most of his time watching television.

He could also remember that things weren't always good. He never saw Uncle Leo. He hated school because the rich kids made fun of him. And he missed his mama.

But things would have been okay if he hadn't started messing up. Hadn't started shoplifting cassette tapes from Kmart. That's when the punishments started.

Vargas looked down at the dashboard clock. It was time to get going. He pulled the Camaro out of the bright lights of the parking lot.

He reached down and turned up the volume on the cassette player. He didn't want to think about this part, didn't want to think about the punishments, but he couldn't help it.

Uncle Leo had told him that he had bad blood in him and that the punishments would get rid of it, teach him to be good, make him stop messing up. But all the punishments did was make him scared and more lonely. It got so he'd do anything not to get the punishment. So he was good. Or good at faking being good because he wasn't sure what good really was. Finally, the punishments had ended.

So did his stay at the big house. Uncle Leo gave him a new place to live. And the only person he saw for the next year was a red-haired man named Rusty. Then, when he turned sixteen, Uncle Leo said he had to start earning his way in the world and gave him a job in the sugar refinery.

It was hard work cleaning the equipment and no matter how much he tried, he couldn't get the stink of burnt sugar out of his hair and clothes. But for the first time in his life, he had his own money. He would cash his paychecks and stuff the money in a Whitman Sampler candy box that used to belong to his mama. Eventually, he had enough to buy the Camaro off an old man over in Jerome. Once, he drove all the way to Naples and wasted his money on a new movie called *Urban Cowboy*. It hadn't been a western at all; just a story about some weird guy who just *wanted* to be a cowboy.

But then, when he was eighteen, he messed up again. He did something really stupid, and he ended up in Raiford. He didn't hear from Uncle Leo again.

Until three weeks ago.

Vargas was coming into the little downtown part of Naples. He slowed down as he passed the fancy shops and restaurants. No one was out tonight, looking in the windows or sitting in the cafes; it was too cold. He drove past a golf course and then turned onto Uncle Leo's street. Funny, how he could remember the way after all this time. He stared at the houses. But he didn't remember it looking like this exactly. He remembered the houses being bigger.

He spotted Uncle Leo's house. The big gate was open and he started to pull up into the curving driveway, his eyes widening as he saw the white car. A fucking Rolls Royce. He recognized it from that hood ornament that looked like an angel. He started to park but then saw a sign for SERVICE ENTRANCE. That's where the maid had told him to go.

He pulled around back and parked next to a big Jeep. The maid was there at the door to let him in and lead him through the huge gleaming kitchen and down a long hall and into a room that looked like an office. Vargas was glad she didn't make him wait in that other room, the one Uncle Leo called his study. He didn't like it in there. It scared him.

He stood in the middle of the office, not wanting to touch anything. He almost didn't want to breathe, but he had to do that so he took small breaths.

Uncle Leo came in through a second door and hardly gave Vargas a glance as he went to stand behind a desk. Vargas was surprised to see Uncle Leo didn't look a bit older. But he was wearing a tuxedo, and the black wool made his gray and white hair and mustache look even more white. It made him look even taller and bigger somehow.

Uncle Leo was just standing there, staring at him. Vargas shifted from one foot to the other. He opened his mouth to say something.

"Take off those gloves," Uncle Leo said.

Vargas looked down at his hands. He had forgotten he even had the gloves on.

"Take off the fucking gloves, Adam," Uncle Leo said.

Vargas slowly peeled the gloves off. They were the cop's gloves. They were nice and fit him good so he didn't want to lose them. He stuffed them in the back pocket of his jeans.

"I expected you yesterday," Uncle Leo said.

"We had to lay low for a day," Vargas said. "You saw the news, right, Uncle Leo?"

Uncle Leo shook his head. "I saw a mess is what I saw."

Vargas felt his face grow warm.

"I asked for one simple hit," Uncle Leo said, his teeth clenched under the mustache. "Put a bullet in Austin Outlaw. How hard was that?"

Vargas's eyes jumped away from Leo to the big windows that looked out over the pool. He could see himself reflected in the panes, his body cut up into pieces.

Byron's voice coming to him: *You can do this, Adam.*

He forced his gaze back to his uncle. "But Outlaw is dead, Uncle Leo. So you owe us money."

Uncle Leo came around the desk and it took him only two strides to reach Vargas. He smacked him hard against the temple, sending Vargas stumbling backward.

"Don't tell me what I owe you," he spat.

Vargas rubbed his head, his eyes burning. "Don't hit me like that."

"Hit you? I ought to shoot you. That would solve everything."

Vargas was silent, trying to figure out what to say next. This wasn't working. Uncle Leo was mad at him and Byron would be too.

"You're a fuck-up," Uncle Leo said. "You always have been."

"Then why'd you give us this job?"

"I gave the job to Ellis. I thought he could do it. I was wrong. He's as stupid as you are."

"Don't say that," Vargas shot back. "Byron isn't stupid. He's smart. He's a smart man. Don't say that about Byron. He didn't mess up. *I* messed up."

Uncle Leo looked at Vargas long and hard. "If I didn't know you better, I'd swear you two were queer for each other."

Vargas felt his shoulder muscles tighten and he fought to hold his uncle's gaze, afraid if he looked away he would know, know that what he had just said was true. And then there would be no money. No boat. And no Aruba.

Uncle Leo finally turned away, walking back behind the desk. He unlocked a drawer and pulled out a large envelope. Vargas waited, his eyes on the envelope, hoping the money was in it but too afraid to say anything more.

"You and Ellis need to leave the country," Uncle Leo said.

Vargas nodded.

"I'll arrange to have you flown out."

"No, wait, Uncle Leo," Vargas said, coming forward. "We got a different plan. We're getting a boat in Everglades City."

"No. You'll just screw it up. I'll have my pilot take you to Canada."

Vargas shook his head, trying to think, trying to digest what was happening. Canada? There weren't any beaches in Canada.

Uncle Leo was pulling money from the envelope. He nodded toward the phone on the desk. "Call Ellis. Tell him to meet you at the airport here."

"I can't. There's no phone where he is."

Vargas heard Uncle Leo sigh, and knew he was mad. He was shoving the bills back into the envelope.

"Then go back and get him and bring him to the Naples airport. I'll have someone meet you."

"What about our money?"

"It will be on the plane."

Vargas hesitated. He wasn't sure Uncle Leo would put the money on the plane. He wasn't sure of anything anymore.

"But—"

"Go on. I want you in the air by midnight."

Vargas slipped out the door and walked blindly down the long hall, and back through the kitchen. He was still shaking as he slid the keys into the Camaro.

Tamiami Trail back to Copeland was nearly deserted, only the occasional glow of oncoming headlights piercing the misty darkness. Vargas drove the speed limit, not wanting to call attention to himself. Byron would be wondering what took him so long. And he would be mad when he found out he didn't get the money, that they had to go back to Naples and weren't going to Aruba. Canada . . . shit, it was cold up there. Byron was going to be real mad about that. But at least they would be able to get away now.

Somewhere up ahead, floating just above the ground, he saw two pinpricks of blue lights. He slowed. The lights grew larger, swirling in the mist.

Damn it. Cops. A road block.

Where could he go? He couldn't just pull off. They'd notice a car sitting on the side of the road by itself.

Wait. The convenience store. He had passed it a mile or so back near Carnestown. He'd go back there. He pulled a U-turn and drove back to the store, parking on the side, away from the gas pumps and neon signs. He went inside, squinting under the florescent lights.

He grabbed a can of orange soda and a bag of BBQ chips for himself and a six-pack of Pepsi for Byron, taking them to the counter. The clerk was a teenager with headphones around his neck.

"That all?" the kid asked.

"Yeah," Vargas said, digging out a few crumpled dollars fron his jeans. "What's going on up the road? Saw a lot of cop cars."

The clerk shrugged. "Beats me."

"I just drove through there," someone behind him said.

Vargas turned. The man behind him was short, old and wearing a red St. Louis Cardinals windbreaker.

"They got some kind of manhunt going on," the guy said. "They caught one of the kidnappers of that little black kid that's been in the news."

Vargas felt a cold prickle go down his back.

"They got road blocks all over the place," the man went on. "Can't get anywhere on highway twenty-nine."

Oh, Jesus. He was going to be sick.

He walked fast out the door, the clerk yelling that he had forgotten his soda and chips. Back in the Camaro, he sat there for a moment, head spinning. He hit the steering wheel with his palm. *Damn it. Damn it.*

There was no place to go. He couldn't go back to Uncle Leo. He couldn't go back to his apartment in East Naples. He couldn't get to Byron and the trailer. He had to find somewhere he could go and *think*. He had to figure this out, like Byron would do. He drew in a breath and slipped the Camaro into gear, pulling away from the neon lights.

The tape was still playing. Vargas switched it off, and the sudden silence engulfed him. There was only one place he could go now, only one place left to hide.

CHAPTER 37

Thursday, January 21

The cold woke him, a slight chill in the air of the bedroom. Louis stirred slowly, pulling the sheet up over his shoulder. He didn't open his eyes. He didn't want to.

He had laid in her arms, a part of him more content than he had been in a long time. But as he fell asleep, it was Ben's face he saw. And he couldn't shake the sickening feeling that Ellis might have been telling the truth.

His arm went out across to the bed to the other pillow, but the sheet was cold. She was gone. The aroma of coffee told him she was still here, somewhere. He slid out of bed and slipped on a pair of sweatpants. He was pulling on a T-shirt as he walked to the living room.

It was empty. The kitchen was empty, too. The porch. She'd be out there.

He paused at the door, hearing her voice. And then, a man's voice, deep with a slight ironic drawl that he recognized immediately. Mel Landeta. He drew back, listening.

"You look good," he said.

"How can you tell?" she said.

"I can hear it in your voice. You're happy. So I know you look good. You always looked good when you were happy."

"I don't think happy is the word for it, considering what's going on," she said.

"But you're happy with him."

She paused. "I like him, Mel."

Louis looked at the floor.

"You want some more coffee?" she asked.

Louis heard the creak of the wicker chair as she got up. He stepped into the doorway. Joe and Landeta looked up at him. Joe smiled.

"Hey, Rocky," Landeta said.

His long body was stretched out on the lounge chair. Black loafers, white socks, faded black pants, an open-collar white shirt, black leather jacket, and yellow aviator glasses.

"Mel," Louis said, giving him a nod.

Louis glanced at Joe. She was in all black: jeans, sweater, jacket. Ready to go for the day. Maybe ready to go back to Miami. She was holding two mugs.

"Let me get you some coffee," she said. She went inside the cottage, touching his arm as she passed him.

Louis looked back at Landeta, wondering why he was here. On the small table between Joe's chair and the lounge sat Byron Ellis's file, Joe's notebook, a three-ring binder with Miami PD embossed on the front, some crime scenes photos of the old people's house, the drop site, and three or four newspapers. The top paper was quartered, Benjamin's photo visible.

"Sit down, would you?" Landeta asked.

Louis sat down in the closest chair, leaving the middle one open for Joe. His eyes moved back to the table and Ben's picture.

"She called me," Landeta said. "Thought maybe I could help."

Louis looked at him, then out past the screening, through the sea oats, to the water. Something bothered him about Landeta being here, but he wasn't sure what it was. Why did she think he needed any help? And why did he know what she looked like when she was happy?

He felt Joe's hand on his shoulder. She handed him a coffee mug. He thought she'd sit down, but she didn't. She went back inside the cottage, closing the front door.

For a minute or so, they sat in silence. Landeta spoke first. "Things aren't very clear right now, are they?"

Louis didn't answer.

"When a case is personal," Landeta said, "you lose perspective because you're operating on emotions instead of logic, anger instead of experience."

Louis took a drink of coffee. Now he knew why Landeta was here. To tell him to calm down. Take it easy. Don't *let* it become personal.

"Mel, I'm okay," Louis said. "I can handle this."

"You get involved. You can't help it."

Louis closed his eyes.

"The boy's not dead," Landeta said. "At least you didn't kill him that night you tried to deliver the money."

Louis looked up. "How do you know that?"

Landeta sat forward, planting his feet on opposite sides of the lounge chair. "Ask yourself one question," he said. "Why did that guy take the chance of coming into Susan's house dressed as a cop?"

"Because he wanted another shot at killing Outlaw," Louis said.

"According to the TV, Outlaw was already dead."

"Maybe they didn't believe the TV report."

"Why wouldn't they believe it?"

"Because they knew I wasn't Austin Outlaw."

"They thought you were Outlaw earlier that night. They thought you were Outlaw at the ransom drop."

Louis was quiet.

"When did they *stop* believing you were Outlaw?" Landeta asked.

"After the noon newscast the next day," Louis said.

"Why did they stop believing?"

Louis was quiet for a moment. "Someone told them."

"Who?"

The answer was obvious. Ben had told them. Ben had seen the newscast and had told them that it wasn't his father who had been killed.

Landeta sipped his coffee. Suddenly Louis didn't mind him being here at all.

The door opened and Joe came back out, carrying a legal pad. Landeta touched her chair, as if to let her know it was okay to rejoin the conversation. She sat down, flipping the pages of the pad.

"I just got off the phone with the Collier County sheriff's office and the M.E.," she said. "First, they're not finished processing the trailer, but so far there is no evidence Ben was ever inside. No prints or strange little objects like paper cigar rings."

"Who owns the trailer?" Louis asked.

"Collier County. Apparently the original owner didn't pay the property taxes and the land and trailer were seized in 1985. The names on the mail box, Raif and Janice Fletcher, were the last known renters in 1980, but the place sat empty for years after they moved. No one can locate the original owner."

"The Fletchers have any kids?" Louis asked.

"Yes, but they'd be in their forties now. Our guy is young."

"Our guy knows that place though," Louis said. "He didn't just find that trailer by chance."

"I agree."

Louis took a drink of his coffee. "Anything else in the trailer to tell us who this other guy is?"

Joe shook her head. "No. It doesn't look like they were there very long."

"What about Ellis's place in Fort Myers?" Mel asked.

"He's been gone from that apartment for over a year. It was just his last known address."

"So we don't know where Ellis has been living since he got out of prison," Louis said.

"Why didn't his parole officer violate him for not reporting?" Landeta asked.

"He wasn't on parole," Joe said. "He served his full sentence."

The porch fell quiet. Louis's eyes drifted to the legal pad in Joe's lap. "Can I see your notes?"

She handed the pad to him. Her writing was easy to read, sharp little strokes that looked more like printing than script. He read down the page until he got to the words AUTOPSY FINDINGS.

"Is this on Ellis?" Louis asked.

Joe nodded. "Two gunshot wounds to the chest."

Louis read on. She had asked about other scars and tattoos and the M.E. had read them off to her: a winged bird looking toward a sun on Ellis's back; two crosses, one on each biceps; a naked woman on his chest; and the words YOUR MINE on the hand.

"Joe, hand me Ellis's file," Louis said. She did and he flipped it open to the distinguishing marks the department of corrections had listed years ago. A bird, crosses, and a naked woman were all there. But the YOUR MINE was not listed. That meant Ellis had gotten the tattoo after the last notation by the state, whenever that was.

"Joe, did the M.E. describe this last tattoo, the YOUR MINE one?"

"He said YOUR was big on the back of the hand and the M-I-N-E was spaced out on individual fingers, above the knuckles."

"Did the M.E. spell out the word YOUR for you or did he just say it?" Louis asked, reaching for a pencil off the table.

"Just said it."

Louis flipped to a clean page in the pad and drew two hands. On one hand he printed the letters BE on the fat part of the hand, putting M-I-N-E below it on the fingers. On the other hand, he put the letters YR on the fat part, with the same M-I-N-E below it.

He held out his sketch to Joe.

"Yancy Rowen had the same tattoo," Louis said. "Only his said BE MINE. B-E . . . or Byron Ellis. Ellis had Y-R for Yancy Rowen"

Joe was staring at the drawings. "They were lovers," she said.

Landeta looked at her. "More like each other's property. The tattoo that says *B-E Mine* means Byron Ellis *is* mine. Y-R, Yancy Rowen *is* mine. The fact that it's on the hand means hands off to everyone else."

Louis was seeing Yancy Rowen's face, the bulging muscles, the agitated jerks of his cuffed wrists when they asked him about Ellis. Rowen had been seething with anger. Or was it something else?

I don't know who his new boy is either.

Louis leaned across Joe again and sifted through the papers until he found Jewell's sketch of the second man. He looked at it. Young. Blond. And white. This was the *new boy.*

And Yancy Rowen knew exactly who he was.

"We've got to go back to Raiford," Louis said, holding up the sketch. "Yancy Rowen knows who this is."

Joe stood up. "Let me cut some red tape up there. I'll be ready in fifteen minutes." She disappeared inside.

Louis was still looking at the sketch when Landeta spoke. "Joe tells me you might have a shot at a job in Miami when all this is over."

Louis nodded. "Yeah. Maybe."

Landeta took off his glasses and started wiping them with a white handkerchief. "Lots of nice things in Miami," he said.

There was something in his voice, a wistfulness, a memory of something he once had but was now gone. And Louis realized that the job he might soon take was the same job Landeta had lost a few years ago because of his declining eyesight. But was there something else he seemed to be re-membering? Was that other memory Joe?

"You should go for it. You're young. Don't be too . . . cautious," Landeta said.

Louis glanced over at him. Landeta was looking straight ahead, out over the low dunes toward the gulf. It was just one big smudge of gray with no delineation between water and sky, and for a moment Louis understood what it was like to see the world as Landeta did, with no sharp edges or boundaries.

Joe came back out onto the porch. "Let's get moving," she said.

"I need to get dressed," Louis said, standing.

She gave him a wave and he went inside. As he looked back over his shoulder and through the door, he could see the lower half of Landeta's body. He saw Joe lean forward, and pick up Mel's cigarette. She took a drag and handed it to him, saying something to Mel that he couldn't hear.

Louis dressed quickly, anxious to get going. Anxious to get back outside. He went to grab his jacket, but it was muddy and still damp from yesterday's chase with Ellis. He grabbed a hooded sweatshirt, wincing at the pain in his shoulder as he pulled it over his head. He seldom even stopped at the mirror, unless he was dressing up, but he caught an image of himself and he took a minute to take it in.

The thin gray light from the windows shadowed his face with dark angles and he suspected, close up, he looked like crap. But standing here now, in snug jeans, sneakers, a hooded sweatshirt, and hair longer than he had ever worn it, he looked . . . young?

Joe came to the bedroom doorway. "Primp too much you'll have ol' Yancy putting the moves on you," she said. "C'mon, let's go."

She left before he could reply. He followed her back to the porch. Landeta was still sitting in the lounge.

"You need a lift home?" Louis asked, looking at Landeta.

Landeta shook his head. "Nah. If it's okay with you, I'll stick around here a while and watch the world go by."

"How will you get home?" Joe asked.

"Same way I got here. Cab."

Louis looked at Joe. She was looking at Landeta.

"See you?" she asked.

"You bet, Joette," Landeta nodded.

She turned to Louis, tossing him the keys. "You drive. I'm going to sleep."

CHAPTER 38

The clang of shackles was the only sound in the small room as Yancy Rowen shuffled to his place at the table. The guards secured his ankles and wrists to the metal loops, then took their positions by the door. Louis took the chair across from Rowen. Joe stood behind him, against the wall, arms crossed.

Rowen was looking at Joe. The whites of his eyes were shot through with tiny red veins, the lids heavy and dark, and there was an intensity in the stare that made Louis glad Rowen was cuffed to the table.

Louis placed a closed manila folder on the table between them. Rowen's gaze moved to it.

"I want to talk to the pretty woman," Rowen said.

"You're not interested in the woman, Yancy," Louis said. "You and I both know that."

Rowen's gaze jumped to Louis's face. "What you talking about?"

Louis took out his drawing of Ellis's hand tattoo from the folder. He slid it across the table, turning it so Rowen could see it. Rowen looked at it and clenched his left hand, the one with the matching tattoo, but there was no way he could hide it.

"You and Ellis were more than cell mates," Louis said. "More than friends."

"You're wrong, man," Rowen said, slumping back. "I ain't no homo. That's a white man's thing."

"Then explain that," Louis said, pointing to Rowen's B-E MINE tattoo.

"It don't mean shit. And it had nothing to do with Ellis."

"How long you been in here, Yancy?" Louis asked.

Rowen was looking back at the drawing. "Twelve years."

"And you were how old when you got here?"

"Look it up."

"I did. You were nineteen."

Rowen glared at him.

"When did you give yourselves the tattoos?" Louis asked.

"I told you them tats mean nothing, nothing about Ellis. Nothing about nothing."

"Whose idea was it?" Louis asked. "I bet it was his. He was older, right? Had already been in here a while. It was his game and he really knew how to take care of a young buck like you, right?"

Rowen's hands jerked against the cuffs, then he leaned as far over the table as he could. "You're one stupid—"

"What was it like that first night, Yancy?" Louis said. "What was it like to lie in a cell, listening to the cries and sounds in the dark, hugging yourself to keep from throwing up, knowing that it was just a matter of time before you became one of their fuck-toys?"

"Shut up. It wasn't like that," Rowen said.

"It was exactly like that," Louis said. "You needed protection. You needed—what do they call it?—a daddy?"

Rowen was silent, his eyes locked on Louis.

"Ellis was your daddy."

Rowen curled his lips. "El kept me alive."

"In all the right ways," Louis said.

"In every way," Rowen said.

Louis opened the folder again and took out the sketch of the second suspect. He slid it across the table.

"Until *he* came along."

Rowen's eyes dipped to the sketch. His body shifted in the chair.

"You were replaced quicker than yesterday's garbage," Louis said. "By *him*."

"It didn't matter," Rowen said, his voice tightening. "I didn't care. Nobody cares in here."

"No, you cared," Louis said. "You and Ellis. You had something different. You belonged to each other in a way none of the others would ever understand."

Rowen's eyes shot back to Joe but he said nothing.

Louis stabbed a finger at the sketch. "He took everything you had."

"He was nothing!" Rowen spat.

"He was something to Ellis," Louis said. "He was younger than you and he was prettier than you. And he was something else you could never be. He was *white*."

"So fucking what?" Rowen yelled.

Louis pulled out a photograph, a full-body color shot of Byron Ellis in the morgue. Ellis had a sheet up to his waist, and the two bullet holes Joe had put in his chest were clearly visible.

He slapped it down in front of Rowen. "Byron Ellis is dead."

Rowen's eyes widened, but he didn't move. Louis watched the veins in his neck pulse for a second or two.

"Who killed him?" Rowen asked.

Louis pointed to the sketch. "He did. Shot him dead, naked in their bed."

Rowen looked away, his jaw tight, lips pressed together, his hands rattling the cuffs. Louis thought he might explode into a rage and he knew if that happened, the guards would end the interview instantly.

"Yancy," Louis said, his voice low. "It is what it is. Nobody's judging you here."

Rowen just stared at the table.

Louis's eyes went to the teardrop tattooed under Rowen's eye. "Yancy, you ever kill anybody?" he asked gently.

Rowen shook his head.

Louis leaned as far over the table as he could and kept his voice very low. "Give us his killer."

Rowen sat perfectly still for a moment, his eyes on Louis. "Tell the bitch to leave," he said.

Louis didn't have to look back. He heard Joe's footsteps moving to the door. When the door closed behind her, he waited.

Rowen took a deep breath. "You think I'm some kind of monster. Or freak fairy."

"No, I don't."

"We ain't no different than you, man," Rowen said. "We just got different options. You got her, I had El."

Louis held Rowen's gaze, silent.

"In this place, you take what you can get when you can get it. Most times, it don't matter from who." Rowen shook his head, eyes on the table. "Then sometimes it *does* matter. Like you said, El is what he is. And he ain't never been ashamed of it."

"And you?" Louis asked. He knew the answer, but he also knew Rowen was ready to talk. Wanted to talk.

Rowen was quiet for a long time. "I ain't so sure what I am," he said finally. "My first fuck was in here and I ain't got nothing to compare it to."

Louis's eyes flicked up to the guards. To Rowen, the guards must have been invisible. It struck Louis odd that Rowen was more embarrassed to have Joe hear this than the two guys at the door.

"Are they any good?"

"What?" Louis asked, looking back.

"Broads. Are they any good?"

"Yeah, they're good."

"I get out in six years."

"Give them a try."

Rowen looked down at the sketch. "Can I hold that?"

Louis looked at the guards. One shrugged. Louis handed Rowen the sketch.

"The boy you said El kidnapped. You find him yet?"

Louis shook his head.

"The kid yours?" Rowen asked.

Louis almost lied to him, thinking it might make a difference. But he'd lied enough to this guy. If Rowen saw through a new lie, he would clam up.

"No, he's the son of a friend. His mother is a defense attorney."

"El won't hurt him."

"It's not up to Ellis anymore," Louis said, nodding toward the sketch. "It's up to him."

Rowen looked back at the sketch, then spit on it. He crumpled it with one of his large hands and tossed it aside. Rowen took a deep, long breath, like he needed strength to say the name.

"His name is Adam Vargas."

Louis waited a moment, then put the photo of Ellis back in the folder. He didn't want Rowen to ask to keep it.

"Anything else you can tell me about him?" Louis asked. "Do you know what he was in here for?" He knew he could find out the offense later, but he wanted to know now.

"Armed robbery."

"Anything else you can tell me about him?"

Rowen shrugged. "He had a mean streak."

Louis looked at him. He wanted to ask, *Don't you all?*

Rowen saw the look. "This was different than most of the guys," he said. "It's like it didn't fit him. Nothing seemed right about him, even like he didn't really belong here."

"He committed an armed robbery," Louis said.

"With a plastic gun, man," Rowen said.

A plastic gun?

"Can I ask you something else, Yancy?"

Rowen nodded.

"How come you never hurt him?" Louis asked. "Or even killed him?"

Rowen shrugged. "I don't know. I ain't no killer. I had a guy offer to do it for me, but I . . . just couldn't. In a weird way, it woulda been like killing a kid."

"Why?"

Rowen shrugged. "It was like the guy never got past thirteen or something."

Louis stood up. "Thank you," he said.

Rowen looked up at him, his face a mixture of embarrassment, anger, confusion, and something else close to pain.

Louis walked to the door. The guard let him out and he stepped into the hall. Joe came up to him quickly.

"Adam Vargas," Louis said.

"Good job. I'll get what I can from the office and meet you outside."

They walked out, escorted by a guard, back down the long hall and through the security check-in area. Joe went in another direction. He checked out and stepped into the cold air outside.

The sky was still a slate gray, the clouds low on the horizon. The wind whipped at his face, the air sharp with the smell of more rain. He leaned against Joe's Bronco and looked up at the prison. It was a cold, white boxy building, the rows of dark windows set in the stone walls like holes that led to nowhere. The constant bang of metal doors, reminding you that you were locked up. The eternal feel of another man's eyes on you.

Rowen's face came back to him. That strange final look, the lips drawn painfully over the teeth, the tattooed tear drop glistening with sweat.

His gaze moved back to the big white building.

Hard, cold grown men who'd sooner shoot you than look at you, drawing teardrops on their faces.

Jesus, he couldn't imagine being in prison. Any kind of prison. Yet, every once in a while, the thought hit him. He could be. Maybe should be.

Major Anderson asked about you. Walk in the door as a detective. Are you interested?

I have some things to work out here first.

Louis knew Joe thought he had meant his relationship, such as it was, with Susan. But he hadn't meant that at all.

There was a gun buried in the sand under the Gumbo Limbo tree in his front yard. The gun was evidence in another case, evidence he had not turned over to the cops.

A young girl was dead. Her confessed rapist and killer was going to go free and there was nothing Louis could do about it. Until the man got accused of another crime. A crime Louis knew he did not commit. And the gun that would prove the man innocent of the second crime dropped into Louis's hands.

He had hid the gun, buried it in his front yard. And the rapist went to jail for another man's crime.

It seemed right at the time, if not legally, then morally. The man needed to be punished one way or another. And the girl needed justice. So he had given it to her.

He had regretted burying the gun almost immediately. But then things got complicated. Time went by. The trial started. Susan had been involved with the case, and he knew she would never forgive him if he ever told her that he had tampered with evidence and obstructed justice in a case that involved her. She had told him once she knew there were lines he would not cross. He knew she'd be disappointed in him to find out she was wrong.

But as job openings came and went in the Fort Myers police department and Lee County sheriff's office, he found that it wasn't Susan's possible disappointment in him that was the problem. It was his own.

He needed to make it right again before he even considered an interview with Major Anderson.

He looked back up at the prison. But he didn't have the faintest idea how.

The red needle on the speedometer was pushing eighty-five as they sped south on I-75. They were heading to East

Naples, to an efficiency apartment that the prison records had shown as Vargas's address after his release. The warden had also given them a thin copy of Vargas's life story, according to the Florida Department of Corrections. Joe read it to Louis during the drive.

Adam Pernell Vargas had entered prison at eighteen, after robbing a store off Alligator Alley. The Alley cut through the Miccosukee Indian reservation, and it was the tribe's small store that Vargas had chosen to hold up with his plastic gun. He had been sentenced to two years, but only served eighteen months. His uncle, Leo Ryker, had offered Vargas a job at his sugar cane processing plant near Clewiston to secure the parole.

The armed robbery was Vargas's first and only charged offense up to now. It struck Louis odd that Vargas had turned so violent after his release, and even chalking it up to Byron Ellis's influence didn't explain it. Ellis's own manslaughter charge had been a personal beef that ended in a gunshot. Nothing in his background suggested he was capable of the damage they had seen this week. But together, these two losers had gone on a bloody rampage. What had set it off?

Louis had a hunch Vargas was the key—and he hoped to find something at Vargas's old apartment. After that, they had an appointment to go see Leo Ryker. Joe had called Ryker's office from the prison, and he had agreed to wait for them at the plant in Clewiston.

"Louis, you okay?" Joe asked.

He nodded, his eyes trained on the road.

"You haven't said much for the last two hours."

"I'm thinking," he said.

She closed the file. "About Vargas?"

"About everything," he said.

"I'm sorry I have to take off tomorrow," she said.

"Can't be helped," Louis said.

Before they left Raiford, Joe had called her own department to check in. She had been told she needed to return to Miami tomorrow for an unexpected court appearance on an-

other case. She would be gone only a day, she had told
Louis. She had been oddly quiet most of the day and he wondered now if she was glad to have an excuse to put some distance between them.

He glanced over at her. She was looking out the window.
Neither of them had mentioned last night, yet the unspoken
questions had seemed to hover in the air all day. Questions
about him and Susan. Questions about whether their own
lovemaking last night was a beginning of something or just a
sudden explosion of need fueled by the tension of a missing
child and her killing of Ellis. He knew relationships started
by cops in the midst of a high-stress case were seldom more
than a series of quickies, fading rapidly when the case was
over.

He knew she wouldn't ask any of those questions. But
then he realized that she wasn't the one who wanted the answers.

He heard Mel's voice in his ear, bugging him again about
being more open, but all he could think about was this morning. *You sound happy,* Landeta had said. Her hand on his
arm. The strangeness in Landeta's voice. *Lots of nice things
in Miami.*

"Joe," he said finally.

She looked over at him, waiting for him to speak. When
he didn't, she did.

"We haven't talked," she said. She shifted in the seat so
she was facing him. "I guess you want to know about Mel,
why I called him. I thought maybe he could help you work
things through about the boy, about—"

"It's okay," Louis said. That wasn't what he wanted to
know. But he realized he had no business asking her the real
question on his mind—whether the past she shared with Mel
had gone beyond work.

She was quiet for a moment. "Plus, I guess I wanted to
talk to him," she added.

"He's a good guy to talk to when things get shitty."

"That's not why I wanted to talk to him."

Louis stayed quiet.

"About ten years ago," she said. "Mel and I had a relationship."

Louis's eyes never wavered from the road.

"I was twenty-five, he was thirty-five," she said. "I was a uniform, he was a detective." She drew in a deep breath. "One night, after three years, he just ended it. Said it's over and walked out my door."

"Joe . . ."

"For the next few years, I was so angry and so hurt I couldn't even look at him. Then I got promoted, and Major Anderson assigned us a case together."

"Joe, if you're trying to tell me that you still—"

"Shut up and listen," she said. "A few days into the case, I could tell there was something wrong with him. A couple weeks later, he told me about his eyes."

Louis rubbed his face, not wanting to look at her.

"He told me he broke it off with me for two reasons. One was that he said he couldn't be a burden to any woman." After a long pause, she went on. "The other reason was that he knew I wanted to get married back then. And he told me I was too good a cop and I loved it too much to be saddled with kids, a house and an old asshole like him."

She smiled slightly. "It turned out he was right. Not about him being an asshole. But that the timing was all wrong for me."

Louis finally looked at her. Her head was down, her hand flat on Adam Vargas's folder.

"I still love Mel," she said. "But not like you probably are thinking. I asked him over this morning so I could tell him something in person that I didn't want him to hear from you."

Her gray eyes were steady on his. He slowed the Bronco, pulling over to the shoulder. He turned to face her.

"Things are pretty charged right now," she said. "And maybe that is a big part of what happened between us last night. But I don't want to get in the middle of something."

"Are you asking about Susan?" Louis said.

"Yes."

He was trying to figure out how to answer. Whatever he and Susan could have been together started to crack the moment Austin walked in. It fell apart when Ben was kidnapped, and it disintegrated last night when Susan's door slammed shut behind him.

"We were never more than a possibility," Louis said.

She nodded. They were silent for a moment. A semi sped past, making the Bronco sway in its wake.

"Look," Louis said, "I'm not a very good dancer."

"Neither am I," she said.

"Okay, you staying at my place again tonight?"

"You want me to?"

"Yes, I do."

Her hand slid across the seat to cover his, holding it for a moment. Finally, he put the Bronco in gear and pulled back onto the road.

CHAPTER 39

They pulled up outside Vargas's apartment to a blur of squad cars and blue lights swirling in the falling darkness. Louis took note of the cruisers: mostly Collier County, two Lee County, and a few from Naples. Lee County Sheriff Lance Mobley was standing in the doorway to Vargas's efficiency when Louis and Joe hit the yellow tape. Mobley saw them coming and came across the scraggly lawn to meet them, collar up, cheeks red, his blond hair whipping around his head.

"The boy's not here," Mobley said. "Neither is Vargas."

"Can I look inside?" Louis asked.

"What for?"

"I might see something I recognize. I know the kid. He's been leaving things. Clues."

Mobley put his hands on his hips and looked toward the apartment. "I want this guy bad, Kincaid. He killed one of mine. I don't need your interference right now."

"Damn it, Lance, what can it hurt?"

Mobley hesitated, then looked at Joe, his eyes dropping to her badge that hung around her neck.

"You must be Detective Frye from Miami."

She stuck out her hand. "Sheriff. Louis tells me good things about you."

Mobley slipped Louis a look as he took her hand. "I don't believe a word of that, but nice try. C'mon. Make it quick."

Mobley lifted the tape and they dipped under it, following him to the door.

The efficiency was tiny. One room with a chipped linoleum floor, faded yellow walls, a patio door smeared with years of grime, a table lamp with a bare bulb and a cheap framed print above an open sleeper sofa. There was a card table littered with orange soda and Pepsi cans, paper plates, and an empty pizza box.

A couple of Collier County detectives gave Louis the once over, but he ignored them, hoping neither of them remembered who he was. He still owed them a statement on the shooting of Byron Ellis.

He walked to the sleeper sofa. The sheets were tangled, pulled from the edges. They were pale blue, thread-bare, dotted with light stains. His gaze moved over the walls. The picture above the sofa was a western landscape with a setting sun, the corners frayed and dried, curling away from the frame. The television was an older model, a layer of dust across the screen. Balanced on top of the TV was a video-cassette recorder, the $399 price tag still stuck to the top. Both the TV and VCR sat on a small wooden stand with a broken door.

Louis motioned to the Collier sheriff, who came forward.

"Have you looked inside this?" Louis asked.

"Not yet."

"You mind?"

The sheriff opened the broken door to the TV stand with the tip of his pen. Louis squatted down to get a better look. VHS videotapes, the blank kind you bought and recorded TV programs on. Someone had meticulously labeled them with the strips supplied in the box. The writing was small and childlike:

> *They Dide with there Boots on*
> *Two Road Together*
> *Butch Casidy and the Sundance Kid*
> *Rio Bravo*
> *Stagecoach*
> *Back in the saddel*
> *The last Roundup*

"There must be fifty or sixty of these," Louis said.

"Think these belong to Vargas or this other guy, Ellis?"

Louis stood up. "They belong to Vargas. The guy's a wannabe cowboy. I bet we find music, too."

"A cowboy?"

Louis nodded and moved to a small cardboard box in the corner. It was full of cassette tapes, most without covers. Behind the box was a stack of old record albums. Louis used his pen to flip through them. Gene Autry, Marty Robbins, Tex Ritter, and a few Louis never heard of. Most of the covers were tattered, and had PROPERTY OF ZELDA VARGAS written on them with black marker. Louis knew from the information Joe had read about Vargas on the way home that Zelda was Vargas's mother's name.

There was a small piece of paper sticking out of the Gene Autry album and Louis pulled it loose by the corner. It was faded, heavily creased from plenty of handling.

GENE AUTRY'S 10 RULES FOR COWBOYS

1. A cowboy must never shoot first
2. A cowboy must never go back on his word
3. A cowboy always tells the truth
4. A cowboy is kind to children . . .

"So you find any clues from the kid?"

Louis looked up to see Mobley standing there. He shook his head, dropping the paper back between the albums.

"Maybe they stowed the kid at Ellis's place, wherever that is," Mobley said.

"Ellis lived here with Vargas, Lance," Louis said.

"This place is smaller than a dog house. Where'd he sleep?"

Louis looked at the bed. Mobley followed his gaze, then his eyes snapped back to Louis. "Jesus, they were homos?" he asked.

Louis nodded.

As Mobley looked back at the tangled sheets, Louis could almost see his brain working to conjure up the images.

"You sure?" Mobley asked.

"Yeah, I'm sure."

"You could've told me."

"I'm telling you now. Has Ellis's death hit the papers yet?"

"This morning."

Louis looked over at Joe, who was talking to a Collier County investigator. "Vargas is going to react somehow."

Again, Mobley followed his gaze. "Frye's name was all over the papers and her face was on TV. You thinking he'll go after her?"

"I think he might if he knew where to find her."

"Where's she staying?"

"My place. Out on Captiva."

Mobley smiled. "Good move, Kincaid. Security wise, I mean."

Louis gave the efficiency one last look around. "Do me a favor. Save anything weird, anything that looks like a kid might have left it."

"The kid was never here, and you know it."

"Look anyway," Louis said. "We've got to get going."

Louis motioned to Joe and was at the Bronco by the time Mobley caught up with him. "Where you going?" Mobley asked.

Louis debated telling him. But he didn't want to find himself back behind the yellow tape, unable to ask questions again.

Mobley put a hand on the driver's side door. "Tell me

where you're going or I'll find some reason to lock your ass up."

"We're going to talk to Vargas's uncle," Louis said, looking back at Mobley. "He gave Vargas his first job when he got out of prison."

Mobley looked around the yard. He didn't have many officers here. This was Collier County and Louis knew Mobley was here only as a courtesy since Vargas's crimes had now touched three counties.

"Where'd you get your information?" Mobley asked.

"Raiford."

"What were you . . . ?" Mobley held up a hand. "Never mind. I don't even want to know. But I want you to take a detective with you."

"I got one with me."

Mobley glanced at Joe as she came up next to them. "This is not *her* jurisdiction."

"It's not yours either, Sheriff," Joe said.

Mobley faced her. "Look, Detective, Collier County has been more than cooperative and professional. I'd expect no less from Miami-Dade."

Joe reached for the Bronco door and Mobley had to step out of the way to let her open it. She leaned in and grabbed her file on Adam Vargas. She handed it to Mobley.

"Knock yourself out," she said. She climbed in the Bronco, but before she closed the door, she looked back at Mobley. "One more thing, Sheriff," she said.

"What?"

"See if you can start keeping up with the rest of us, okay?"

Louis went around to the passenger side and got in. Joe watched Mobley slap the folder against his thigh and walk away.

She reached down and started the Bronco. "I need to go back to your place and start packing if I'm going to make that court appearance tomorrow morning," she said. "Can you handle old Uncle Leo alone?"

"No problem," Louis said. "I won't be back till ten or eleven, though. Why don't you walk up to Timmy's and grab dinner."

"Sounds good," she said.

"I'll wake you when I get in."

"That sounds good, too."

CHAPTER 40

It hurt. And it was hard to see in the dim candlelight, and the ink was getting all over his hands.

Vargas leaned closer to the mirror, feeling the warmth of the fire from the stone fireplace on his bare back. The cabin smelled good with the wood burning.

Not much had changed in the cabin, except it was real dusty. In the closet, he had found some clothes that he had left years ago. He had tried them on, but they were too small. Just like the cabin itself was small. Smaller than he remembered.

He dipped the straight pin again into the pool of ink that had spilled from the plastic pen.

He could hear the man on the TV talking again but even if he looked, he knew he couldn't see him very good. His face was hidden behind a snowstorm of static. Earlier they had shown pictures filmed from a chopper in the air, and he had been able to pick out the green and white trailer and cops swarming around it like cockroaches. He had seen the swamp buggy overturned in the water, and the gurney with the black body bag.

And he had seen her, seen the woman with the gold

badge, and heard the guy on TV say, "The suspect was shot and killed by Miami-Dade Detective Joe Frye."

Talking about Byron dying like it was nothing.

At least Byron had gone out kicking, gunning that old buggy down the road, making them chase him. It must've been something to see.

He pulled back and let out a breath, looking at his reflection and then down at the broken pens and ink in the sink. He wasn't sure if Byron would want him doing this, marking his body, but it was *for him*. He would understand.

The newscast was ending and he knew it was almost seven. It was dark now, too, but he hadn't turned on any lights. He wasn't that far away from the trailer. And he knew there were still cops there, probably looking for him now. But they would never find him out here, unless they knew where to come or asked Uncle Leo. But Uncle Leo wouldn't tell them.

Unless Uncle Leo was mad at him now.

He felt his hand tremble as he carefully pricked his skin. He was tired. It had been over twenty-four hours since he had left Byron in the trailer and gone to see Uncle Leo. He was supposed to have brought Byron back to the airport, back to the plane and the money last night.

But he had kind of lost track of things since yesterday. He couldn't remember the last time he ate or slept. He didn't even know where he got the pens and the pins. Everything after the stop at the convenience store had been a blur.

Vargas stepped back from the mirror and picked up the candle, holding it close to his face. The teardrop on his cheek was finished.

He carefully dabbed the little dots of blood away with a piece of toilet paper then went to the TV, shutting it off. He set the candle on the wood plank floor near the bed and picked up the small cassette player and the tapes he had brought in from the Camaro.

He had some time to kill.

He sat down on the floor and stuck in one of the tapes. He leaned back against the bed. The dark cabin began to fill with the sadness of singing cowboys. He didn't fast-forward it, like he usually did, to get to his favorites. He pulled out his knife and started sharpening the blade with slow, smooth strokes.

For the next hour or so, the music played.

Sometimes, if he liked the words, he'd sing along, softly, keeping time with the whetstone scraping against the blade, like the brushing sound drummers made with their cymbals. But mostly, he just listened.

They sang about lonely journeys ending under golden red skies. Broken hearts. Broken dreams. Building nests in the west with the stars peeping down. Pale Montana moons. Cowboy heavens. Silver-haired daddies.

He laid his head back on the bed, silent tears burning the tender skin under his eye.

He didn't like remembering the days in the trailer, but sometimes when the music played, he couldn't help it. That's where he had first heard the music, first met his heroes.

Long, hot Saturday afternoons watching the old westerns. Evenings filled with *Bonanza, Gunsmoke,* and reruns of *Paladin,* his mama's favorite.

Sometimes, when she was drunk enough, she'd talk about how handsome the cowboys were. How handsome *he* was. And sometimes she'd mention the summer she spent in Arizona in 1964, the summer before he was born. And she would talk about a man named Sonny.

Then one night his stepfather put a bullet through the TV and the cowboys disappeared.

For months after, the music was the only sound in the trailer. Sometimes, he and Mama would sit on the porch, the sky ablaze with red and yellow, and they could hear the records playing inside. Sometimes if she remembered the words, she would sing along with them. But most times she just listened. Like he was doing now.

Once she had pulled him out of bed at three A.M. and tried

to teach him to dance. But she had gotten mad because he was clumsy and sleepy and he stepped on her new red shoes. And she had started hitting him, slapping at him, like she did sometimes in the middle of the night, just out of nowhere, just for nothing, crying and screaming about things he knew nothing about.

But he never got mad back. Not at her. She was like the music. Empty. Sad. Beautiful.

Then one day the music stopped.

He had been used to Mama going away for a couple nights in a row. He knew she sometimes drove over to Fort Lauderdale to get what she called "a boost," and sometimes she and a man would come back to the trailer and the man would stay for a few days, then he'd be gone. But when she went that last time, she didn't come back.

Five days later, a cop and woman came to the trailer. They told him Mama was dead. They had found her in an alley in Miami. They didn't tell him how she died, but a few years later Uncle Leo told him she had been shot dead behind a bar.

Vargas stared at the log beams in the shadowed ceiling, his throat so tight he couldn't swallow.

That had been the worst time of his life. Until now.

Suddenly the cabin was quiet and the music was gone again. It took him a moment to realize the cassette player had stopped and the fire had burned out. For a few minutes he didn't move, then he slowly stood up, wiping his face with the back of his hand, smearing the ink.

Maybe when this was all over he would go out west. Maybe Uncle Leo would fly him to Arizona instead of Canada. Maybe things would be better out there.

But first he had something to do.

He stood up slowly, running a finger along the edge of the blade. Then he put it in its sheath and pulled on some clothes and shoes. He took an old hat off the rack, too. They might be looking for him now and he couldn't afford to get caught. Not yet.

He squatted and sorted through the cassette tapes on the floor, finally finding the one he wanted to play in the Camaro.

He left the cabin, huddled in his jacket, and started hiking back out to the road, where he had left the Camaro.

It didn't take him long to get back to the car. It was cold and he walked fast. He had hidden the car in some brush, covering it with branches. He pulled the branches off, then stopped to take a long look up and down the narrow road. The wind was whipping the trees and the darkness was dense, no light anywhere to be seen.

He got in the car, started it up, and slipped in the tape. It wasn't the Marty Robbins version. It was his own version, recorded by him singing into the little microphone inside the cassette player. He had changed the words.

> *So we beat the drum slowly*
> *and played the fife lowly.*
> *And we wept in our grief,*
> *as we carried him along.*
> *For we all loved that cowboy,*
> *so brave and so handsome.*
> *Yes, we loved that young cowboy,*
> *although he done wrong.*

CHAPTER 41

The sugar fields rose up around him, the wind-whipped cane stalks undulating like huge dark waves. The night sky was a black shroud with no moon or stars. The dark had a peculiar denseness to it out here, like it would absorb any kind of light or life.

Louis had driven northeast from Naples, finally hitting the deserted service roads that cut through the monotony of the cane fields. Then for an hour, nothing, just the walls of cane and the black night. Finally, he saw a pinprick of distant lights that grew into a glowing cluster. As he neared, the lights and a building took shape, appearing like an ocean liner moving on the black sugarcane ocean.

The Bronco's headlights lit up a chainlink gate and a big sign that read CANE CORP. Beyond, Louis could see the refinery, a huge building that throbbed green in the orange glow of the parking lot lights. Boxcars sat empty on the scars of tracks that crisscrossed the grounds. A slow trickle of men coming out of the building streamed out in the lot and dissipated into the night.

Louis picked up Joe's files off the passenger seat and got out. He could feel a misty rain on his face, but it was warm. It took him a moment to realize it was coming from the refinery. His nostrils burned with a sharp smell—sickly sweet with an acrid undertone.

In the reception area, a security guy gave him a badge and pointed the way down a hallway lined with plaques and awards touting the sugar industry's achievements and contributions to Clewiston, "The Sweetest Town on Earth."

At the end of the hall, Louis knocked on a door with a gold plate that read LEO RYKER.

He was about to knock a second time when the door opened. A short man with a lean tan face and thin red hair stuck his head out.

"Yeah?"

"Louis Kincaid. I'm here to see Mr. Ryker."

"Well, he's—"

A voice from within the room: "It's okay, Rusty. Let him in."

The man stepped aside and Louis went in. It wasn't a grand office, not what Louis would have expected of a man who ran the second largest sugar cooperative in the country. A man who started out buying up muck land around Lake Okeechobee and now was worth ten million dollars and living in a mansion on the Naples waterfront. A man whose money had helped reelect Reagan and was rumored to have the secretary of agriculture on his speed dial.

Louis had learned all of this from Joe. She had called her Miami office and ordered up a quickie dossier on Leo Ryker. She had read it to him on the drive back to Captiva to drop her off.

"The guy came from the same stock as his nephew," Joe had told him.

But as Louis considered the man standing before him, it was hard to see any connection between Leo Ryker and the professional loser Adam Vargas.

Leo Ryker was in his late forties, tall and lean. He was wearing sharply creased khakis, a heavy gold watch, and a navy polo shirt with the Ralph Lauren logo over his left pec. He worked out and was proud of the fact. His thick hair and mustache were variegated gray, his face sun-reddened, and his blue eyes shrewd. Leo Ryker looked like a man sure of his place on earth, the kind who didn't give a rat's ass what anyone thought of him.

The wood-paneled office was like the man—polished, masculine, no-nonsense.

Except for the photographs.

Louis couldn't help himself. He stared at them, at the photographs of the men holding up the heads of big, black, hairy boars with long snouts and curling tusks. The men wore fatigues or T-shirts and ball caps and were holding crossbows or knives. Louis picked out the red-haired Rusty as one of the guys behind Leo Ryker in all of the photos.

Ryker saw him looking and smiled. "Ugly, aren't they?" he said.

"Yeah."

"Wild boar," Ryker said. "They're considered a nuisance around here. Some things just need killing, right, Rusty?"

He was hovering in the background and came to life at Ryker's prompt. "Yes sir," he muttered. "Hogs is stupid animals, sir."

"Do you hunt, Detective?" Ryker asked.

"Only when I'm forced to," Louis said. He moved away from the photographs.

Ryker was looking behind Louis, to the door. "I thought there were two of you coming?" he asked.

"Detective Frye couldn't make it," Louis said, extending a hand. "I'm Louis Kincaid."

Ryker shook his hand with a tight, controlled grip, then moved to his desk, motioning for Louis to take a chair in front of the desk. Ryker sat down. Louis remained standing.

"What is it you need to know about Adam?"

"Is this a good likeness of your nephew?" Louis asked, pulling the sketch out of Joe's files and laying it on the desk.

Ryker looked at it. "That's pretty close."

"When is the last time you saw him, Mr. Ryker?" Louis asked.

"I haven't seen Adam since he started working here in . . ." He looked at the man leaning against the wall. "Rusty, you remember when that was?"

"No sir, I don't."

Ryker looked back at Louis. "I just remember his parole officer contacting me. So I put Adam to work at night cleaning equipment."

"Have you had any contact with him since?" Louis asked.

"Once. About a month after he started, he asked me for some money."

"Did you give it to him?"

"I didn't want to, but I gave him a couple hundred. Adam is . . . he doesn't have much direction in his life. I try to help him when I can."

"Is he still working here?" Louis asked.

"As far as I know." Ryker looked at Rusty. "Do you know, Rusty?"

"No sir. You want me to call his supervisor?"

Ryker turned the phone around for the other man to use and looked back at Louis. "I have over two thousand people working here. I don't keep in contact with Adam."

Louis was thinking about Ryker's dossier, the fact that the man had no wife, no kids, no relatives at all.

"Why not?" Louis asked.

"Excuse me?"

"Adam Vargas is your only nephew," Louis said. "Why don't you keep in touch with him?"

Ryker stared at Louis. "I don't see where that's any of your business."

Louis let it go. "What was your relationship with his mother? Brother-sister?"

Ryker paused a moment. "His mother Zelda was my sister."

Louis had a vision of the trailer back in Copeland. If Zelda Vargas and her son had ever lived there, he was sure Leo had never visited. Or maybe Ryker had lived someplace similar once and when he made his money vowed he would never go back to Copeland or any other hellhole on the edge of the swamp.

Rusty hung up the phone. "He hasn't clocked in for eleven days, sir."

"Thank you, Rusty. Why don't you wait outside. I'll give you a lift home."

Ryker waited until Rusty was gone before he spoke. "I knew Adam would blow it again."

"Again?" Louis said.

"I took Adam in when he was thirteen, right after his crazy mother was killed," Ryker said, leaning back in his chair. "The kid had no place to go."

"How did that go?"

"He was moody, strange. I always thought Zelda was mentally ill. Maybe Adam is, too. He was always getting into trouble. Got caught shoplifting once."

"Where was he living then?"

"With me, in my home. Adam ran off after two years. I didn't hear from him until I got a call from some guy saying he was a parole officer and that Adam had put me down as a relative who would give him a job."

"So you didn't hear from him from the time he was fifteen until the time he got paroled from Raiford?"

Ryker started rocking in the leather chair. "No."

"What about when he was arrested for the armed robbery at eighteen?" Louis asked. "He didn't ask for help then?"

Ryker was working hard not to show it, but Louis could see it in every little movement of his body. The hunch of his shoulders, the jut of his jaw and the squint of his eyes. He was getting pissed.

"My error," Ryker said calmly. "He did ask if I could get him out of it. Wanted me to make restitution to the store."

"You can't buy your way out of armed robbery," Louis said.

"This was a small store on the reservation. I was told the

Indians didn't want to deal with a nontribal offender and had turned him over to Broward County for prosecution. They said they would drop the charges if they got reimbursed."

"How much?" Louis asked.

"Excuse me?" Ryker asked.

"How much was the restitution?"

Ryker took a long time answering. "One hundred and eighty-three dollars."

Louis stared at Ryker, but he was seeing a flash of a younger Vargas, walking through the gates of Raiford, easy prey for men like Byron Ellis, and worse. For less than two hundred dollars stolen with a toy gun.

"I had to teach him a lesson," Ryker said, crossing his arms over his chest.

"Did he contact you from prison?" Louis asked.

"He wrote letters."

"Did you read them?"

"I threw them away."

"Did he keep writing?"

Ryker sat forward. "What can that possibly matter?"

"We don't always know what matters," Louis said. "Did he keep writing you letters?"

"Every week," Ryker said.

"But you haven't seen him since he got out?"

"Only when he took the job and that one time when I gave him that money. That's all."

"Do you even know where he lives?" Louis asked.

"No."

"We found out he had been staying in an abandoned trailer in Copeland," Louis said. "You know anything about that place?"

Ryker looked surprised. "Copeland? That's where he was living when Zelda died." He shook his head. "Like I said, he's probably nuts."

"Is there anywhere you can think of that Adam would go now?" Louis asked. "Some place he may have lived when he was younger?"

"No."

"Do you know a man named Austin Outlaw, Mr. Ryker?"

Ryker stood up slowly. "No."

"What about a Byron Ellis?"

"No."

Louis pulled a small snapshot of Yancy Rowen from the stack of papers and held it out to Ryker.

"I don't know him either," Ryker said.

"How did you know this *isn't* Ellis?" Louis asked.

Ryker hesitated just a beat. "I just assumed it was."

"You said I don't know him *either.*" Louis said. "Which tells me you knew it wasn't Ellis. Which tells me you know what Ellis looks like."

Ryker's blue eyes sparked with anger, but his voice was calm. "You misunderstood, Detective."

Louis glanced at the photographs on the wall, then walked to them. "It takes a real man to hunt wild boar, doesn't it?"

"It takes a certain kind of man," Ryker said.

Louis faced him. "But a real man, right?"

"That's an old-fashioned way to put it, but true enough," Ryker said.

"I don't see Adam in any of these photos," Louis said. "Did you teach Adam to hunt?"

"He didn't want to learn," Ryker said.

"Suppose that was because he was gay?"

Ryker didn't move. But in his eyes, Louis saw first disbelief, but then hard realization of a truth that he hadn't seen coming, but should have.

"Byron Ellis and your nephew were lovers," Louis said. "They kidnapped a boy and killed six people. And we're trying to figure out why."

Ryker straightened his shoulders. "I can't help you. You need to leave. It's late."

"Just one last question, Mr. Ryker," Louis said. "When we called, why didn't you ask us *why* we wanted to talk about your nephew?"

"I just assumed he was in trouble again."

"But you never asked what he *did* this time."

"I didn't care what he had done."

Louis picked up a pen from the desk and scribbled down the phone number for the sheriff's department on a small pad of paper.

"If Adam doesn't know he's wanted, he will soon. If he contacts you, we'd appreciate it if you'd call us."

"He won't come to me," Ryker said.

Louis tossed the pad on the desk. "I think he will."

He turned and walked out. Ryker was lying but Louis wasn't sure about what. It was obvious he didn't care for Adam Vargas, but there was something wrong with the other answers. And Ryker *knew* who Byron Ellis was.

Louis walked toward the parking lot, digging for Joe's keys. As he neared the Bronco, he saw a woman standing under an aluminum rain shelter, near a sign marked EMPLOYEE SHUTTLE.

She was young, wrapped in an old brown raincoat, her head bare. As he walked past, she looked up at him and gripped her plastic 7-Eleven bag tighter. She was striking looking, her black hair long and straight around her round, brown face.

Another face jumped out at him.

A woman on TV, a week ago, that Friday he was waiting with Susan for Austin and Benjamin to come home from the ice cream place. The woman on TV had been found dead off Alligator Alley, a rape-murder.

He remembered being annoyed that the newscaster had called the woman black because it was obvious to him that she wasn't black at all. She had looked Hawaiian, Polynesian. She had looked a lot like this woman.

He turned and walked back to her. She watched him approach, pulling her plastic bag to her chest.

"Excuse me," he said.

She backed deeper into the shelter.

Louis glanced around the parking lot. There were plenty of parked cars for the swing shift workers, but no one else waiting. And no bus in sight.

"Are you waiting for a shuttle?" Louis asked.

She nodded, still not looking at him.

"What time does the shuttle come?"

"I missed the six o'clock one," she said. "Now I have to wait for the next one."

"When is the next one?" Louis asked.

"Eleven," she said.

Two hours from now. "Can I ask where you are from?" Louis asked gently.

Her eyes met his. They were brown, wary, but not really frightened. "I live here," she said.

"No, I meant originally," Louis said. "Where is your home?"

"Pohpei," she said.

"Where is that?" he asked.

"Micronesia," she said.

Louis was stunned. The woman read his silent stare as threatening and started inching away.

"Wait, please," Louis said. "I won't hurt you, please."

When she looked up at him, her eyes were welling.

"What's the matter?" he asked.

"I don't know." She pushed her long hair back from her face. "I don't know. I'm just tired. I'm very tired."

There was no bench, no place to sit. "Let me give you a ride home," he said. He pointed to the Bronco. "That's my car there."

She looked at the Bronco.

"Please," Louis said. "I won't hurt you."

Maybe it was his voice. Maybe it was just her exhaustion and the thought of standing two more hours in the cold rain. But she finally nodded. Louis led her to the Bronco.

They were out of the parking lot and into the blackness of the cane fields. She murmured some directions, telling him to stay on the service road, that she lived just a couple miles ahead. Then she was quiet, pressed against the passenger door, the 7-Eleven bag tight in her hands. In the reflected dashboard light Louis could see now that she wasn't as young as he first thought, and that there was a flatness in her eyes that didn't come only from fatigue.

"What is your name?" Louis asked.

"Margareth Likiche." The last name came out sounding like "le quiche."

"What do you do here?" he asked.

She glanced at him.

"What work do you do here?"

"I clean the bathrooms."

Louis looked back at the narrow road. He switched on the high beams and with each pass of the wipers, he could see the undulating cane walls.

"Micronesia," he said. "That's a long ways away from here."

She was silent.

"How did you get your job here?" Louis asked.

Still nothing.

"Did someone bring you here?"

She looked at him. "Why are you asking me these questions?"

Louis hesitated. "I'm an investigator."

"Is this about the dead woman?"

Louis glanced at her but she was staring out the windshield now. "Yes," he said.

"I heard things. They say she was sliced open with a cane machete. They say she was trying to get away so they killed her."

"Who?" Louis asked.

"The men who brought her here."

"The same men who brought you here?"

She didn't answer.

Louis could see some lights ahead. He only had a few more minutes to talk to her. "How did you get here?" he asked. "How does it work?"

Louis heard her let out a breath and the rustle of the plastic bag in her lap.

"My family lived in Uman and we were fishermen and

farmers," she said. "We were poor but we managed. I am the oldest child and I was in school and one day, this man—a recruiter—told us about a program where we could go to the United States and they would pay for me to go to college."

Louis slowed the Bronco to buy time.

"Four of us signed up and went with him on a plane. He told us that we would learn to be nurses and make good money working in hospitals."

She shook her head slowly. "It was not what they promised. We were crowded into a little apartment far away from everything. We were sent to work in a nursing home. We emptied bedpans, lifted the old men into their beds, cleaned the old women when they dirtied the sheets. We did the work no one else would do."

"You were paid?" Louis asked.

"Four dollars an hour," she said. "But they took money out of our paychecks for our uniforms, food, electric, and the bus that took us to work. I tried to leave, but the recruiter told me I had signed a contract and couldn't leave until I paid it back."

"How did you come to work here?"

"After a year, they said we could make more money working at the sugar house." She let out a tired breath. "Someone bought my contract and I came here. Now there are many Micronesians here. They work in the fields and the sugar house. There are new ones coming all the time."

She was quiet for a moment, then pointed. "That is it," she said.

Louis pulled into the gravel lot. There were four low-slung green concrete buildings clustered around a dirt yard. Most of the small windows were bare, a few draped with sheets for privacy. The place had the despairing look of some of the public housing Louis had seen in Fort Myers, except for the towering walls of cane stalks that imprisoned the complex.

The woman was looking out the windshield at the weak lights coming from the windows.

"I want to go home," she said softly.

"Can you?" Louis asked.

Her eyes glistened in the dashboard lights. "I asked once. They told me I can buy out my contract. Six thousand dollars. Where does a person get six thousand dollars?"

She pulled up the collar of her raincoat and looked over at Louis. "Thank you for giving me a ride," she said.

Before Louis could answer, she got out, shutting the door. Louis watched her cross the path of his headlights, crouched against the wind. He watched her until she disappeared.

He sat there, peering out the windshield, watching the ugly green building blur and reappear with each swipe of the wipers. The instincts that had kicked in when he first saw her standing at the bus stop had mutated into an anger. Margareth Likiche was no better than a slave, kidnapped from her home with no way to get back. There were hundreds, maybe thousands, just like her working in shitty jobs no one else wanted to do. And there was a dead woman just like her laying in the Broward County morgue.

It had all started with that dead woman.

Wallace Sorrell and the secretary in Little Havana. The pizza delivery kid. The old people. The cop. They were all dead. And Ben was still missing.

Because of Austin.

Louis jerked the Bronco in reverse, the tires spitting gravel.

CHAPTER 42

The living room was quiet and dark, except for the flickering orange glow of a fire in the fireplace. The house smelled of lavender air freshener, the odor of sweat and stale coffee banished.

The cops were banished, too, standing their watch out in the cold rain. Susan wasn't letting anyone in now, into her home where they could drink her coffee, eat her food, intrude deeper into her life and her pain.

Louis looked toward her closed bedroom door. No light. He looked at Ben's door and saw a sliver of light under the door.

He drew in a breath to calm himself. The long drive back to Sereno Key had given him enough time to cool off; he wasn't going to bust in and beat the truth out of Austin while Susan was asleep in the next room. He would tell him quietly to come to the Florida room or outside.

Louis took a breath and pushed open the bedroom door.

Austin was standing at Ben's bed, a new suitcase open on the lower bunk, stacked with folded clothes. He looked up as Louis came in.

Louis's eyes flicked to the dresser. The black Vuitton

purse lay open, stuffed with bills, a dark blue passport nearby.

"You sonofabitch," Louis hissed. "You're walking out on her."

Austin looked at the bed, then the window, anywhere but at Louis.

"Does she know? Or are you just going to sneak out while she's asleep?" Louis asked.

"You're not supposed to be in this house," Austin said. "I'm going to get one of the cops—"

Austin started for the hall, but Louis put up an arm, blocking the door. "I have some questions."

Austin knocked his arm aside. "Fuck your questions."

Louis shoved him in the shoulder. Austin shoved back, a flat two-handed push to the chest. Louis winced but came back with both hands, gripping Austin by the shirt, forcing him back against the top bunk.

"What started all this?" Louis said.

Austin struggled to get free, but Louis jerked hard on the shirt, swinging him around and slamming him into the dresser. Austin's head bounced backward and the mirror behind him splintered into a spiderweb of glass. Ben's London bus, plastic transformers, and painted Styrofoam planets crashed to the floor.

"What did you do to piss these guys off?" Louis demanded.

"I told you I don't know!"

"There's a dead Micronesian woman in the Broward County morgue with her throat slashed."

"So what?" Austin said, pushing at Louis's fists.

"You brought her here," Louis said. "You brought her here and you know who killed her."

"I don't know—"

Louis smacked him. "Maybe *you* killed her. Or maybe you arranged to have Vargas do it and now Vargas wants you dead."

"Who?"

"Vargas! Adam Vargas."

"I don't know anyone named Vargas!"

"Byron Ellis?"

"No!"

"What about Leo Ryker. Know him?"

Austin stopped struggling, his eyes widening. He recognized *that* name.

"No," Austin said. "I don't know him either."

Louis punched him, and Austin stumbled sideways, falling into a telescope and landing on the floor. He stayed there, wiping at his lip.

"You lying bastard," Louis said. "Tell me what's going on or I'll beat you to a fucking pulp."

"Oh, Jesus . . ." Austin's eyes moved to the hallway. Louis turned.

Susan was standing in the doorway, hands in the pockets of her white robe, her hair a wild spray of black. Slowly, she pulled her nickel-plated revolver from the deep pocket of the robe and pointed the gun at Austin.

"Tell him what he wants to know," she said.

"Baby," Austin whispered.

"Tell him!"

Austin dropped his head back against the wall. "Blackbirds," he said softly. "We call them blackbirds."

"Who?" Louis asked. "What are you talking about?"

"That's what they used to call them in Australia," Austin said quietly. "It started a long time ago when the farmers couldn't get anyone to work in the cotton and sugar fields so they would go to Fiji or the Solomon Islands and kidnap the natives." Austin looked away. "They brought them back as indentured servants . . . blackbirds."

"What about now? What about the people *you* bring?" Louis asked.

"Same thing. No one wants to work in the fields or lousy jobs here either, so we bring them from Micronesia."

"On false promises," Louis said.

Austin shook his head. "You don't understand. They're hired into good jobs."

"They're enslaved."

"They got it good. Half of them don't want to work anyway."

Louis took a step toward him but stopped, uncurling his fist. "Who was the woman on Alligator Alley? Did you bring her here?"

"Yeah. Her and two others."

"Who were they for?"

"I don't know," Austin said.

"Don't lie," Susan said.

Louis glanced at her. She was holding the gun steady.

"Christ, I swear I don't know," Austin said. "I started getting phone calls back in November. Some guy wanting to know if I'd make a special delivery of three young women. Cash only. No paperwork. No questions."

"And you *agreed* to this?" Louis asked.

"He kept calling and he kept offering more money," Austin said. "I finally said yes. I found three girls who didn't have big families, didn't have any relatives over here, three I figured he'd like."

"Three he'd *like*?" Louis asked.

Austin looked at the floor, drawing a ragged breath. "Hell, I figured he was looking for prostitutes or sex slaves or something like that."

"You bastard," Susan whispered.

Louis looked at her, wondering if he should take the gun away from her. He decided not to.

"Who called you?" Louis asked.

"I don't know," Austin said. "It could've been any one of fifty guys we've worked with over the last few years. He could've been an independent who heard about me."

"Could it have been Leo Ryker?" Louis asked.

Austin glanced at him, then looked away. "Maybe. We've

worked with Cane Corp. before, but I never met the guy so I couldn't tell you for sure."

"Who *did* you deliver the girls to?"

"I was told to meet a man on Alligator Alley. He was supposed to give me the money, and I was supposed to give him the girls."

"What did he look like?"

"He was . . ." Austin leaned an arm on the upper bunk. "He was the same guy that came in here dressed as a cop."

"Adam Vargas."

Austin shrugged. "I didn't know his name. But when the sketch was done, I recognized him as the guy who . . ."

"Who what?"

"Killed the first girl," Austin said. "He killed her right in front of me, had her laying over the front of the car when he cut her throat."

Susan let out a small gasp, and fell gently against the door frame, lowering the gun.

"What did you do then?" Louis asked.

"I got the hell out of there," Austin said. "Left the other two girls with the guy and bailed."

Louis could only stare at him.

"Well, what would you have done?" Austin said, looking from Louis to Susan. "He would've killed me next. I saw him do it."

The bedroom fell silent. Susan was staring at the floor, the gun limp in her hands. Louis reached over and took it away from her, sticking it in his belt. He looked back at Austin.

"Why didn't you tell us all this when they first took Benjamin?" he demanded.

Austin shook his head and his words came out in a whisper. "Because I never believed Ben was alive . . . not after the first night. Not after what I saw that guy do out on the alley."

Louis stepped closer to him. "You were wrong. He was alive two nights later and I think he's still alive."

Austin looked up at Louis, tears in his eyes. "I don't."

"Is that why you're leaving?" Susan said.

"There's nothing else I can do here," Austin said.

"My God, what's wrong with you?" Susan said. "Even if our son is dead, they will find him. Don't you want to be here when they *do* bring him home?"

Austin went to touch her but she pulled away and he dropped his arms. "I don't know if I can face them bringing him home."

Susan bit her lip, tears streaking her face. "You're right. You were never there for him when he was alive. Why be there for him when he's dead."

"That isn't what you can't face," Louis said.

"Stay out of this," Austin snapped. "This is between my wife and me."

Louis reached for the passport. Austin tried to take it from him, but Louis jerked it away.

"You're afraid they're going to charge you with something," Louis said. "You're afraid of going to jail."

Austin glared at him. No tears now. "Give me my passport."

Louis put a finger in Austin's chest. "Let's name a few possibilities. Accessory to murder, conspiracy to commit murder, obstruction of justice. Kidnapping? Slavery? Smuggling? Transporting of illegal immigrants?"

"Bringing those people into this country is legal. I can't control what happens to them after that."

"The cops won't see it that way."

Austin held out his hand. "Give me my damn passport."

Louis held the passport out to Susan. "Your choice, Susan. Let him go or make him stay."

For a moment, she didn't move. Then she put out her hand and Louis gave her the passport. She curled it tight in her fist, and picked up the Vuitton purse off the dresser.

"Baby, c'mon, don't do this to me," Austin said.

She turned and left the bedroom.

Austin started after her, but Louis stepped in front of him.

"No."

Austin's eyes dropped to Susan's revolver in Louis's belt.

"Try it," Louis said.

Austin spun away from him, and leaned against the bed with both arms. Louis watched him for a moment. Head down, arms tight, his breath shaky.

Louis left the bedroom, closing the door behind him. Susan was standing in front of the fireplace. She turned to face him as he came up behind her, holding out the passport and Vuitton purse.

"Take these," she said. "I don't want him to find a way to get them back."

Louis took the bag, stuffed the passport inside, and zipped it. He looked back at her. She was silhouetted against the dying flames, the glow giving her whole body a soft orange aura. He couldn't see her face clearly.

"Please thank Detective Frye for me," she said.

"Detective Frye?"

"She called me this morning," Susan said. "She told me about . . . timing, a TV newscast . . . that Ben must've said something . . . must've been alive . . . and that . . ."

"Hush," Louis whispered.

"She didn't want me to think you . . ."

He pulled her to him, and she laid her head on his shoulder.

CHAPTER 43

Vargas couldn't feel the cold anymore. As he crouched in the shadows at the side of the cottage, he couldn't feel the cold or the rain running down the back of his neck, soaking his denim jacket. He was shivering, but it was a shiver of anticipation.

Byron would have been proud of him. He had done things right this time, had used his brain and thought things out.

First, he had stolen a car. He couldn't risk being seen in the Camaro anymore. Then, after he drove out to Captiva, he had found a bar without very many people inside. The waitress was nice and helpful when he told her he wanted to hire the black private eye but didn't know where he lived. She had even gone out in the parking lot to point down the road to the cottage. He had been careful to smile and thank her.

The rain was coming down harder now.

He blinked it away and crept up to look in the bedroom window. There was a light on inside and through the gap in the curtains he could see the corner of an unmade bed and beyond into a bathroom. He could hear a TV on out in the living room. But he had seen no one inside.

He slipped down against the side of the cottage looking out toward the front yard. He couldn't see the gulf, but he could smell it, almost taste the salt in the cold air. And he thought about Byron and how much Byron liked beaches.

If he had time, he'd leave her body there. Out near the water. Kinda like a tribute.

A phone rang, inside the cottage. Two times, then it stopped. Vargas rose and peered in. There was no one in the bedroom but he could hear a voice.

Then, there she was. She came into the bedroom, carrying the phone, the cord snaking behind her.

She looked different than she had on TV. She was tall and her hair was down around her shoulders, not in a ponytail like it had been on TV. She was wearing black jeans and a little T-shirt thing. Her gun was on her belt.

He heard Austin Outlaw's name. Then his own name. Then she hung up the phone and set it on the end of the bed.

Vargas's eyes shot back to the bedroom doorway. He saw no one else. When he looked back, she was gone. He moved to try to get a better angle and suddenly, she was back, coming out of the bathroom now, pulling the T-shirt over her head. She wore a little black bra, and she discarded that, too. Then the gun belt, and jeans came off. Then the black panties.

Her body was pale. She was skinny, too, but not so much that she looked sick. She picked up a white bathrobe and put it on, disappearing back into the bathroom.

Vargas put his fingers on the bottom of the window and tried to lift it. It opened easily and quietly. He climbed inside, drawing his knife. There was only one light on, a small blue lamp on the dresser near the door. He could hear the shower running.

The phone rang again. His heart jumped, and he spun first toward the bathroom door then back to the phone. He had to stop it. He hurried to the bed, grabbed the cord, and cut it. When he looked back, she was coming back into the bedroom, still in the robe, but carrying a towel.

Her eyes locked on him, then went to the knife in his hand.

"Vargas."

He didn't answer her. He moved to her.

She started sidestepping in her bare feet, wrapping the towel around her forearm as she moved, her eyes never leaving his face. He thought first she was going to run, but then her eyes gave her away. It wasn't the door she wanted.

It was the gun on the bed.

She lunged to the bed but he caught her robe and flung her backward. She smashed into the dresser, knocking over the lamp and sending bottles crashing to the terrazzo floor.

He came at her, but she threw up her towel-wrapped arm, deflecting the knife. He grabbed her robe to keep her from twisting away, and his knife plunged into her shoulder.

She screamed and spun back. He brought the knife up again. Then something smashed into the side of his head— glass shattering, stabs of pain, darkness. He reeled back, his hand on his face.

Blue glass all over the floor, the broken lamp laying there. His hand red. Blood . . . *his* blood.

Now the bedroom was dark but in the light spilling in from the bathroom, he saw something white move. She was going for the gun. He threw himself at her and they fell against the wooden footboard of the bed and onto the floor. Her hands caught the edge of the spread, and she pulled it down with her. Everything—clothes, shoes, suitcase, and gun tumbled to the floor.

She tried to scramble away but he was quick and shoved her back against the footboard.

He stabbed at her, the knife plunging into the robe, her arms, the floor. She was hitting him, kicking him, and he tried to get control, tried to pin her against the wooden slats. She slid down, trying to get away, trying to shield herself.

He was above her, on his knees, his left hand flat on her chest, and for an instant he could see her face, eyes wild, skin and hair streaked with blood. He brought the knife down, not caring where it hit.

Her hands flew to his wrist, and she stopped the downward thrust of the knife, her elbows locked and shuddering under his weight.

He tried to pull back to free the knife, but she held on.

Shit. Shit!

He hit her with his free hand, hard on the jaw. But she held on, her fingers tight on his wrist. He rose higher on his knees to get leverage and she brought up a knee, trying to wedge it against his chest.

Strong . . . she was so strong. Not like that little thing out on the Alley. But he was stronger. And he was mad now, blind mad.

He shoved her knee away and threw all his weight behind one last thrust of the knife.

But the knife didn't go down, didn't hit flesh. His gloved hand crashed through the bed slats. He couldn't move it, couldn't get free.

He threw out his free hand to break his fall against the bed. The knife was still wedged between the slats, and he couldn't pull it out.

Motherfucker!

He locked eyes with her for a second. Not wild now. And not afraid.

He was twisting his hand, trying to free the knife. Then a blow to his gut doubled him over and emptied his lungs. Another kick to his stomach and the knife dropped from his hand. He fell backward, gasping.

A blur of white and he knew she was getting away, but he couldn't breathe, couldn't move fast enough.

She was tossing the clothes and sheets, looking for her gun.

He started to crawl after her, but she grabbed something off the floor.

He caught the glint of black metal. *Shit, the gun!*

He struggled to his feet and he ran toward the living room. He was at the door when he heard the explosion, felt a bullet rip into his shoulder blade. He tumbled forward, crashing out onto the porch and ripping through the screen door as more bullets popped behind him.

The cold rain hit his hot face as he ran. He found his way back to the road, staying in the shadows. Finally, he fell into the sand behind some bushes. He sat still, his lungs burning, head pounding, his shoulder smoldering.

Get away . . . he had to get away. Get back to the mainland.

He had to get to the airport so Uncle Leo's plane could take him away.

CHAPTER 44

Louis pulled the Bronco into the gravel drive and turned off the engine. The living room light was on in the cottage, but the bedroom was dark. She was probably asleep. He got out and hurried onto the porch. He stopped.

The front door was wide open and the TV was on.

He stepped inside, looking around the living room.

Nothing was out of place, but . . .

He heard a noise. A moan that for a second he thought was the cat. Then it came again.

He stepped toward the bedroom, drawing his gun. He slipped around the corner, leveling the Glock in the darkness.

"Joe?"

"Here."

Her voice sounded small, weak.

His left hand went out to turn on the blue lamp on the dresser but he couldn't find it. He moved to the bathroom, pushing open the door. Light flooded into the room, across the terrazzo floor, the bed, and over her.

She was sitting on the floor at the foot of the bed, her legs drawn up, gun resting on her knees. Her face was dark, puffy, her hair wet, limp around her face. His white robe was streaked with blood.

"Vargas," she whispered. "He's gone."

Louis went to her, dropping to one knee. He took her gun and set it on the end of the bed and holstered his own.

He touched her chin, gently, carefully, tilting it up to the light. Her cheek was cut, ugly bruises forming around her right eye, and her lip. Blood and glass speckled her hair.

Something started to burn inside him, burning his chest, his eyes.

"I hurt him," she said. "Shot him."

The burning in his eyes were tears. *God, her face was . . . Jesus.* He tried to take a breath, but that burned, too.

"How long ago?"

She didn't answer.

"Joe, how long ago?"

"Thirty . . . minutes . . . maybe."

Louis looked around for the phone and grabbed the cord, pulling it to him until he saw the severed end.

He stood. "I'll be right back. I've got to call for help."

He hurried to the cottage next door, fumbling for the keys he used as the resort's security guard, and let himself in. His hands were shaking as he dialed the number to the sheriff's office. When he got back, she had her gun back in her hands. He took it away from her again.

"Where else are you cut?"

She leaned forward and he could see the back of the robe was soaked in blood.

"Oh God," he whispered.

He started to ease the robe down but she flinched. "Hold tight," he said. He gently pulled the robe open around her neck. The skin on the back of her shoulder was slashed open, the gaping wound oozing blood. There were three or four more smaller cuts around her collar bone and chest.

The burning inside him was growing, hardening now into pure anger. He had to take several small breaths to stay calm.

"Help me," she said. "Help me up."

He lifted her gently and tried to lay her down on the bed, but she pushed him away, wanting to sit up. He helped her scoot across the mess of sheets, grabbing a pillow off the floor to wedge behind her back. She leaned back against the headboard, shutting her eyes.

He reached across and switched on the small lamp on the nightstand.

Her face was a horrid chalky white. He was worried she was going to pass out. He put a hand to her forehead. Her skin was like ice. He quickly got the blanket off the floor and covered her.

For the first time, he got a good look at the bedroom. Blood was smeared across the terrazzo floor like a wild red painting. The picture frames were bent, the glass shattered. The blue ceramic lamp was crushed, the pieces scattered, the shade twisted. The bedspread, sheets, and his clothes were splashed with blood.

Every part of him raged with anger.

He wanted to kill him.

He walked to the dresser and jerked open a drawer. He pulled out a box of ammo and the extra magazines for the Glock. He started shoving bullets into the empty magazines. He could hear sirens.

"Louis."

"I'm going after him, Joe."

"Louis."

He spun to her. "Goddamn it, Joe, the sonofabitch hurt you. He hurt Ben, he hurt Susan. He was *here!* He came in here and did this. He was here."

"Louis . . . don't."

He ignored her

"This isn't how you do it. There are rules." He could hear the pain in her voice.

"I don't have any rules right now."

He stuck the loaded magazines in the back of his jeans and put the box of bullets in his jacket pocket.

The sirens were loud now, close.

"Where?" she asked.

"What?"

"Where are you going?"

He didn't answer. He was going to start with Uncle Leo in Naples. If Vargas was hurting now, he might do what he had always done—run back to Uncle Leo. But if he told Joe that, she might send the sheriff's office right behind him. And they'd have to notify Collier County. And they'd have to fight for a warrant. And Vargas would get away. Again.

"I don't know," he said.

He heard footsteps and voices on the porch.

"Rescue!" someone yelled.

"In here," Louis yelled back.

Two men rushed in. They took one look at Joe and surrounded her, blocking Louis's view of her face.

Another siren was coming. The sheriff's office, probably. Louis started to turn away and spotted Joe's shield on the floor. He bent to pick it up, using his finger to wipe a smear of blood off the gold. He glanced at her, but she couldn't see him. He stuck the shield in his pocket.

He went over to Joe. She was still on the bed, a blood pressure cuff on her arm, the two paramedics hovering. The whole right side of her face was swollen and red. He wanted to hold her. He put one hand gently on her hair instead.

He could read her eyes, read what she was trying to tell him. Don't go.

But not *don't leave me;* don't go do what you're going to do.

He gave her a soft kiss on the top of her head and left the cottage. He was just a half-mile down the road when he passed a Lee County cruiser going in the opposite direction. He kept driving.

CHAPTER 45

Vargas was crouched in the caboose, the last car on the children's train in Lakes Park. He was soaked through and shivering. The pain in his shoulder was just a steady, pounding throb now. There was no sound except the rain on the metal roof of the caboose. There was no light, except the small white lights floating up in the dark sky. He struggled to focus on them. Streetlights . . . that's all they were.

He had lost track of time but he had the feeling it had been hours since he had left the cottage. He could remember dragging himself back to the car and speeding east, trying to get to I-75. But then he had seen the spotlight sweeping the trees along Summerlin, and he had heard the police helicopter. He knew they would find him, knew there would be road blocks ahead. He knew it would be impossible to get to Uncle Leo.

Then he saw the park. And he *knew* it. He had been in this same park just six days ago. He could hide here, in the dark trees, out of sight of the helicopter and its light. And he knew there was a phone here, too.

Uncle Leo?
Where are you?
Lakes Park . . . Fort Myers . . . I'm hurt.

What happened?
They're looking for me. Helicopters. Cops.
Silence.
Uncle Leo, please, I'm scared.
Silence.
Please.
Stay in the park. I'm coming.

Uncle Leo was coming. Vargas tried to look at his watch, but the glass was fogged and he couldn't see it. God, he was cold, so cold. He closed his eyes, struggling to stay awake.

When he opened them he saw the white lights again. No . . . low now. Headlights.

He crawled from the caboose, easing his way to the road as the lights grew closer. He stayed behind a tree until the car passed and he could see the shape. It was square, boxy. A Jeep . . . Uncle Leo's Jeep.

He watched the taillights until they were just specks, then he saw the Jeep do a U-turn and come back his way. He stepped onto the road, into the headlights.

The Jeep stopped.

Vargas started toward the passenger door, but the driver's side door opened.

"Uncle Leo?"

"Stay where you are, Adam."

Uncle Leo was coming toward him, his black rain poncho billowing in the wind, huge and shiny and dark.

"Uncle Leo, I'm cold."

Uncle Leo stopped in front of him, face shadowed by his hat. He put a gloved hand on Vargas's left shoulder and pushed him down.

The wounded shoulder exploded with pain, driving Vargas to his knees.

"I'm sorry. I'm sorry," Vargas cried, holding his hand over his shoulder. "I was coming back, I swear."

Uncle Leo walked behind him. Vargas didn't dare turn, didn't try to get up. A hand came down firm on the back of his neck. Then a hard, icy jab at his temple.

"What are you doing, Uncle Leo?"

"You're going to shoot yourself, Adam," Uncle Leo said. "Just like your crazy mother did."

"Oh, God . . ."

"Shut up."

Vargas hunched forward, trying to gulp back his tears but he couldn't stop them.

"Don't cry, you fucking faggot."

He knew. Oh, God, he knew.

"Sit up. Act like man, goddamn it."

Vargas didn't move. Uncle Leo jerked on the collar of Vargas's denim jacket and pulled him upright. The barrel came back against his temple, harder this time.

Vargas closed his eyes, his heart hammering. "Stop! He's alive!" he yelled.

"Outlaw?"

Vargas held his breath.

"Do you have him?" Uncle Leo asked.

Vargas nodded.

The gun moved away from his head.

"Take me to him," Uncle Leo said.

CHAPTER 46

Her face was round and brown, her eyes dark and suspicious as she looked out at him through the leaded glass of the door. Louis held up Joe's gold shield again so she could see it better.

"Police, ma'am. Please open the door," he said, raising his voice over the sound of the rain.

The door clicked open and she stared up at him, clutching the lapels of her pink robe. She opened the door just enough to let him in. Louis stood, dripping on the white marble. The foyer was illuminated by a gold chandelier, but the rest of the house beyond looked dark. Normal for any house at two A.M. Not normal for Leo Ryker's house if he were hiding his murdering nephew.

"I need to speak with Mr. Ryker, please," Louis said.

"It is very late," the maid said. She was Micronesian, an older version of the woman he had talked to at the refinery.

"I know. This is official police business. Get your boss, please."

"He isn't here."

Louis tried to gauge if she was lying, but her smooth face gave nothing away. "What about his nephew? Is he here?" he asked.

She shook her head.

Louis's eyes went to the dark rooms beyond the foyer. He could see the outlines of furniture in the huge living room and floor-to-ceiling windows that looked out onto the black expanse of the gulf.

He saw a sliver of light beneath a closed door down a short hallway to the left. He started toward it.

"Wait! You can't—"

He ignored her, going to the double doors and pushing them open. Shaded lamps cast shadows. Heavy wood book-cases and a massive desk. A sprawling map behind the desk. Thick green carpet under his feet. A bank of French doors. And heads . . . animal heads.

Louis stared up at them. They covered almost every inch of the dark paneled walls. Birds of every size and shape. Small game from badgers to fox. Antelope with great spears of horns. Deer with towering racks of antlers. Water buffalo with giant hulking heads. Rams with graceful curls of horns as thick as a man's thigh.

Louis's eyes settled on the black hairy head of a boar. Its glass eyes stared back, dead and black.

He didn't see the small man with the red hair sitting in a chair in the corner. Rusty rose slowly, staying in the shadows. He just stood there, calm, slightly stoop-shouldered.

"Is he dead?" he asked.

"What?" Louis said.

"Is he dead?"

"Who?"

Rusty wiped a hand over his face.

Louis took a step toward him. "Who?"

"Adam," Rusty said quietly. "Is he dead?"

"Why would he be?"

Rusty held his eyes. "You're a cop, right?"

Louis ignored the question. "What are you doing here?"

Rusty emerged from the shadows, moving toward the desk by the windows. He moved slowly, head down. At the desk, he hesitated then picked up a brandy snifter. He raised it to his lips, started to take a drink, then grimaced and set the glass down.

"I can't," he said softly, shaking his head.

Louis's eyes went to the bottle of Pierre Ferrand cognac and the second glass on the desk. He knew Leo had been here, been here with Rusty. "Can't what?" Louis asked.

Rusty had turned away. "I can't do this for him," he said softly. "Not this time."

"Can't do what?" Louis asked.

Rusty was just standing there, looking at him.

"Talk to me, Rusty," Louis said. "Things will go a lot easier on everyone if you do."

Rusty's eyes roved over the room, looking up at all the animal heads.

"I've known Leo for nearly twenty years," he said. "I was a guide working out of this crummy camp up at Okeechobee. Leo used to come out with his friends to hunt hogs and they hired me to take them out. He paid good. Real good."

Louis didn't have time for this, but he forced himself to listen.

"He brought me into the business about five years ago." Rusty gave a small shrug. "Don't get me wrong, I was grateful and the money is damn good. But being inside in a factory all day ain't what I call life."

The wind crested, sending the blades of the palm fronds slashing against the tall windows.

"Why are you here tonight, Rusty?" Louis asked.

"Leo called me. Asked me to come."

"What for?"

Rusty wouldn't look at him.

"You said you can't do something, Rusty? What *can't* you do?"

Rusty's eyes went to one of the animal heads mounted on the wall behind the desk. "That was his first kill," he said, pointing to the boar. "I was one of the guides on that hunt. That's where I met Leo."

His eyes drifted to a larger boar with tusks. "He got a

taste for it real quick. Pretty soon after, he hired me as his personal guide."

Rusty shook his head. "Hogs weren't enough after a while. So we'd go up to this place up near Ocala, this private lodge where they brought in big game from Africa and places and then you could pick what you wanted to go after and pay by the kill."

He pointed to one head. "That there's an African Impala. Cost Leo five thousand. Over there's a wildebeest. Cost more than seven thousand for that one."

Rusty let out a long breath. "Some men just got more money than they know what to do with, I guess."

"You didn't answer my question," Louis said, trying to be patient. "Why'd Leo call you tonight?"

"He wanted me to go get Adam," Rusty said. "Adam called here around two and then Leo called me to come over. He said he'd give me a thousand dollars to go get him."

"From where?"

"I don't know. I told him no."

"Were you supposed to bring Adam back here?"

"No," Rusty said. "He wanted me to take him out to Starvation Prairie."

"What's that?"

"A place on some land Leo owns. He has a hunting cabin out there."

"And do what?"

Rusty shook his head. "I don't know. I was just supposed to meet Leo there."

"Where is this place?"

Rusty shook his head slowly. "Man, you'd never find it."

Louis looked up at the map behind Leo's desk. "That Leo's land?"

Rusty nodded.

"Show me where this prairie is," Louis said.

Rusty went to the map and pointed to a blue area. "That's Fakahatchee Preserve. State land." He indicated the sprawl of yellow below it. "That's Leo's land. The north part is swamp, but the south part is open higher ground. That's why they call 'em prairies." Rusty was silent for a moment. "That's where the best hunting always was."

When he looked back at Louis, his eyes held memories, but Louis couldn't tell if what Rusty was remembering was something he cherished or wanted to forget.

"Take me there," Louis said.

CHAPTER 47

The drive was endless, stretching deep in the blackness, the cypress trees along the side of the road rising up like monsters in the headlights.

Tell me where Outlaw is, Adam.

I'll show you when we get there, Uncle Leo.

Tell me now.

I tell you now, you kill me now.

Vargas closed his eyes. He was exhausted. His face was starting to swell from where the lady cop had hit him, and the wound in his shoulder ached. It was only the growing knot of fear in his belly keeping him awake.

The Jeep pulled off the gravel road, hitting a bump that jarred new pain into his shoulder, then came to stop. For a second, Vargas could see thickets and trees stretching endlessly before them. Then the lights disappeared.

"All right," Uncle Leo said, turning in his seat. "Where is he?"

"With the women," Vargas said.

"Why?"

Vargas felt dizzy. "What?

"Why did you bring him here? Why didn't you just kill him like I told you to do?"

Vargas struggled to think. "I thought you'd want to be sure this time, Uncle Leo. I thought you'd want to see him yourself."

Uncle Leo was quiet for a moment, staring out into the darkness. "Get out," he said finally.

Vargas climbed out and closed the door. Uncle Leo walked to the back of the Jeep, then reappeared, holding a Coleman lantern and his crossbow.

Vargas looked at the bow. "What's that for?"

"We're going blackbirding, Adam."

Vargas stared at him. "What?"

"I'm going to have a little fun while I'm cleaning up your mess." Uncle Leo nudged him with the tip of the bow. "Walk."

Vargas started into the brush, pushing aside palm fronds and branches. Even in the darkness, he knew where he was. It was the path that led to his cabin and the shack. It was the same path he had taken the two women down that first night after he picked them up on the alley.

Vargas could hear the crunch of Uncle Leo's boots behind him, feel his own heart pounding in his chest. What the hell was he going to do when they got to the shack and Uncle Leo found out he had lied, found out that Outlaw wasn't there?

They had reached the fork. Vargas stopped.

"What's the matter?" Uncle Leo demanded.

Vargas couldn't move. Couldn't think.

"Let's go," Uncle Leo said, poking him in the back with the bow.

Vargas started down the fork, more slowly now.

"You know, Adam," Uncle Leo said. "Maybe I should've taken you hunting a long time ago."

"I've killed things before," Vargas said weakly.

"But you haven't hunted."

Vargas was quiet.

"If I had taken you hunting, maybe you wouldn't have turned out to be such a fuck-up," Uncle Leo said. "Hunting helps a boy understand himself at his most primitive level. Helps him know what he is."

"I know what I am."

Uncle Leo laughed. "Yeah, you're a queer."

Vargas turned around. "Is that why you're going to punish me?"

Uncle Leo stopped and held the lantern up so he could see Vargas's face.

"Is it?" Vargas asked. "Is that why?"

Uncle Leo leveled the crossbow, the tip of its arrow an inch from Vargas's belly. "Let's get to where we're going, Adam," he said. "It'll be light soon."

Vargas turned and walked on, throwing aside the branches. The ground became more solid, and he knew they were close. Close to the shack. But also close to his cabin.

He wiped his face, trying to clear his mind, trying to come up with a plan. His cabin . . . that's what he would do. The cabin was less than a half mile from the shack. He would take Uncle Leo to the shack and tell him Outlaw was tied up inside. And when Uncle Leo went inside to get him, he'd run. Run to his cabin. Then he'd figure out how to get away.

Vargas stepped through a cluster of trees and stopped, the shack a few yards in front of him. Uncle Leo came up next to him and turned up the knob on the lantern, bathing the shack in light.

Vargas had seen the shack in daylight many times. But now, in the dark, illuminated by the white lantern light, it looked different—its rotting gray planks seeming to expand and contract like a breathing animal, its warped door hanging open like a slit of a black mouth.

"He's in there," Vargas said, nodding.

Uncle Leo took a step toward the cabin. Vargas glanced toward the trees on his left.

"Open the door, Adam."

Vargas hesitated, then pulled on the old door. It was hanging on one rusted hinge and opened easily. Vargas took a step back.

"Now go in and bring him out," Uncle Leo said.

"What?"

Uncle Leo pulled a small flashlight from his jacket and tossed it at Vargas. Vargas caught it and stared at Uncle Leo.

"Go in and bring him out here."

Vargas looked at the shack then back at Uncle Leo. He shook his head slowly.

"Get in the shack, Adam."

Vargas shook his head harder.

Uncle Leo leveled the crossbow at Vargas. A sharp zip. Vargas jumped back against the shack. When he opened his eyes, the arrow was in the dirt between his legs.

"I said, get in the shack." Uncle Leo drew out another arrow.

Vargas dove into the shack. He pulled the door shut behind him, throwing his weight against it, trying to catch his breath.

Dark. He couldn't see anything. But he could smell. He gagged, hand to his mouth.

It smelled like . . .

It smelled like the trailer did when his stepfather was gutting the hogs.

Hog blood in the dirt. On the sink. On his stepfather's hands.

It smelled like . . .

It smelled like the other one, the other shack.

You stay in there. They'll get you if you don't.

Outside, Uncle Leo laughed. And Vargas knew that Uncle Leo had never believed him that Outlaw was ever here. He just wanted to bring *him* here. But not to just punish him this time. To kill him.

Vargas started to shake. He fumbled with the flashlight, finally turning it on. He forced himself to move the beam up, over the walls.

Big metal hooks.

You tell anyone, I'll hang you up just like them hogs.

The light jumped down, over the wooden skinning table.

Knives. Lots of knives. All sizes and shapes. Brown with rust. Brown with blood.

This here is your birthday knife, boy, a skinning knife.

Take your pants down, boy.

Don't you dare tell on me, boy.

Shoot yourself. Just like your crazy mother did.

You're a queer, that's what you are.

Laughter. Laughter.

He couldn't even tell anymore if it was coming from inside his head or outside the door. He dropped the flashlight. His hands came up and he held his head, squeezing his eyes shut. Something shattered and the pieces fell around him, bright pieces of things that glittered in the dark and then disappeared.

He took his hands down. He opened his eyes. In the beam of light he saw a knife. It was standing on its tip. He stared at it, fascinated. He focused on the edge of the blade, hearing the clean sound the blade made on the whetstone, feeling it getting sharper, feeling his mind getting clearer, honing all his thoughts to one shining purpose.

Vargas jerked the knife out of the wood table. He looked at the door.

"Uncle Leo," he called out.

No answer.

"Uncle Leo! Come in here. I think Outlaw is dead."

Another short silence.

"Drag him out," Uncle Leo yelled.

"I can't Uncle Leo. My shoulders hurt. Open the door for me, Uncle Leo, so I can back out."

Through the cracks in the boards, he could see Uncle Leo set the lantern on the ground. But he didn't put the bow down. He carried it sideways in one hand.

Vargas set his flashlight on the table, the beam pointed at the door. He slid up against the front wall, knife poised.

He heard footsteps, then saw Uncle Leo's fingers come around the edge of the door. The door creaked open. Uncle Leo gave the door a final shove and Vargas moved into the doorway. Standing on the raised floorboards, he found him-self looking down at Uncle Leo. He moved slightly so the flashlight beam hit Uncle Leo full in the eyes.

Uncle Leo blinked in the beam. He saw the knife, and the crossbow flew up to block it but Vargas was quicker, plung-ing the knife into his belly. Vargas grabbed Uncle Leo's neck with his other hand, jerking his body tighter. And deeper onto the long rusted blade.

Uncle Leo gasped, his eyes rolling up to Vargas's face. They glistened with anger. And disbelief.

Vargas twisted the knife, pushing it deeper, his gloved hand warm and wet as it nearly slid inside the wound.

The crossbow tumbled to the dirt. Uncle Leo hands came up, his fingers gripping Vargas's denim jacket, his face close, wet, his breath hot against Vargas's face.

"You bastard," Uncle Leo whispered.

Then he went limp, falling against Vargas. Vargas tried to step back, but he was off balance and Uncle Leo was heavy. Vargas fell backward, Uncle Leo's lifeless body crushing him to the floor of the shack.

Uncle Leo was wheezing, his head limp against Vargas's shoulder, his hair damp against Vargas's cheek. The knife was still inside Uncle Leo, sandwiched between their bod-ies.

Vargas didn't move. Didn't want to move.

He stared up at the hooks on the wall, feeling Uncle Leo's breaths grow thinner and thinner.

Then they stopped.

Vargas closed his eyes, then after a moment, rolled him off. He sat up, scooting back against the wall, his gaze drawn to the bright white light outside.

He felt a jump of panic, thinking maybe he was the one who had died and the white light was the one that came and got you. Then things came back into focus and he knew it was just the lantern outside he was seeing.

He heard something, something moving outside. Sounds

in the brush, something out there. He stayed as still as he could, his ears straining to hear what was out there.

Just stay in the shack, Adam, and they won't get you.

He opened his eyes and in one quick move, scrambled across the floor. He grabbed the lantern and the bow and drew back inside the shack. He pulled the door closed as tight as he could get it, and held it for a second, listening.

He couldn't hear them anymore.

He turned, and sat back down next to Uncle Leo.

Some things just need killing.

Tears brimmed his eyes. His skin burned and he closed his eyes tight. He jabbed the tip of the knife into the wood floor with every whisper.

Act like a man.

Act like a man.

Act like a man.

Gonna teach you, boy . . .

He looked over at Uncle Leo's body. Slowly, his hand shaking, he reached over and slit the black poncho up the middle.

CHAPTER 48

"That's Leo's Jeep."

The headlights picked up a bulk of dark green on the side of the rutted road and Rusty pulled his truck in behind it. Louis couldn't see anyone in the Jeep or in the heavy brush.

"All right, Where'd they go?" Louis asked.

Rusty pointed into the darkness. "There's a path there. It leads out to a clearing."

"What's there?"

"A cabin. Leo used to bring his buddies out here when he was hunting hogs. He ain't used it in a long time though."

Louis looked at the blackness, then down at the CB radio on Rusty's dash. "Does that work?"

"Yeah. Who do you want to get a message to?"

"Lee County sheriff's office. Just get them out here."

Louis started to open the truck door but Rusty grabbed his arm. He reached back and pulled out something dark. "Wear this. There's a cap in the pocket."

Louis hesitated then took the camouflage rain jacket. He got out of the truck and put on the jacket and the ball cap. The rain was starting to pick up again.

Rusty came around the front of the truck. He was training a flashlight into the brush, his head hunched down in his collar.

"I ain't been out here in years," he said.

Louis pulled Susan's revolver from the waistband of his jeans and put it in the right jacket pocket. Zipping the jacket, he slipped the Glock from his holster.

"Okay, let's go," he said.

Louis could barely make out Rusty's back as he followed him into the dark brush, so he watched the jerk of his flashlight against the trees. The rain splattering on his jacket sounded deafening in the silence.

"How far?" Louis asked.

"About three-quarters of a mile."

If there was a path, Louis couldn't see it. But Rusty was moving easily through the heavy brush.

"The news said Adam kidnapped that boy," Rusty said. "That true?"

"Yes," Louis said.

"And killed all those people?"

"Yes."

"I'm not sure Adam would do all that on his own. Someone else had to have been behind it."

"Someone was," Louis said. "Leo."

"Leo? Why would Leo want all those people dead?"

"He wanted *one* person dead, Rusty." Louis said. "Vargas let it all get out of control."

Rusty was quiet.

"That's why I think he wanted you to bring Vargas here tonight so he could protect him. Hide him from the cops."

"No," Rusty said. "Maybe he would have once, but not anymore."

"Then why would Leo bring him out here?"

Rusty stopped and turned. "To kill him. To solve the problem for good."

"Problem? He took Vargas in when he was a kid."

"Yeah, but he didn't really want him around. He told me once Adam was nothing but white trash."

Louis could see just enough of Rusty's face to know Leo

probably had included him in that category even if he had never said it.

"Adam got in trouble a lot," Rusty said, moving on. "Nothing real bad, just normal kid shit. But Leo got sick of it and worked up a really good punishment."

Rusty swung the flashlight beam slowly over the black trees. "Every time Adam acted out, Leo'd bring him out here and put him in a shack out on Starvation Prairie. He'd leave him here for days."

Louis stared at him. "Locked in a shack?"

"No lock. Didn't need it. Leo just told him if he left the shack the hogs would get him." Rusty was quiet for a second. "No lights, no food. No one to hear you cry."

"How long did this go on?" Louis asked.

"About two years. The last time, Leo left him out here a month. When we came back to get him—" Rusty took a breath. "I don't know, it was like the boy was just broken. He crawled out, crying stuff like I'll be a good boy."

"So Leo took him back to Naples?"

Rusty shook his head. "No, he moved him to the cabin in the clearing. He was alone but at least it was a real place to live. I used to come out once a month and bring him food and stuff." Rusty paused. "He seemed okay, I guess."

They came to a wide clearing. It was dark but Louis could make out the outline of a cabin set back against the trees.

"That was Adam's cabin," Rusty said, pointing. "He lived there till he was eighteen and went off to prison. No one's used it since."

Louis went to the door of the cabin. The rain made it impossible to hear if anyone was inside. He crept up to a window and stole a look. Dark. One room. But it looked empty. He slid to the door, Glock ready. The door gave with one hard kick and he swung the gun in.

Nothing. No movement or sound. He ventured in, his eyes sweeping the dark room. He saw a lamp and then the wall switch. He slapped it on and the room came to life.

Rough wood walls and floor. A small bed with a wad of
sheets and blanket. A table with some soda cans and potato
chip bags. A TV near the fireplace. A cassette player and a
scattering of tapes on the floor.

Louis went to the tiny bathroom and switched on the bare
bulb light. The white sink was stained blue. There were broken Bic pens in the basin and wads of toilet paper stained
blue and red.

Switching off the lights, Louis left the cabin and went
back to Rusty waiting in the middle of the clearing.

"Where's the shack?" Louis asked.

"There's three of 'em spread out over the hunting grounds,"
Rusty said. "One is about a half-mile from here, the second
is a couple of miles northwest of that one, and the third is
way out on Starvation Prairie. That's the one where Leo used
to leave Adam when he was a kid."

"That's where they'll be," Louis said.

"I'm not sure I could even find that one anymore, especially in this weather. We need to wait till daylight."

Louis looked at his watch. Five-twenty. The sun wouldn't
be up for another two hours. And the rain was not letting up.

"I'll try the closest one," Louis said.

Rusty pulled something out of his jacket and held it out.

"Compass," he said. "The path is probably long gone.
Head due west and you'll come to the shack."

Louis took the compass. He turned up the collar of the
camouflage jacket against the rain.

"Be careful," Rusty said. "Leo took his crossbow."

CHAPTER 49

Louis kept the flashlight down, trained on the muddy ground. The branches above him rustled violently, spraying water. He was probably a quarter-mile from the cabin when he saw slits of light.

The shack was a blur against the darkness, but the light he saw seemed to be coming from gaps in the boards. Louis flicked off the flashlight and moved closer, easing up against the right side of the door.

The rain made it impossible to hear. And there were no shadows moving across the light inside. He waited. Seconds. Maybe a minute. Nothing.

He grabbed the door and flung it open, staying well outside but swinging himself to where he could see in the shack. Gun leveled at the doorway, he waited for a response.

A gunshot. A shout. But there was nothing. Except a blur that was slowly coming into focus.

In the white glow of a lantern inside, he saw something hanging on a large metal hook on the back wall.

A body.

Red. Limp. Dripping.

The head tilted to the shoulder. The shirt cut away, small pieces of cloth still clinging to the body. Narrow ribbons of peeled skin hung from raw, red muscle, from the chest and arms.

Jesus. It was Leo Ryker.

Louis backed away, fighting to keep the Glock level. He forced his eyes away from the body.

More skin shavings on the floor. And a black poncho and the lantern, sitting in a pool of blood. Two more hooks—empty—screwed into the wall on either side of Ryker's head.

That was all Louis could see from his position outside the door. He couldn't see the inside walls, couldn't see if someone was hiding inside. He knew he had to go in.

But he waited, frozen in place, only his eyes moving, moving over the wood exterior of the shack and the unwavering, thin lines of light.

Then suddenly one of the cracks to the right of the door went dark and a second later, lit up again.

Someone inside had moved.

Louis moved forward to the doorway, then quickly stepped inside, swinging his gun to the right.

The knife came down at him. He caught Vargas's arm and spun him around, slamming him against the wall. Louis braced Vargas behind the neck with his forearm, beating Vargas's hand against the wall until he dropped the knife.

Louis pushed Vargas's shoulders harder against the wall and searched him. Then he spun Vargas around to face him, the Glock pressed against his jaw.

"You sonofabitch," Louis hissed.

He belted him with the butt of the gun. Vargas stumbled, but didn't fall, didn't even look up.

Louis pulled him up and flung him outside the door. Vargas fell backward, sprawling in the mud. Louis dropped a knee to Vargas's chest and jammed the gun against his forehead.

"Where's the boy?"

Vargas just stared at him, blinking against the rain.

"What happened to him?" Louis yelled.

Nothing.

"Talk to me, you bastard!"

Nothing.

"Talk to me or I'll blow your head off! Where's the boy?"

"He died a long time ago," Vargas whispered.

Louis felt the tip of the gun barrel tremble against Vargas's forehead. He stared down at the blur before him, pushing the gun harder against Vargas's skull. He was seeing Ben's small slashed body, seeing Joe's blood on his bedroom floor, seeing this man inside Susan's house in a fucking cop's uniform.

He wanted to kill him.

He squeezed down on the trigger, the gun shaking in his hand.

No. Don't.

Louis pulled in a hard breath and jerked the gun away from Vargas's head. He straightened slowly, walked a small circle, staring out into the darkness. Finally, he looked back at Vargas.

"Get up."

Vargas managed a sitting position.

"Get all the way up. Show me where his body is."

"I can't."

Louis put the Glock back to Vargas's head. "Get up or I *will* shoot you."

Vargas didn't move. Didn't react.

Louis spun away from him. *Damn it.* He couldn't leave him here. He hadn't brought his cuffs and there was no rope to tie him up with. He knew he couldn't drag him very far. And he knew he *needed* him. Ellis was dead; there was no one else to tell him where Ben's body was.

Rusty. He'd signal Rusty. He lifted the Glock to fire a shot. But then he heard something. Soft at first, then louder.

A humming.

The bastard was humming.

"Shut up."

Words now. Slow. A western song.

Louis faced him. Vargas had crawled to the side of the

shack and was sitting against it, his head down, legs crossed, his voice cracking as he sang.

Louis watched him for almost a minute.

The gun belt. The small plastic cowboy toys. The record albums in the efficiency. The cowboy rules.

Louis pulled in a slow, shuttering breath, trying to calm himself. Joe shot through his mind, the way she could talk to Susan, the way she had of questioning people, getting what she needed out of them, things even they didn't know they had inside. He drew in another deep breath. All right . . . he'd get this sonofabitch talking.

"Some cowboy you are," Louis said.

Vargas stopped singing.

"That's what you want to be, right?"

Vargas shrugged.

"You don't have a horse or a gun," Louis said. "What kind of cowboy uses a knife? What kind of cowboy kills women? And kids?"

Vargas looked away from him.

"You're a bad cowboy," Louis said, hitting him in the shoulder with the tip of the gun.

Vargas didn't seem to care. He drew his knees up and started rocking, like Ben did when Susan got on him about something.

"Cowboys have rules, don't they?" Louis said tightly.

No response.

"Rules! Cowboys have fucking rules, don't they?"

Vargas picked at his jeans. "Yeah."

"You know those rules?"

He nodded.

"Say them for me."

Vargas looked up at him, then away.

"You know them. Say them!" Louis gritted his teeth.

Vargas hesitated, then slowly started repeating Gene Autry's rules. When he got to the one about being kind to children, he stopped.

"Nobody obeys that one," he said quietly.

"Where did you leave him?" Louis demanded.

Vargas ran a hand across his face, looking out into the darkness. "I buried him behind the trailer."

Louis closed his eyes. He had known it was coming. Vargas had said only minutes ago he had killed Benjamin, but there had still been hope that maybe it had been another lie. But there was a hard finality in Vargas's voice that told Louis it wasn't a lie. Not this time.

"Get up. Let's go," Louis said.

Vargas shook his head. "I can't."

"Don't start this shit," Louis said, walking to him. Vargas leaned away from him, bringing his hand above his head.

"I can't," Vargas whimpered. "I can't . . . tell. I can't tell. I can't tell."

Louis leaned down in his face, yelling over the rain. "Tell what?"

"It's a secret," Vargas whispered, looking up.

Vargas's eyes were watering and he was fighting hard not to cry. He drew his knees to his chest, wrapped his arms around them, and put his head down. His shoulders shook with small sobs.

Louis stared down at him.

Yancy Rowen: It was like the guy never got past thirteen or something.

I'll be a good boy. I'll be a good boy.

"Vargas, look at me."

No response.

Louis lowered himself to a squatting position in front of Vargas. He took another deep breath and forced himself to soften his voice. "Adam, look at me."

Vargas looked at him quickly.

"Tell me the secret," Louis said.

"I can't."

"Why not?"

"The hooks."

Louis glanced at the shack. "Those hooks?"

"I don't want to hang on a hook."

"No one's going to hang you on a hook."

"He will," Vargas said quickly. "He told me he would. That's why I killed him." Vargas lowered his forehead back to his knees, curling his arms over his head.

"Who was going to hang you on the hooks?" Louis asked.

"That's why I did it. I had to do it before he did. That's why I killed him and buried him."

Louis felt his heart stop. "Who?"

No answer.

"Who? Who'd you bury?"

Vargas whispered something Louis could barely hear.

"Your stepfather? Is that who you killed? Is that who you buried behind the trailer?"

Another hoarse whisper. "Yes."

Louis stood up slowly. He looked at Vargas, huddled against the shack, arms over his head. He looked small, no bigger than Benjamin. *The boy died a long time ago . . .*

But Louis knew the man was gone, too, fractured, the pieces now so scattered that even Vargas could no longer fit them together.

"Adam."

Vargas didn't answer him.

Louis touched his shoulder.

"Where's the boy you and Ellis took from the park?"

"Who?" Vargas asked, looking up.

"The little boy in the park. Benjamin."

Vargas hesitated, like he was trying to remember. "With the women."

"The women?" Louis asked. "The three women you got from Austin Outlaw?"

"Two. There's only two now."

"They're alive?"

Vargas nodded.

"Take me there, Adam."

"Uncle Leo will be mad."

"Uncle Leo won't know."

"But I won't get my money," Vargas said, wiping his face,

smudging the bluish-black mark under his eye. Louis could see now that it was not a bruise but a smeared teardrop tattoo. And he heard Yancy Rowen in his ear. *Ellis won't hurt the boy.*

"Adam," Louis said firmly. "What would Byron want you to do?"

"I don't know."

"He'd want you to save the boy, wouldn't he?"

Vargas thought about it for a minute. Then he nodded slowly.

"Take me there now, Adam," Louis said.

Vargas wiped his face, then struggled to his feet, bracing himself against the shack. Louis went quickly back into the shack, not looking at the body hanging on the hook as he grabbed the lantern.

He came back out, wiping his face with his sleeve. He held out the lantern. Vargas stared at it for a moment, like he didn't realize what it was, then took it. He looked up at Louis.

In the white glow of the lantern light, Louis could see his face clearly. It was a ghastly mask of dirt and blood, lined with tears and rain. The boy was gone and for a moment Vargas looked exactly like the monster he was.

Vargas turned and started toward the trees. With a final look back at the open door of the shack, Louis followed him into the darkness.

CHAPTER 50

Friday morning, January 22

Louis walked behind Vargas, watching him make his way through the brush, following a path only he could see. Vargas was carrying the Coleman lantern and sometimes he would stumble and stop to rest. Louis would give him a few seconds, then prod him forward.

He wanted to move faster. He wanted to get to Ben as quickly as he could, even though a part of him dreaded what he might see. Vargas had told him he hadn't been back out to see Ben and the two women since Tuesday night. That meant they had gone two full days without food or water. If Vargas's memory could even be trusted at this point.

Even covered with the camouflage jacket, Louis could feel the chill through to his bones, as if it had always been with him. What had Ben endured? Was he even still alive?

A light gray was coloring the sky behind them. Louis looked at his watch. Six fifty-seven. One week gone. One week of opening doors to find nothing behind them. Now it was almost over.

"Is Byron really dead?" Vargas asked.

"What?"

"You guys lied to the TV about Austin Outlaw. Maybe you lied about Byron."

"Yeah, he's really dead."

Vargas stopped, head down, his hand on a tree.

Louis came up behind him. The light was at Vargas's back and Louis could make out tiny bits of human skin and blood in Vargas's hair. The left shoulder of his denim jacket was stained black. The wound from where Joe had shot him had begun to bleed again. Louis poked Vargas with the Glock.

Vargas moved on. "Do you think we were wrong?"

"Killing people is wrong."

"No, I mean him and me. Do you think *that* was wrong?"

Louis didn't want to answer him. But he didn't want him to stop walking, either. "There's no right or wrong to stuff like that," he said.

Vargas was quiet for about twenty feet. "Uncle Leo thinks it's wrong."

"So you killed him?"

Vargas stopped again, head down. "Oh God . . ."

Was he just now remembering what he had done?

"Adam?"

"I . . . I shouldn't have done that."

"You shouldn't have done any of this."

Vargas faced him quickly. "But I *had* to. I *owed* Uncle Leo. He asked me to do a simple job," Vargas said, his voice tightening. "And I fucked up. Just like I fuck everything up."

"Walk."

Vargas turned and moved on, still talking, more to himself than Louis.

"And he said I was a stupid idiot, and now *he* had a problem because there was a witness to me killing the woman. And he told me, you're going to fix the problem, Adam, you're going to find Outlaw and you're going to kill him. I'll give you more money, he said, but Austin Outlaw's got to die."

"Why'd you take the boy?" Louis asked.

Vargas shook his head. "We didn't want to. We sat outside the black lady's house for a whole day and we saw Outlaw put his suitcases in the trunk and put the kid in the car, too. So we figured he was taking him back to Miami with him."

"He wasn't," Louis said.

Vargas ignored him. "But Byron didn't want to make that long drive again, so we tried it at the park and we held onto the kid figuring Outlaw would come back. But he never came. And then when the kid told us it wasn't his daddy out there with the money that night, we knew that the TV was lying to us and we had to get inside the house to find out for sure. That's why we stole the cop's uniform and that's why—"

"Shut up," Louis said.

Vargas immediately fell silent. They heard only the rain for a while until a dull sound rose from the graying sky. It grew louder and Louis looked up.

Two helicopters swept over the trees with a rush of wind. Louis glimpsed the green and white colors of the Lee County Sheriff's Department on the second one before they disappeared.

He looked back to see Vargas squinting up at them and he had the feeling Vargas was beginning to realize that there would be an end to this very soon.

"Where are they going?" Vargas asked.

"They'll land at the cabin. Then they'll start their search," Louis said.

Vargas gave the sky a long look, then turned and moved on.

They had walked close to another quarter mile when Vargas stopped again, looked to his right, then dipped around a tree. Louis first thought he was trying to escape but when he reached him, Vargas was standing in front of another shack.

It looked the same as the first one. Small, gray, rotted wood. But this one had a padlock on the large rusted latch.

Louis moved quickly to the door, grabbing the lock.

"You got a key?"

Vargas patted his pockets. "I lost it."

Louis pressed his face to the wood, trying to see through the cracks. But they were too narrow and the inside too dark.

"Ben!" he shouted.

No answer.

"Are you in there? Is anyone in there?"

Nothing.

Louis stepped back and took aim at the lock from the side so he wouldn't be shooting inside the shack. The first bullet missed, hitting the grass not far from where Vargas was standing. Louis fired again—a flurry of shots that pelted the latch, lock and ground. Finally the latch snapped loose from the brittle wood, and the door swung open by itself.

No one came out.

Louis glanced at Vargas. He was watching the sky.

"You go in ahead of me," Louis said.

Vargas shook his head. "I don't go all the way in. I set the food inside the door and lock it again."

Louis edged toward the door. "You're safe!" he called. "I'm a cop. Come out."

He heard someone crying. Whoever was inside wasn't going to come out. Standing at the door, he clicked on the flashlight.

A glint of metal . . . a steel bucket. A tumble of old dirty blankets on the wood floor. Plastic water bottles, fast-food wrappers. The smell of urine.

The beam picked up a face. Brown. Female.

She was cowering in the corner, hands covering her face. Her blouse and skirt were filthy, her feet bare. He swept the flashlight over the small shack. No one else.

Keeping the Glock on Vargas, Louis motioned to the woman with his other hand.

"Please. Come out. It's okay."

She wouldn't move. Louis held out his hand.

"I won't hurt you," he said softly. "Come out, please."

She moved slowly, stepping out to the grass. Her black

hair hung lank and dirty, her hands were wrapped in fabric ripped from her skirt. Louis could see where she had torn the skin on her fingers trying to somehow claw her way out.

She blinked against the bleak light, her body shaking in the cold rain. She saw Vargas and pulled back, terrified.

"He won't hurt you," Louis said.

Her eyes went to his Glock trained on Vargas. Vargas's expression was blank as he stared at the woman.

"Where are the others?" Louis asked her.

Her eyes were still on Vargas. "He took her."

"Who? Him?" Louis asked, pointing the Glock at Vargas.

She shook her head. "No, a big man with gray hair and a mustache."

"Who did he take? The other woman?" Louis asked.

"Yes, Fubina. A man came three nights ago. He stripped her and took her outside. He called her a blackbird and he told her to run," she said.

The woman was trembling. She was frozen with the cold but it was more than that. In her dark eyes, Louis could see the terror of what she had seen, imagine what she had felt. He knew now what she knew. Leo Ryker had brought the women here not for sex but for sport. He had hunted them.

"What about the little boy?" Louis asked.

"He was here," the woman said, "but he ran away."

"When?"

"A while ago, when he heard the helicopters," she whispered, wrapping her arms around herself. "He said he knew they were here for us, that they must be the police."

The woman glanced nervously at Vargas. "The little boy begged me to go with him, but I was too frightened."

Louis looked at the sky. The sun was up now, a soft white blur behind the gray clouds. It was easy to tell which way was east and it made sense that if Ben were following the choppers, he'd head toward the sun, like they did. But he couldn't have seen them. He would have only heard them.

"Which way did he go?" Louis asked.

She looked at the shack, then started to walk around it, toward the rear. Louis motioned for Vargas to move and they followed her.

She stopped and looked at a broken board in the back wall. The hole was no more than eight or nine inches wide.

"He got out there," she said. "And went that way." She was pointing south, toward a dense thicket of trees and tall brush.

"We need to go after the boy," Louis said to the woman. "I need you to stay here."

"Oh, no, please no," she said. Her eyes were wide, scared, filling with tears.

"The rest of the police will be here soon."

"No," she said, grabbing his sleeve.

He pulled away gently. He took Susan's revolver out of his pocket and shoved it in his belt. He quickly slipped off the camouflage jacket and wrapped the woman in it. "Stay here. I promise someone will come soon."

He turned to Vargas. "Let's go, Adam."

Vargas was staring off into the brush, in the direction the woman had pointed. He hadn't moved a muscle; he was frozen in place. He seemed to be growing smaller, pulling into himself.

"Adam," Louis said. "What's wrong?"

"I can't."

"Can't what?"

"Can't go there."

"Damn it! You're going!" Louis grabbed his arm but Vargas pulled back.

"No! They're out there!"

Louis drew back, wiping his face. Then, suddenly, he knew. The boars. He was talking about boars.

"Adam, I can shoot them," he said, trying to sound calm.

Vargas wasn't moving.

Louis could see it in Vargas's face, see the fear, see the absence of whatever it was that carried people through, whatever it was that had carried Ben through.

"You can do this, Adam," Louis said.

Vargas shook his head. His skin had grown whiter, his fists clenched. He was backing up, his eyes tearing, mouthing something Louis didn't at first understand. Then he saw the words, silent on Vargas's lips. *I'll be a good boy . . . I'll be a good boy.*

"Adam," Louis said sharply.

Vargas's eyes slowly focused back on Louis, then dropped to the revolver in his belt.

Louis was frozen in place. His mind understood what Vargas was thinking, but he couldn't bring himself to do it. He looked at the woman standing there watching them, shivering in the camouflage jacket. He thought of Ben, somewhere out there in the woods, shivering and alone.

He pulled in a deep breath and pulled the revolver from his belt. He emptied the cartridges, putting them in his jeans pocket. He held the gun out to Vargas.

Vargas stared at it for a moment, then took it, resting it easy in the palm of his other hand. Louis could see something in Vargas's eyes, something just past confidence, something close to courage.

"Take me to the other shack, Adam," he said.

But Vargas wasn't moving. He was staring at Louis's chest, staring at Joe's badge hanging there.

The last thing Louis wanted to do was to let this murderer wear Joe's badge. But it wasn't the murderer looking at him; it was the boy.

Louis slipped the chain up over his head and put it on Vargas. He fought back the sickened feeling in his stomach.

"Let's go," Louis said.

CHAPTER 51

Starvation Prairie was an empty expanse of reedy brown grass and scrub bush, dotted with squat palmetto palms and spindly pines. There were no lush green plants, no splashes of colored flowers, no blue-shadowed marshes hiding white egrets. Whatever survived here did so only with the greatest grit and the lowest expectations. It was a place that was exactly like its name—a place somewhere just on the edge of death.

Louis heard a helicopter and looked up. Another chopper was coming from the east, but he knew it wouldn't see them. It was searching too far north, back over the thick trees.

Vargas was slowing down, stumbling. The bloodstain on the back of his jacket had grown larger. He had been strangely quiet the last thirty minutes. No more talk of Uncle Leo or Byron Ellis. No more humming. Then, suddenly, he started talking again.

"Why do you want to find the kid so bad if he isn't even yours?" Vargas asked.

"Because I care about him."

Vargas seemed to think about that for a minute before he spoke. "He's lucky."

Louis didn't answer him.

A few more feet, then: "There gonna be a lot of cops there when we get back to the cabin?" Vargas asked.

"Yes."

"Am I going back to Raiford?"

"Yes."

Vargas stopped. He was a silhouette against the misty gray light, the gun hanging in his hand.

"They have the electric chair there, don't they?" Vargas said.

Louis hesitated. "Yes."

Vargas started moving again. For a moment, Louis thought he heard him humming again, the same tune he had sung before. Then he stopped again. Louis came up next to him. He could see a dark shape in the distance. The third shack.

Louis tried to hurry, but Vargas was lagging and he didn't know if it was fatigue or fear keeping him back. He pulled him along, finally letting go of him when they reached the shack. Vargas sank down on the ground, exhausted. He was just sitting there slumped in the tall grass, staring at the shack.

Louis called out Ben's name. There was no answer. He reached for the door, then drew back.

The odor. He knew that smell. Decaying flesh. But there was something else, too. Chemicals . . . weirdly familiar, like a morgue.

He opened the door.

Oh, God . . .

Hand to his mouth, Louis backed off, a rotted stench filling his nostrils. He stood, gulping air, staring into the dark interior.

He drew his flashlight and shined it inside, but the beam was weak and he had to move closer. The wood floor was stained a dark deep brown with old blood, but it was clean, swept.

Louis pulled the front of his sweatshirt over his nose and stepped inside, moving the flashlight over the walls.

Empty hooks. Flies buzzing.

The beam moved over the table.

Bottles. Bloodstains. Tiny pieces of dried flesh.

And a human head.

It was laying on its side, the long black hair tangled and matted. The skin was puffy, discolored, deeply dimpled on one side, smooth and preserved on the other. The eyes were . . . flat. Black. Glass . . . the eyes were made of glass.

Just like the animal heads on the wall of Leo Ryker's study.

The light was trembling. Louis realized it was his own hand shaking.

He had seen the dead before. But never the desecrated. He had known killers before. But he had never seen such cruelty. He knew this was the third Micronesian, the woman Leo Ryker had taken from the shack and hunted. What had the woman endured? What had she thought as Ryker stripped her naked, threw her out in the cold, and told her to run for her life? What had she felt when the arrow hit her?

What in the hell had been going on here? Had Leo Ryker looked for new thrills behind hunting? Had he tried to preserve a human head for his trophies?

Louis looked back at Vargas. He was sitting in the tall grass, sitting there staring at the shack, rocking slowly.

What the hell had he seen in this place? What had he endured?

Vargas had covered his head with his hands. Louis backed out of the shack, closing the door.

CHAPTER 52

There had been no sign of Ben. Louis was leading the way now, Vargas trailing as they made their way back toward the cabin. The rain had stopped but the sky was still a muddy gray and the sound of the helicopters was growing louder. Louis heard a groan behind him and turned. Vargas had fallen. Louis walked back to him.

In the full morning light, Louis got his first good look at him. He lay face up in the brown grass, covered in mud and dried blood. His pale skin was dirty, swollen with bruises and cuts. His hair was matted with mud. The only thing brighter than the gold badge on his chest was his blue eyes.

Louis bent down and helped him to his feet. They walked on, Louis looking toward the sun to find their way back to the clearing.

He heard the muted sound of helicopters first, then voices. They stopped behind the trees, the cabin visible beyond. A helicopter sat on the ground. Louis could hear another in the air. There was a large four-wheel drive vehicle parked near the cabin. Dogs barking. Cops were everywhere.

But Louis saw nothing that looked like joy. Nothing that resembled the rescue of a lost boy. They hadn't found Ben.

Louis looked at Vargas. "I need the badge back, Adam."

Vargas took it off his neck. "Guess we don't want them to get the bad guys and the good guys mixed up, huh?"

He dropped the badge in Louis's hand. Louis slipped it in his back pocket.

"And the gun," Louis said.

Vargas looked back at the cops. "You ever heard the song 'Blow out the Candles'?" he asked.

Louis started to say no, but Vargas was gone. Breaking through the brush, into the clearing, the empty revolver raised in his hand.

The cops turned.

Vargas pointed the gun at them.

Louis rushed forward, his shouts drowned out by the dogs and helicopters. "It's empty!" he yelled, waving his hands. "Don't shoot! It's not loaded!"

His words were lost in the volley of gunshots.

Vargas was hit, dropping first to his knees, then backward to the ground, the revolver still clutched in his hand. Louis stopped running, his eyes locked on Vargas.

As the echoes from the gunshots faded, Louis heard voices. Shouts. Screams. Demands for him to drop his weapon.

He lifted his hands over his head, the blur of uniforms in front of him coming into focus. He tossed his Glock to the ground and they were all over him, throwing him to the dirt. Knees jammed in his back, his face shoved to the mud.

He heard Sheriff Mobley close by, screaming at his deputies to back off. Then the cops were gone.

Louis rose first to all fours. Then to his knees. He glanced at Vargas, then looked away, drawing a hard breath. Mobley dropped down in front of him.

"What just happened here?"

"His gun wasn't loaded," Louis said. "It wasn't loaded."

"Where'd he get the damn gun?"

Louis closed his eyes, a cold ache moving through him. "Is Ben here?"

"No. No sign of him. Kincaid, what the fuck's going on here?"

"There's a woman," Louis said. "She's in a shack out there. You need to—"

"Where?"

"Northwest. Head northwest and go get the woman. She's one of the . . . one of the . . ."

"One of what?"

"And there's another shack," Louis said. "On the prairie. You need to go there, too. Leo Ryker was—"

Mobley put both of his hands on Louis's shoulders. "Calm down."

Louis closed his eyes, Mobley's hands steadying him.

The voices suddenly changed. The talking turned to shouts. The shouts rose to cheers.

Louis opened his eyes, struggling to his feet.

Beyond the cabin, in the trees, he saw them. Two figures walking toward the clearing. One small, one larger. One boy. One woman.

They were coming out of the trees, silhouetted against the morning mist. They were holding hands. Benjamin . . . and the woman.

Louis moved toward them, first in disbelief, then filled with a rush of relief so strong it brought tears to his eyes.

He wanted to scoop Benjamin up, hold him tight against him, be the first face Benjamin saw. But he couldn't get there. Uniforms blocked his way and he couldn't break through.

And then Benjamin was gone. Picked up by cops and emergency personnel, hustled toward the helicopter, his small face barely visible above their shoulders, his eyes searching the crowd.

Louis called to him, but Benjamin didn't hear him, didn't see him.

Benjamin and the woman were pushed into the helicopter and the door slammed closed. The chopper lifted off, rising straight up, then swinging right, over the trees, disappearing into the thin fog.

CHAPTER 53

They gave him a dark blue windbreaker with POLICE in big yellow letters on the back. He told them he didn't need it—the rain had stopped and the cold was finally starting to break. But then one of the cops pointed out his sweatshirt was dark with mud and blood.

Louis was wearing the windbreaker when they dropped him off at Lee County General. He endured a quick exam and then went immediately upstairs to the third floor pediatrics wing. But the cop outside Benjamin's door said the doctor was in there and to come back later.

He took the elevator up to the fifth floor. Joe's door was open. She was sitting on the bed, stuffing things in a black tote. Her hair was pulled back in a ponytail and she was wearing tennis shoes, gray sweatpants, and a big Miami Dolphins sweatshirt that he recognized as his. The left sleeve hung limp, her heavily bandaged arm secured beneath.

She looked up. His heart gave.

The whole right side of her face was swollen. There was a small butterfly bandage above her eyebrow.

She smiled. "Thought you'd never get here," she said.

He came in. "How you feeling?"

"Don't know. They got me pretty doped up. But all things

considered, not too bad." Her gray eyes searched his face. "How about you?"

He shook his head slowly. She didn't press it.

She closed the tote bag. "I'm just waiting for prescriptions, then we can get out of here. Chief Wainwright's sending a car."

Louis sat down on the side of the bed next to her. Joe's hand closed over his. For a moment, they just sat like that, the sounds of the hospital filtering in from the open door.

"I heard what happened out there," she said. "But I want to hear it from you."

Louis wanted to tell her. But he was so tired and things were such a blur he wasn't sure where to start.

"How'd he get Susan's gun?" Joe asked.

"I gave it to him."

She slowly pulled her hand away. The question was there in her eyes. But that's all that was there.

He reached back into his jeans pocket and pulled out her badge. He held it out. "I gave him this, too."

She took it. She stared at it, her thumb rubbing the gold embossing. She looked up at him, the question still there in her eyes.

"It was the only way to get to the boy," Louis said.

"Which boy?"

"Both of them."

He knew he'd have to explain everything later. And he knew he would have to have faith she'd understand.

She gave him a small smile. "Where'd you get the windbreaker?"

"Some cop took pity on me," he said.

"Looks good on you."

A nurse came in. She gave Joe some prescription slips and had her sign a form on a clipboard. She left and returned pushing a wheelchair. Joe stared at it.

"I don't need that," she said.

"Sorry, rules," the nurse said.

Joe looked at Louis, then sat down in the chair with a

sigh, clutching her tote. The nurse pushed Joe out to the elevator. Louis's eyes watched the floors light up.

"Can we stop on three? I need to go see Ben before we leave," he said to Joe. "You mind?"

"Of course not."

They got off on three and the nurse let Louis wheel Joe down the hall. Louis could see the door to Benjamin's room standing open but as they neared, Joe raised a hand.

"Louis, wait a minute."

They stopped just outside the door. Louis could see in, just the foot of the bed. But he could hear Ben's voice. Then Susan's soft voice in response.

And then Austin's.

A second later, Austin came into view. He sat down in a chair near the foot of the bed. He was dressed in a fresh yellow shirt and slacks. He was smiling, holding a stuffed bear. Suddenly he looked up and saw Louis. His dark eyes narrowed slightly, then he looked away.

Louis just stood there, rooted to the floor. He felt a warm hand cover his.

"Louis, let's go," Joe said quietly.

Austin looked back at him for one second, then he rose, disappearing from Louis's view.

A second later, Louis heard Ben. A tentative laugh.

"Louis, let's go," Joe said.

Her hand was still on his. She curled her fingers between his. He gave a slow nod and they turned, heading away.

Louis held the double glass doors open and the nurse pushed Joe's wheelchair outside. Louis walked her to the curb, scanning the parking lot for a dark Sereno Key cruiser. His eyes stopped instead on a white and green patrol car. But the gold letters on the side panel didn't read Lee County. They read: BROWARD COUNTY.

Two men stood outside the cruiser talking to Sheriff

Mobley. They wore white shirts and ties, covered with dark green windbreakers, BROWARD COUNTY stenciled on the back. Detectives.

The men turned and walked toward the entrance to the hospital. Louis told Joe he'd be right back and went over to intercept them as they neared the hospital door. Mobley heard him coming and turned.

"Detectives Phil Ward and Fred Turner, Broward S.O.," Mobley said. "Guys, this is Louis Kincaid."

Their expressions told Louis they had heard his name a lot in the last few hours. One extended a hand and Louis shook it.

"They're here for Austin Outlaw," Mobley said.

"What are the charges?" Louis asked.

"Conspiracy to commit murder," Ward said. "Transporting of illegal aliens and a few more."

Louis looked up at the hospital. "He's with his son."

"We won't cuff inside the room," Ward said.

"The kid will know you're cops. He'll know what you're doing and he's already been through hell," Louis said. "Let me go up and bring Outlaw out."

Ward hesitated and looked at Mobley. Mobley gave a nod. Louis motioned to Joe that he'd be right back and he led the cops back upstairs to Ben's room.

He knocked, hoping Susan would come to the door. When she didn't, he knocked again, louder. The door opened a crack and Austin peered out.

"We need you to step out here," Louis said quietly.

Austin's eyes flicked from Louis to the three cops behind him but he didn't move. Susan's face appeared behind Austin.

"Now," Ward said.

Austin came slowly out the door, followed by Susan. Austin looked at Louis as Ward pulled him forward to cuff him.

"This is how you get rid of the competition? You turn me in to the cops?" Austin said, staring at Louis.

"*I* turned you in," Susan said.

Austin's eyes jerked to Susan. "You? How could you do that to me? I'm his father. He needs me. He loves me."

Ward started moving Austin down the hall.

"He'll hate you for this, Susan," Austin yelled.

Susan turned and walked back into Ben's room, closing the door.

Louis followed the detectives downstairs and watched from the curb as they put Austin into the cruiser. Louis went to Joe, who was waiting in the passenger seat of a Sereno Key police car. She rolled down the window.

"Can you give me ten minutes?" Louis asked. "I just want to see Ben."

Joe nodded and Louis headed back upstairs. Just outside Ben's door, Susan met him, hands raised.

"What's the matter?" Louis asked.

"He saw you," she said. "He saw everything from the window."

"Shit," Louis said softly. "Can I talk to him?"

She shook her head. "He saw *you* down there, in that jacket. He thinks *you* arrested his father."

Louis stepped back, his eyes going to the closed door. He could hear Ben crying. And he wanted to go inside, he wanted to hold him, talk to him, tell him that it was all going to be okay.

Susan stepped in front of the door. "I'll explain things to him when the time is right," she said.

"Susan—"

"No, Louis," she said. "You need to go. Please."

Louis turned and walked away.

CHAPTER 54

One week later

His suitcase lay open on the bed. Issy had made a nest in his shirts but he let her stay. He looked around the bedroom. Everything else was already packed.

Joe had left to take one last walk on the beach. She had been taking the walks every day. They helped her heal, she told him. He could tell she was eager to get back to Miami.

So was he. Things had gone well with Major Anderson, and in the series of interviews that followed. There would still be a battery of tests and weeks of certification. But at the end of it all, he would be given a gold badge.

Issy got up, stretched, and jumped off the bed. He closed the suitcase. There was only one thing left to do.

He went to the porch, watching Joe heading away down the beach. He pushed open the screen and went out into the yard. Kneeling under the gumbo limbo tree, he started scooping out the sand.

It was still there, right where he had buried it over a year ago. He pulled the thick plastic evidence bag out of the hole, brushing off the sand. He stood, holding the bag, feeling the hard contours of the gun inside.

Back inside the cottage, he left Joe a note saying he'd return in an hour.

When he pulled up in front of the Sereno Key police station, Jewell was just getting out of his car. He was in jeans and a T-shirt, carrying his uniforms in cleaner's plastic over his shoulder. He recognized Louis's Mustang and waited, pulling off his sunglasses.

"Hey, Jewell," Louis said.

"Good afternoon, sir."

Louis was looking at the uniforms. "What's going on?"

Jewell shifted from one foot to the other. "I'm glad I ran into you before you left. I need to tell you something."

He hesitated.

"What is it, Jewell?"

"I sent Adam Vargas to your cottage. I told him where Detective Frye was staying."

"What do you mean? How?"

"The day he was in the house, he asked where everybody was. I told him she was staying with you on Captiva."

"Shit, Jewell," Louis said softly.

"She could've been killed, and—"

"She wasn't."

Jewell looked toward the station. "I came here to quit, sir."

Louis's eyes went to the uniforms slung over Jewell's shoulder. "Don't do it, Jewell."

"Sir . . ."

"You take that badge off something goes with it, and it's really hard to get it back," Louis said.

Jewell looked back at the station, then at Louis.

"You can be a good cop, Jewell," Louis said. "Don't let this get to you."

Jewell hesitated. "I like being a cop. I don't want to quit."

"Then don't."

Jewell let out a long breath. Then he nodded and stuck out his hand. "Thank you, sir."

Louis watched him walk away, back to his car.

Wainwright was tilted back in his chair, eyes closed, sunlight on his face. Louis closed the door behind him and Wainwright looked up, bringing his feet down off the desk.

"Didn't expect to see you for a while. I thought you went to Miami."

"I'm back wrapping up some things," Louis said.

"How's Detective Frye?"

"Getting better."

"And the boy?"

"I haven't seen him."

Wainwright's eyes dropped to the plastic evidence bag in Louis's hand. "What's that?"

Louis set the bag on Wainwright's desk. "I need you to do something for me, Dan. I need this to be found here on Sereno Key with no connection ever made to me. And after you process it, it needs to find its way to Mobley."

Wainwright picked up the bag, feeling the shape. "This is a gun," he said.

"Yes."

"And what will happen when Mobley gets it?"

"Mobley knows this gun. And he knows it will free an innocent man from prison."

Wainwright looked up at Louis. "You hid evidence?"

"Yes."

"Why?"

Louis took a moment. "I didn't know how else to get her justice."

Wainwright was silent, studying Louis's face. "Why'd you bring it to me?"

"Because you've crossed lines, too," Louis said. "You know what it's like."

Wainwright set the bag on the desk and sat back in his chair, staring at it. "And you think doing this will clear your conscience before you take that job in Miami."

"Something like that," Louis said.

Wainwright hesitated, then opened a desk drawer. He put the gun in and closed it. "I'll take care of it."

CHAPTER 55

Louis looked to the left as he drove along the beach road, watching the sun as it began its slow descent into the gulf. The air was still cool and the sunset was going to be lost behind the heavy cloud bank that hung over the water.

He hurried, wanting to get back to Joe. They had planned to go to Timmy's Nook tonight for their final dinner on Captiva.

When he pulled in, he slowed, seeing Susan's old silver Mercedes in front of his cottage. In the softening light, he saw Joe and Susan standing by the car. And then Benjamin sitting on the step of the cottage watching Issy playing in the sand.

He parked behind Susan's car, cut the engine, and got out. Susan and Joe watched him as he came up the gravel path. Benjamin looked up. There was nothing in his face, no expression, no happiness, nothing at all.

But he was here.

Louis came up to Joe and Susan. There was a second of awkward silence before Joe spoke.

"I think I will go for a walk," she said, glancing at Louis.

Louis and Susan watched her head over the low dunes. Susan looked back at him. He had hoped to tell her about him and Joe before she learned it from someone else but there hadn't been time. It was obvious from her face that she knew now.

"Susan," he said, glancing toward Joe as she headed down the beach.

"I like her," Susan said quickly. "She's good for you."

Louis couldn't think of a damn thing to say. It hadn't worked out for him and Susan and they both knew it. But they were both okay with that.

Susan looked at Benjamin, hunched on the porch steps, then back at Louis. She started to say something then just gave Louis a long, hard hug.

"Thank you," she whispered. "Thank you so much."

He held her for a moment, his eyes tearing. Over Susan's shoulder, he saw Benjamin watching them. He pulled back gently.

"How's he doing?" he asked.

Susan's smile faded. "He's very angry," she said softly. "He talks to me about the things that happened to him. He asks about the woman he was locked up with, what happened to her, and he even asked about the McAllisters. But he won't talk to me about his father." Susan looked at Benjamin, her lower lip quivering. "I think he hates me."

"He needs time," Louis said.

She was still looking at Benjamin. "He asked me to bring him here," she said.

Louis looked at Benjamin. He was drawing circles in the sand with a stick.

"Go talk to him," Susan said.

Louis walked slowly over to the step where Benjamin sat. When he looked back at Susan, she was walking away, heading out toward the beach.

Louis looked down at Benjamin. "Can I sit down?" he asked.

Benjamin shrugged. He was dragging the stick through the sand at his feet.

Louis sat down on the step. Benjamin didn't look up, didn't move away when their shoulders touched.

"What are you drawing?" Louis asked.

"Nothing."

"You feeling okay?"

Benjamin waited a moment. "I'm scared a lot."

"Of what?"

"Being taken again," he said softly.

Louis shut his eyes for a second. It was very quiet except for the soft hiss of the surf.

"Why didn't my daddy come back for me?" Benjamin asked.

Louis looked at him. "What do you mean?"

"At the park? Why didn't he come back? We waited a long time."

Louis cleared his throat, unsure he could talk.

"Maybe . . ." Louis said slowly. "Maybe he wanted to, but he just couldn't."

Benjamin stared at the sand, the stick motionless.

"The blond man said Daddy was a coward," Benjamin whispered.

"These were bad guys. They wanted to hurt your father," Louis said. "Being afraid doesn't make you a coward."

Benjamin looked up at him. "Ma says *you* came," he said. "She says you never stopped looking for me."

Louis's throat tightened.

"I looked for Daddy when I found the helicopters," Benjamin said. "But he wasn't there. Were you?"

Louis nodded.

Benjamin leaned over, his head against Louis's shoulder. For a few minutes they just sat like that, the soft evening breeze against their faces.

"Ma says you're moving and you're going to be a cop again."

"Yes."

"Will you come and see me sometime?"
"Yes."
A long silence.
"I love you, Louis."

CHAPTER 56

It was still dark when he slipped out of Joe's bed. He looked back at her. Her face was in the shadows, a shaft of moonlight falling across her shoulder. Her two cats were curled at the bottom of the bed.

Pulling on a pair of sweatpants, he left the bedroom. Out in the dark living room, Issy looked up at him from the sofa, then went back to sleep. His eyes were drawn to the sliding glass doors and the lights beyond.

He went out onto the balcony. Miami was spread out below him like a carpet of lights. A police siren wailed and died in the distance. A warm breeze came up, wrapping itself around him.

He leaned on the railing.

Oh man . . . this is going to be tough.

He felt the press of her breasts on his back and her arms wrapping around his chest.

"What's the matter?" she asked.

"I can't stay here," he said softly.

She hesitated. "I have a feeling you're not talking about my apartment."

Louis turned to face her. "I need to know he's going to be all right."

"He'll be all right, Louis," Joe said. "Kids are resilient. They're stronger than you think."

"They're more fragile than you think, Joe. Especially boys."

"He has a strong and loving mother."

"And no father."

Joe took a step back. "You can't be Ben's father, Louis."

"I know that," Louis said. "But I can be something."

She just looked at him.

"I don't want him to grow up scared," Louis said. "I don't want him to grow up angry. And I don't want him to not trust people because his mother can't. I just want . . ."

Louis shook his head.

Joe took another step back. "You've waited a long time for this. How can you just turn your back on everything?"

Louis knew she meant the job—and her.

Her eyes teared up. He went to her, wrapping his arms around her, crushing her against him.

"I need you, too," she whispered.

He closed his eyes and buried his face against her neck.

"I'll be three hours away," he said.

She pulled back and wiped her eyes. "Two if you drive fast."

He cupped her face in his hands and kissed her.

The road in front of him was straight and flat, cutting a cruel slash across the gut of Florida. No curves, no hills, nothing to relieve the sadness of the journey. The sun had crept below the visor, making him squint as he headed west.

He glanced at the odometer, calculating how many miles he'd come. And how many more miles he had yet to go. He'd be back in Captiva before sunset.

His thoughts were jumping between Ben and Joe.

He was thinking, too, of Phillip Lawrence and he realized he had never thanked him. How did you thank a stranger for stepping in and saving your life? How did you thank a foster father for being a father?

There had been other boys in Phillip's house. Other boys who had come out whole because of him. But Louis had also seen the others. The broken boys. Seen what they could do. What they could become.

He drove on, the sun sinking lower into the west.

Ben and Joe. They were both in his head, but Joe was there in his heart. His eyes flicked up to the rearview mirror. He missed her already.

A rest stop came into view. He hesitated, then let up on the gas, pulling off Alligator Alley. He stopped in front of the pay phone and got out.

The low slanting sun had turned the saw grass into a rippling river of gold. The blades whispered in the wind. He started to pick up the phone to call her. But then he stopped. He was thinking of the picture, the one of the little boy Joe carried behind her badge. The boy she couldn't save.

He went back to the Mustang and opened the passenger door, popping open the glove box. It took him a minute to find it in all the junk. But finally, he pulled out Benjamin's picture, the one Susan had given him the night he disappeared.

He looked at it for a moment, then took out his wallet. He folded the photograph carefully and slid it behind his license.

Back in the car, he started the engine and pulled out of the lot. At the edge of Alligator Alley he stopped. He looked left, across the flat grass to where the gray edge of the coming night was shading in from the east. Then he turned the Mustang west, heading home.

ABOUT THE AUTHOR

P.J. Parrish has worked as a newspaper reporter and editor, arts reviewer, blackjack dealer, and personnel manager in a Mississippi casino. The author currently resides in Southaven, Mississippi, and Fort Lauderdale, Florida, and is married with three children, three grandchildren, two cats and a dog. P.J. Parrish is currently at work on the next Louis Kincaid thriller. Please visit the author's Web site at www.pjparrish.com.